MW00881773

RIDGEVILLE SERIES
Volume Two

CELIA KYLE
NEW YORK TIMES BESTSELLING AUTHOR

Head Over Tail

CHAPTER *one*

"Backbones are like assholes. Everyone's got one. You just have to find yours. The backbone, not the asshole. I'm assuming you know where you asshole is. If not, we have bigger problems." – Maya Josephs, Prima of the Ridgeville Pride, who swears ta god that she will slap her last name on her unborn twins' birth certificates if her mate doesn't marry her soon.

Maddy Lane's kidnappers had been all about kung-fu fighting and fast as lightning.

She was not a kung-fu *hi-ya!* kind of gal and tended to lean toward run-and-hide.

Now, a ton of minutes post-kidnapping, she'd decided that being abducted was not an enjoyable experience and she really needed to learn how to wield a judo chop.

She kinda figured the kidnapping adventure needed to come to an end. Any time. She was totally ready. In all the romance novels she'd read, the heroine would be spirited away by evil-doers and then rescued before anything bad could happen to the poor, defenseless waif.

She hadn't been rescued…not that she'd been missing all that long.

But still. Bad stuff had happened.

She tongued her lower lip, wincing when the muscle encountered the oozing wound that would make it hard to smile for a while. Her head throbbed to the hella fast beat of her heart. One of the assholes in the SUV was the cause of both discomforts and she'd love the chance to repay him.

Eventually. When she gathered enough nerve to fight them. Which would probably be never, but a girl could hope.

Maddy twisted her arms, rubbed her wrists against her bindings and searched for any give in the material. Snippets of pain from the movements registered, but she couldn't worry about those feelings. Not when her life was at stake. Because, really, she wanted to do the whole "living" thing a little longer.

The SUV took a sharp left and she was thrown against one of the men. A piercing ache erupted in her chest and a small whimper escaped without conscious thought.

Okay, she could add bruised or broken ribs to her list of injuries. Lovely.

The man she leaned against didn't respond to the sudden additional weight. But, as low as the sound had been, it caught the attention of one of the other males.

A beefy hand wrapped around her upper arm, yanking her upright once again. "Hey, pretty. Shut it. We don't need no shit from the boss' kitten, got it?"

She squeezed her eyes shut as the prickle of tears gathered behind her lids. She willed the moisture to recede. There was no way she'd let the men see her cry.

The male released her and she stifled another sound, a deep groan that had built in her chest as he'd held her tight. The palm had been covering a bruise, nothing more, but that additional ache just piled on with the others in her body.

Maddy felt like a bruise from head to toe and back again. Sure, she figured they'd tried to be easy with the whole "sneak in and grab her" thing, but she'd been asleep when they came for her. And when she slept, she forgot to be afraid.

She hadn't heard them outside her home, disabling her alarm. Or when they'd picked the lock on her back door. Or when they'd crept through her house. Or when they'd secreted into her bedroom.

No, it wasn't until that first brush of a foreign breath on her skin that she knew her space had been breached and she'd awoken a tad...upset.

That wasn't even right. Upset was a word her parents used. Angry maybe? Pissed worked even better. Okay, fucking enraged.

And they hadn't been expecting that reaction. Hell, if push came to shove, Maddy hadn't been expecting it either. She was a cower-er by nature...

Well, they'd woken her and then they'd had to deal with her. More importantly, they had to deal with Maddy's lioness. The cat had been less than pleased with all the males crowding her space.

Hell, she didn't remember most of what happened between waking in her bedroom with a man looking down at her and sitting in the SUV. Obviously, it hadn't been pretty.

Maddy took as deep a breath as she dared, pain in her chest flourishing with the move. She needed to stay calm and figure out where her life had gone to hell.

And the quickest way to do that was tap into the wonderful powers she hated and put them to use. Her abilities were the source of her life's hardships, but they had their uses.

True, being a Sensitive meant she could do more than a "normal" shifter. She could sense turmoil in the pride, soothe others in need and glean knowledge that shifters may want to keep hidden.

Guess how many lions, hell shifters, avoided her?

All of them.

Ding, ding, ding… Johnny, tell her what she's won!

When shifters weren't taunting and being mean to her, they were keeping their distance, afraid she'd somehow lay some voodoo smack-down on them.

Well, except Maya. The pride Prima had a knack for cutting through B.S. and had a habit of telling the other cats to get the fuck over themselves.

Maddy wanted to be her when she grew up.

Sensitives were needed, essential, but they were also the physically weakest of the cats which left her at the mercy of the others. True, the Prima had put an end to all that, but the fear lingered.

Damn her fear. She really needed to find her backbone like Maya had told her.

Backbones are like assholes…

Fuck it. She'd find it later. For now, she needed the metaphysical "lay of the land".

One last breath and she let her consciousness float. Honestly, that was the only way to explain it… She just drifted in her head, the two halves of her mind twining in the cool darkness, picking and poking at one another until they twirled together and became one.

The lioness, the cat that ached for retribution and blood, calmed with the first touch of Maddy's human thoughts while Maddy's human half became stronger with the stroke of her beast's fur. They worked well together. Always had. Always would.

If only you'd work with me more often…

Maddy gritted her teeth. The only bad part of the whole process was that now she had the cat's voice in her head. Joy. Oh, look, another "benefit" to being a Sensitive, she got to talk to the cat instead of getting vague emotional impressions like everyone else. Goody.

You love me. Stop pretending.

She did an internal eye roll. *Can we get on with the show?*

5

Fine.

The cat now focused, they worked together and her innate power flowed through the small space, poured over each body. She'd heard others describe the touch as being stroked by their mother, cleaned and snuggled when they were cubs.

The twitches and jerks of each male's body eased. She opened her mouth, tasted the air and gauged their response. The dominance that permeated the air had lessened, but hadn't disappeared.

Better than nothing. She was just thankful they hadn't taken a bite out of her yet. Not everyone's animals reacted well to getting poked and prodded by a Sensitive, so she was glad one of them wouldn't be going all growly on her in such close quarters. Then again, she wasn't even sure they knew who, or what, they'd kidnapped.

With another thought, a tendril of power slithered between each body, tapped the two behind her, the two beside her and the two at the front of the vehicle until their minds were wide open.

And then she dug.

She didn't like what she found.

Out of the six males, one was a hyena, another a polar bear, two wolves and the group was rounded out with a pair of mountain lions.

All of them worked with a single man: Alistair McCain, the leader of Freedom.

She nearly groaned aloud with the news and her cat was right there beside her, feeling exactly the same.

About a week ago, the man had orchestrated her wererabbit friend Carly's kidnapping. They'd gotten the rabbit back, extremely bloody and hurt, but back just the same. Actually, from what she'd been told, Ricker, the council's tracker, had gotten her back. But whatever. The male had been after Alistair for some time, had hunted him to Ridgeville and had been pivotal in Carly's rescue. Then, he'd disappeared, back on the hunt for the crazy male.

And when she meant crazy, it was in the literal sense.

Freedom was…insane. Their beliefs were based on the destruction of the shifter clans and removal of all hierarchy. They felt individual shifters could govern themselves. They didn't need Primes, Alphas or Bucks. Which, considering the fact that the movement had a leader while trying to destroy the existence of leaders…struck her as a bit odd.

Kinda contradictory. But no one had ever said they were all that smart.

Okay. So, Freedom had her. Lovely. Now, she just needed to pluck out a handful of thoughts here and there.

Tiptoe through the window…er…their heads.

Maddy sent a tendril toward the hyena and took a peek…

Fucking bitch. Fucking dug her puny assed nails into my shit. Fucking whore. Gonna fuck that bitch's shit up once Alistair's through with her. Fat piece of shit…

Okay, she totally wasn't a whore. Seriously. She hadn't even taken part in the Gaian Moon, let's-get-pregnant fuckfest in like, forever. And yeah, she did claw the ass, but he'd slapped her! And, hey, she wasn't fat. Seriously.

7

More cushion for the pushin', maybe. Okay, a lot of cushion.

Asshat.

With an internal harrumph, she moved on...

A peek into the polar bear's head revealed a red haze, blood on the brain, and she sensed that his gums ached, beast desperate for release. He wanted to rip the hyena apart for touching...her. Huh. Careful...oh so careful, she extended a ghostly representation of her hand into the male's mind, stroked and pet his bear to ease him away from the killing edge.

By increments, the man's body relaxed, shoulders easing down as the thirst for blood slithered from the bear's thoughts.

Instantly, the aggression in the SUV lessened, floated back to a reasonable level and the remaining shifters seemed to slump into their seats.

With nothing left to glean from the bear, she moved on, touched the remaining males.

The mountain lions held lust balanced by an intense fear of Alistair's wrath at her state. Apparently, they'd been directed to kidnap her very nicely.

Right.

The wolves were occupied with their hate of cats, Maddy included, but accepted that pleasing and supporting Alistair was a means to an end. They wanted to go lone because of...something, but the wolf laws demanded death to those who didn't belong to a pack and so they'd

8

been stuck. It was either jump in with Alistair, and the chance at freedom, or face sure death from the wolves.

After touching each male, she slithered back into her own body and let the cat slink back to her place inside Maddy. They were exhausted. No, exhausted didn't quite cover things.

Poking around in one brain wasn't all that hard. Poking and soothing, a little worse. Poking around in six heads and bringing a polar bear back from the edge of murdering everyone in the SUV? Well, that was like running a five minute marathon. Twice.

Had she mentioned she wasn't all that into exercise?

Uh, yeah.

Maddy let the seat welcome her, sunk into the soft leather and leaned her head against the bear's shoulder. If he'd been pissed about the others hurting her and he held a decent amount of fear of Alistair, she figured she'd be safe. For a little while.

With a yawn, she closed her eyes. She could do the whole scared shitless she-cat thing after she'd had a nap.

Sometime later, she jolted, the rough rocking of the truck yanking her from sleep to awake in a blink.

"Easy…" The voice of the man beside her was a low rumble. Soft and sweet, the tone was incongruous when she considered who was speaking. "We're at the compound. You'll meet with Alistair soon."

Great.

Unable to speak, she jerked her head in a quick nod. So, she'd soon figure out why she'd been taken.

Twisting and turning down a half-dozen roads, they pulled up to a large iron gate and eased through the opening. A huge home spread before them and the SUV pulled behind the home and right into...a sunken drive. The truck continued on its path, into the earth and leaving civilization behind.

Well, wasn't that just peachy.

They traveled deeper into the earth for another few minutes before parking beside a handful of other vehicles.

Various shifters milled about the trucks, watching their approach. The moment the SUV stilled, the males went into action, alighting from the vehicle, and the polar bear tugged her along.

She wasn't about to fight him.

Now was not the time to find her backbone.

Maddy stumbled from the elevated truck and the bear caught her before she met the ground. "Thank you" rested on the tip of her tongue, but she bit it back. She didn't have to be polite to kidnappers. She was pretty sure that was a kidnap-ee rule. If not, it should have been.

She'd head to the library as soon as she was rescued and double check. Hell, she'd write her own manual if she needed to... *What to Expect When Shifters Break into Your Home, Beat You Up and Kidnap You* by Maddy Lane

Had a nice ring to it...

She almost smiled. Almost. Of course, the inclination quickly got squashed by the echoing roar that split the cavernous room.

"You *dared!*"

Everyone's focus swiveled toward the source of the voice and Maddy whimpered, sliding behind the polar bear and putting his large body between hers and the newcomer's.

While she'd had to consciously enter the other male's minds to discover their feelings, this other man's intentions and emotions slammed into her like a Mack truck. It wasn't anger. It was more. Rage, molten hot and pure, spewed from the shifter and her two halves warred inside her.

The human wanted to run and hide, cower in the presence of such emotion, such aggression. The cat ached to soothe the beast, knowing that his outburst hurt others, caused strife within the pride. Okay, not pride, per se. How about strife in their fucked up menagerie? Fuckedagerie?

Suddenly, the screamer was before them, his hands on the polar bear's shoulders, claws slicing into skin, and he tossed the large male aside as if he weighed nothing. Which left her with a death-craving lunatic.

Go team Dead Maddy!

Without conscious thought, the cat lunged inside her head, forced a joining. Then her power poured from her, right into the enraged male. Hands, more than she possessed on the physical plane, stroked the man's polar bear. It snarled and snapped at her attempts to soothe him, ghosted teeth reaching for her, aching to sink into her flesh. She and the cat dove past the beast's defenses and put her hands on his

11

fur, grabbed him by the ruff. And that fast, the animal's rage dissipated as if it'd never existed.

The man's blood-red mind cleared, the haze of desperation for death receded, leaving a single, calm polar bear in the male's mind.

Immediate danger eliminated, the lioness in Maddy's mind retreated and the human half of her slumped, exhaustion overtaking her. The man could catch her...or not.

When her world tilted, she realized he'd swept her into his arms and cradled her against his chest.

A deep voice emanated from the man holding her, the sound sending a vibration through her body. "And this is why I brought her here."

...*I brought her here.*

Well, goody. She'd just fainted into the arms of Alistair McCain. Wasn't that just fucking perfect.

* * *

Ricker Croft tossed back the remainder of his Jack, draining the glass in one big gulp. Not that he wanted to swallow the searing liquid. But appearances had to be kept up, and the small town at the base of Willow Mountain had pegged him as a heavy drinking shifter in hiding.

He needed to keep it that way.

At least until he found Madison.

Damn. Madison Lane, five feet of sweet-as-pie lioness who was at the mercy of Alistair McCain. He'd never been so angered at having a tip pan-out as when the news about Madison's kidnapping had come to light.

Of course, he just guessed at her disposition, but he'd never known a Sensitive that wasn't gentle and accommodating, happy to do as others asked.

Alistair had nearly killed Carly Thompson-Landry just over a week ago. Since then, Ricker had followed the coward around North Carolina and then lost him near the South Carolina border only to have the piece of shit circle back and kidnap the tiny Sensitive.

Fuck.

The bartender, a slim fox who lived up to her species name with her trim body and model-like looks, poured him another glass with a seductive smile and wink. "Here you go, baby. Let me know if you need anything else."

Information.

Not that he'd say the word out loud. Nah, he'd sit around the bar, keep his ears open and listen for gossip. Disgruntled worker bees tended to talk and he found Freedom members to be particularly unhappy most of the time.

Hopefully a human, or shifter, would unload on him soon.

It being a Friday night, the place had filled up pretty quick, men taking their places at the bar top and ordering heavy drinks.

It wouldn't be too long now.

A man, human, that he'd seen hanging around the bar the last night or two approached him, slid into the stool to his left and waved a couple fingers at the bartender.

"Cat." The human had a deep, smoke tinged voice.

"Human."

The man grunted, but had no other response.

The fox sauntered over and slid a glass filled with two fingers of liquor across the smooth wood. Bourbon from the smell of it. "Here ya go Jimmy."

"Nice night." The human nodded at the bartender, stinking of sweat and loathing.

Well, Ricker didn't care for the man either. "Uh huh."

"It'd be better if your kind weren't crowding our mountain."

"And I've been thinking that we'd all be better off if y'all left us to the wilds. Funny how shit works, huh?" Ricker took a sip from his glass, hands loose. He either had a man with a verbal message or one whose information came with a couple of fists the minute he exited the bar.

Ricker kinda hoped for fists. He had a lot of frustration built from his tracking and wouldn't mind taking a bit of it out on the stinking human.

The guy grunted again and he wondered if the man wasn't part ape. "I'd be happy if y'all left Nelson all together and avoided Willow Mountain, that Flick place in particular. Tommy Flick was a good boy and y'all are turning his granddaddy's home into one of your heathen places." He took a sip of his bourbon, set the glass carefully on the polished wood. "Seems y'all can't even stay with your own kind anymore. Disgraceful. Bears and cats. Fucking dogs. We ought to take y'all out back and shoot ya. Then you bring in another slut…"

He hated prejudiced hicks with nothing better to do than drink and act ignorant.

Instead, he hitched the side of his mouth up in a half smile and shrugged. "Yeah, well, sometimes sticking with a pride doesn't work."

The man grunted, took another sip and slid from his seat. "Gonna get outta here before I decide to take a little target practice. You just tell your friends to get the fuck out or we'll send you on your way ourselves."

With that, Jimmy abandoned his drink and disappeared into the crowd, slithering like a snake between bodies, then right out the front door.

The man had been sent. No doubt. The town of Nelson more than likely had a faction of the Humans for Shifter Extermination, the HSE, settled within town limits. Apparently, the good ole boys had a problem with a mottled group of shifters making their place home and assumed Ricker was one of them.

Good of them to assume since it helped his cause. However, his newest problem became keeping a quiet balance between the HSE and Freedom while he liberated the "slut" that had turned up recently.

At least he had a place to start.

Ricker waved the fox over, slipped a hundred dollar bill beneath his glass and slid the money and empty tumbler across the bar. "Tell me about the Flick place."

The woman leaned over the hard surface, low-cut shirt displaying a large swath of her tanned cleavage. Ricker's cock didn't even twitch. "What kind of business do you have there, baby?"

He raised a single brow. "I think the occupants and I might have some common interests."

A wide smile split her features.

Contact initiated.

CHAPTER *two*

"Some shifters don't understand that "no means no". If that's the case, teach them that a nine millimeter Glock means no." – Maya Josephs, Prima of the Ridgeville Pride and a crack shot.

Maddy woke on the floor in a small room with only her pajamas and a blanket between her and cool concrete. Her head spun and the cat growled in the back of her mind. The bitch was pissed. Well, human Maddy wasn't feeling much better. Alistair had paraded her through the compound's living room and forced her to touch each and every one of his shifters, calm them and implant feelings of absolute trust in Alistair. Then, after she'd passed out from the exertion, he'd apparently tossed her into this cell.

Remaining still, she kept her lids lowered and swept the room with her gaze. The area was sparse, only holding a small table, the pallet she lay upon and a toilet. Spying no one, she opened her eyes fully when…

A whimper, barely a sound at that, cut through the silence and was followed by a soft shuffle. Another look around the room revealed the source of the noise. Hidden beneath the table, pressed into the corner and tucked into a small ball sat a woman.

Maddy could see trembles and shudders wrack the fragile body, and she ached to go to the woman. Without asking, the cat joined her and they seeped into the woman's consciousness.

Fear, hunger, hate… They mingled and mixed inside the sweet fox's mind. Maddy couldn't identify the female, couldn't even pluck events from her memory, but she could soothe the poor creature. With the ghosting of a touch, she swept away the fear, calming her. There was nothing to be done about her hunger and Maddy figured that hating their captors couldn't hurt anything.

And yes, they were both captives… Maddy could sense a kindred spirit in the fox, recognized her for what she was. A Sensitive.

As Maddy retracted her metaphysical touch, the woman slumped and the shivers ceased torturing her slim body.

"Th-Thank you."

"You're welcome."

Maddy remained silent for another few moments as the stranger collected herself. "I'm Maddy. Madison Lane. How long have you been here?"

The woman raised her head and Maddy bit back a whine. Death and despair lurked in the fox's eyes.

"Two years, maybe? Not sure exactly. He," she swallowed. "Alistair took me from Hayes in South Carolina and then…" A tear slithered down the female's cheek. "Then they used me, broke me. I can't do anything anymore…"

Broke me.

18

It wasn't easy to break those like her, their power was one of birth and not artificial, but she'd heard stories…

"What's your name?"

"Elise Mara."

Maddy pushed herself to a seated position and leaned back against the stone wall of their prison. "Well, Elise Mara, we're going to get the heck out of here."

The woman raised her eyebrows, eyes wide. "We can't. We don't… You're like me. We aren't made for violence. We listen and do as we're told and—"

Maddy shook her head. "Nope. My Prima has been working with me, helping me find my back bone. Which, in case you were wondering, is above our asshole." She winked at Elise. "Everyone's got one, we just have to find ours."

"Assholes or backbones?" She didn't miss the smile playing around the fox's lips.

"I'm hoping you know where your asshole is, so I'm guessing it's the backbone we have to work on." That earned her a giggle from Elise and Maddy smiled. Maybe the tiny woman would be okay. Maybe. "Another thing we'll learn to use is our middle finger."

"Middle finger?"

Maddy figured she could keep Elise occupied with Maya-isms while she scoped the room, poked and prodded at the door as well as seeped into the minds of those surrounding their prison.

"Yup. According to Maya, it takes, like, a gajillion muscles to be scared shitless and only four to give a guy the finger. I tend to add 'suck it', but that's just me. We just need to do a little finger-robics."

Look at her, she could be all optimistic and confident and shit. She just hoped she could keep up appearances until help arrived. Or until she died. Whichever came first.

Maddy prayed for help.

"What are they gonna suck?"

She scoffed. "Toes. Duh. You know, after you've tromped through mud puddles and your feet are all stinkdified."

The echoing thud of wood hitting metal yanked them from their conversation and they both turned their attention to the visitor.

Hello asshole. The hyena from the kidnapping squad stood framed in the doorway, hair disheveled, bruises marring his face and, upon further inspection, a very large bulge behind his jeans.

Broke me. Elise's soft voice flitted through her mind.

Lust poured off the hyena in waves, blanket after blanket of the cloying emotion choking her, and she pushed past those feelings to delve into the crazy fuck's mind.

Hate.

God, did everyone hate everyone in the freaking compound? She'd just finished calming the fucker. The least he could do was stay "fixed" for more than five minutes. They seriously needed a time out and some kumbaya shit.

With a gentle, metaphysical hand, she reached out to soothe the man…only to have a real claw-tipped paw physically wrapped around her throat as the male lifted her from the ground.

"Nu uh, little cat. You did that once. Jasper won't let you play in his head again."

Really? The guy had to talk about himself in third person?

"Jasper should kill you now, she-cat. Think of how much fun it would be to bathe in your blood." The hyena cackled, evil laugh echoing off the walls and Maddy decided she was officially creeped the fuck out.

She also realized she couldn't breathe. She clawed at his hold, fingers and human nails digging into the flesh of his arm and hand, searching for purchase. She wheezed and coughed, scraped at his skin in an effort to get away.

On the other side of the room, poor Elise had huddled beneath the table once again, valiantly trying to curl her already tiny body into an even smaller ball.

And Maddy couldn't blame her. Before the months she'd spent in Maya's care, Maddy had been the biggest pussy known to pussy-dom. Seriously. She was like a Timex watch in a totally bad way. Her body took a licking (literally sometimes) and kept on ticking…until the next time a pride member took a swipe at her for shits and giggles. Most of the pride members were nice, but there was spoiled meat on a carcass. It'd taken Maya's influence on both their Prime, Alex, and the pride, to get them to treat her as more than a whipping boy, er, girl.

With one, last, evil smile, he dropped Maddy and she crumpled to the ground in a gasping heap.

"Pity Jasper can't kill you quite yet." He turned away from her as if she were of no consequence and crouched near Elise. "Come fox. You know it is better for you if you don't fight. Not better for me, but I don't wish to break you further."

Lust, hot and powerful, filled the room once again until Maddy nearly gagged on the stench.

God, he was going to…

Struggling to her feet, she croaked out two words that would probably change her life forever. "Take me."

*

Ricker slipped into the house through an unsecured window, movements silent thanks to his inner tiger. He and the cat had trained for these situations, working together in a synchronization that not many possessed.

He was the best at what he did, the greatest tracker in the history of the council, and the only male trusted with the job of hunting Alistair McCain.

The bartender had been most forthcoming with information. Suspiciously so. She'd claimed it was because Alistair had done her fox clan—her skulk—harm, but still Ricker was cautious. He wasn't about to go in with guns blazing so he could get himself shot.

He envisioned the layout of the home he'd studied, plans courtesy of an illegal trip to city planning, and recognized that he was in the first floor library. He had to get down a hallway, into the basement and then down a subterranean passage that led to the compound hidden beneath the earth. Old Mr. Flick had been a survivalist nut job and had taken his bomb shelter building seriously.

Piece of slaughtered Zebra.

Not.

He patted himself down, double checked the placement of his weapons and then crept to the door. It stood slightly ajar, a two inch gap giving him plenty of space to see into the darkened hallway. He opened his mouth and tasted the air, confirming what his eyes were telling him.

There had been no one in the area in the past two hours. Maybe longer.

He eased the door open, just enough to slither through the opening and into the confined area.

Ricker stuck to the wall, his heart rate and breathing even as he moved toward his destination. The shadows cradled him, hiding his progress.

Fifteen feet down the hallway opened to the home's entryway. To his left lay the front entrance and, to his right, the grand staircase leading to the upper floors. More importantly, just beside the stairs there was the path to the kitchen and, ultimately, the basement.

He just had a few Freedom members to get through first.

Ricker scented the area once again, tasted each fragrance and cataloged them. A lion stood watch just outside the front door. He was weak, easily overtaken if necessary.

He didn't want it to be necessary.

If anyone died this night, it'd be Alistair due to his position of leadership in Freedom, along with those who stood in his way while he hunted for Madison. The others could be rehabilitated. At least, that's what the council desired.

He kept to the wall, steps not making a sound as he crept along the hard surface and toward the back of the house. A glance at the front door revealed that the guard still hadn't spotted him. Good. He hoped to at least get into the compound undetected.

The shadows of the stairs enveloped him as he neared his destination. At the open entrance of the kitchen he lowered to a crouch. He pulled a tiny mirror from a pocket. Easing it along the floor, he inched it into the doorway, making out the shapes occupying the room.

And make them out he did. His deep inhale confirmed what he saw. Two males, both wolves, sat around the kitchen island, cups of coffee steaming before them. They were silent save their breathing and Ricker settled in to wait, thankful for the council's recent invention that masked his scent from others. He'd neutralize the wolves…at the right time.

It didn't take long.

The scrape of wood against tile signaled one of the males rising and the thump of footsteps neared him. He only had an instant to subdue the guard.

The man stepped around the corner, cup at his lips as he sipped at his drink and it was all the distraction he needed. In one fluid movement, Ricker gripped the man's head and gave it a fierce twist. His inner tiger lent him a bit of strength to make the killing quiet and fast, the coffee cup hitting the carpet with a muffled thud.

He caught the wolf's weight and lowered the body to the ground, stretching the male straight against the baseboard and out of sight.

One left.

Ricker dared a glance into the room and found the other wolf still sitting on his stool, back to the door and he rolled his eyes. Hadn't Alistair trained the men in any way?

It was no fun killing stupid people.

He edged forward, hands at his sides and loose, ready to dispatch another. It took two steps and a wrenching pull to eliminate the wolf, and Ricker ignored the pang of guilt that came with every kill. It seemed to magnify and weigh down on him more and more with every death.

Ricker navigated the kitchen with ease and found the entry to the basement without a problem. He paused long enough to listen for any other surprises and heard no one, so he headed down the dark staircase and found…nothing.

Oh, the area was dusty with worn furniture scattered about as well as some electronics, but otherwise, it was completely empty and didn't appear to have been used recently.

Did Alistair not realize…

Well, he hoped the polar bear had no idea about the bolt-hole entrance to his "impenetrable" compound.

Ricker strode to the brick wall and stared at the stones. To the casual observer, it was simply a decoration for the room, a faux finish that was meant to be pleasing to the eye.

It also happened to be a door.

With care, he pressed a handful of bricks, in precisely the order described by the bar's fox. While he'd gotten the plans from the city, the handy-dandy code came from the bartender. Thank God for pissed off women.

The wall opened with a soft whoosh. Cool, stale air wafted over him.

Ricker had a feeling the weight of guilt would be nearly debilitating before the night was through, but to save a sweet, innocent Sensitive, it'd be worth every slice of pain.

CHAPTER *three*

"To err is human, to love is divine. But fucking with a chick that grows fur and claws is a mistake. Show 'em how big that mistake can be." – Maya Josephs, Prima of the Ridgeville Pride who, regardless of the ginormous belly, is happy to show off her claws.

Jasper hadn't taken Maddy. No. He'd leered at her, promised that she'd enjoy his company someday, but he had a craving for his sweet Elise.

The fucker would die. Painfully. Twice if she could manage it.

She was pretty sure Carly had found some voodoo witch priestess chick after the fuck up with Alistair and Andrew. Andrew had sold Carly out to Alistair and then he'd been killed by the Freedom leader. Carly had wanted to bring Andrew back so she could kill him again. Slowly. With lots of tourniquets so she could cut off bits and pieces without him bleeding to death.

Apparently, being kidnapped turned cute bunny shifters into blood thirsty beasties.

Maddy was proud of her.

27

As soon as she saved herself from her current kidnapping, she'd get with Carly on how to properly torture and dismember a hyena.

Maddy padded to the door and pressed her ear against the hard surface. The cat helped her send tendrils of power flowing into the hallway. Her beast had been so close and ready to pounce that it took barely a thought to leap into action.

Instead of being stuck wandering the hallways, her mind flitted through walls, touched and stroked each shifter she encountered, hunting for knowledge about their location. More importantly, Elise's location.

Her earlier encounter with Alistair's men hadn't given her the opportunity to dig through their heads. She needed to find a very, very weak mind. With luck, she could drop a lovely thought into the shifter's brain and that person would wander over to check on her. With even more luck, release her.

Maddy hadn't really used that particular talent in a while, not since she'd convinced her aunt to hand over the cake bowl for her to lick. That tricked had earned her a stomach ache and a spanking to end all spankings.

Here kitty kitty...or beary beary...fuck it. Come here one of you ass-sniffers.

Her search went on, one mind after another, until she'd touched at least twenty-five and that was just within the general vicinity.

Fuck.

Panting, energy quickly draining from her exertions, she pushed on.

Another few feet, another few shifters and then…

Ding, ding, ding! We have a winner!

A male, fierce and determined, had one thing on his mind. Finding her. A deep look into his thoughts revealed his motivation and she was relieved to find out that he wasn't craving a quick tumble with a Sensitive chick. Nope, he was her Search and Rescue.

Thank God. She had been seriously losing faith in her favorite romance novels.

Hardcore.

Okay. She'd found him, now she had to get this insanely strong tiger male to her without risking his life in the process.

Here kitty, kitty…

The tiger in the male's mind roared in displeasure and Maddy felt a sickening rage take over the animal. Apparently "kitty" was not a name the cat preferred.

Well, too fucking bad. She needed saving, damn it.

As pissed as the male happened to be, she still felt him move through the compound, his consciousness nearing her with each passing second until he stood before her door.

"Step. Back." He bit off the words, growl in his throat.

Well, apparently kitty was pissed.

Goody for him.

She was angry, too, damn it. She'd tell him so. Eventually. Maybe.

Maddy did as he asked, placed six feet between her and the door, and waited. It didn't take more than a moment for the tiger to break through the obstacle. He stepped into the cramped space, large body taking up the majority of the room.

Oh, heaven on two legs. The tiger was just over six feet in height with long, dark blonde hair and piercing green eyes that seemed to encapsulate the room with one sweeping gaze. He had broad shoulders, a heavily muscled chest and thick legs. She could only imagine the wealth of power he held tightly leashed.

He was delicious. Like a popsicle on a scorching summer day and she wanted to lick him from head to toe and then suck on the wooden stick until she got all of the flavor and…

Dominance and fury filled the area and her body trembled with the need to cast her eyes to the floor and expose her neck in submission.

Then again…maybe not.

No. Fuck that. She was Maddy, hear her…something. Hear her not cower? Maybe?

Internally, Maddy gave the big growly guy the middle finger. Ha! Take that!

Externally…she turned into a pussy and lowered her eyes.

Yeah, she really needed to work on becoming a bad ass. One step at a time.

And then…oh, drop her to the floor and fuck her now…the tiger's scent drifted toward her on the cool air and her body tensed.

The guy smelled like chocolate. Not Hershey's. Nope, the high end, frou frou, spend-an-arm-and-a-leg-on-the-fucking-gold-box shit. And she knew without asking that it was the male's natural scent and that he didn't smell like her fave thing evah because he'd sprayed choccy cologne all over his body.

A deep shudder made its way through her limbs and arousal, hot and fiery, stole through her. The lioness was desperate to bathe in the man's fragrance, lick him from head to toe and back again. Maddy wanted to rub against him, purr as she stroked him and begged for a single touch from the tiger.

Her pussy grew moist and achy, need growing with her every breath.

Oh, come to momma.

Her lioness was in full agreement. The cat rolled around in her mind, exposed her belly and wanted to give the man a purred invitation.

Maddy watched as the tiger's expression shifted, changed before her eyes, from fury, down to "normal" anger and then slid into…desire.

She licked her lips and bit back a smile as his entire focus shifted to her mouth.

"Hi." Her voice was husky, deep and tinged with need.

The male's nostrils flared and his mouth parted, probably to taste the air, and she knew he'd recognize her arousal.

Sue her. She was a woman and he was one hunk of bend-me-over-do-me-now fuckaliciousness.

He opened his mouth farther and his single word broke through the silence. "Mine."

Oh. Well.

Wow.

Then, before she could sputter a response or voice her disbelief since her cat hadn't made a peep about mates, the she-bitch did some uttering in her head. Loud. Roaring really.

And it had one word on the brain. *Mine.*

Huh.

Look at how totally fucking accurate romance novels turned out to be! She was the damsel and her super-hunky lover was rescuing her.

Growly demeanor and overpowering dominance forgotten, Maddy took two steps and launched herself at the tiger. He caught her plump frame with ease, arms holding her and hands cupping the curve of her ass. She wrapped her legs around his waist and plastered her mouth over his.

Well, for all of a second since, hello, there was Elise to save. Fisting her hand in his hair, she wrenched his head back, his growl telling her he wasn't too happy with the interruption.

"Fucking later. Escaping now."

The tiger opened his mouth baring his fangs, but a blaring siren cut off his words and they both froze. The stranger lowered her to her feet. He spun and placed his back against the wall as he tugged her toward the doorway, his body tense.

Yells, growls and roars echoed along the halls and she worried that her tiger's presence had been discovered.

He paused near the portal and she watched him scent the air, his shoulders tensing even further. "Humans."

"Fuck."

She felt rather than heard his chuckle. "That's one way of putting it, Kit." He paused, quite for a moment. "We'll use them to cover our exit." He turned to her, eyes intent and full of a deadly seriousness. "You stay on my ass. Period. I will blister your bottom if you even think of doing anything I don't tell you to do. Got it?"

"Got it." She whispered, fear and anger warring within her. She was all about getting out alive, so she'd ignore his ordering her around. Yeah, she wasn't keen on being captured again, but the man didn't have to be so growly.

Plus, she really hoped he was exaggerating the whole "blister" thing since she was intent on disobeying him the second they got down the hall. She'd touched enough minds to know the layout of the compound and exactly where the hyena had taken Elise.

So, yeah.

Her mate headed right after leaving the small room, moving fast and sure down the hallway, free hand clutching a gun. His long strides ate up the path and Maddy practically jogged to keep up with the man.

Had she mentioned she didn't "do" exercise? And that she had uber short legs?

Huffing and jiggling, Maddy kept pace with the big cat, eyes scanning the various corridors as she sent tendrils of her powers through the space. With the alarm, she wasn't sure if Elise was still with Jasper or if he'd hauled her somewhere else.

Found you!

Apparently even the threat of invasion didn't deter the piece of shit.

At the next split in the hall, two men came tearing around a corner. Maddy wasn't sure if they were human or shifter and, apparently, it didn't matter to her mate. The tiger raised his gun and released a handful of shots, the deafening sound echoing off the concrete walls.

Her mate distracted, Maddy took her chance. She jerked her hand from the male's grasp and broke into a run, desperate to find Elise. She wasn't leaving without the timid fox. A roar followed her, but her lioness lent her strength and speed. Her short legs ate up the ground, bare feet slapping against the smooth surface.

From memory, she navigated the twists and turns, shoving men aside, ducking their grabs as she raced toward her destination. The heavy thud of the tiger's steps grew closer with every breath, but she was determined to save the woman, come hell or high water. Or crazed shifter.

Another turn, through a cavernous room and to the other side. Men fought around her, grappling, tearing into flesh, the blood of humans and shifters alike assaulting her senses.

And still she ran. Another fifty feet. Then twenty-five. The door was in sight.

The lioness shoved to the fore, shifting Maddy's bones, gifting her with wicked claws, elongated fangs and furious strength. The fox's emotions called to her in a desperate plea for help, the woman dying a little more with every passing second that she was alone with the hyena. Maddy hit the door at a dead run, ramming her shoulder into the steel and the frame gave way with a squealing protest.

Adrenaline fueled her rage. She recovered in an instant and took in the room in a lightning fast sweep of her gaze.

The sick male hovered over a nude Elise, her trembling body nearly as pale as the sheet under her small frame. The man's jeans barely clung to his hips, ass bared, and he swung his attention to her with a snarl.

"What—"

Maddy didn't give him a chance to utter another sound. As if she'd grown wings, she flew at the male. Arms outstretched, she hauled the piece of shit from the Sensitive and threw him against the wall, his head colliding with the hard surface with a resounding crack.

She followed him to the ground, teeth bared, and closed her mouth around the male's neck, sinking fangs into him until she hit bone. Then, she pushed deeper.

The hyena tried to shove her away, hands digging into her shoulders, but she refused to release the predator. Not when she had him where she desired.

His attention focused on her mouth, she brought her claws between his legs and wrenched the flesh she found from

35

his body. It took one grasp and pull and he'd never rape another again.

One last swipe along his inner thigh and she severed his femoral artery.

Have fun bleeding out, fucker.

Whining and whimpering, the male released Maddy's shoulders and turned his attention to stemming the flow of blood from his body.

He'd be dead by the time she left the room with Elise in her arms.

Maddy took a single step toward the cowering woman and the tiger burst into the room, face a study in fury. His cheeks had sharpened and stripes of orange and black covered his arms.

He growled deep and the sound was quickly followed by a snarl as he neared her.

Maddy ignored him. He was her mate and she figured he'd focus on getting them to safety before he got to blistering her bottom.

"Come on, Elise. Time to go."

"Ma-Maddy?"

Maddy nodded. "Yes, sweetheart." Wiping her hands on her pajamas, she then leaned down and snagged the woman's shirt from the ground, thankful that it hadn't been coated in the hyena's blood. "Here, Elise. We gotta get."

A soft gurgle and sickening squelch came from behind them, but she ignored the sound. With the big cat in the room, she didn't think they were in any danger and if Ricker was the cause of the noise, she didn't even want to know what he'd done to the hyena.

"Y-you're covered in blood."

"It's all his." She dropped the shirt over the woman and tugged it down. It barely covered her ass, but it'd have to do. They seriously needed to get on the road. Grabbing Elise's hand, she turned toward her mate. "We're ready."

Without a word, the tiger seized her hand and then went to the door. He scanned the hall and stepped into the passage. Maddy stayed on his heels, Elise's hand in hers, as they navigated the compound. Around one corner, then another, they twisted and turned through the space. The male fired on those that approached, leaving the bodies where they fell and Maddy didn't have even a twinge of sympathy for them. She knew their intentions, their emotions and desires nearly choking her, and she didn't have an ounce of pity.

Sliding around another corner, the tiger wrenched a door open and shoved them inside.

"This is a closet." She hissed the words.

"Quiet." His voice was a low growl, the word accompanied by a wave of dominance that had sweet Elise whimpering.

Maddy pulled the woman behind her and glared at her mate. She opened her mouth to tell him exactly what she thought about his meanie-ness, but snapped her teeth together when the wall slid aside to reveal a tunnel.

"In." He bit off the word.

She sensed that the "blistering" may have turned into something a bit more painful and decided to do as he asked. She slid past him, a cowering Elise in tow.

The tiger followed, the portal sliding shut with his passing. Then they were following him again, trudging up an endless line of stairs.

Again with the exercise. The she-cat had retreated which meant the bitch wasn't helping Maddy put one foot in front of the other any longer.

After countless minutes, the tiger stopped and she immediately did the same, careful to steady Elise.

The big cat looked at her over his shoulder, glare in place, and she took that as a sign to keep her mouth shut and ass put.

He touched the wall, hand pushing various spots, and then it slid aside. He stepped inside the space and then motioned for her to follow.

The next moments went by in a blur. They dashed through a large home, the space seeming to be completely empty. Well, besides a couple of dead wolves, but she figured they were courtesy of their escort.

The tiger led them into a back room and through a window. Then it was a mad dash to the tree line.

Maddy's bare feet collided with dry leaves, twigs and rocks, but still she kept moving, weaving around trees and bushes as they traveled deeper into the woods.

Huffing, she remained practically glued to the tiger's ass, matching him step for step.

Elise lagged behind her, but she held tight to the fox's hand.

No man left behind. Okay, woman…shifter…body?

Finally, what seemed like hours later, they came upon a black SUV, windows darkened, and Maddy nearly sobbed in relief when the tiger unlocked the vehicle.

With a handful of stumbling steps, she pulled the fox to the back door and shoved her into the truck before following her. The moment Maddy settled, Elise scrambled to her side, almost crawling into her lap and she held the smaller woman close.

"Shh…we're safe now. Safe, sweetheart."

The tiger started the SUV, popped it into gear and they tore from the area, racing past trees until they turned onto a paved highway. Maddy stroked Elise's back, she and the lioness working to ease the woman's fear to a manageable level and cease the shudders wracking her body.

Woman calmed, she directed her next question to her mate. "Who are you?"

"Ricker Croft."

Maddy paled. The man who'd saved her friend Carly had come for her. The one male rumored to be the most dominant and fierce of all shifters had broken into hell and pulled her out. And he was her mate.

She was in deep shit. With a red bottom.

CHAPTER *four*

"There are a ton of rules floating around, follow half and plead ignorance if you're caught. You're cute and you'll probably get off with a warning." – Maya Josephs, Prima of the Ridgeville Pride. And still ringless.

They'd dropped Elise with her family. The foxes were waiting at the street for the timid woman, a couple of the males ready to escort her out of state to heal.

Maddy nearly begged to take her with them, but one glare from Ricker quelled the urge. Okay, a glare and a brush against his mind. The male was still pumped with rage because she'd put herself in danger, but it was tempered with a good dose of fear at almost losing her.

She was seriously tempted to tone his anger down a bit, but she didn't think her mate would care for her mucking about in his head. Again.

Their SUV raced down the highway and they hadn't exchanged a word since he'd revealed his name. Which was fine with her. Captivity hadn't been all that fun and she was good with existing in her own head for a while.

She opened her mouth to ask where they were going, but was silenced when he took the next exit, the large vehicle hugging the curve and then pulling into light traffic. They traveled another half-mile before they turned into the parking lot of a hotel. He backed into a parking spot and popped the vehicle into park.

"You will lock the doors when I leave. When I come back, you will unlock them. You will not touch anything in the SUV and I will find you here when I return. Understood?"

Well, what crawled up his ass and died? Or what crawled up his ass, period? He obviously had not learned about the pleasures of his prostate so...

The deepening of Ricker's glare pulled her from pondering his rear end and she nodded her agreement. She'd really have to talk to him about stopping the whole ordering thing. Just as soon as he no longer looked like he wanted to maim her.

One last dark gaze and he leapt from the truck, slamming the door. He stood just outside and didn't move until she hit the button to lock the doors.

Well, untrusting much?

But, Maddy stayed put and watched as people traveled in and out of the front entrance to the hotel, keeping her eyes peeled for Ricker.

Before long, he emerged, all long-legged grace. He seemed to glide over the asphalt, body moving easily as he crossed the parking lot to her. His eyes nearly glowed in the darkness of night and a shiver of desire throbbed in her veins.

She had no idea how she could get hot and bothered by a furious tiger. It had to be one of those bad-boy, rough, angry sex fantasies or something.

As he reached for the handle on the door, she hit the button to unlock the vehicle and let him in.

Ricker cut her a glance, but remained silent, pulling the car from the space and driving around the building. What, not even a "good job"?

When they stopped, his gaze combed over her body in a slow sweep. Without uttering a word, he reached into the backseat and grabbed a blanket, tossing at her.

"Wrap yourself in that, then grab the duffel."

Maddy did as he demanded and wondered when he'd get over his little snit. She kinda liked the idea of a mate, but wasn't too keen on him being all asshole-esque.

When he nodded and climbed from the SUV, she took that as a sign that she could do the same. Bag in hand, she half-fell from the vehicle (cause, hello? Short). Ricker caught her just before her bare feet collided with the asphalt and swept her into his arms with ease. There was no grunting or groaning as he accepted her weight. Nope, he lifted her as if she were light as a feather.

He thumped the door closed with his hip and strode toward the sliding doors of the building, not pausing as he passed through the portal and then through the building without any hesitation.

"You scoped out the building." Her mate glanced at her, single eyebrow raised and she returned the expression. "Before you came for me. You could get through this place blind."

He jerked his head in a tight nod. "But that won't be necessary because you're going to stay where I put you and I won't have to chase you through a compound filled with humans and shifters slaughtering each other, will I?"

Well, someone was still Mister Cranky-pants.

Maddy opened her mouth to say…something…when he paused at a door and lowered her to her feet. She swayed, suddenly more tired than she'd ever been, and slumped against him.

Without missing a beat, Ricker, wrapped an arm around her shoulders and hugged her close while he slid the keycard into the door handle and let them into their temporary home.

Home.

God, where would they live?

Hell, would she let him live? No matter what stupid stunt she'd pulled, he should have been over his pout by now. And if he didn't stop telling her what to do soon…

Ricker shoved the door open and led her into the space, her feet sinking into the plush carpet with every step.

Instead of leading her toward the bed, he paused by the bathroom and shuffled her into the small area, tugging the blanket from her body as they moved. A flick of the light switch illuminated the room and she gasped at her reflection.

Blood.

Everywhere.

The red, coppery liquid had dried on her skin, trails lined her mouth and neck, and the life giving fluid had soaked into her top. A glance at her hands revealed even more red stains and her pajama bottoms sported the burgundy hue.

Pure, predatory satisfaction coursed through her veins at what she'd done. True, the presence of the blood disgusted her, but the reason behind it pleased her lioness to no end.

He'd died. At her hands.

"Easy, Kit." The soft rumble of her mate's voice cut through her and she met his eyes in the mirror, his gaze saying more than words could express…worry, fear, anger, possessiveness. All of it clouded his features.

"I know you said you weren't hurt, but I need to strip you. Need to check myself."

His voice was soft, gentle, and completely incongruous with his motions. Jerky tugs pulled at her top and then bottoms. She watched, detached, while her plump body was displayed to her mate.

Although his emotions remained in turmoil, tender hands stroked her, slid along her curves and tenderly traveled over her skin. Unbelievably, her body responded to his soft touch, arousal flickering to life and spiriting through her limbs.

God, even exhausted, she wanted him, ached to finish what they'd started. She didn't know him from Adam, but her lioness was desperate to sink her teeth into the man and claim him.

She whimpered and Ricker was quick to soothe her. "Shh… I've got you."

Gentle, so fucking gentle she was sure she was dreaming, the male scooped her into his arms and carried her to the shower and then lowered her to her feet. She leaned against his heavily muscled body, inhaling his sweet scent and he reached around her and fiddled with the faucet.

The rumble of running water filled the space, but she didn't care. Not when she had her hands on her male. The aftermath of the night was closing in on her and all she wanted to do was sink into her mate's hold. Nothing else mattered but him. Nothing.

After a few, brief moments, Ricker returned his attention to her. "Going to turn on the shower, Kit."

"Maddy." She grumbled against his chest, unwilling to lose her spot.

"Madison, then. Here it comes."

A soft patter of water rained down on her back and she let the warm fluid soothe her aches, the pain of her tense muscles washing away with every droplet that skimmed her skin. She moaned, luxuriating in the feel of getting clean, the stench of the hyena's blood dissipating.

"Shh…" Ricker must have interpreted her sound as distress.

She'd put the man through hell; the least she could do was let him know he didn't have a crying girl on his hands. With any other man, she probably would have burst into trembling tears already, but Ricker made her feel a hundred feet tall, as if she shared in his strength.

Maddy nuzzled his chest, inhaled more of his flavors and then raised her head to focus on his face. "I'm fine."

"Yeah?" The right side of Ricker's mouth quirked up in a half smile.

She nodded.

His large hands skimmed her back, blunt fingers tracing her spine, sliding over one vertebra after another until his palms rested at the top curve of her ass. "You feel fine, but I'm not sure about the rest of you, Madison."

"I really am good, oh striped one."

That earned her an all-out smile. "I like it. What happened to the sweet, timid little Sensitive your pride told me about?"

Now, she smiled. "Maya is teaching me how to be a bad ass."

"Uh huh." He barked out a laugh. Barked. Heh. "I can believe it. If you're fine, turn around and we'll get you washed."

At the mention of getting clean, Maddy was reminded of one thing: she was naked. Amazingly, Ricker was not.

"You're still wearing clothes!" Oh, all of that yummy black leather was getting ruined. And she'd had such high hopes at seeing her mate sweaty and shirtless in nothing but his pants and boots with his badass guns all strapped on and…meow.

"It was dressed…" Her mate leaned down and brushed his lips across hers in a chaste kiss. "Or naked and claiming you against the wall. I didn't think taking you while you were still covered in blood was very romantic."

Oh. Oh, her growly man was all sweet and gooey. She practically swooned like those brainless twits in her favorite regency romance novels.

Ricker pulled back and gave her a mock glare. "But if you tell a single soul about how nice I'm being and ruin my reputation, I'll warm that ass until you can't sit for a week."

Maddy rose to her tiptoes, nipped his lower lip and spoke against his mouth. "Promises, promises."

Her mate narrowed his eyes and clenched his jaw, vein throbbing along his temple, but didn't say a word. Nope. Instead, he forced her to turn around and face the warm spray of the shower.

Ricker at her back, she leaned into him, relaxed against his body and let the water wash away the bulk of Jasper's blood. Pale pink rivulets danced over the floor of the tub and Maddy watched the evidence of the night slither away.

The tiger shifted behind her, but remained a solid presence for her to rest on.

In her periphery, she watched as his arms came into her line of sight, hands coated in soapy bubbles. "Lemme clean you up, Kit."

Oh. Touches. Mate touches. Yay!

Those large, work-roughened hands cupped her breasts, her flesh overflowing his palms as he massaged her. Fingers danced over her slick skin, soap sending the remnants of her struggle down the drain until only her pale complexion remained.

Ricker's digits didn't move on though. No, he toyed with her nipples, traced tight circles around the hardening nubs.

48

He tormented her with barely there touches, calluses glancing her sensitive skin and she arched into his strokes.

She needed more of him. Much more.

Every tease of her nipples sent a spear of desire to her pussy, forcing her passage to become slick and wet, readying her body for his possession. Her clit throbbed and twitched, ached for his touch.

Ricker leaned his head down, chuckled against her shoulder and then grabbed her flesh between his teeth. He didn't break the skin, but the gentle sting was enough to add to her need.

"Greedy, Madison."

"Ricker." She whimpered and arched into him even more. His hands continued their torment, slick soap easing his attentions. Round and round, his fingers traced her heaving breasts.

"Don't interrupt while I'm washing you, Kit. This is serious business."

She giggled. Couldn't help it. Of course, the giggle turned into a high-pitched gasp when he squeezed her nipples between thumb and forefinger. Both hands gave her breasts the same torturous treatment and she couldn't decide between begging for more or begging him to stop.

She voted for more.

"Yes. More. Need." The pain added to the pleasure, stoked her arousal higher and made her that much more desperate for him. The hard shaft nestled against her ass reminded her that he seemed to want her just as much.

"I've got you." He rumbled against her ear, vibrations traveling through her from head to toe and back again.

"Ricker. Want." He'd reduced her to single word sentences. God, what would happen when he fucked her? Would she end up a drooling pile of satisfied goo? She kinda hoped so.

He plucked the nubs, squeezed hard and tugged on them in tandem. She arched her back to follow his movements, unwilling to lose the contact. Pleasure followed every shift of muscle, every strain of her body.

When she didn't think she could take any more of the stinging pain, he eased his hold, stroked the abused flesh with a soothing touch and a rush of ecstasy flooded her pussy.

Her heat pulsed, tightened and wordlessly begged to be filled. His hard cock remained firm against her ass and she ached to have him free, throbbing against her palm and then sliding deep into her. She wanted his possession, craved his domination.

"Shh…" Ricker abandoned her right breast, let his hand wander further south until the pads of his fingers rested at the top of her slit, close, but not touching her nether lips. "Is this where you need me?"

"Yes!" She screamed the word, the sound echoing off the tiled walls.

His response was a cocky, male chuckle.

A single finger teased the area, digit sliding between her sex lips a half inch and then retreating, tormenting the aroused flesh. In and then out, her body heated with every rub of the roughened member over the delicate area. She writhed against him, rose onto her tiptoes, chasing the contact and whimpering at each withdrawal.

"Damn it, Ricker." She and her lioness joined, growling and snarling at his teasing.

He laughed. Fucker. The man laughed entirely too much and she'd tell him so. Just as soon as he made her come.

But then…then his finger delved deeper, the tip nudging her clit and she moaned at the contact. The barely-there touch sent a piercing spear of delight through her pussy and her heat released more of her slick cream.

Ricker kept up his tormenting strokes, brushing the bundle of nerves with every pass, but going no deeper.

Didn't matter. She could come from him rubbing her clit. She just needed more.

"Please…"

Her mate rocked his hips, sending his leather clad cock sliding along the crack of her ass, a deep groan quickly following the move. "You already know how to get me, don't you, Madison?"

His finger dipped a little deeper, his baritone voice washing over her. "Is that what you want? Want me to pet this pretty little pussy? Do you know how good you smell? All hot for me. You want me to slide deep into your cunt, don't you?"

She whimpered, but couldn't manage a single word. Each question resulted in his digit gliding closer to her heat, stroking and caressing her flesh with a penetrating touch.

"Tell me, mate. Will you squeeze me tight when I finally slide into you? Will you come for me?" He spoke against her shoulder, teeth grazing her heated skin, sending arousal spiraling through her body. "Will you come on my hand? On my cock?"

"Yes." She groaned. Moaned. Fuck, her throaty voice devolved into a needy, desperate, do-me-now sound.

Ricker reached deep between her thighs, that digit circling her opening and her pussy clenched in response, eager to pull him within her body.

"Beg me."

"Bastard." She hissed and brought her hands to his forearms, determined to force him to do as she desired.

"Nah, Kit. Just a man who wants to hear how bad his mate wants him. Do you want me, Madison?" He ran his tongue along the shell of her ear. "Tell me."

Maddy growled low. "I want you. I want you fucking my pussy with your fingers, your cock. I want to come on your hand, your dick, fuck... I just want to come, Ricker."

"Mate."

A deeper growl grew in her chest. "Mate."

That teasing finger penetrated her then, slid right into her heat and stroked her inner walls, sent her arousal soaring with the breach. He slipped in and then retreated, shallow and then deeper, tormenting her with the touch.

Maddy rocked her hips, rode his hand as much as he would allow, and it wasn't enough. Not nearly.

"Ricker," she whined.

The single digit disappeared, and before she could protest, it was replaced by two, stretching and filling her, pressing against nerves she'd forgotten. The pads of his fingers stroked her inner walls, the rough texture forcing her pleasure points back to life and she tightened around him.

He slid his fingers from her pussy and then back in a slow pace that tormented rather than satisfied. He repeated the shift of his digits, inching into her heat and then back out. Each movement rocked the heel of his hand against her clit, sending shards of bliss-tinged pleasure along her spine.

Her longing for him grew, her body thirsty for his with every mocking stroke. He knew what she needed, but refused to give in.

"Damn it, Ricker." She rocked her hips, rode his palm in an effort to come.

"Not yet." He nibbled her earlobe. "I need your agreement, first."

He plunged deep and curled his fingers, pads rubbing along her G-spot and she screamed in response. The overwhelming pleasure rocketed through her core and her breath stilled in her chest.

"Anything." Seriously. Whatever he wanted. She just needed to come already.

"You were very bad back at the compound and you need to promise to listen to me whenever I tell you to do something. You take direction from me." His voice held a dark promise, but his words stilled the blood in her veins.

"No." It was the only answer. Period. Full stop. She'd found most of her backbone, damn it. She'd killed a man for goodness sake.

She'd proven she could take care of herself and learned that no one was the boss of her.

Except the pride's Prime, Alex. And the Prima, Maya. But other than them, she was the boss of herself, thank-you-very-much. She wasn't about to revert to the cat that got ordered around. He'd been telling her what to do all night, which had been fine since it'd kept her alive. But carte blanche? Fuck no.

"What?" Ricker's ministrations halted.

The man sounded truly astonished. Well, woohoo for him.

Maddy grasped his wrist and pulled his hand from her body, stepped out of his embrace.

"No." She turned and backed up until she met tile. "I think I can take things from here."

His thunderous gaze met hers and she refused to back down, flinch and grovel at his stare. The warm water from the shower pelted him and she saw that his shirt was soaked through, revealing the wicked lines of his chest and abdomen. His leathers were plastered to his thighs and his cock was outlined by the wet material.

She almost whimpered. Almost.

With an internal shake of her head, she got back to the topic at hand.

They would be mates…eventually…

Her momma had given her one piece of advice about men and mating, and she'd held it close to her heart from that day forward.

"Maddy Lane, don't you do something for your mate that you aren't ready to do for the rest of your life. You wash his socks once and he'll want 'em washed 'til the day you die. It's the way men are. You remember that. For. The. Rest. Of. Your. Life."

"I'm ordering you, Madison…"

She snorted. "You can try."

Ricker's eyes darkened to near black, death written in every feature and not one bit of her was afraid. "Sensitives can't disregard a direct order and I'm—"

Maddy's inner lioness didn't care for his words and pushed forward. She'd been in "grow a backbone" training right along with her human half and had a little somethin'-somethin' to say about her mate being an ass.

"This Sensitive thinks you can shove your orders up your ass. Wait, you've already got a steel rod there, don't you? Maybe you can quit being a dick long enough to pull it out. While you work on that, I'll be taking a shower. Alone."

Ricker's eyes drifted closed and he took a single deep breath. He wrenched aside the shower curtain, stomped from the tub and yanked the curtain back into place. At the thundering slam of the bathroom door, Maddy resumed her position beneath the spray.

She'd either done a ballsy, O-M-G-awesome thing, and it'd all work out in the end, or she'd fucked up royally and hopefully Maya could help her fix things.

Either way, she had to remember…

55

For the rest of your life…

*

Ricker glared at the closed door.

That…that woman!

A steel rod up his ass? And why the hell hadn't she listened? That's what Sensitives did. They were given orders, did as others asked. They were a necessary part of the pride, but they also listened. They did not tell their mates "no". Hell, they didn't tell any shifter more dominant than them "no". It just wasn't done. True, she'd only half done what he asked during their escape, but he figured that'd had more to do with rescuing Elise than flat-out brushing him off.

But then, she was…and then she'd…and…

Fuck it. The little lioness was perfect. Perfect for him. Hell, perfect in general. From the tip of her pert little nose all the way to her pink painted toes. And everything in between. And when he meant everything, he meant everything. She had curves on curves and he wanted to lick and nibble every lush inch of her.

How the hell had he gotten so lucky?

His mate was all soft curves with an ass that hugged and cradled his dick and breasts that overflowed his hands.

And those lips… When he'd taken a nice, long look at those luscious lips, all he could think about was sliding his cock into her waiting mouth.

Hell, even her eyes were sexy. All flashing blue and bright in the shower when she'd gotten her back up. He wasn't sure what he'd done wrong, but part of him wanted to do it again just so he could watch her eyes shine with anger.

The woman was…his. Good and bad and he had a feeling that she'd be a whole lotta bad.

He couldn't wait. His cock throbbed in agreement as he thought of turning that rounded bottom over his knee and warming her skin until she begged for him. The tiger wanted her pushed to her hands and knees the moment the spanking was finished so he could mount her, claim her and connect them forever.

Ricker stared at the door separating them and, with a sigh, he stomped away from temptation. He grabbed the duffel he'd brought along for the ride. It held their necessities, a change of clothes for both of them as well as toiletries and a chocolate bar that the Prima had said Madison would kill for.

He wondered if handing over the sweet would make her more amenable to completing their mating.

Ricker tugged off his weapons, the waterlogged metal clinking as it hit the bed. Then he went after his sopping wet clothes, letting them fall to the carpeted floor with a squishy plop. He'd trash everything before they got back on the road. His hunting blacks weren't exactly conducive to being under the radar while they traveled.

With quick efficiency, he laid out Madison's clothing and tugged his own free of the bag. Just as soon as his little mate emerged, he'd take her place and then…

Nude, he padded to the room's closet and snagged a clean towel, wrapped it around his waist so he wasn't bare when she appeared. He trapped his hard cock between his body and the cotton, figuring he'd be in a state of constant arousal when around his mate. He'd better get used to it now.

Shower still running, Ricker snagged the secure cell phone from the bag, one of many that he kept around when he went on a hunt, and he dialed the first number from memory.

Two rings and the call was answered. "From Click to Ship, how can I help you?"

Ricker recognized the voice of his long-time friend, Lia. He wanted to drill the woman on how to get his mate to come around, but stuck to their planned script.

"Hey, this is Tommy Jenkins. I know I called y'all earlier today about losing my package, but I just wanted to let ya know that I found it all safe and sound. I actually found two in my box, but forwarded the one that didn't belong to me on to its rightful owner."

"Excellent Mr. Jenkins. Just to confirm, you found your box and you won't be submitting a claim for damages? You also forwarded a secondary package?" Lia was all business, but he could hear the relief, as well as curiosity, in her voice.

"Nope, we're good. And the other box is on its way home. Have a nice night."

"You, too, Mr. Jenkins. And thank you for working with Click to Ship." The soft click of her ending the call reached his ears and he hit the "off" button on his end.

Now, rinse and repeat.

Ricker searched through the phone's memory and found the number he'd been searching for, hit the "send" button and waited.

Barely half a ring sounded and then the call was answered. "O'Connell."

"Mr. O'Connell, Tom Jenkins. Just wanted to let you know I found that package. I thought it'd been lost, but I stumbled across it today and I should be able to deliver it soon."

The Prime's gusting breath of relief flew over the phone lines. "Thank god. She's—The package is okay?"

"As okay as can be expected."

"Th-Thank you." Ricker could hear the emotion clogging the lion Prime's voice.

"Not a problem sir. I'll give you a call later with an ETA. Have a nice night." Ready to end the call, his thumb hovered over the "off" button, but the Prime's voice brought him back.

"Wait. Tell…tell the package—" The Prime's voice was cut off and a whispered argument ensued until he heard the unmistakable sigh of resignation from the Prime. "Just a minute."

Next, he got blasted by a feminine voice that could only be the Prima. "Listen. You tell the package that she's a kick ass bitch and we're totally having margaritas the minute she gets home so she can tell me all about how those bastards ended up bleeding all over her floor. Cause she's fucking awesome, right? I totally know those 'Grow a Set' lessons were working. And—"

"Wait. Grow a set?" Did she mean…

"Yup. Everyone gives her shit because she's a Sensitive. Being sweet and caring is not an invitation for everyone else to show their asses and walk all over her and tell her what to do all the time. You understand that, right? Because if you don't, I'll make you understand when you bring my box back. Just see if I don't." Part of him wanted to laugh at the idea of the tiny, very pregnant Prima tearing into him, but the other half was thrilled that Madison had a protector in the woman. "Oh! I have a new quote for her, ready?"

"Ready?"

The Prima growled. "Write this down."

Ricker looked in the drawer of the bedside table and snagged a pad of paper and a pen. All hotels had their stationary stashed in the same places. "Go ahead."

"Life is hard. It's even harder if you're stupid. You're not stupid so buck up buttercup and show the guys that your balls, and SAT scores, are bigger than theirs." The snippet of knowledge was followed by a purely feminine giggle and a snort from Alex. "Did you get it?"

"Yup."

The soft click of the bathroom door opening drew his attention and Ricker feasted on the sight before him. Madison's skin was flushed from the heat of her shower and droplets of water clung to her skin, giving it a soft glow. He ached to lap up each pearl of the fluid, dry her with his tongue. And, thinking on the Prima's words, he felt some of his prejudices and preconceived ideas melt away. She wasn't just another lioness. She wasn't simply a

Sensitive. She was his. And he'd been an ass. "I've definitely got it now, thanks."

Before the Prima could keep gabbing in his ear, he ended the call and set the phone on the table. A tug on the page he'd written on released the note. Ricker padded toward his mate and slid the piece of paper into her hand.

"Here, Kit. Maya had a message for you." He leaned toward her and dropped a kiss on her forehead. She stiffened, but didn't pull away. Well, that was a step. Tiny, but still a step. "There're some warm clothes on the bed. If you're tired, go ahead and crawl on in." He glanced back at the single, king-sized bed in the room and internally winced. Well, it was his own fault he wouldn't be seeing any relief any time soon. "I'll get in when I'm done, but I'll keep my hands to myself."

Their gazes clashed and he watched the emotions flittering across her features. Hope, wariness, exhaustion and…that something he couldn't quite identify.

Another kiss on the top of her head and he forced himself to finish his walk to the bathroom.

Because he got it now… He just needed to get her.

CHAPTER *five*

"They say good boys are found in all corners of the earth. What the idiots never realized is that the fucking earth is round. Then again, it doesn't matter. 'Cause it's the bad ones you really want." – Maya Josephs, Prima of the Ridgeville Pride. Had she mentioned she still had no ring?

Ricker's cock hurt. No, not just hurt…it felt like it was about to burst into a million pieces and not in the I'm-about-to-come way.

At all.

And it was his fault.

After his shower he'd crawled into the king sized bed and rolled to his side, watched his sweet mate sleep. For hours.

The tiger had been manageable while she slumbered, the cat knowing their woman needed rest after her ordeal. Of course, then she'd rolled into his arms, snuggled her soft body along his and rubbed against him like she was a cat begging to be pet.

The furball in his head had nearly overpowered him. Only his fierce control had kept the beast at bay through the hours and he raced from the bed the moment his alarm had sounded.

They'd only managed a four hour nap, but they had to get on the road. There was no telling if Freedom or HSE had managed to track them. He'd figured that the two groups would fight for a while and that had been the only reason he'd stopped for a rest.

The male shifter at the check-in desk had assured Ricker he'd call if anyone came looking for them and the proximity alarm on the SUV hadn't alerted him to any tampering. But he'd rather be safe than sorry.

Hence a bundled up Madison sitting in the front seat of their new wheels, cradling a cup of coffee as if it were the choicest cut of beef.

Lia had done her job after their phone call. The unassuming car, turbo-charged and sporting a few hundred non-factory horse power, had been waiting in the parking lot for them. Stocked with the usual, they now had plenty of cash, several changes of clothes and enough tech and firepower to get them through to Ridgeville.

Not that Ridgeville had been his first choice in places to run, but Madison belonged to Alex until Ricker managed to claim her as his mate. Which meant what Alex said was law.

A soft whisper reached across the center console and tickled his ears, but he missed the words. "What?"

Madison cleared her throat. "Um, do you have kids? Cubs? Because Neal had cubs and didn't tell Carly and that caused all kinds of shit to hit the fan. He was a bit of a man-whore, too, but the kidlets pushed Carly over the edge for a while."

Her eyes remained glued to the road in front of them, but he could sense the heightened tension in the car. Her pulse pounded in her veins so loud, he could hear it over the road noise and the tang of her worry assaulted his nose.

"No. No, I don't have any children." He kept his eyes focused on the asphalt. "I'm typically tracking during the Gaian Moon, so I never take part in the festivities."

Well, "festivities" was one way of putting it. Every six months, the Gaian Moon pulled at all shifters, enticing and urging them to mate and create life to fill the ranks. It was nature's way of ensuring that shifters didn't dwindle and die off.

Madison took a sip of her brew. "Okay."

She went quiet again, leaving them in unsettling silence.

Ricker reached across the car and stroked her free hand, twined his fingers with hers. She stiffened for the barest of moments, but quickly relaxed into the touch.

The tiger purred at her acquiescence, anxious to touch, stroke and pet what belonged to them.

Before he could lose his nerve, Ricker shoved an apology from his lips. "I'm sorry about last night, Kit. It was wrong. How about stupid? I'm an idiot?"

He tried to make it a joke, but a glance at his mate revealed that she wasn't finding him amusing.

"Is that a question? Or do you really believe it. Because, let me tell you another Maya-ism. Apologizing doesn't mean that you're wrong. It just means that you're tired of arguing and are ready to move on. Just make sure that the other person thinks you're sincere."

Ricker winced. He was sorry, but her words had a ring of truth he couldn't deny. How many times had his father told him to apologize to a woman even if he didn't mean it?

"I was an ass. I tried to seduce you into agreeing with me and also tried to use what I know of Sensitives against you to force your promise. I truly am sorry."

Quiet descended on the vehicle once more and he could practically feel Madison's mind turning over his words, spinning and pouncing on them, looking for an untruth.

Finally, after what seemed like hours, she spoke. "I want to touch you. See if you're sincere. See if this is even a good idea or if we should simply part ways in Ridgeville."

Ricker squeezed her hand and flashed a wicked smile, tossing her a wink for good measure. He smiled even wider when his flirting was met by a bright blush to her cheeks. If he let his true emotions show through, she'd see a broken man, see the pain the idea of not mating with her had caused.

"Baby, you can touch me all you want, whenever you want."

"Not physically, idjit." She rolled her eyes and a tingling stroke of something brushed his mind. "Touch you." She nibbled her lower lip. "I know I did it without permission back at the compound, but I do like to have a shifter's agreement before I go poking around in someone's head."

Ricker took a deep breath, chest expanding and slowly deflating as he considered her request. Yeah, he'd felt her all right, but he'd brushed off the sensation. He'd been so focused on finding her that the trespass had been the least of his worries.

66

Now, he had to agree to regain a crumb of her trust and prove that they were meant to live side-by-side.

"Okay. But I'll warn you now that some of what you find might not be pretty. My life hasn't been tiger cubs and roses, Kit."

Her answer was a small nod and then her eyes fluttered closed. From what he remembered, her little peek wouldn't be painful, just...odd. So, he didn't bother pulling over or slowing his speed.

Which was a mistake.

Madison's first brush was like a gentle wind, unseen hands stroking and easing his agitated tiger until the cat was a docile as a kitten. Her next touch was more firm, deeper, stronger. He took a deep breath, calming his heart as the strange sensations spread through him. The third foray went even further, fingers delving into private places, areas that he'd long ago cut off from himself.

Ricker saw his first mission, then the loss of his best friend when Alistair had attacked the council five years ago. Rescuing Lia from Freedom's clutches and finding her bloody, beaten and repeatedly raped. Hunting Alistair to the small cabin that held Carly Thompson and seeing how much of her blood coated the wood floors.

Finally, the sheer terror he'd felt at watching his mate race from his side and ducking between fighting males. The worry and rage that had overtaken him at the thought of her being in danger and the resolve to keep her safe.

Madison's response was a soft gasp and he saw her open her mouth, eyes wide. "Ricker—"

Any other words she might have said were cut off by the rough slam of another vehicle against their car. The crunch of metal and shattering of glass surrounded them.

The first thing Ricker did was grab his mate by the back of her head and force her to bend low. "Down. Stay there."

Amazingly, she complied without a single protest.

He should have let her fuck around in his head from the jump off.

Ricker looked in the rearview mirror and swept the situation with his gaze. Three males, possibly four, occupied a blacked-out SUV. Based on the sharp lines of their faces, he decided they were shifters, probably Freedom members.

Lovely.

Thank God he'd left a gun in the center console. A quick snatch and the pistol rested in his palm.

The truck swerved around them, pulling up along the driver's side and he watched as a body emerged from the backseat window, holding a gun as he hung from the vehicle.

He didn't hesitate. In one smooth move, he hit the brakes and extended his arm. Two pulls of the trigger and the window shattered as the bullet shot through the glass and into his target. A double tap, straight to the male's head.

One down, three to go.

Ricker hit the gas, thankful for the mods on the car that let them breeze past the SUV without trouble. Behind them, the truck jerked from side to side, but the driver quickly regained control and returned to the chase.

With them at their back door, he put his mate to work.

"Madison, grab the guns and magazines from the glove compartment."

He couldn't spare her a glance, but he could feel the roll of her emotions and assumed that their connection remained. Their fight with the Freedom assholes hadn't allowed her to completely disconnect. He accepted her fear, stark terror at the prospect of dying, but he also welcomed her trust in him, the blatant belief that he'd get them through this unscathed. Well, fuck if he wouldn't try.

With shaking hands she did as he asked, carefully pulling the handguns out along with a few magazines that Lia had left for them. Damn, sometimes he could just kiss the woman who saved his ass.

A low growl came from the passenger seat and he remembered their open link. And…that thought about Lia went right out the window.

When he saw that she'd gathered everything they needed, he kept on with the instructions. "Good girl. Put that stuff in the center console, but I want one of those guns in your hands, okay? If you need to use it, hold on tight with both hands, then point and shoot. I don't expect you to be perfect, I just want you to hit whatever you can, okay?"

Attention divided between what lay in front of them as well as behind, he didn't see a response. "Words, Kit. Do you understand?"

"Yeah. I've got it. Grab. Point. Shoot."

"Good girl." The moment the words left his mouth, they were rammed again, harder this time, and he nearly lost control of their car.

Of course, the fuckers had to be as predictable as fuck and the driver brought the SUV alongside them again. The passenger window was rolled down, revealing a man cloaked in black holding a submachine gun.

And then it was rinse and repeat. He and the gun operated as one, the need to aim no longer necessary after all the time he'd been playing this game.

Pop, pop.

Two down, two to go.

Instead of dropping back, the SUV lurched forward, the large block of metal roaring past them and Ricker went into action.

"Get back down, Madison." His mate didn't utter a peep.

As he'd expected, the larger vehicle swerved in front of them and threw up the back hatch, exposing the two remaining males. A driver and one passenger.

And that fucking submachine gun. He wasn't sure if it was a full or semi-automatic, but he wasn't keen on finding out.

"It's going to get rough. Hold on."

While the male rocked in the SUV, the truck shaking and jerking as it traveled, Ricker took a risk and raced up to the vehicle's back end. Grip on both the wheel and his gun firm, he shot right through the front windshield.

And then they were assailants no longer.

Four pulls of the trigger, fast and furious, was all it took to end the threat.

The SUV swayed, no one controlling the behemoth any longer, and then hit the ditch, flipping until it finally rested against the trees lining the highway.

Ricker didn't stop.

"Madison? I need you to grab the phone out of my bag in the back." As his mate struggled to do as he asked, he kept any eye on their tail. Thankfully they'd been in the middle of God's nowhere and hadn't attracted attention. There was no sign of the police and he prayed it'd stay that way. His gun wasn't registered, the council having manufactured his weapons themselves. No trace. No slug catalogued in IBIS that'd lead them back to shifters.

"I'll give you the freakin' phone just as soon as I get all these burning metal thingies off me!" Her voice was high-pitched and shrill.

For the first time, he noticed her squirming and wiggling in the seat. "Kit, it's called brass and if it's hit your skin, it's already done all the damage it's gonna do. The phone, Madison."

She grumbled something about setting the phone on fire first, but she did hand it over.

He laid it in his lap and reached for her hand, squeezing her fingers gently. "We're going to be fine. The brass doesn't hurt that bad and I'm gonna get you somewhere safe."

"Says the man who didn't end up with burning bits of metal down his shirt."

Ricker almost smiled. At least his mate wasn't screaming and crying in the face of violence.

"I'll kiss it all better later. But right now I need you to think about something for me. Did you pass out at some point? Do you have any scrapes you don't remember? Are you itching anywhere? New bumps? I think they injected a tracker into you at some point; we just have to find it." He spared a glance for his mate and watched the blood drain from her face. "Easy. The minute I know where it is, I can cut it out. Quick and simple. You just need to find it for me."

"I…" Her hand slipped from his and got to work, rubbing and pinching her body from head to toe. It wasn't long before she crowed in victory. "Found it!"

Her hand was beneath her shirt, cupping her breast and Ricker bit back his building growl. "Okay. Give me a minute and I'll get it out of you."

Ricker snatched up the phone and, with the press of a button, his call went through, Lia answering on the first ring. "Click To Ship."

"It's Jenkins. I've had a problem delivering the package. It seems there's more than what I ordered inside. I'm going to stop and re-box, but it'll take a little extra time. I also hit a speed bump and have some damage to my car, so I'm going to stop over in Ames, just across the South Carolina border."

"I see." The line was quiet for a moment, the click of keyboard keys coming over the line. "I've got a friend in the area who does some car work and you can probably crash there for the night if you need to."

"Sounds good. Let them know I'll be there in the next few hours."

The hit of a button cut off anything else Lia might have said and Riker steered their beat up car onto the off-ramp and into a rest area lot. He parked them as far away from others as he could and then grabbed the med bag from the backseat.

"Okay, Kit. Lift your top and we'll get this over with quick."

He would have added painless, but that would have been a lie.

CHAPTER *Six*

"Anything worth doing should be done slowly. Twice. Or three times. It depends on how good he is." – Maya Josephs, Prima of the Ridgeville Pride. She has also decided that being pregnant sucked. That is all.

Pain lingered on the underside of Maddy's breast, but she pushed it aside. Ricker had dug the little tracking-capsule-chippy thing from her breast and crushed it beneath his boot. Then he'd hustled her into the car and they got right back onto the road, traveling as fast as legally possible. Maddy had remained quiet through the journey, unwilling to distract him.

Hours later, the wound had healed, but the ache lingered. She didn't have much more time to focus on her pity party. Not when they whipped onto a dirt road and trundled through the forest.

Before long, Ricker pulled them up to a log cabin with a wide front porch. Two rocking chairs decorated the space along with a swing and Maddy sighed. This was her picture perfect home. It was a nice little place hidden in the woods where she could relax and just "be" without any worries about the pride, her job or the outside world.

As if the space held magical powers, she felt tension and worry drain from her, the tightness in her chest fading away with every breath.

The moment the car stopped, she leapt from the vehicle and raced around the car, wide smile on her face. "Are we stopping here? It's gorgeous! Can we stay for a while or is this a layover?"

Feelings not her own slithered into Maddy's mind, hope, happiness, exhaustion…

Mate…

The word was a whisper, the voice familiar, yet not, and she whirled on her tiger. "Ricker? What the—"

It had to be coming from him, but how?

Worry bombarded her and then the male was striding toward her, fierce thunder in his gaze. "Madison?" In two steps, she was cradled in his arms, one large hand cupping the back of her head, pressing it to his chest, and she listened to the solid beat of his heart. "Are you okay?"

"I don't know. I can feel…you."

Anxiousness came from him and his pulse stuttered. "I felt you after the fight. I didn't tell you because I liked knowing how you were doing and I figured that you'd close it off when you were ready."

"Close it off? I'm not even open." She pulled back to stare at him, eyes wide.

They gazed at each for what seemed like hours, emotions bouncing back and forth like a tennis ball.

This had definitely not been included in the "What to Expect when a Sensitive Mates" instruction manual. At all.

She was totally writing that book when she got home, too. She'd open her own little *were* bookstore for unsuspecting furballs.

A wide smile split Ricker's face, mirth twinkling in his eyes. "There's an instruction manual?"

Maddy stuck out her tongue. "No fair plucking things outta my head."

Her mate leaned down and brushed his lips over hers, a sweet, gentle touch that she felt all the way to her toes. Arousal, quick and hot, burned through her in a flash and she couldn't withhold the moan that gathered in her chest.

"I like being in your head. Like that I can feel how hot you get when I touch you." Ricker nipped her lower lip and a whimper escaped her throat. "How good do you think it'll be between us? I can sense what you need and give it to you, Kit. Anything you want, it's yours."

His cock hardened against her, long, thick and ready and the only thought in her mind was…bed. The tiger's free hand stroked her back, traveled along her spine and then cupped the abundant curve of her ass, fingers kneading her flesh.

Maddy rocked her hips against him, savored the low hiss that escaped his lips and reveled in the growing arousal between them.

"There's a bed inside, just say the word."

She licked her lips, want and need pounding through her veins and the cat focused on its singular desire. "Word."

That earned her a snort from her mate and then he had them in motion, his fingers twined with hers as he stalked toward the cabin, his long strides eating up the ground. At the door, he paused and gave her his attention, eyes serious, and tingles of apprehension and concern filtered through to her.

"Stay here for a minute? Please? I need to check out the interior. I don't scent anyone in the yard, but I don't want to—"

God, the man was tripping over himself while he tried not to offend her or order her to stay put.

Maddy placed her fingers over his lips. "It's fine. Go make sure we're safe so we can knock boots and get on with the show."

"Knock boots?" His lips twitched.

"Shaddup and get moving, mister." She mock glared and he stiffened to attention, giving her a military salute.

"Sir, yes sir." With a laugh, he opened the front door and headed inside, leaving Maddy to look over their temporary home. She approached the railing and leaned against the wood.

Had she mentioned perfection? The air was filled with the fresh scents of the forest and the wind carried the soft twitter of the birds that surrounded their space.

Peace. The entire area wrapped her in peace.

Then she was wrapped in pure, unadulterated desire, a desperation for sex that she'd never felt before.

Mate...

The word whispered through her mind, the combined voice of her mate's human and tiger voices danced across her consciousness and she sensed Ricker moving closer. Relief that the home was safe and empty slithered into his thoughts, but the need for her overpowered anything else he may have been feeling.

And his ache fanned hers.

The squeak of the front door swinging open was followed by the steady thump of her mate's boots against the solid wood of the porch, his steps purposeful as he neared her. He didn't hide his approach, nor his thoughts.

Attraction, lust, burning desire and…something more than mere caring. Maddy wouldn't classify it as love. Mating wasn't the same as falling madly in love with a person's other half. It was hormonal, a beast's drive to procreate.

But, she hoped for an enduring love like her parents…like Maya and Alex or Carly and Neal. There was always hope.

As her mate neared, she turned toward him, her back against the porch railing and she looked her fill.

She had no idea how she'd ended up so lucky. The man was strength and dominance tempered with sensitivity and vulnerability. A brush of his mind revealed his anxiousness, his tiger's desperate ache for her as well as its acknowledgement that she was nothing like the Sensitives they'd encountered in the past.

Ricker's body moved with sensuous shifts of muscle beneath skin, his clothing tight enough to reveal the ripple of his body as he approached. His shirt clung to his chest and abdomen, the outline of his washboard stomach easily visible. She still wanted to trace those depressions, travel further south and see if he had deep lines at his hip bones that pointed to his groin.

A glance at his face revealed her desire mirrored in his features. His green eyes had darkened and neared black as he gazed at her. Tension filled him, his strong jaw clenched tight and the tick of a vein easily visible.

It went beyond need now, his body demanding her, his emotions showing her that she had become a necessity to him, to his cat.

Her pussy pulsed at the thought, the idea that he craved her as much as she craved him. An ache built between her legs, moisture gathering and body preparing for his possession. The musky scent of her arousal filled the air between them, and Ricker's nostrils flared, his chest rising as he took a deep breath.

"Madison…" His voice was a deep growl, the baritone vibrating through her and settling at the juncture of her thighs.

Ricker… She whispered into his mind, needing the connection. She'd been surprised at their presence within each other's heads at first, but it seemed so natural now. So necessary.

A final step brought him within a foot of her, his sweet chocolate-y scent surrounding her like a blanket and then she was lost. Waves of emotion traveled between them, growing and compounding until she couldn't differentiate between the two of them.

Ricker cupped her cheek as he gazed at her, eyes intent on her face while they communicated without words. The claiming was imminent, the cats undeniable in their need to bind them together.

She licked her lips, throat suddenly dry, and the movement caught his attention. He traced her mouth, thumb sliding back and forth. She lapped at his digit, pulled it in and suckled him. He pressed against her then, brought his body flush against hers and she could feel his hard length. He was ready for her, thick and solid, and her pussy clenched, leaked more cream and soaked her panties.

His other hand stroked her arm, fingers petting her heated skin and leaving goose bumps in their wake. He caressed her, arousing her further, until he cupped the fullness of her breast, plucked her aching nipple and the touch was reminiscent of their brief shower.

That thought reminded her of her anger and Ricker was quick to soothe her.

"None of that, Kit. This is just me asking. Will you mate with me? Let me discover this sweet body? I'll make you so happy, Madison. I swear it." He slid his thumb in and out of her mouth, mimicking what she craved, and he groaned. "I know we'll probably fight and butt heads, but you'll always come first. And I'll try very, very hard not to be an ass."

Maddy nipped his thumb and giggled, the remnants of anger dissipating with every breath and beat of her heart. "Take me inside, Ricker. I want you to be mine."

*

Ricker's dick nearly split his jeans. Her words washed over him, wrapped around his cock and stroked him from root to tip. He throbbed within his pants, the hardness begging to be released, and his tiger roared in approval.

Her sweet, pink tongue laved his thumb, sucked and teased him and he couldn't wait to have her plump lips wrapped around his cock.

They wanted her, craved her like their next breath and Ricker didn't want to spare another second.

He abandoned her breast and retraced his path until he snagged her hand and moved toward the door, anxious to sink his teeth into his mate, share a bite and claim her forever.

Ricker didn't waste time on showing Madison around the cabin. Nope, he kept her moving through the space, past the living room, kitchen and dining room and then down the hall to the bedroom. The place was a nice size, not too small or too big. Perfect for a safe hideaway.

The master bedroom was large with a massive king sized bed that would easily fit them, and he had every intention of using each square inch of the soft surface.

A handful of feet into the space and he tugged on Madison's hand, brought her in front of him. He looked her over, amazed that God would gift him with such a beautiful woman, a female perfect for him in every way.

Her pretty blue eyes sparkled in the dim light and a soft blush stained her cheeks. He wondered if the pink hue covered her from head to toe.

He couldn't wait to find out.

A rush of embarrassment stroked him and he realized that Madison had caught a hint of his feelings.

"Kit, don't you know you're perfect?"

She licked her lips and he ached to kiss them, but he refrained. If he started kissing now, he'd never get to see her peaches and cream skin, never be able to take his time exploring her from head to toe.

"No one's ever… I'm not… My hips are…" The red intensified on her face and he rushed to reassure her.

"Madison, I love every curve of your body." He released her hand and cupped her breasts, held their weight in his palms and stroked her nipples until they hardened against his thumb. "Your breasts are gorgeous. Big enough to fill my hands…my mouth." He abandoned her chest and moved south. "You waist fits me, fits you. It's got a sweet little dip and it leads me right to your hips and ass. Damn, Kit, don't you know that I love your ass? It's got this lush, heart shape and my hands itch to hold it." He let his gaze bore into hers and his voice lowered to a growly baritone. The cat needed his mate. Now. "I want to bend you over, Madison. Want to stare at your ass as I take you. Grip your hips while I fuck your sweet pussy and spank you until your cheeks are red and you're screaming in pleasure."

A shudder wracked her body, traveling through her in tiny twitches and he savored her soft gasp.

"Do you want that, mate? Do you want me?" He grabbed her ass, kneaded her abundant flesh. His cock was pounding now, near hurting where it pressed against his zipper.

"Yes." Her voice was a whisper, but he heard it just the same.

Triumphant, he reached for the hem of her shirt, but had his hands brushed away by the she-cat. Desperate need flowed from Madison, the feelings overwhelming his, and he let the lioness take the lead.

83

Ricker couldn't decide which he preferred, this eager dominance of the lioness or the gentle compliance of the hotel. Both memories made his dick inexplicably harder.

Madison tugged and yanked on his shirt, pulling the hem from his jeans. He reached back, grabbed a handful of the material and pulled it free of his body. Tiny hands, soft and sure, stroked his shoulders, fingers sliding along his skin. His shaft pulsed and he felt sure he'd stained the cloth with his pre-cum.

He didn't give a fuck. Not when his mate's touch traveled to the closure of his jeans and freed the button, lowered the zipper and his cock sprang free of its tight confines.

Then that hand…that perfect, soft, delicate hand…encircled his length, wrapped around his hardness and stroked him. She pumped his cock, squeezing just below the tip and tracing his slit with the pad of her thumb.

Sparks of arousal and desire encircled his balls, an ache he'd never known joining in with the sensations.

Wonder and hunger sank into him. His mate's desire joined his, and he groaned at the powerful feelings.

"Madison, need you, Kit. So bad." He watched a smirk form on her lips.

"You'll just have to wait a little longer, won't you?" Her gaze strayed back to his face and she winked.

Minx.

Madison abandoned his cock and she hooked her hands along the waist of his jeans, yanking the material down his legs. He kicked his boots free, then the pants, and stood nude before his mate.

Her gaze traveled over him, her look almost like a touch as her attention moved from head to toe, pausing on his cock with each pass.

Ricker palmed his cock, stroked himself as she'd been doing only moments before, and she focused on his movements. Madison's eyes darkened before his eyes and her pale tongue snaked out to lap at her lips.

"See something you like, Kit?"

His mate growled and yanked his hand from his cock. Before he could blink, she jerked him around her and shoved him onto the bed. His large body bounced against the cushioned surface and he smiled at his ravenous she-cat.

Madison followed him down, kneeled between his spread thighs and opened her mouth. Her heated tongue licked him from balls to tip, flicking over the fluid-topped head and teased his slit. Propped on his elbows, his gaze remained riveted to her actions, watching her while she repeated the caress. She lapped at him, talented muscle tracing the throbbing vein on the underside of his dick, end of her tongue flicking just beneath the head. The action yanked a groan from him and he couldn't resist the need to touch her.

He rested his weight on one elbow and brought his hand to her head, sifting his fingers through her hair and cupping her skull. "That's it, Kit. Lick me. Suck me."

Madison moaned against his aroused flesh, sending jolts of pleasure along his dick, and his balls drew up tight against his body, pulsing with the need to release his cum. His mate rose, positioning her body so that her mouth hovered over the head.

"Suck it, Kit. Suck my cock."

With a twinkle in her eye, she sheathed him in her mouth, slid her lips along his dick and swallowed him down.

"Fuck, that's it. Suck it like a good girl."

Arousal, searing hot and sharp, tore through him and he recognized the feelings as coming from his mate. Her body was scorching, pussy aching and desperate to be filled. But she wasn't ready to give up his dick.

Funny, he was in full agreement.

Madison wrapped her hand around his cock, squeezed his shaft and followed the movements of her mouth. She rose and fell along his length, wet mouth sucking him, palm sliding over him, twisting and tightening while she pulled. She moaned and flicked her tongue along his hardness.

Then her other hand came into play. She cupped his balls, gently clutched the sensitive flesh and sent splintering shards of pleasure through him.

Ricker tightened his hold on her hair, fisted the strands and flexed his hips. She groaned and took more of him, her throat swallowing around his invasion and he tenderly fucked her sweet mouth. In and out he slid between her lips, gasping and moaning with every suck and brush of her tongue along his cock.

"Suck it. S'good."

Pleasure and pride rushed at him through their connection and he pulled the feelings close.

With each pull, he eased closer to release, balls preparing to empty into his mate's luscious mouth. Tendrils of mutual pleasure coursed through their connection and Ricker embraced the feelings, let the ecstasy of her possession fill him from head to toe.

He wouldn't come in her mouth. No. But he'd revel in the sensations for as long as he could.

The wet slide of her along his length continued, his hips shifting and pushing in and out of the moist cavern. His groans of pleasure mixed with hers, creating a seductive music that filled the room.

"Madison… Kit…" He gripped her tighter for a brief moment and lifted her mouth from his cock, forced her to release him and her attention settled on him. Beneath his gaze, her tongue snaked out and lapped at the head of his cock, gathered each droplet of pre-cum as it formed. "Kit, need inside you."

Ricker loosened his hold the slightest bit and Madison took advantage of the momentary give and slid from his grip, slithering off the bed to stand between his knees. Hand empty, he encircled his cock, pumped his dick while his mate stripped.

Fuck, he'd come before he got inside her if she didn't hurry.

Layer after layer disappeared before his eyes. The top was tossed aside to reveal the lace cups of her bra, the thin material barely concealing her lush breasts. Then her pants disappeared, her ass wiggling as she inched them over her hips and down her thighs.

Ricker's mouth watered at the sight of her. Covered in scraps of lace, her hidden flesh taunted and teased him.

The tiger, anxious for its mate, shoved against his wall of control and the bones in his face cracked and shifted. Prickles traveled along his arms and chest and he knew without looking that the cat's stripes had formed along his body. A purr built in his chest at the sight of his lioness.

Anxious to sink deep into her heat, he pushed to his hands, leaned forward and reached for Madison. He needed her naked. Now. His gums ached, fangs descending and pricking his lower lip, the cat not willing to wait any longer.

She slapped his hand away. "I don't think so. You've been telling me what to do all this time. I think it's my turn."

*

Hot desire burned Maddy's veins. Her mate's ache flowed over her like a living thing and she rejoiced in the feelings he projected.

He wanted her. Ached for her. His long, thick cock throbbed and pounded…for her. So many years of being the chubby chick that shifters picked on were washed away with his gaze, the flood of his emotions shoving them from her mind.

At her words, Ricker had stilled, hand frozen and fangs peeking from between his lips. "Madison, you don't know what you're doing."

But she did. Empowered by his desire, she reached for the straps of her bra and eased them down her arms and then flicked the clasp between her breasts. With the next breath, she popped free of the lace confines and the tiger's gaze immediately zeroed in on her exposed flesh. She let the bit of silk slide from her arms to fall to the floor.

She hooked her fingers into the hem of her panties and smirked. "I think I do."

Maddy eased the soft fabric from her hips, let the knickers drift to the carpet and then stepped free of the undergarments. Nude before her mate, Ricker's thoughts bombarded her.

Pain. Need. Desire. Attraction. And a possessiveness that thrilled her to her core. She was his, just as he was hers.

She stepped closer, pushed on Ricker's shoulders and her mate flopped back without hesitation, gaze locked on her. With care, she crawled atop him, thighs on either side of his hips and hands now resting on his pecs.

Legs spread, she lowered her hips, hissed when her wet pussy connected with his hard, hot shaft, the length nestling along her cleft. Maddy gripped her mate's chest, fingers squeezing the hardened muscle while she slid over his cock, veined length stroking and petting her slick heat.

"Need. Kit. Please." Ricker begged. The big, bad council tracker writhed beneath her, hips flexing, dick throbbing against her vulnerable flesh.

She rocked, coated his hardness in her cream, shivered and shuddered each time the head of his dick nudged her clit.

Ricker's hands settled on her hips, nails pricking her skin and showing her how much closer he was to losing control. The sharpened lines of his cheeks stood out against his features and the orange and black dusting of fur only served to arouse her even more.

He held onto his tiger by a thread, the beast raging against the mental walls that held him back.

Maddy wanted the cat free.

Loosening her hold on her lioness, the beast surged forth and the tips of her fingers shifted into claws, just long and sharp enough to prick her mate and draw blood. At the same time, she pressed down on his hips, rocked and flexed, stroking him with her pussy.

"Fuck! Madison!"

"Right here." She repeated the motion, embraced the quakes of pleasure. "Right here."

Ricker's grip tightened and she watched as his eyes flashed amber, a true sign that the cat lurked.

"Madison…" His voice was barely recognizable, deep and gravely as he spoke around his lowered fangs.

Willing to go easy on the big guy, she leaned down, lapped at the droplets of blood peppering his skin. The coppery tang of his blood burst over her tongue, bathed her taste buds in his essence and she took delight in the flavor.

"Kit. Mad—Fuck."

Maddy lifted her head, eyes intent on her mate. "Come inside me, mate."

She didn't have to ask twice. One of Ricker's hands abandoned her hip, reached between them to grasp his erection and placed the head at her opening. Nice and slow, she pushed back, pussy enveloping him in her heat, cradling his length. He stretched and spread her like no other, settling into her as if his cock had been made for her alone.

Then again, he had been made to be her mate.

Inch by inch, she engulfed him, welcomed him into her body. His heavily veined shaft stroked her inner walls, slid over the nerve endings that sent pleasure coursing through her. Maddy's arousal grew with every breath as the head of his cock pushed deeper and deeper into her pussy. She accepted more and more of him until she held his full length.

Hips resting against Ricker's, she paused, reveled in his possession.

Her mate raised his head, gaze intent on where they were joined. "Damn, Kit. Do you know how good it is to be inside you?"

Maddy laughed. She couldn't help it. "About as good as you feel inside me?"

Before he could utter another word, she raised her hips, letting his cock slide free of her heat as she climbed. A groan tore from Ricker's chest and she echoed the sound. His cock stroked her walls, seared pleasure spots that she'd forgotten existed and sent her bliss soaring into the sky.

She retraced her path, accepted him back into her body and his intimate caress repeated.

His hand returned to her hip, both of them now gripping her hips and forcing her into a mutually pleasurable rhythm.

Up and down she moved, pussy clinging to his dick while she rode him. With every fall, her clit brushed his pubis, the pressure sending shards of ecstasy along her spine. With the next lowering of her body, she pressed down harder than before, ground her pussy against him and moaned with the rising bliss.

"Yes…" She hissed, unable to keep quiet.

Her pussy clenched around his invasion, pulsing and milking his cock. She rose and dropped followed by a hard circle of her hips. Okay, two circles. Make that four.

"Fuck. Madison. That's it." His face was harsh, mouth more pronounced and stripes evident over his features. "Take it. Kit. Come on my dick."

Madison was all for that idea. She took from him instead of giving, granting herself permission to be selfish and demanding. Claws pierced her skin, the scent of her blood joining Ricker's, and the pain and flavors of their fluids added to her need.

With every inch up and down, every twitch of her hips, her release inched closer. She panted and moaned, body shifting to her desire rhythm. Harder and faster she moved, chasing her orgasm, determined to come on his cock.

Ricker's heaving breath matched hers, his expression a mixture of pleasure and pain. A lesser woman would have run in the other direction, afraid of the barely constrained strength.

Maddy wasn't a lesser woman.

Plus, she seriously needed to come.

She rocked and flexed her hips, thighs burning while she increased her tempo, determined to give and take the looming ecstasy. It was so close. So…fucking…close.

Pace growing again, one of Ricker's hands left her hip and snaked around her, palm cupping and kneading her ass cheek, encouraging her.

And then not.

His palm abandoned her, only to return with a resounding smack. A hot sting snaked through her, circled and centered on her clit.

"Fuck!" She half-screamed, the sound coming out more as a growl.

"Doing that, Kit." Another slap followed his words, heat immediately on its heels.

"Ricker…" She whimpered, pain intensifying her pleasure.

Smack.

"Right here."

Smack.

"Hurts." She whined, not sure if she wanted him to stop or continue. With every fall of his hand, her pussy clenched and milked his cock, sending her closer to the edge of release.

Smack.

A full-body shudder overtook her, muscles twitching with the need to come. Her clit throbbed, ached and practically begged. Not much longer…

Smack.

Maddy whimpered, cunt spasming.

Her gaze remained focused on her mate, watched the changes that slinked over his face with every lowering of his hand, each collision of his palm and her ass. Desperate need covered him and she could see that he held on by a thread. His breathing was shallow and heavy, huffing and puffing through his gritted teeth.

"Need. Ricker."

"Come for me. Come on my cock, mate."

A full-body moan built within her, the vibrations merging with the heat from his spanking, the pleasure of his cock and the pressure against her clit. Her pace increased and he matched her movements, hand raining down on her with every fall of her body.

Over and again, she repeated the motion, each shift of muscle shoving her toward the edge. Her gums ached and she felt her sharp fangs descend. The cat was ready, anticipating the moment she could pounce and strike at the man beneath her, claim him as hers.

Another rise and fall, up and down, smack and sting. Her pussy milked him in a steady rhythm, clenching around his shaft and begging for his cum.

More and more she gave and took, racing toward the edge, ready to leap and embrace the pleasure he was throwing at her. She convulsed around him, chains of spasms overtaking her as...as she came.

With a shout, the dizzying explosion of her release shot through her veins. Bliss engulfed Maddy while pulsating waves of ecstasy filled her from head to toe. She shuddered uncontrollably, pussy squeezing him as tremors of pleasure seized her body.

Without hesitation, she struck, leaned down and sank her razor sharp fangs deep into the spot where neck met shoulder and bit him as deep as she dared. Her teeth sank

94

through the flesh with ease and his blood flowed into her mouth. She swallowed the fluid, welcomed that part of him while her saliva mixed in with his essence.

He belonged to her.

Distantly, a shout met her ears, a purely masculine moan immediately following and then a fierce pain gripped her. Ricker repeated her claiming, the hurt instant and overwhelming.

She screamed, not in agony, but in pleasure. Another orgasm, stronger than the last, blew through her like a tornado and dragged her in its wake. Her pussy clenched in rhythmic convulsions, body no longer her own. And her cat…the lioness roared in approval as their mate took them, filled them with his seed and marked them as claimed.

His hips remained sealed to hers, snug and tight where their bodies joined as his dick pulsed inside her sheath, seeming to grow with every twitch. She could feel him filling her, his cum coating her inner walls. Her beast purred, savoring the scent that accompanied their love making.

Panting, breathless, she slumped against him, exhausted and spent.

Good sex could be hard on a gal. O-M-G-fucktastic sex was killing her.

The chest beneath her twitched and then the vibrations from Ricker's voice slid through her. "O-M-G-fucktastic?"

Maddy didn't even raise her head. Hadn't he heard her thoughts? She was dying for fur's sake. "Word."

"That all you got?"

She cracked an eye open and tilted her head until she could see him. "Unless you feed me or unbreak my vagina, that's all I got."

That earned her a swat to the ass. And damn if her pussy didn't tighten. Stupid vagina. It didn't even realize it was broken.

"You're a shifter, Kit. You'll be ready again in an hour. Faster if I feed you." The corner of his mouth quirked up in a half-smile. "So, what can I make you? Because I want you again."

The hardening of his cock within her sheath confirmed his words.

Damn. She'd need vaginal rejuvenation if he fucked her like that every time.

Maddy wondered if Ricker made enough to keep a vajayjay specialist on retainer.

Her mate's voice flitted through her mind…

Yes…

CHAPTER *seven*

"Live by the three "F" rule: If they don't fuck you, feed you or finance you, they don't matter." – Maya Josephs, Prima of the Ridgeville Pride, who is getting fucked. Regularly. Without a ring. Bastard.

Maddy woke with a groan, stretching her arms high above her head and flexing her toes as she shifted from a sated sleep to fully conscious.

Being conscious was overrated.

Aches and twinges of pain were sprinkled through her body, reminding her of everything she'd been doing for the last several hours. More importantly, who she'd been doing.

That thought brought a smile to her lips and a delicious throb to her overused pussy.

God, she hadn't realized that when Maya had been gushing about all night sex that the woman hadn't been kidding. After the initial claiming and a quick nap, Ricker had woken her with gentle passion, sliding into her and making love to her for hours. Over and again, they joined, shared pleasure and then collapsed back into a sated sleep.

But, since she was alone, he couldn't have been that exhausted.

The alluring scent of coffee reached her nose and every hint of fatigue danced away.

Mmm...coffee.

With a groan, she rolled toward the edge of the bed and pushed until she was sitting on the mattress, feet dangling over the side. Dude. That had been hella hard.

A quick scoot had her sliding from the soft surface and she swayed on her feet, eyes half-closed while she shuffled toward the bedroom door. Half way across the room, she scooped Ricker's shirt from the floor and pulled it on, satisfied that it at least covered her ass. Being naked during sex and being naked at the breakfast table while holding scorching hot liquid were two totally different things. Burned boobies were not on the day's menu.

Maddy padded down the hallway, nose leading the way as she hunted the goodness that was caffeine. It didn't take long to find her prey...and her mate. More importantly, her prey.

One step into the kitchen she froze and took in the sight before her. Her mate stood in front of the stove, shirtless with jeans barely clinging to his hips and exposing his muscled back. Arousal flared to life and she wondered if she'd ever get used to the man. They'd made love mere hours ago and she wanted him again already.

Contentment from Ricker filled her mind with happiness quickly behind, and she found her emotions echoing his, falling into sync without conscious thought.

Maddy padded toward him, drinking in his appearance, and then pressed against him. She wrapped her arms around his waist and let him take her weight as she rested her front against his back. She let her hands wander, stroke his pecs and then trail along his abdomen. Her last stop was the waist of his jeans and she hooked her thumbs over the worn cotton, fingertips spread over his lower abs.

"Mmmorning." She nuzzled his back, rubbing her cheek back and forth over his smooth skin.

"Hey, Kit." He leaned his head back and his hair tickled his face. "Coffee's to your right and I've got eggs and bacon for us."

"More bacon than eggs?" She asked after snagging a cup of the bitter brew.

Ricker barked out a laugh. "Of course. I know how to feed my mate."

Mate. She loved that word.

Before long, Ricker had breakfast for them, a plate piled high with the bacon. He'd tugged her to his lap and she settled against him with a sigh. She reveled in his touch, the feeling of security that filled her as his arm encircled her.

Ricker gave her bite after bite of the salty meat, sprinkling in bits of eggs.

Quiet surrounded them and she simply enjoyed being in his presence, relished the serenity that his closeness imbued. Every so often, his lips would ghost over her skin, brushing her neck or forehead while they sated themselves with food.

When the plate was finally empty, she turned on him, rose enough until she could straddle his thighs and gave him her full attention.

"Hi."

"Hi, back." He held a small smile.

"What are we doing today? Running from the bad guys? Do I finally get to use a gun?" She leaned forward and nipped his lower lip, grinding her pussy over his semi-hard cock. "Or do you have something else in mind?"

That earned her a growl and a swat to her ass. "Insatiable wench."

This time, she brushed her mouth over his, flicking her tongue out to taste her mate. "Only for you."

Ricker cupped her ass, kneading her plump flesh and forcing her body to grind against his, rubbing her bare pussy over his dick. Desire burning hot and fast shot through her body, the desperate ache for her mate shooting high with every breath. Her heat clenched and grew moist with the evidence of her arousal. She whimpered against his mouth, aching for him.

"Ricker…" She couldn't stifle the moan that grew in her chest.

Her mate increased the pace, the slow back and forth grind over his now hard cock. The rough cotton abraded her sex lips, the cloth zipper flap settling along her slit and stroking her clit with its rough texture. The sliver of pain the contact created served to increase her pleasure as it scraped the bundle of nerves.

A cool draft bathed her ass as the tiger lifted her thin shirt, baring her cheeks to the room. His callused hands grazed her, fingers digging into her plump flesh, forcing her to acquiesce to his speed. Each shove forward rubbed her clit and each rock back caressed the nub sending bolts of ecstasy through her veins.

Maddy captured his lips in a fierce kiss, shoved her tongue into his mouth and tasted the very essence of her mate. She drank from his mouth, absorbed his moans and responded in kind, taking and giving pleasure as much as she could.

Ricker's fingers teased the crack of her ass, tips delving between her cheeks, touch inching closer and closer to her hole. When the digits finally connected with her forbidden entrance, she whimpered against his lips, unsure and excited at the same time.

She wrenched her mouth from his, panting and whining, absorbing his breath as he inhaled hers. "Ricker…"

He spoke against her lips, tongue occasionally flicking out for a taste. "Do you want me here, sweet mate? Are you naughty and want me buried deep in your ass? Filling you up?"

Another whimper stole through her, the very idea of having him in her forbidden entrance both exciting and scaring her in equal measure. The thoughts, coupled with his touch and stimulation of her clit had her racing toward release. Her heat clenched and throbbed, aching to be filled and claimed by him.

A single fingertip traced her asshole, circled the virgin nerves and traced the ring of muscle. "You want it, don't you?"

Maddy pushed back against his touch, encouraging him without words.

One of his hands left her and then slammed down on her ass cheek causing a fierce sting to race through her body. It joined her arousal, her need, and sent it flying high. "Lemme hear you, Kit. Do you want me to take your ass?"

She lapped at his mouth then nuzzled his cheek, burying her face against his neck. She didn't want to answer, didn't want to admit that she craved the illicit touch.

Her silence earned her another swat. Not that she minded. No, she definitely didn't care when the slow burn ran along her veins and joined in her pleasure. She kept with Ricker's pace, back and forth, clit twitching and throbbing with every glance of the cotton.

Mouth shut, another smack landed and a soul-deep groan left her chest. "Ricker."

"I want back here, Kit. Gonna sink in nice and slow, spread you wide for me. I'll get you safe and then your ass is mine. Isn't it?"

Smack.

A tremble danced through her followed by a shudder that slid down her spine. The pure pleasure of his touch, the combination of pleasure and pain, urged her orgasm closer.

"Isn't it?"

Smack.

She was breathing heavy. Panting against his neck, alternating between desperate whines and needy groans.

Ricker forced her to lower further over him, shove her exposed pussy to the rough textures of his jeans while his finger rubbed her virgin asshole.

Smack.

Maddy's body trembled, bliss from his touch nearly overwhelming her with each passing moment. A ball of arousal encompassed her, surrounded her and grew with every breath, every rock of her hips. Ecstasy pumped through her veins, pulsing and gathering, surrounding her pussy, clit and ass.

Her gums ached, fangs elongating and she scraped them over Ricker's neck, glanced his vulnerable skin with her sharp teeth.

Smack.

"It's mine."

A tremor of pleasure bolted along her nerves and she let her mouth venture to his shoulder, scratching at where she'd placed her mark mere hours ago.

God, the sensations were growing. Her pleasure and the pain mingled, surged and embraced her until she didn't know where each sensation ended and the other began. Her orgasm raced forward and she couldn't hold back, couldn't keep the growing ecstasy at bay any longer.

Ricker, her seductive, dominant, gorgeous mate struck her again, palm colliding with her abundant flesh with a resounding spank.

Smack.

Maddy could only utter a single word. One syllable. "Yours!"

And then it was over. She sank her teeth into Ricker's shoulder, fangs slicing through skin and muscle with ease and the coppery sweet flavors of his blood poured over her taste buds.

At the same moment, the dam restraining her orgasm broke and flooded her with indescribable pleasure. Her pussy clenched in rhythmic spasms as if begging, no demanding, to be filled. Uncontrollable shudders wracked her body, muscles twitching and jerking as the explosive climax sprinted through her veins. The molten sensations of her release crested and then retreated, only to surge forth once again.

Ricker didn't stop.

His blows continued to rain on her ass, finger teasing her asshole and she kept rocking over his hardness, grinding her soaking pussy against the ridge of his hard cock. More and more he gave; more and more she took.

The still lingering orgasm grew, sending her higher than before until the strong, lovely sensations claimed her once again. She screamed against the flesh in her mouth and then tore her lips from his shoulder, shouting her second completion to the room.

A fierce growl joined her yell and her mate stiffened beneath her, cock pulsing against her pussy, twitching against her overheated flesh. The salty, musky scent of his release reached her and she sighed, slumped against him and let Ricker take her deadweight. She lapped at his wound, savoring the remnants of his blood as their breathing slowed and the last vestiges of pleasure seeped from her body.

Ricker's finger left her asshole and both hands snaked beneath her shirt to trace her spine, palms sliding over her skin with gentle strokes.

She hummed and snuggled closer. Reveled in the security of being in her mate's arms.

"I'm going to make sure you keep your promise, Kit."

She raised her head and looked him in the eye. "You'll have to catch me first."

With that pronouncement she jumped from his lap, squealing when his fingers caught her shirt. She shoved the thin material over her head and kept running, heading toward the bedroom and, hopefully, lube.

Because, hello? The ass is not a self-lubricating orifice.

And that had been an embarrassing lesson from the school nurse during Sex Ed.

Maddy dashed down the hallway, intent on her goal and unwilling to lose. The lioness was determined to win this small battle and the chase had simply rekindled her need for the tiger. It wasn't like running through the forest, mate nipping at her heels with one goal in mind: her submission.

They'd mate that way someday.

Hopefully soon.

She rounded the corner into the master bedroom and launched herself at the bed, scrambling for the bedside table. Wasn't that where everyone stashed their goodies?

Her fingers wrapped around the handle. Ricker pounced on her with a growl, his now nude body aligned with hers from shoulders to toe, his reawakened cock nestled between her ass cheeks.

"Got you…"

She wiggled her butt, teasing him with what he desired. "Maybe—"

A shrill song broke their play, the annoying tune colliding with their passion and dousing it in an instant.

Groaning, Ricker rolled from her and crawled off the bed. He padded to the other side of the room and dug through their bag, exposing his luscious ass to her gaze. Damn, she really wanted to nibble, scrape her teeth along that curve and see if he tasted as good as he smelled. And then she'd work her way to the front and swallow—

"What." Ricker's back was stiff and straight, muscles that had been languid and loose were now tense.

Ooh. Her cock blocked mate wasn't happy about being, er, cock blocked. If she strained she probably could have listened to both sides of the conversation, but she figured she'd find out soon enough.

"Am I in charge of this operation? She's my—"

Maddy could, however, hear his teeth grinding.

"I don't care. She's—" He growled. Then snarled. Which was kinda hot, if she was honest. "Fine." He bit off the word, probably imagining it was the head of whomever he was speaking with.

Sighing, he dropped the phone back into the bag and then propped his hands on his hips, his breathing audible in the silence. In and then out, he breathed deep and even. Poor guy. Hell, poor her!

No nookie for them!

With a final exhale he turned toward her, his cock down to half-mast and slowly softening further. "Apparently a certain someone's Prime has demanded that we hurry our asses along. A certain someone's Prima has decided we should have been in Ridgeville by now. Your Prima has said jump."

"And Prime has said 'how high?'." She rolled to her back and stared at the ceiling. "Alex needs to fuck her more. If she was exhausted, she wouldn't care that we were taking a fuck break."

She heard his snort. "Yeah, I'll be sure to pass that along."

"Pussy."

She felt rather than heard him close the distance between them and then his palm cupped her heat. "No, this is a pussy. My pussy." His mouth descended and lips captured her nipple, sucking and tonguing the hardened nub.

Maddy moaned and arched into the caress, sifted her fingers through his hair and fisted the strands. She spread her legs wider for his touch, lost between the sensations of his mouth and hand. She panted and writhed, desperation growing with every breath.

"Yes, yours…"

He released her breast with a soft pop and one final lick before giving her his attention, gaze intent on hers. She rocked against his palm, aching for him, pussy desperate to be filled with him once again. Passion glazed his eyes and she thought for sure he'd give the Prime a big "fuck you" and take her anyway.

His hand slid from between her thighs and quick as a blink, he had her on her stomach and his palm came down on her ass with an echoing smack. "Now that we've got that settled, let's hit the road."

Ricker moved away from her and she lay there, eyes staring at nothing in particular as she replayed the past handful of seconds. That...that...

"Asshole!"

Her curse rang through the room and her mate, the crap eating jerk that he was...laughed.

CHAPTER *eight*

"Money can't buy happiness, but it can buy self-defense lessons, a big assed gun and bitchin' clothes. And, if all else fails, borrow their pen and stab them in the eye." – Maya Josephs, Prima of the Ridgeville Pride, who has yet to use the whole "pen in the eye" thing, but hasn't ruled out the possibility.

Part of Ricker, the part that had some semblance of sentimentality, felt happy at the reunion between his mate and her friends. Maya, Carly and Maddy hugged and gushed, talking over each other as they relayed what had happened in the few days his mate had been in captivity.

The other part of him, the tiger that longed to sink deep into their lioness, hated every single one of 'em and it was getting harder to keep the cat at bay. It had some lovely ideas about tearing them limb from limb so that the two of them could be alone and…

"Come on, Ricker. You won't get anything out of that group for a while."

Ricker looked over at the Prime and raised a brow, glancing back at the women who surrounded his mate and then the male once again. He sighed, knowing he'd been defeated by three women who were barely tall enough to hit his shoulder.

"Damn it. Lead the way."

Alex preceded him down the hallway and toward the front of the house. Masculine voices grew louder as they drew closer. The male led him into what he assumed was the living room and found Maya's off-duty guards sprinkled throughout the space, drinks in hand.

"You guys know Ricker." Alex waved a hand and then slumped into a nearby seat, catching the beer that Brute tossed to him with ease.

Ricker echoed the move, settled at one end of a nearby couch. Brute threw a can his way and he plucked it from the air, popped the top and took a deep swig. It was ice cold, bitter and exactly what he needed. Another deep drink and he lowered the can to rest on his knee…and noticed that every set of eyes in the room were trained on him.

"So." Alex began, probably trying to stare him into submission.

Yeah. Right.

"So?" Ricker countered with one of his own stares, eyes intent on the Prime's. Sure, Alex was the big boy on the playground, but he and his tiger towered over the lion in the "my balls are bigger than yours" department.

Neal, Carly's mate, cleared his throat and pulled Ricker's attention toward him. "So, you mated Maddy."

Statement. Not a question. Well, at least they recognized her change in scent.

"I did. She's mine now." Alex snorted and Brute, big fucker that he was, snickered. "What? You know something I don't?"

Deuce joined the conversation. "Uh, yeah. You know Maya's been giving her 'bad ass' lessons, right? Have fun with that whole 'mine' thing. And trying to tell her what to do. She's kind of a raving bitch now. Don't bother giving her instructions of any kind or—"

Snarl on his lips, Ricker launched himself from the couch and right at the cocky lion, claws unsheathed and ready to tear into the fucker. Even if he agreed with the other lion's assessment, no one was going to say anything bad about his Madison. The woman was perfect, if a little mouthy and unable to listen worth a damn. Every curvy, short inch of her belonged to him.

Mouth open and fangs flashing, he took two steps and reached for Deuce, tiger looking for blood. This is what males did. They defended, protected and went through anyone who stood in their way to accomplish it.

Four sets of arms corralled him before his nails encountered Deuce's neck, tips a mere hairsbreadth from the man's skin and Ricker growled his displeasure. He yanked, pulled and fought the hands that held him, the tiger craving the blood of the other man.

"Never say another word about her again. Never." His beast was just below the surface. It prowled and poked at his control, just waiting for a chink in the wall that held him at bay.

Deuce had held his ground, arms held high, palms out and face paler than a ghost. Had to give the guy some credit for not running. Or pissing himself. With Ricker's level of

111

dominance, he'd had more than one fierce male lose control of his bladder when Ricker got mad.

Ricker really hated the smell of piss.

"You got it man. Nothing doing."

Ricker narrowed his eyes, studied Deuce's face for any hint at deception. His nose worked double-time, scenting the air surrounding them, searching out a lie. Worry, apprehension and something that Ricker had labeled as "freaked the fuck out" hit his nose. The stinging tang of a lie was nowhere to be found.

Smart man.

Ricker pulled at the hands holding him, a quick jerk of his body, and smiled at Deuce's flinch.

Alex's voice broke into the silence that followed Deuce's apology. "Well, that's fun," the Prime deadpanned. "Ricker, do you think you can refrain from killing Maya's guard for now? She tends to get attached."

Tendrils of the lion's dominance graced his skin. And while he could have brushed off the suggestion, he chose to listen and release the tension thrumming through his body.

Damn, he hadn't realized his possessive and protective instincts were gonna turn him into a raving lunatic when it came to Maddy.

The hands retreated and Ricker turned his back on the other male. The offense forgotten. At least by him. He was sure Deuce would remember the lesson. At least for a little while.

He moved back to the couch and sunk into the cushions once again. The earlier process repeated, Brute throwing him a new beer since he'd spilled the other on the Prime's carpet. Since the man hadn't bitched at him yet, Ricker figured cleaning could wait.

Ricker popped the top of the can and took a deep swig of the bitter brew. Just what he needed. He rested the can on his thigh, laid his head against the back of the couch and let his eyes drift closed, let the security of being surrounded by strong males lull him. He didn't have to be on guard, didn't have to wait for the next shoe to drop or a crazy shifter to come crashing the door, guns blazing.

He could take a break. And let his mind wander to his mate. Since the fire-fight, she'd been in the back of his mind, tethered to him and he relished that connection. She was happy, almost giddy, and he could practically feel the purr of her lioness in his mind. The cat was happy, Madison was happy and life was good.

The men's voices raised once again, Harding and Wyatt giving Deuce shit about being an asshole.

Alex agreed.

Neal had to add his two cents. "It's the beer, man. Fucker drinks light beer. How can we expect him to be smart if he does dumb shit like drink light beer? We ought to revoke his man card and cut off his balls while we're at it."

Ricker raised his head and looked around the room. "Light beer? Seriously? You guys should have told me that before I went after him. It's like picking on the runt of the litter." He took a sip of his beer. Regular beer. Not that mamby pamby bullshit. "If I'd known, I wouldn't have tried to gut him. Seems wrong to attack the defenseless…"

An empty can came flying at his head and he caught it before it struck him, crumpling the aluminum with ease. It was a light beer can.

Fucker.

Ricker felt Alex's focus on him and he turned his head toward the Prime. The man was letting him, a more dominant feline, camp out in his territory. For now. The least he could do was show a bit of respect.

"A little touchy are we?" He flashed Ricker a smirk and raised a brow.

"'Fuck you' would be the wrong response, huh?"

Alex snorted. "It would."

He chuffed and extended his legs, thighs spread, and settled deeper into the cushions. "Fine. A little. She's just… Damn." Ricker rubbed his chest, an ache building in his heart, and he was quickly swamped in feelings he didn't want to identify. 'Cause seeing them for what they were would just cause a hell of a lot of problems. Like giving up his man card because he'd become pussy-whipped by his little woman. "Does it get easier?"

That smirk grew to an all-out smile. "Nope."

He'd been afraid of that.

*

"So, freakin' dish already!" Maya's voice was a loud squeal, quickly quieted by a spoonful of ice cream which was followed by a deep moan. The woman was huge, pregnant with twins, and had decided that she could exist solely on ice cream through her entire pregnancy. Alex kept trying to

114

feed her veggies and meat, but apparently, he hadn't been successful on the "balanced diet" front.

Maddy laughed and snatched one of the unclaimed cartons from the freezer. After grabbing a spoon, she settled into a kitchen chair and dug into her pint of goodness. There was nothing better in the world than Jen & Berry's. Except maybe sex. But even then, it was a very close call.

"I got kidnapped." She shrugged, pretending indifference. She was anything but. The bastards had stolen her from her home, assaulted her and forced her to use her powers on perverted shifters.

Yeah, not fun.

But at least she got a mate outta the deal. Ricker... How the hell had she gotten so lucky? Well, maybe "lucky" wasn't the right word. He was hot. No doubt about it. And growly and dominant. Which added to the hotness. But what she liked about him also pissed her the hell off. He was so...frustrating. He had expectations as to how she should act and she'd worked hard to blow Sensitive stereotypes out of the water.

"Yes, you got kidnapped. Which you totally rocked at by the way." The Prima interjected. "I made Alex take me along when he checked out your house and there was blood, like, everywhere. It was freakin' awesome."

Carly nodded her agreement, but didn't look up from her pint. Since she was another preggers chick, Maddy didn't take offense. The lady had a constant craving for the stuff and no one, ever, came between Carly and ice cream.

Maddy took another bite of the creamy goodness and then waved her spoon at the Prima. "Thank you. But I couldn't have done it without y'all. I mean, Maya, you taught me to be a bitch and Carly, you taught me how to kick ass."

Maya mock-glared at her. "I'd take offense to that statement if it wasn't true. Bitch."

"Whore."

"What, like you didn't climb Ricker the first chance you got." The Prima raised an eyebrow.

Maddy's face burned because that's exactly what had happened. One sniff and she went King Kong on the man, climbing him like the Empire State Building.

Rawr.

"Anyway. Yes, I kicked butt and did the Macarena on their asses, thank-you-very-much. And, yes, I played 'King of the Mountain'…" That earned her snickers all around. "…with Ricker. Even better, I totally killed a guy."

She could joke her way through this. She could.

Carly finally looked up from her sugary treat. "Score!"

Carly raised her hand and Maddy gave her a high-five, quickly followed by one with Maya.

"Yup. It was this fucker who totally spoke in third person. What is up with that? Anyway, they threw me into this room and there was another Sensitive there. The guy had raped her repeatedly over the last two years while she was held captive and came to take her again while I was there. When Ricker busted me out of that room, I hunted the asshole through the compound and took him out." She frowned. "I had no idea that it would be so bloody. I mean, fighting those other guys was a little icky, but that guy," she shuddered, memories of her cat's thirst slinking through her mind. A gentle stroke, a soothing touch, floated through her connection to Ricker and the horror of the hyena's death was brushed from her mind. "That was gross-tastic with a side of puke-worthy. Blech."

Maya, the most bloodthirsty of any lion Maddy knew, was leaned toward her, eyes alight at the prospect of hearing the gory details.

"Anyway. He's dead. I'm not. And Elise is with her family." She took another bite of her Karamel Sutra ice cream. "Oh! I told her she could come here if things weren't all 'happy-happy' at home." Maddy poked at the frozen confection. "The thing about it is…" She glanced around the table and found her friend's gazes intent on her. "She's sort of a fox."

"Fox as in, wow she's hot and we should watch our men around her? Ready to bitch-slap them if they look too long?" Maya didn't look the tiniest bit upset about the idea.

Carly broke in with her own question. "Or fox as in, grr grr?" She made claws out of her hands and reached for Maddy.

Maddy nibbled her lower lip. Way back when Carly was seven, she'd gotten mad at her parents, shifted and run into the forest. Hours later, she came back dragging the body of dead fox. Shed told her mother that foxes did not play fair. "Uh, grr, grr? I swear, though. We'll totally get her to promise not to eat you in a bad way. Or anyone in your warren." She held up three fingers. "Scouts honor."

Carly's face went blank. "You were never a scout."

117

Maddy sniffed. "I would have been if my brothers hadn't chased after me that time we went camping. I couldn't control my shift and—"

"And you came back to camp nekkid." Maya, the bitch, smirked.

"Fuck you."

"That's Ricker's job."

Maddy growled. "Then go fuck yourself."

Maya licked her spoon. "That's Alex's job."

Carly snickered. "And boy did he ever."

"Anyway. If she wants to join our band of wackiness, she's welcome. But she has to bring her own ice cream." Aw, sometimes Maddy really loved Maya. When she wasn't snarking at her.

"And she has to understand that there will be no destroying of my kitchen if she comes to my house." Carly pointed at her with her spoon. "Maya still hasn't gotten the walls fixed and it's been months."

Maddy wasn't going to laugh. Really. The Prima hadn't taken the news of her pregnancy well and, after plopping into a chair in Carly's kitchen, had kicked off her shoes to get comfortable. There were now dents in Carly's wall. Oh, and the freezer door was missing which was why ice cream parties were now being held at the pride house instead of Carly's place.

Maya had been really freaked.

"Agreed. No eating rabbits, her own ice cream and no destroying of private property."

That wasn't enough for Maya. "No public property either. I like Genesis just the way it is. If she needs a chew toy, we'll buy her one. The tables at the club are off limits."

"Chew toy?" She choked on a bit of ice cream.

The Prima looked at her with wide, not-so-innocent eyes. "Well, she's from the Canidae family, right? So are dogs. Dogs chew on things. Hence, chew toys. I'll put some in her welcome basket."

Okay then.

CHAPTER *nine*

"In a fight, don't go away mad. Make them cry first. Or bleed. I prefer bleed, but whatever works for you." – Maya Josephs, Prima of the Ridgeville Pride, who actually has done the whole "bleed" thing. For Maddy even.

Alex and Maya had growled, snarled and practically ordered Ricker and Madison to stay with them at the pride house. Well, Maya had wanted them there and Alex was merely trying to give his pregnant mate exactly what she'd desired.

But Ricker had won.

He needed time with his sweet, non-biddable mate, and he hadn't thought that would have happened at the pride house. Not with lions traipsing in and out of the home at all hours and most of them wanted to check in with Maddy.

It'd taken everything in him not to snarl at the males who'd hugged her and welcomed her home.

Every. Thing.

Ricker glanced at his mate from the corner of his eye, saw her eyelids droop while he navigated the streets of the tiny town. They passed home after home, little Victorians that eventually bled to ranch style houses and finally those that had a good bit of land surrounding them.

From what Madison had said, she'd inherited her house from her grandmother (which frustrated her brothers to no end) and she'd lived there ever since.

He turned into the gravel driveway, tires crunching over the loose stones, and pulled up to the home, right next to what he assumed was her little car. It looked at least ten years old and he made a mental note to look into getting her a new one.

"Don't need a new one." She grumbled and stretched in her seat before removing her seatbelt. "That one does just fine."

He narrowed his eyes. Maybe being connected wasn't all it was cracked up to be.

Madison snorted and hopped from the SUV. Her hopping reminded him that he needed to return the truck to the council. They'd had the car replaced after leaving the cabin. He'd have to buy something closer to the ground so she wasn't jumping from the car everywhere they went. Winter in Chicago, the council's headquarters, made the roads and sidewalks slick. He climbed from the vehicle, mind rolling with preparations. The last thing he needed was for his mate to slip and hurt herself. Hell, by then she'd probably be pregnant with their cubs and no way would anything happen to them.

Madison, half way to the house, glanced back at him, smile playing on her lips. "What has you so happy?"

Ricker couldn't fight his shit-eating grin. He closed the distance between them, wrapped his arms around her and tugged her close. He loved the feel of her body against his, those lush curves cushioning him.

He nuzzled her neck, rubbing his scent on her and inhaling her fragrance. Damn, he'd never get enough of her. Ever. "You. Pregnant with my cubs."

"Yeah?" Madison snuggled and wiggled against him as if she wanted to crawl inside his skin. She sounded so unsure of herself, disbelieving, that he wanted to hit whoever had made her doubt herself.

"Yeah, Kit. You and me? We're it. I want you by my side, big with my cubs. Forever."

He settled his chin on the top of her head, rubbed it back and forth. Emotions were pouring from Madison and he worked at sorting through them. He tossed aside the disbelief. He'd spend the rest of his life proving that he wanted her, and only her.

Hope just added to his anger at those who'd beaten her down as she grew up. His mate should believe him, believe that she was worthy of his devotion. Hell, she should grab him by the nuts and demand her due.

Then, buried so deep he'd almost missed it, was a kernel of feeling that made his breath hitch. It wasn't love. No, he readily admitted he wasn't quite to that level either, but it was a start. Something more than "like" and just under the "L" word and he was relieved he wasn't the only one feeling that way.

She tilted her head back, face upturned. "Forever?"

He didn't think he'd ever get tired of staring into those blue eyes. "Yeah, Kit." He closed the distance between their mouths, brushed his lips over hers in a ghost of a kiss. Once, twice and then he lingered, tongue stroking the seam of her lips. He needed a taste, just another reminder of his mate's flavor.

Madison's hands clutched his shirt, tugging on him, and he lowered willingly, aching for more from her. He slipped his tongue into her mouth, swept into the moist cavern. He drank from her, a groan building in his chest. Another swipe, deeper still, exploring her moist heat, lapping and sucking her tongue, mimicking what was to come.

It'd been too long since he'd been inside her, slid into her pussy and made her scream. The idea made his cock harden in his jeans, press and struggle against the confines of his pants. Madison wiggled against him, rose to her tiptoes and rocked against his length. The cradle of her thighs hugged him, teased and tormented him.

He shifted his hold, cupped the fullness of her ass and brought her more firmly against him, nice and snug. She whimpered into his mouth and his knees nearly buckled, her need bleeding through to his mind and amplifying his. The scent of her arousal taunted him, teased him with what was to come.

Because now that they'd started (again), he wasn't about to let them not finish.

Ricker gripped her tighter, took her weight into his palms and pulled his mouth from hers.

"Wrap your legs around me, Madison." His voice was more tiger than man, beast on the edge and needing to claim their mate once again.

Madison lapped at his mouth and nipped his lower lip, doing as he asked. "Please."

Mate in his arms, he strode toward the house, intent on finding a bed. Now. His arousal was roaring through his veins, cock pounding hard and ready to burst. Madison surrounded him in her scent, her taste, her lush curves pressing against him.

He stomped up the wooden steps and across the porch, right up to the front door. Unable to wait another moment, he pressed her against the hard surface and dove back in for another kiss.

Heat bounced between them, tongues licking and teeth nibbling, exploring and discovering everything anew. Her hands clutched at his shoulders, pulled him harder against her and he couldn't help but obey. His balls ached, dick pulsing as the heat of her pussy seared through his jeans. He knew he'd find her wet and ready for him, sweet pussy begging for his touch, his mouth, his cock. Fuck, he wanted it all. He craved her body like a drug.

Ricker rocked against her heat, slid his cloth-covered length along her pussy and smiled at her groan. Pulling his lips from hers, he spoke against her mouth, hips keeping a steady rhythm.

"Like that, Kit? Like my cock against this hot pussy? You want me there, don't you? Want my dick in your cunt." A gasp escaped her just as a tremor wracked her body and Ricker didn't fight the grin tugging at his lips. "Like that? Do you want me to tell you what I'm gonna do to you, Kit?"

"Yes." Madison wrapped her arms around his neck and pressed her face to his shoulder, her hips grinding over his cock, keeping their arousal rising with every breath.

"I'm going to take you into this house and right to the bedroom. No stopping along the way. As soon as we cross the threshold, you better be ready for me because once I start, I won't stop. These jeans, the ones keeping my cock out of your soaking pussy? They're shredded, Kit. Gone." He pushed hard against her, seam rubbing hers and giving her more friction. "Panties too. Then I'm going to taste this sweet pussy. My pussy. It belongs to me, doesn't it?" She nodded against his heated skin and he continued. "You're gonna come in my mouth, Kit. Scream my name. Then I'm going to fuck you. You can't wait for my cock, can you? Your needy little cunt is going to suck me in." Ricker kept the words low, body moving and keeping her on edge. Fuck, his cock hurt. The tiger inside was loving the hell out of their game, enjoyed making their mate needy, wet and hot. But it was hell on his dick. "I'm going to ride you hard. Shove my dick in and out of your tight little cunt until you scream. Or maybe I'll take your ass."

"Ricker." She clawed at his shoulders, half-shifted nails slicing through his shirt and right down to skin.

"You wanna know why, Kit?"

She nodded and nipped his neck, the coppery scent of his blood wafting into the air.

"Because you're mine."

Ricker didn't give her a chance to reply. A quick loosening of his control on the beast gave him a little extra strength and he half-turned, Madison still in his arms. It took barely a nudge to bust the door open, sending splinters flying into the house. But he didn't care. The tiger wouldn't let anyone near them while they loved on their mate. Ricker the man would slide his cock into her ass while the tiger

126

remained alert. He had not doubt the cat would roar if someone interrupted them now.

"Hey!" Madison growled against his neck.

"I'll fix it. Just as soon as you come on my tongue, Kit." He brushed his lips across her ear. "Don't you want me to make you come? Lick that needy clit?"

A whimper was her response.

Following his nose, Ricker navigated the home, thumping across the living room, past a kitchen and then down the hall. Her scent grew stronger with every step, the sweetness tinged with the stench of cleaning products. They'd told him they'd cleaned everything and he was glad for it. There was no way he could've brought his mate to a tainted space. A handful of steps into the room and he tossed his mate to the bed, her body bouncing on the soft surface, legs spread.

"Damn, that's pretty. Get ready, Kit. I'm gonna make you scream."

*

Uh, yes, please.

Maddy watched her mate whip his shirt over his head, exposing hardened muscles. She still hadn't gotten the chance to lick and taste each line. And from the way he was staring at her, she didn't think it'd happen any time soon.

Next, he kicked off his shoes and shucked his jeans, leaving him nude before her, long, thick cock hard and ready. He reached down to stroke his shaft, pump his dick from bottom to top and then rubbed his thumb over the tip.

Whimpering, she licked her lips, aching for a taste of him once again.

"Next time, Kit. Right now, I'm hungry."

Ricker reached for her then, popped the button on her jeans, tugged the zipper and then yanked the cotton material from her body leaving her clad in skimpy lace panties.

"Shit, Madison." His voice was a deep growl and she watched as his fangs grew.

Ricker put his knee on the bed and leaned toward her, gaze intent on the juncture of her thighs. She spread her legs, anxious for his mouth on her, tongue lapping at her heat.

He eased his other knee to the soft surface and kneeled, lowering his elbows to the mattress as he positioned himself before her pussy. He nuzzled her inner thigh sending shards of arousal through her, feelings centering on her cunt.

Then…oh, fuck. Then she watched as he opened his mouth, exposed those wicked teeth and nibbled her tender flesh, silk and lace stretching over her labia. A groan vibrated through her and her need increased, cunt releasing more and more cream with every breath, soaking her panties. The salty musky scent of her desire filled the air, competing with the aromas of Ricker's arousal.

Her mate sucked and lapped at her covered pussy, moaning with every brush of his tongue over the wet fabric.

"S'good." The rough rumble of his voice sent shockwaves through her and she couldn't stop her hand from lowering to his head, fisting his hair and directing him as she desired.

"Ricker…" She rocked her hips against him, forcing that wicked mouth where she needed him most.

"Need." The single word was followed by the tug and rending of cloth, the cool air suddenly stroking her wet pussy. He hissed. "Yes…"

Then he was back, flexible muscle flicking her exposed clit, tonguing the bundle of nerves. She flexed her hips, rolled them, forcing his touch to remain where she needed him most. He wrapped his lips around the nub, sucking and tapping. Her pussy clenched, more cream easing from her needy hole. She ached to be filled, stuffed and fucked by her mate. She couldn't get enough of her male.

Ricker shifted and his fingers teased the opening of her pussy, circling heat, toying with the desperate nerves surrounding her entrance. He tempted and teased, going round and round as she writhed beneath him.

Desire blossomed and filled her, nipples hardening and begging for attention right along with her cunt. With her free hand she cupped her breast, pinched her hardened nub and tugged, adding a delicious slice of pain to her growing arousal.

Those tormenting fingers left her pussy and she whined at the loss. She wanted to be filled and stretched, wanted him to pet her G-spot until she came on his hand.

"Shh…gonna give you what you need, Kit." Ricker's soaked fingers traveled south, digits circling her back hole and she tensed. "Easy. Give it to me, Kit."

129

Oh god. She'd never had a lover there, yet…yet she craved this level of submission. The she-cat wanted to hand over the power to their dominant male, lay beneath him as he took their ultimate surrender. The forbidden thrill of having him fill her ass brought another level of arousal forward and she shuddered.

Maddy forced herself to relax, to release the clenching of her body until his fingertip could slip past the first ring of muscles surrounding her hole.

"Oh."

"That's it. Lemme in. Gonna make you fly and make you mine, Madison."

Ricker pushed deeper, entering her further and she shivered with the explicit penetration. He brought his mouth back to her clit, tormenting the nerves as he eased in and out of her ass. She kept her legs spread, fingers toying with her nipple, hand buried in his hair while he stoked her need.

His finger disappeared and she groaned at the loss, only to moan when two pushed into her hole, spreading and stretching, sending a stinging burn through her. She gasped and twitched, pain merely adding the bliss building in her body. He resumed his previous pace of thrust and retreat, scissoring and stretching her.

"God. Yes. Need." She barely recognized her voice, words coming in stuttered spurts as the pleasure of Ricker's touch invaded her body. She rocked against him, enjoying his wicked penetration. His rhythm increased, moving faster as he worked her asshole, the burning stretch quickly replaced by pure ecstasy with every passing second.

130

He gave her clit a hard suck and released the nub, flicking it with rapid movements. "That's it, Kit. Gonna fuck your pretty ass. Gonna sink deep and pound my mate until she comes."

"Ricker!" Her empty pussy clenched and a spear of bliss shot through her at his words. The desperation for him grew to incredible heights.

His fingers disappeared and were replaced with three, the cream from her pussy still giving him just enough lubrication for his gentle invasion. The burn of his penetration increased with the added digits and she bowed her back, body fighting between retreating and pushing closer.

Fuck, she needed. His touch was shoving her toward completion, pleasure rolling and building within her, filling her from head to toe with ecstasy. Her virgin hole was desperate to be stuffed with his cock, spreading her as she fully submitted to him.

Pain from the stretch receding, she moved in counterpoint to his thrusts, pushed and shifted until she was taking full advantage of his actions. Each shove elicited a moan, a deep groan that joined with her heavy pants.

Her clit throbbed and twitched, his tongue dancing over the nerves, the flicks adding to her ever growing bliss. She released her breast and propped herself on her elbow, keeping her eyes trained on Ricker between her thighs as her male licked and sucked her clit, fucking her ass with his fingers, each flex of muscle taking her to new heights.

"Please. Close. Need."

"Know what you need." The growl reverberated through her pussy.

Each breath, each plunge of his fingers, every pull on the sensitive bundle of nerves buried in her folds shoved her closer to release.

Ricker's eyes burned bright, the shifting and sharpening of his features showing her how close his tiger was to the surface and her she-cat responded. The crunch and crackle of bone told her without words that her lioness wanted to play with her mate, wanted to give and receive pleasure from their male.

With the presence of her cat, Maddy's pleasure shot higher, growing until she could barely breathe, and she sobbed with the overwhelming sensations. With her outburst, Ricker increased his pace, harder, faster, deeper…he gave her more and more of himself. She writhed and wasn't sure if she was trying to get closer or further away. The ecstasy was taking over her every move.

The heat of his touch burned her, sent fire through her veins until breathing became difficult. Sensation after sensation piled upon her, burying her in pleasure. Her pussy rhythmically clenched and tightened on air. Her asshole mimicked the movements, sucking on his fingers. Clit aching and throbbing, it pulsed beneath his tongue, twitching with his every touch.

"Come for me Madison."

The deep rumble of his voice was what shoved her over the edge. Maddy came with a scream. Her back hole tightened on his fingers, pussy sucking and begging to be filled while pleasure-tinged fire seemed to burst from her clit and then flow over her nerves. Every shift and tightening of muscle increased the ecstasy inside her, forcing her bliss to grow with every breath.

She screamed his name, begged and pleaded for more. Anything, everything. She needed it all from her mate as the fireworks of her release crashed through her body. Muscles jerked and spasmed, no longer controllable. The sensations overwhelmed her, wrenched control, her shattering release exploding and breaking her into a million pieces.

Her body was no longer her own and she was a slave to the pleasure her mate created. Glorious waves of her climax ebbed and flowed, filled and retreated only to crest again.

Minutes passed? Hours? Eventually Ricker slowed his movements, mouth leaving her over-sensitized clit, lapping gently at the nerves as he slid his talented fingers from her ass. With gentle touches he brought her down from her peak and her breathing eased until she no longer gasped and panted.

Sated beyond belief, she slumped against the bed, wrung out from her powerful release and she only had one thing to say.

"Wow."

She raised her head enough to look at her mate and found him kneeling between her thighs, hand stroking his cock as he stared down at her, smirk in place.

Smug bastard. Totally earned. But he was still smug.

"Not done yet, Kit. Where's your lube? It's time your mate claimed your ass."

Her traitorous pussy tightened and her ass mimicked the spasm. Greedy bitches.

Not that she was complaining or anything.

Maddy managed to raise a hand and wave toward her bedside table. "In there somewhere."

Ricker shifted and she watched through slitted eyes as he dug into her drawer-o-sexy-times.

He glanced at her, eyebrows raised. "I think my she-cat is a kinky kitty, isn't she?"

"They're personal massagers." At least, that's what she kept telling herself.

She got a hum in response. "Right now, I'm all the 'personal massager' you'll need."

"Do you know how cheesy that sounded? I mean, really?"

Ricker growled, grabbed the lube and pounced on her, teeth bared.

Was it so wrong that she thought his fangs were hot?

Her mate eased down her body, fangs scraping along her heated skin, caressing her with his dangerous teeth. He scratched and teased her, tracing her curves as he traveled south. Each touch rekindled her arousal and her heart rate increased, sending pulses of bliss through her veins.

When he was once again kneeling between her legs, he dropped the bottle of lubricant and gripped her thighs. In one smooth move, he brought her legs up and then flipped her to her stomach, exposing her to his gaze.

Maddy wiggled and shifted, trying to get her knees beneath her and raise her ass so she could give herself to him completely.

She got a growl for her efforts.

Again, totally wrong that she found that hot. Totally.
Maybe.

*

Ricker gripped his wiggling mate's hips, dug his fingers
into the rounded curves of her body and yanked her into
the position he desired. Her knees were draw up, but
spread wide, ass titled and open for him. The pink rosette
of her hole beckoned his touch, his cock.

One hand stroking one plump cheek, he reached for the
lube with the other, popping the top and then drizzling the
viscous fluid along her crack. Madison whimpered,
squirming due to the cool lubricant. Her soft sounds
quickly melted to moans as he stroked the separation of
her cheeks.

He palmed her ass, thumbs teasing her hole, sliding first
one digit and then the other, alternating, as he tormented
her. With every thrust, more of the lube slid into her body,
preparing her for his cock.

His length throbbed in time with his heart, pounded and
pulsed with the need to sink deep into his mate. He
alternated thumbs, push and pull, stretching while
lubricating her passage. Her hands were fisting the sheets,
face buried against the comforter, moans coming in rapid
succession.

Fuck, it made his dick hard. Hell, she made his dick hard.
With her tender moments and ferocious growls, he didn't
know how he'd lived before her.

"Ricker, damn it."

He slid both thumbs into her hole and pulled them apart, broadening her passage. "Yes, Kit?"

"Bastard. More."

He chuckled. "No, Madison. Mate." He drew them further apart. "And when I'm ready."

She whined. "But I need you. I'm ready. It hurts. Please."

Ricker pulled his hands from her tempting ass and grabbed the lube once again. With a few squirts, he had enough of the liquid to coat his cock and another bit for her hole. He wanted his Kit to feel only pleasure as he claimed her in this final way. Pain didn't have any place in their lovemaking. Unless Madison earned a spanking…

He eased closer to her, stroking and petting her back as he lined up the head of his dick with her hole. "You ready, Kit? Ready for me to shove my cock into your ass? You want it, don't you? Want me to take you?" He nudged her opening, slid the tip in past the first ring of muscle and then back out again. "Tell me you want my cock in your ass, Madison." She whimpered and pushed back, but he held her firm. "Tell me."

"Please."

"Please what?" His fangs elongated further, tiger pushing forward, eager to claim what belonged to them.

"Please fuck my ass." The words came out in a rush, but he got what he wanted just the same.

"That's a good girl."

Ricker held her hips still and pushed forward, gently entering her in increments, unwilling to harm his mate.

Inch by inch he fed her his cock, welcomed her warmth. Her ass clenched around him, milked him and encased him in velvety heat. With a small retreat, he pressed forward once again, her body swallowing more of his length with every thrust.

"So tight. S'good." His balls pulled up against his body, tense and ready to release into her waiting hole. His dick was harder than ever before and the tiger clawed and scratched against the inner walls that held him at bay.

The stinging pain of bone shifting and reshaping joined in his pleasure, the cat shoving past bits of his control.

Deeper into her and then back out. Then deeper still. He sunk into his mate as she welcomed his invasion, body lax beneath his while he gently fucked her hole. He gave, she took.

Sweat coated his brow, the effort to hold back both his release and the cat nearly overwhelming him. His breathing came in heavy pants, and pleasure burst through him with every exhale.

Finally, his hips were flush with her cheeks, cock buried in and surrounded by her velvety softness. He rested there, let her grow accustomed to his full possession and he rocked his hips in a gentle shift of his body. His balls swung against her dripping pussy, coating him in her abundant cream and he remembered what her cunt felt like wrapped around his dick.

Later.

Later he'd compare the two. Maybe twice. He had to be thorough.

Seconds ticked by and then his mate became impatient, her shallow pants quickly turning to begging whines. He stared down at her spread before him, head flush with the blanket, waist tapered to the wide flare of her ass and his dick snug in her back hole.

The tiger roared in approval.

Yeah, Ricker the man was pretty fucking pleased as well.

"Move." She whined. "Please?"

"Since you asked so nicely…" He tightened his grip on her hips and did as she asked: pulled his hips back, cock sliding from her ass, and then pushed forward once again, her body accepting him fully.

Ricker repeated the slow motions, unwilling to harm his mate with rough fucking during her first time. He started gently, in and out, then again, balls tapping at her clit and pussy with every entry.

"Fuck. Madison." His breathing picked up to a hurried pace, balls aching for release, dick twitching within her passage.

"Yeah. Harder. Need." Her voice was breathless.

Growling, he gave her what she needed. Fuck, he gave her what he needed. Conscious of his mate's body, he increased his pace, fucking her harder. The bed shook in response, picking up the rhythm of their bodies. The wood of the frame creaked and groaned with his every thrust, but he only had eyes for the vision of his dick disappearing into Madison's ass.

She swallowed him, accepted him into her body and trusted him not to harm her and that level of trust floored him. His mate submitted, accepted and believed he'd never cause her pain.

And he valued the gift she'd given him.

Cock and balls aching, begging to empty, he leaned over her, braced one hand on the bed and used his hold for leverage. The new position gave him more control, enabled him to push deeper, harder. And he did.

With flexes of his hips, he plunged in and out of her, relished the moans and gasps that escaped Madison's lips as he pleasured her. The slap of skin on skin mingled with the sounds of their breathing, creating a sex-filled symphony.

More and more he gave. More and more she took.

Pleasure filled his veins, pumped through his body with every beat of his heart and thrust. His dick throbbed, picking up the same rhythm.

"Fuck. Madison. Come Kit. Come on my dick."

Her ass rippled around him, milked his shaft and stroked his hardness as he plunged in and out of her back entrance.

"Gonna." Her voice was reedy thin.

"Yeah, Kit." He puffed out the words, balls more than ready to follow his mate in release.

The tingles of ecstasy had grown to full-blown spears, racing through him and striking each nerve with pleasure as it passed. His dick was ready, thickening with the impending climax.

Then it was there. The scream of pleasure from Madison filled the room, the sound quickly echoed by the convulsing of her ass around his cock, practically begging to be filled with his cum.

He didn't disappoint.

Roaring, howling, he then groaned in satisfaction, jerkily thrusting in and out of her as he gave in to his orgasm. His cock swelled and twitched within her walls as wave after wave of his seed coated her ass.

Trembling explosions of bliss wracked his body, muscles spasming while her hole continued to caress him. He pulsated within her, throbbing as each tremble forced more and more of his cum from his body, making his climax seem endless.

Eventually, and hell if he knew how much time had passed, Madison stilled beneath him, tiny tremors skittering through her frame. His breathing eased with hers, bodies cooling, sweat drying as they recovered from their orgasms.

God. Damn.

He'd never get enough of her. Never get enough of his lush mate, sinking into her body and making her scream. Their connection intensified with their every touch until he didn't know where he ended and she began. They'd fed off of each other's emotions as she'd cradled him and he'd never had a more moving experience in his life.

Look at him getting all poetic and shit.

A snort and huff pulled him from his thoughts and he leaned down to nuzzle Madison. "What?"

"Poetic?"

"Hush or I'll decide that I want your ass all nice and pink."
He squeezed her shoulder and trailed his hand along her
spine as he pulled from her body.

"Promises, promises." Madison rolled to her back then sat
up and nipped him, teeth sliding over his chest.

He didn't respond, dick too tired to do anything about her
teasing. Exhaustion was finally catching up with him, their
mad dash suddenly weighing down on his body.

Closing his eyes, he sunk into their connection. She
soothed the savage beast, took the edge off the tiger's need
to dominate and destroy anyone who pissed him off.

Ricker rolled from the bed and fetched a warm, wet
washcloth then returned and cleaned them both up before
flopping into bed and pulling her close.

The council would love her. He figured they'd spend a few
weeks in Ridgeville and then they could pack up her
belongings and ship them to Chicago. His apartment
wasn't that big, he was a simple guy, but Madison would
need more space for all her…stuff.

He'd get her settled, maybe take another handful of weeks
off after the move before he got back to work. They had
Stone figuring out what the fuck went down at the
Freedom compound, but Ricker had a few ideas of his
own. He'd cuddle a little longer and then go hunt up a sat
phone. No sense in keeping his opinions to himself. He
wasn't actively working, but it didn't mean he didn't have a
brain.

Ricker glance at his mate once more, smile on his lips as he
realized how lucky he was. The other trackers would be

jealous that a coldhearted roughneck like him had landed the sweet Madison.

Yeah, two weeks here, just enough for her to have one last run with the pride at the full moon, and then on to Chicago. He could have Lia scope out a new place. She'd always been good at that sort of thing. She could decorate it too and—

"Chicago?" The word cut through the silence, Madison's anger an almost physical presence in the room. "Lia?" His mate spit the word like it was an offensive bite of food.

Wow. Look at how quick he managed to ruin a perfect fucking after-sex daze.

Fuck. He knew better than to mention another woman's name when he was in bed. Now he needed to make sure he didn't even think about another woman.

He cleared his throat. "Uh, Lia is one of the mission coordinators. My call-in. She was the one, uh, you saw that got hurt? When you went digging? She's not... We've never..."

A fraction of Madison's tension melted away, but her body was still stiff against him.

"And Chicago?" She slid from his arms and, as much as it hurt him, he let her go. "Ricker, I'm not sure about moving. I know we never talked about it. We just went all bitey with no forethought. But the idea of moving to a big city like that and the council. It—"

"Scares the shit out of you." The pain pouring through their connection would have brought him to his knees if he'd been standing.

Madison nodded. "Yeah."

The rumble of a truck pulling into the driveway cut their conversation short. Ricker jumped from the bed, hand going to the gun on the nightstand as he settled on his feet. He grabbed Madison's hand and shoved her toward the corner so he could block her body from attackers and…

His mate was laughing. And he had a deep suspicion it was at him.

He turned and glared at her bright wide smile.

Most shifters, especially women, would cower when faced with his glare. The crazy woman smiled.

"Ricker, it's my family. Hear that other car? And the Harley that pulled in just after? Momma, Daddy and my two brothers just pulled in." She snuck past him, smile still playing on her lips. "Get dressed. They're gonna see the broken door and come in growling and snarling if we don't show them that we're okay."

Madison dug through a nearby dresser, tugging out clothes and slipping into the scraps of cotton.

He scowled again. He really liked his mate naked and ready for him.

Then he remembered that she probably wasn't going to be "ready" for him any time soon. Sure they'd have to put the question about Chicago aside for the moment, but it'd come back and bite him in the ass. Soon.

Madison took two steps toward the bedroom door and he snagged her hand before she could escape. "We can talk about Chicago, Madison."

A look of sadness crossed her features and she simply nodded, tugging her hand from his and padding from the room.

CHAPTER *ten*

"If he's your guy, he's your guy. Just make sure you tattoo your name on his furry ass so everyone else knows who he belongs to. You could pee on him and mark your territory, but a tattoo is permanent." – Maya Josephs, Prima of the Ridgeville Pride, who has decided that neutering her mate was a viable option.

Maddy sat at her kitchen table, coffee in hand as her mother puttered around her kitchen. It was just something mommas did. They puttered, poked and somehow created delicious meals out of a near empty pantry.

Maddy loved it.

With her two brothers and father in the other room, she enjoyed the quiet of sitting with her mom and bathing in the serenity that always flowed from the woman.

Cookies baking (and she had no idea how that came about), her mother settled across from her, those knowing eyes focused on Maddy.

"So."

Maddy grimaced. Grilling from her mother was more about parental stares than words and she knew she wouldn't get outta this without spilling all.

"So, hey, I got mated." She tried to smile wide, super big and everything. It didn't work. Nope, her mother frowned, deep lines forming around her mouth and eyes narrowing.

"And my baby isn't as happy as she should be."

She forced her smile a little wider. "Of course I am. I found my mate. Everything is perfect and…"

Her mother shook her head. "Don't try to feed me crap, Madison Margaret Lane. I gave birth to you. I brought you into this world and I'll take you right back out of it if you don't start telling the truth."

So she did.

She unloaded about the kidnapping. She skipped over the whole "make all the Freedom members happy" portion of the show.

Tears formed in her mother's eyes.

Then about offering to be raped so that little Elise would have been left alone. Then saving the sweet fox and gutting a hyena in the process.

The tears disappeared and were replaced with pride.

She added in rejecting Ricker in an, uh, "delicate moment". She wasn't talking about sex with her mother. Finished or otherwise.

Maddy got a smile for that one. "I think I love our Prima. I'm gonna make her a cake and some cookies."

That was big praise coming from her mother. The woman was a blue ribbon winning baker and anything that came out of her kitchen caused oral orgasms.

Seriously.

Then there was the actual mating at the safe house. Again with the glossing over of "delicate moments". She skipped over the whole driving and getting shot at part. She considered that a kissing cousin to "delicate moments".

Mating talk made her mother's smile go super nova.

Kaboom.

Then the recap ended with getting home.

She skipped the whole "Chicago" issue.

Of course, her mother was like a bloodhound mixed with a piranha. She scented blood in the water and she was chasing after it. "Well, where's the rest? You should be glowing. You've got a fine man in the living room being grilled by your father and your brothers and he hasn't been chased out yet. But I'm not feeling a whole lotta happy coming from my baby girl and I know those men in the living room are aware of it as well. So, give me all of it."

Maddy slumped into the chair, defeat washing over her. "He wants to move to Chicago."

An ache at leaving her family, her pride, blossomed in her chest. Then again, she knew that Ricker needed to be in Chicago for his job. He was the best tracker the Council had, one of the toughest lines of defense against Freedom and the HSE. She couldn't imagine the shifter world without him protecting them all.

Her mother reached across the table and Maddy slid her hand onto her mom's, drawing comfort from the touch. "You knew you'd mate outside the pride. You knew you there was a possibility you'd have to go with him when that happened."

"I know. I just hoped he'd be like daddy and come here." Tears pricked her eyes. "I don't want to leave you."

Her mother scoffed. "It's not leaving. Chicago is only a few hours away by plane. Your daddy and I can come and visit and I have no doubt that your brothers will come and make sure he's treating you right. Probably when you least expect them."

This time Maddy scoffed. "They'll visit, all right. To meet women and party."

A twinkle slid into her mother's eyes. "They'll give your mate hell, too. It's a brother's prerogative."

With a sigh, she let her mother's love sink into her. "I don't want to leave."

"But you will. You're head over tail for that young man and you'll follow him to the end of the earth."

Maddy wasn't quite ready to admit that her mother might be right. The woman was a gloater.

The timer on the oven dinged and Maddy pulled her hand free of her mom's, thankful for a reason to escape her mother's searching gaze. "Lemme get those. The guys will be in here any second for a quick bite. I have no doubt that they worked up an appetite grilling Ricker."

Just as she opened the oven, all four men came tromping into the kitchen. A quick look over her mate revealed that he was physically unharmed and a brush of his mind showed her that there was calm, affection and something more occupying it. In two steps he was next to her, his face pressed against her neck and a shadow of hair scratching her tender skin.

His scent enveloped her in a blanket of reassurance, each brush of his head against her bathing her in his essence. "Hey, Kit."

"Hey." She nuzzled him in return, taking his strength. She sunk into him, the rest of the room forgotten.

A rough cough interrupted. "Yeah, 'hey' all around. Brat, you gonna give out the cookies now? Or do we have to throw down?" Her brother, Paine, interrupted, but she chose to ignore him.

Too bad Ricker didn't.

A snarl silenced the room and her mate's comforting touch disappeared. "Don't touch her."

Wow. He-man much?

Maddy set the cookie sheet down and wrapped her arms around his waist, rubbing her hands over his flat abdomen. "Shh… He's just being an ass. Besides, I can take him."

Her other brother, Darius, howled. "So true. Remember that time she treed your ass, P? Ricker, your girl chased Paine to the top of our old oak and wouldn't let him down until Mom told her she wasn't gonna get any cookies until she left him alone."

Heat burning her cheeks, she rested her forehead against Ricker's back. "In my defense, he told me I had cooties and that Grayson would never like me because I was a stupid girl."

A growl built in her mate's chest. "Grayson?"

"Uh…" Oops? A laugh came from Darius and he sounded more like a hyena than a lion. She looked around her mate and glared at her oldest brother. "Shut up, asswipe." She stuck out her tongue. She was juvenile. So what?

"Grayson?" Her mate's voice was quiet. Way too freaking quiet. Like, who-do-I-need-to-hunt-down-and-kill, quiet.

"It was a crush. I was young and he was sixteen and he's not my mate, you are, and—"

"He's Alex's Second." The deep voice of her childhood crush filled the room and she wondered what she'd done to God now.

Ricker's body tensed, weight shifting as if he was ready to go after Grayson, but Maddy kept her arms locked around him. No, she wasn't deluded enough to think she could keep him still if he really wanted to be free, but a girl had to try.

Peeking under her mate's arm, she gave the pride second a small smile. "Hey, Gray. How ya doing?"

See, even if her mate was ready to go all homicidal, she could be nice and shit.

"Mine." The voice was deadly soft, but held a whole fuck-ton of intent behind the single syllable.

Mom, the epitome of a people pleaser, and totally used to diffusing angry males, butted into the tense situation. "Well, isn't this fun! Anyone want cookies?"

150

A bite of a cookie, a bite outta Grayson, another bite of cookie, another bite out of the second.

Ricker could see the pluses in his plan.

The tension in his mate's body told him she didn't agree.

Great.

With a concentrated effort, he eased the tiger from the surface, forced the beast into its cage until the need to murder the male before him left his body. The breath he'd been holding eased from his lungs and his muscles relaxed in slow increments.

With his mate at his back, her soothing presence urged the process along. Maddy's fear for the male before her irked him, but a deeper look revealed that her worry was centered on what would happen to him if he killed Grayson.

The male, big and dominant, wasn't a true match for Ricker, so it wouldn't have been too hard. But the council could have a teeny-tiny problem with outright murder.

The man approached, hand outstretched, smug smile on his lips. Bastard. "Grayson Shor, pride Second and Maddy's high school crush, apparently."

"Ricker Croft. The man who will gut you if you look at Madison as anything other than a sister."

Ricker heard something that sounded suspiciously like "possessive asshole" from behind him, but he ignored it. Yes, he was possessive. And yes, he was an asshole when the need arose. Right now, he needed both, so he shoved it all together.

Instead of looking scared, hell worried, the lion laughed out loud. "Funny, Stripes, you're funny. So, do I smell Mrs. Lane's cookies or did you buy one of those smelly candles?"

Madison's mother went into action then, bustling around his mate's small kitchen. The woman got Grayson settled in a chair and then the family was chatting with the pride's second, ignoring Ricker and his mate.

He pried his lioness from his back and brought her to snuggle against his chest, head tucked just beneath his chin.

Fuck, the mere thought of her even liking another male had sent him into a rage. Madison belonged to him. Him. Not some measly second. She needed a strong male to protect her, even if she didn't let him do his job very well when she decided to go running off, aggravating the hell out of him.

But he was the only one she'd ever aggravate again, damn it.

"Little possessive are we, He-man?"

He placed a finger beneath her chin and forced her to meet his gaze. "You're mine, Kit. I can't stand the idea of another holding your affection."

"It was a long time ago, Ricker. Besides, you're my mate now. There's no one else for me."

Ricker moved his hand, stroked her plump lower lip. "I know I've got your soul, Kit. But I want your heart, too."

152

Madison's heart stilled and then the rapid tattoo of the muscle filled his sensitive ears. "What if I want yours?"

"Then I think we'd have an even exchange."

Tears pooled in his mate's eyes and he ignored the prickle behind his own. Men didn't cry.

"Aw, they're having a moment." The feigned high-pitch of Paine's voice interrupted them.

Ricker smiled when he watched his mate give her brother a one-finger salute.

"Mooommm... Maddy's flipping me off..." Her brother whined.

"Nu uh, I'm telling you you're number one, butt wipe." She blew the male a raspberry.

Ricker knew of a lot of things he'd like to do with that pink tongue.

A cookie came flying at them and smacked into his temple. With slow shifts of muscle, he turned his head to glare at the offending lion. He almost ruined the effect by smiling when all of the blood drained from Paine's face. He held the male's gaze for a few moments until Grayson broke the spell.

"Aw, give the kid a break, Stripes." The second popped a cookie into his mouth and didn't bother swallowing before he continued. "You're smooching on his sister." Another cookie passed his lips. "Thanks for the munchies Mrs. Lane. I just stopped by to check on Maddy and invite her and Ricker to a run tomorrow night. Alex is gathering everyone and I wanted to see if the little lady feels like going."

"We'll be there. Together." Ricker didn't bother keeping the growl out of his voice.

Madison was his and he'd be damned if the woman went anywhere near other men without him. Other naked men. Sure, shifters were nonchalant about nudity, but it didn't make him want to parade his woman in front of the males. She was so beautiful, so perfect and he didn't want to give her the chance to hunt up someone else.

Mating be damned, he was an insecure fuck.

CHAPTER *eleven*

"You can like a guy, but you can't love him. At least, not until he says it first. Or, if he's a furball, not until he brings you something dead and drops it at your feet." – Maya Josephs, Prima of the Ridgeville Pride, who, in addition to no ring, hasn't had anything dead dropped at her feet. What-evah.

Maddy munched, thankful for the picnic table the pride always setup at each run. It was what she did when she was nervous. She was a muncher. A connoisseur in muncherism. The munchtastic mistress of munchlandia. The…

"Dude. I eat less than you and I'm eating for three. What the fuck?"

There went the quiet munching. With a sigh, she set the plate of food on the table and turned toward Maya. "I'm just…munchy."

Maya raised an eyebrow. "Really? 'Cause you only eat like that when you're sad. Or worried. Or angry. Or…"

Maddy rolled her eyes. "Yeah, yeah. If I'm not happy or horny, I'm hungry."

155

"I could have done without the horny part. Just sayin'."

"And I could have done without hearing how strong Alex is because of the fact he can fuck you against the wall. Or the fact that you got pregnant on the Genesis office's carpet. Or…"

"Shaddup." Pink tinged Maya's cheeks. "Back to you. Tonight's a happy night. You get to run with your man and maybe get your nookie on if you can escape your fam. What gives?"

The thoughts that hadn't been far from her mind since the morning before rushed forward. Visiting with her family had forced her to realize just how much she'd given up by mating with Ricker. Never again would she stand around the clearing watching her friends chat and laugh before their run. No more watching her mother bake or making fun of her brothers. No ice cream parties with Carly and Maya.

None of it.

"I'm moving to Chicago." The words were hollow, a part of her dying inside. She was very close to loving the man talking with Alex, but the separation from the pride would still hurt. Hell, she did love him, but she wasn't about to say that out loud.

He hadn't dropped anything dead at her feet yet.

"What?" Maya's screech yanked everyone's attention to them and heat seared Maddy's cheeks.

"Shush!" She wrapped her fingers around the Prima's arm and dragged her into the forest. "You know Ricker is the best tracker the council has. They depend on him to do all the killing messy stuff."

"Killing messy stuff?"

"Fuck you. You know what I mean." She huffed out a breath. "His job is there. It's important. I can't take him away from there simply because I don't want to leave my family and friends."

"Of course you can. It's a woman's prerogative. We get our way. Why else would god give us pussies if we weren't supposed to use them to control men? It's in the Chick Bible." Maya looked at her like she was an idiot.

Maddy returned the expression. "What if what happened to me happens to someone else? Alistair wanted me because I could calm his members and I'm not the only Sensitive in the world. If I hold Ricker back, how long will the next woman be held by those psychos?"

Tears pooled in Maya's eyes and spilled down her cheeks, nose burning bright red as the woman started to cry. The Prima sniffled and whined, opening her arms and engulfing Maddy in a tight hug. Well, most of a hug. Maya's belly was mega-huge which kept them from getting too close.

"I'm going to miss you."

"I know, I'll miss you, too."

"I don't want you to go." Maya's arms tightened.

"But I have to."

"You better not forget your lessons. I want weekly reports on who you were mean to."

Maddy chuckled. "I promise."

The rumble from the gathering quieted, signaling that Alex had called their attention. With one last squeeze, they released each other and returned to the clearing side by side. At the edge of the forest, Maya broke off and waddled through the center, taking her place at Alex's side.

Maddy skirted the edges, unwilling to draw attention to herself by cutting through the middle of the rough circle the pride had formed. In a handful of minutes, she was at Ricker's side, not far from where Alex and Maya stood.

Her reached for her hand and twined his fingers with hers, giving them a gentle squeeze. When she raised her head to stare into his gaze, he gave her a soft reassuring smile. This would be her first run with Ricker. And her last with her pride.

All eyes trained on Alex, her Prime.

"Welcome, Pride!" Cheers met Alex's words and he waved his hand to silence them. "As many of you know, our sweet Madison was taken from us." A low rumble of growls filled the clearing and he nodded. "I agree. I agree. We were fortunate that Ricker Croft was able to return her to us and we have embraced our delicate Sensitive once again. Her abduction proves our need to be diligent. To become strong fighters. Men, women and children need to learn to defend themselves. And it's a sad day that we ask this of our little ones."

Damn, Alex had the whole political schmoozing speech thing down.

"To that end, we have a male who has requested to join the pride." Maddy's heart stuttered in her chest then picked up a frantic rhythm. "His strength will strengthen the pride. His knowledge will increase that of the pride. And most important, his heart will belong to a member of

158

our pride, tying us together." She squeezed Ricker's hand, afraid to hope that her Prime spoke of her mate. "Ricker Croft, step forward and kneel."

Ricker's hand went slack in hers, but still she held on, fingers tight around his. "You have to let go, Kit." He leaned down and brushed a kiss across her temple. "I can't stay with you forever until we get this out of the way."

Nodding, she forced her tense muscles to ease, then watched as Ricker's smooth gait took him to Alex. He kneeled as instructed and she brought her hands to her lips, forcing her sobs to remain quiet.

He'd sacrificed it all. His career. Those he could save. Everything.

For her.

Maddy was torn between elation and sadness over others who could possibly face the same fate as she did. Kidnapped and held by Freedom or the HSE. But the other part of her, her lioness, purred and rubbed in her mind, happy that they could keep their family and their male.

"Do you pledge yourself to the pride? Do you vow to use your body for its protection and your heart for its care?"

"I do."

With flourish, Alex whipped a blade from his side and held out his hand to Ricker. Even though Maddy knew what was next, her she-cat still bristled at what was to come.

"Ricker Croft, give me your hand." Her mate, her strong, dominant, bull-headed male, extended his arm toward Alex. The Prime sliced his own wrist and then Ricker's, quickly pressing their arms together. "Blood to blood, heart to heart, fur to fur, I welcome you to my pride."

The roars of her pride mates covered her, their joy nearly overwhelming her. The moment Alex released Ricker, she ran to him, raced to his side and launched her body at her male. As before, he caught her with ease and held her close. She buried her face against his neck, filling her lungs with his scent.

"Ricker... I can't believe... How?"

"I couldn't take you away from them, Kit. I figured it out. It'll be a lot of work, but it'll be here and that's what matters."

A sob escaped her lips and she tightened her hold when it felt like he was going to release her. She didn't want to let go. Ever.

Unwilling to put voice to her words, Maddy let her mind do the talking... *I love you.*

"Thanks."

She felt amusement coming from her mate, but that wasn't what she was looking for. She bit him. Not hard or anything. Just a nip. –ish. Okay, only a tiny bit of blood hit her tongue. Promise.

"Ouch, woman! Okay, I love you, too." He rubbed his chin over her cheek. "I can't believe you made me say it in front of everyone. I've got a tough guy image to uphold, you know."

"Hey! You two love birds about done snuggling? The pride would like to run sometime this century." Alex's voice ruined their moment.

Maddy wondered if she could kill the Prime and get away with it…

Ricker must have caught her thoughts… "Maybe next time, Kit. I've got a mind to strip my mate down to fur and chase her through the forest."

Oh. Well.

Maddy released Ricker and then turned to the gathering, throwing her arms high. "Let the run begin!" Then she dashed toward the tree line, giggles trailing after her.

Along with Alex's roar. "I start the run, woman!"

"Maybe next time!" She waved behind her as she neared the forest. Her nerves quickly shifted to arousal and excitement, her mate's heavy tread on her heels as he chased her.

Besides, it wasn't like she was worried about her Prime's anger. Ricker had saved her once. He could always do it again.

Plus, she was a total badass beyotch now.

End of Head Over Tail

Note from the Author

Here are a few other Maya-isms for your reading enjoyment. They didn't manage to sneak into this book, but they're too good not to share.

"Being a lion doesn't make you a pussy. You make you a pussy. So, grow a set and kick some ass."

"Courage is like a muscle. Become a bodybuilder. Though, I'm not sure if steroids would work with this."

"Smile, it's the second best thing you can do with your lips. The first involves politely telling people to be nice to you before you kick their ass. You thought I was gonna say blow jobs, right? Naughty beyotch. You can do the whole blow job thing, too. Just not to the peeps whose asses you're kicking. Unless it's your mate. Sometimes they deserve it. The ass kicking, not the blow jobs. Unless you guys are kinky like that and then you can do both."

"If worms had guns, birds wouldn't mess with them. The same thing applies except you're a lioness and have claws. And everyone else is wormy… Wait. Does that make sense? It doesn't, does it? Fuck it. You've still got claws and I'll buy you a gun."

FIERCE IN FUR

CHAPTER *one*

"The best laid plans of foxes and felines often go awry. Or fucked up beyond all recognition. But that second one isn't very kid-friendly, is it?" – Maya Josephs, Prima of the Ridgeville Pride who is very, very pregnant and very, very unmarried.

Somehow, Brute's baby sister had morphed from an adorable, toddling cub to a bloodthirsty bitch of gigantic proportions. His mother assured him this happened when lions hit their teen years.

Brute didn't recall being such an ass.

His mother told him it was because he'd been born with a dick.

And that had ended that discussion.

"Honor," he sighed and rubbed the top of his head, palm tickled by his growing hair. It was time to bust out the Bic again. "Explain to me why slaughtering Jenner would be a good thing. Just one more time."

Their parents were vacationing in Florida, which left family matters squarely in his court.

"Because." His baby sister, all of sixteen, snarled at him like a full grown lioness. Why did his parents keep having cubs after him? Why?

"I can't go to the Prime with 'because' when one of the Prima's favorite lions suddenly turns up dead during a run. That would upset the Prima, which upsets the Prime, and then things get bloody and I have to clean up the mess." He raised a brow. "Try again."

Honor stomped her foot and Brute could have sworn that the tile cracked beneath her. Damn, their mother was going to be pissed. Not as angry as she would have been if Honor had succeeded in ridding the world of Jenner, though. So, he figured he'd be thankful for the cracked tile.

"Brutus." His name was uttered between clenched teeth.

Now, anyone outside the family knew not to use his given name under threat of blood and gore. Unfortunately, that didn't apply to family. His momma had laid that law down long ago.

"Honor." He kept his tone strong, but level, gaze centered on the little bit of lioness before him. He couldn't show fear. It didn't matter that sweat was dripping down his back, sliding and settling at the base of his spine. No fear in the face of the enemy.

You are a fierce lion. You are the king of the jungle. People run when you roar. Stay strong...

"But—"

166

One of Brute's other sisters, Emma, waltzed into the room, nose buried in her e-reader.

"She saw Jenner hitting Genesis last night with Maya's friend, Gina Ernst." Emma turned her e-reader off as she slid into her seat at the kitchen table. "And they were cozy."

Honor pointed at her younger sister, every muscle in her body tense. "See! He needs to die. No, dying is too good for him. What did Carly do to that guy when she was kidnapped? I wanna do that." Another stomp of her foot.

Brute sighed and gave Emma his attention. She was the family angel while Honor was the family… Psycho Hose Beast Demon from Hell. "Translation?"

"She thinks he's her mate."

God save him from females. He swung his attention back to his now screeching sister.

"You bitch!" Honor launched her lithe body across the kitchen and Brute snagged her around the middle with ease, holding her back so that all of the Mauers remained intact until their parents returned.

The she-cat in his arms scratched his forearms and beat her heels into his shins, fighting his grasp with everything her little body had. As if she'd be able to break his hold.

"He is my mate, you whore!"

Little Emma, calm as always, diverted her attention from her toast to Brute. "Can a virgin be a whore?"

"When you let any male sniff at you and buttfu—" Brute slapped a hand over her mouth and growled low, Honor freezing in his arms.

"Emma, have you…" The males in the pride knew better than to sniff after his sisters, but he couldn't control every human. And then there were the bunnies…

His youngest sister gave him a wide-eyed stare, nose wrinkled. "Uh, ew."

Brute let out a sigh of relief. Good, he wouldn't have to kill anyone. Today.

Snarls and growls filled the room then. All from Honor. God, he couldn't wait until her hormones settled. Better yet, he couldn't wait until his mother returned. He'd rather be doing anything other than wrangling two young lionesses. Anything. Having his fingernails ripped out with pliers ranked higher on his list.

"Everybody decent?" A thumping knock against the front door as it was pushed open followed the greeting and Brute sighed in relief, almost losing his hold on Honor in the process.

Grayson could get him out of this mess. The pride's Second always managed to calm females. Brute figured it was because the male had fucked so many, but he didn't really care how the other lion came by his ability. He just wanted his sister calm. And not trying to kill anyone.

"Yeah, we're back here."

The Second stepped into the kitchen, gaze sweeping the room before settling on Brute. "What's doing, big guy?"

Emma didn't look up from her breakfast, e-reader once again on before her. "Honor wants to kill Jenner because she thinks he's her mate and she saw him going into Genesis with Gina Ernst. Brute said no because it'd upset the Prima which would upset the Prime which would end with bloody things for Brute. And because I don't believe her, I'm a virgin whore." Emma gave Brute her attention. "Anything to add?"

His mother should have left the thirteen-year-old in charge.

Another outraged yell and wiggle snatched his attention and he tightened his grip on the wriggling Honor. "Damn it."

"Stop." The Second's voice was low and calm, a simple but powerful order that everyone followed without question.

Grayson's attention turned to Honor in particular. "Jenner is not your mate."

"But—"

"He's not. Period." Grayson's eyes flared to amber for a moment before settling back to brown. There was more to his expression. Something Brute absolutely refused to acknowledge. He had his suspicions, but his parents could deal with it when the time came.

Honor slumped in his arms, the fight gone, and he released her. She didn't say a word, but her sadness filled the kitchen, practically choking him with the emotion.

"Are you…" Her voice was so small, and Grayson's expression softened.

169

Right. He really wasn't touching the situation between the two of them with a ten foot pole.

As long as Grayson didn't touch his sister with a two hundred million foot pole, they wouldn't have a problem. Hell, any pole. The one between the lion's legs in particular. At least, not until she'd gone into her first heat and could sniff the man herself, find out if Grayson was what Brute thought he was.

Her mate, more than likely.

"Yes, I'm sure."

That earned Grayson a glare.

Which the male ignored as he turned his attention to Brute. "Alex sent me. It seems that the Prima had a 'brilliant idea' and has decided on a road trip."

"Okay." The woman was about ready to pop out the set of cubs she was carrying and she hadn't let her pregnancy keep her from doing whatever the hell she wanted. "What has she done this time?"

"We think she's gone to Virginia."

"Think?" He raised his eyebrows.

"Pretty much."

Brute propped his hands on his hips, closed his eyes and let his chin drop to his chest. With a deep breath, he returned his attention to the Second. "Okay. Let's get going."

"What about…" Grayson waved a hand to indicate his sisters.

"Fuck." He ran his hand over his bald head for the second time that day, and it wasn't even seven yet. "Can you two manage to get through a single day without drawing blood?"

The two of them looked at him with wide, innocent eyes. As if he hadn't just held a homicidal she-cat in his arms and the other one hadn't managed to hack the school's network and give everyone in her math class an "A" the first day he had been in charge.

He really wasn't fooled.

"Well?" Brute demanded.

Two sickeningly sweet smiles, including dimples, were tossed his way. "Yes, Brute."

It was creepy.

Instead of commenting, Brute simply glared and then spun on his heel. "Gimme five minutes." He took a step toward the hallway and then thought about what he was doing. Instead of passing by Grayson, he snatched the man's arm and dragged him along. "I don't trust you."

The Second growled at him. "That's disgusting."

"Okay, I trust you. I don't trust her. Ever."

"I heard that!" Honor's outraged voice roared through the house.

Brute's parents couldn't return quickly enough. Closing his eyes and begging for patience, he led Grayson deeper into his parent's home. "Come on, let's go save Maya from her most recent 'awesomesauce idea'."

She'd been having way too many of those lately.

* * *

Elise hadn't quite figured out what to think.

There'd been a plan. A good one, even. All week she'd been covertly FedEx-ing her belongings to Ridgeville, stopping by the shipping store on her way back from therapy.

Ugh. Therapy. She'd have to find someone else to see once she got to Ridgeville. Ever since she'd returned after being rescued from Freedom, she'd been in therapy. With a non-shifter, non-Sensitive psychologist. The woman didn't know what the hell she was dealing with and no matter how Elise had tried to explain, the woman just wasn't getting it. Which was why she was hell-bent on getting to Ridgeville. She hoped (prayed, really) that Maddy, as another Sensitive, could help her. That the lioness could dull the edges of her memory, ease her pain and panic so that she could get back to living a semi-normal life.

Maddy had agreed to help her any way she could.

The Ridgeville pride's Prima, Maya, had as well.

Except Elise had been caught trying to leave town and had called Maya, begging to move up their timeline to, like, now.

Because the only group not on board was her fox Skulk. And currently, they were making their displeasure known.

Maya, in all her nine-months-pregnant-with-twins lioness glory was growling and glaring at five of Elise's Skulk members, her parents among them. While they, in turn, glared at Maya (lioness), Maddy (another lioness and bad

172

ass), Carly (a rabbit, go figure), Gina (look, more lions) and herself (fox-ish) as if they were the devils incarnate.

"You're not leaving." Her brother, Gavin glared at her.

"Am to." She sorta glared back at him.

"Not." His lips tightened.

"To."

"No—"

"Enough." Maya's roar cut through their arguing. The Prima took a deep breath and let it out slow, rubbing her belly as she repeated the process. "Now, Elise has requested to join our pride—"

"She's a fox." Her father harrumphed.

"So? We've bought her chew toys." Maya countered.

That had been the wrong thing to say.

"What?" Elise's dad.

"I never!" Elise's mom.

Gavin growled, baring his canines.

The other two, the Skulk Alpha Male and Female, laughed. And that got everyone's attention.

Every set of eyes focused on Elise's leaders and the Alpha Male broke the sudden silence, wiping tears of laughter before speaking. "Elise, you have our permission, with good tidings and happy hunting, to go to the Ridgeville Pride. With their acceptance, we offer your release."

The quiet remained. For one beat and then two.

Then all hell broke loose.

Her parents started yelling over each other, her brother kept on growling and then everything got better when Maya clutched her burgeoning stomach and roared over them all.

"Oh shit, I'm in labor."

Carly moved until she stood between Elise's fox family and Maya, glaring at the Prima. "You're not in labor."

"I am." The lioness snapped.

"No, because then Alex would kill you." Carly sounded way too calm.

"It doesn't change the fact that I'm going to be dropping the twins in the driveway if we don't get moving." The Prima did not sound happy. "Everyone in the car. We're going home."

The group of women spun on their heels and headed back toward the massive SUV they'd brought along and Elise froze, not sure where she belonged.

Maya solved the problem. Crawling into the truck, she settled into the passenger seat, rolled down the window and then smacked the side of the car. "Elise, I'm not dropping the kidlets on the concrete. Getcha ass in the car."

"But…" She glanced back and forth between her Alpha Male and the Prima. There was a ceremony and…

The lioness rolled her eyes. "Blood to blood, let's get furry and blah, blah, blah, you're in the pride. Let's go. I need to get married before I have the kids and I can't do that without Alex."

Gavin stepped forward, hand raised and a mischievous smile in place. "I'll marry you."

"And Alex would gut you. Funny how things work." Maya flashed a toothy smile. "Mount up, bitches."

Elise spun around and reached for her parents, hugging them each in turn before going for her brother. He snatched her close, wrapping his arms around her in a fierce hold, and buried his face in her hair. "Gonna miss you."

She blinked back the tears in her eyes. "Me too."

Maya's sigh reached them. "For the love of gawd. I will buy chew toys for everyone and the whole world can visit if we could just get on the freakin' road."

Chuckling, she released her brother and grabbed her bag from the ground. She raced toward the waiting vehicle. In two seconds, she had her suitcase stowed and was settled in the backseat, waving while the SUV pulled from the curb.

She'd miss them, without a doubt, but going to Ridgeville felt right. Perfect. Wrapped in cotton with the Skulk wasn't going to help her get her poop in a group so she could get back to living.

With Carly driving, it took minutes to hop onto the highway to leave Elise's corner of the world behind.

Maya grunted in the front seat and then released a long, slow breath. "Okay then. Elise, meet Carly and Gina. You know Maddy and I'm the head bitch in charge. Even if I'm a cat."

Elise smiled. This wasn't a woman tiptoeing around things, treating her as if she'd break.

Maya kept on going. "Carly's a rabbit and there will be no eating of the rabbit. Unless it's the girl-on-girl kind, in which case, I don't wanna know and her mate, Neal, would probably bitch."

Carly snorted. "He'd probably wanna watch."

"True. Anyway." Maya waved a hand toward them. "Gina's the only unmated in the car. You can bunk with her or we can find ya a place to stay. Whatevs. But, if you're getting munchy with Carly, you may wanna stay with her."

"Uh," Elise cleared her throat. "No munching if that's okay. And I have a job. At Drool and Dine. Seno said I could live above the diner until I found a place in town."

It'd taken two weeks to psych herself up enough to call the man and make the arrangements. Maddy had helped her along, feeding her information on jobs in the area and hooking her up with the diner owner.

"Huh. Look at that. All self-sufficient and everything. Better than some of the cats at the pride house." Maya tensed, shoulders tight, and then relaxed. "Just so you know, Seno's a big assed bear, but sweet as pie. Sorta like my Brute."

"I thought your mate was Alex." She slapped her hand over her mouth, cursing herself for the word vomit. That

176

was borderline questioning her Prima and no one questioned those more dominant than themselves.

Elise's heart pounded, blood pulsing through her veins while she waited for the Prima's response. She could handle pain, a lot of it, she just hoped the correction would be swift and fairly bloodless.

"Oh, he is. Brute is one of my guards. He's like freakin' King Kong. All big muscles and growly, but he's sweet as a satisfied kitten." Maya relaxed into the front seat, hand stroking her belly. "Seno is the same way. Mostly. Just don't touch his knives. He's got some weird relationship with them. It's kinda freaky. But he's sweet. Really."

Maddy gave Elise a look that said Maya was lying. Or crazy. Or both.

"Uh, okay." Elise tried to keep the skepticism out of her voice.

Maya flicked the radio on then, twisting, poking and turning knobs until she slumped against the seat once again.

That didn't last long.

Oh, the labor continued, the tightening of her belly and the huffing breaths as she worked through the pain of birth. But between contractions, Maya started dancing and singing with a pen as a microphone.

And so it went.

Hee hee hee hoo.

She "brought sexy back" with Justin Timberlake. The contractions were five minutes apart.

177

Hee hee hee hoo.

She wanted to know if men wished their girlfriends were "hot like her" with the Pussycat Dolls. Okay, still five minutes. That was good, right? Or was it four minutes. Damn it, Elise's watch might have been slow.

Hee hee hee hoo. Followed quickly by a "O-my-fucking-gawd-kill-me!".

Then it was Alejandro by Lady Gaga and she told everyone not to "call her name" and then explained the music video with hotties wearing high heels and faux fucking which the Prima found weirdly hawt but the couldn't tell Alex cause he'd look at her funny. And he definitely wouldn't wear heels for her. Unfortunately.

Elise figured being pregnant had rotted the poor lioness' brain.

And she decided never to have babies. Ever.

"Hey, guys?" Carly's voice rose above the singing and hee-ing. "We got someone following us." Oh shit. Oh shit. Oh shit. "It's a red, beat up truck."

Elise looked behind them and sighed. "It's my brother. He's annoyingly protective, but he shouldn't cause a problem. I'm really sorry and…"

"It's all good, puppy." Maya's voice was strained and suddenly a fragrance filled the SUV, something that Elise wasn't familiar with but put the other occupants on alert.

"Maya?" Carly's voice was soothing, calm.

"Oops?" The Prima's voice was small.

"Oops, how?" That was Maddy pushing into the conversation.

"Uh…"

Gina butted in. "Oops my water broke while we're still an hour from home? That oops?"

"Hey, I'm the head bitch in charge here. No growlies."

Maddy whipped out her cell phone. "I'm calling Alex."

"Prima said no!" Maya's roar filled the SUV.

"Prima can't kick my ass at the moment and I figure I've got a few days to hide before you come after me. So pft on you." Elise watched as Maddy openly defied her Prima and dialed, Alex answering in a single ring. "Hey, uh, Alex. The thing about it is…" She pulled the phone away from his ear and looked at Elise. "He'll calm down in a minute. He just has to get this out of his system." A minute, then two, passed and finally Alex's voice quieted. "Right. Well, we're pulling into a rest stop at mile marker seventy-two. If you'd like to be married before the babies are born, I'd recommend grabbing a minister and hurrying." Not waiting for Alex's response, Maddy ended the call and flashed a bright smile. "So, Elise, you used to be a nurse and we've got a kick ass first aid kit. Tell me, how do you feel about catching babies?"

CHAPTER *two*

"When in doubt, bite the things that scare you." – Elise Mara, former Sensitive who has yet to figure out how to bite her own shadow.

Brute ended up driving. Grayson had stayed behind to "manage the pride".

Brute had called him a pussy.

The Second hadn't argued.

Alex was in the passenger seat, claws unleashed and ripping into the leather that surrounded him. Both Neal and Ricker had tagged along, the males furious that their mates had left without telling them where they were headed.

So, basically, he was locked in a moving box of metal with three shifters who were inches from losing control.

Brute went a little faster.

"Do you really think she'll give them 'Josephs' as a last name?" He'd never heard the Prime so unsure before.

181

"Naw. She has to know how you feel. You did get her a ring two months ago. It doesn't quite fit anymore, but she has it." Honestly, it didn't fit at all. Poor Maya's fingers had swollen to baseball bats and she couldn't even fit the circle of gold and diamonds on her pinky.

"Yeah. Right." Alex nodded.

Another mile passed, then two and Brute finally caught sight of the rest stop. Not slowing a bit, he pulled onto the off-ramp and roared through the parking lot, squealing to a halt right behind the women's SUV. Alex launched himself from the vehicle before it'd even rocked to a stop.

An echoing roar shook the area, the sound even sending tremors through the ground, and it sent everyone scattering.

Well, mostly everyone. Carly, Maddy, Gina and a male he didn't know scuttled aside, retreating to the sides of the vehicle. Another woman stayed put, her back to them and focus intent on the rear of the SUV.

Alex stalked forward and Brute rushed around the truck, quick to slow the Prime. "Easy now." Neal and Griffin stepped forward to help, grabbing Alex's arms. "Birthing lions don't need the upset. Calm."

The Prime took a deep breath. "I'm calm." Another breath. "Calm."

Uh huh.

Brute released his leader, but kept to the man's side as they approached the other SUV. Coming alongside the back of the vehicle, they got the first look at what they were dealing with.

A pint sized woman, the female reaching no higher than his shoulder, was standing between the Prima's bent legs and… Brute was quick to turn his back wishing he could unsee what he'd just seen. "Uh, Alex…"

Another roar shook the ground.

The unknown female snarled right back and Brute glanced over his shoulder to get a good look at the little thing. The scent of Maya's birthing surrounded them, so he wasn't quite sure what she was, but there was no doubt an animal lurked beneath the surface. A human couldn't have snapped at the Prime that way.

She was short, no doubt, but it was her curves that called to him. Her body was lush, a roundness that he knew would cradle him, welcome him. Her brown eyes flashed and darkened as she glared at Alex, standing up to the larger male, and a surge of protectiveness rushed forward. He wouldn't let the Prime yell at her, no matter what he was going through.

Brute took a step forward, ready to put himself in Alex's path, but he shouldn't have bothered.

"Shut. Up. Are you pushing two watermelons out of your vagina right now? No? Then you don't get to make a sound." Seeming to be done talking, she whirled back to Maya.

A glance at Alex revealed their Prime's mouth hanging open.

"Alex! Get the fuck over here so I can castrate your furry ass." Maya's voice was strained, tired and furious all at the same time.

The Prime took a step toward his mate and the tiny woman snarled at him. "Side door. You can sit at her head."

Brute cautiously eased toward the woman, attention shifting from Alex to Maya's pint-sized protector and back again. "Is there anything I can do?"

It was wrong that he prayed she'd turn and look at him. Wrong that he wanted her full attention. The brief glimpse at her plump lips, those shining eyes and rounded frame just weren't enough for him.

It was equally wrong that, as his Prima lay in the SUV in pain, he could think of nothing but giving the smaller woman pleasure. A lot.

"I'm good. Can you find Gavin? Any second now Maya is going to remember…"

His voice overlaid Maya's. "Gavin?"

"Where the fuck is the priest?" The Prima roared, clutching her belly and pushing herself up until she was sitting, legs splayed wide.

"He's not a priest Maya. Remember? He's an internet ordained minister." The woman's voice was soft, soothing as she stroked the Prima's leg.

Then Brute was hit with the full force of his newest obsession. Her eyes weren't brown, they glowed near amber. Her lips weren't just plump, they were juicy berries begging for his kiss. Her pert nose attested to her sassy nature and he couldn't wait until that attitude was unleashed on him. He ached to scent her, roll her flavors over his tongue and see if she was what he believed.

His mate.

Maybe.

Brute had never felt such an attraction, a bone deep need, for another woman.

Keeping his back to Alex and Maya, he leaned toward the female. "Gavin?"

She eased away, putting a few inches between them, and he tried to shove away the hurt. He knew he was a big guy. Hell, he scared half the pride and that included some men. But from her...the ache grew in his chest.

After a moment, she responded. "My brother. He followed us because he's a pain in the butt. He hopped on his computer and got ordained with the Triumphant Life Church while we waited for you guys to show up."

Brute was struck dumb for a moment. "What?"

"Yup. You can do anything on the internet and Maya wasn't too optimistic that her mate would remember a minister." Her golden eyes strayed to him before shifting back to Maya. "Was she right?"

"Yup. He was too worried about her to... Anyway. I'm Brute. One of Maya's guards."

A tiny laugh escaped. "Right. King Kong mixed with a kitten."

Brute wasn't sure how to take that comment.

"I'm Elise." The woman leaned toward Maya. "And we're ready for the babies. It's about time to push, Maya."

"Not without getting married first, damn it. This fucking cat is saying 'I do' or these babies aren't going anywhere. I will cross my legs. Just see if I won't."

Elise stepped back and opened her mouth. "Gavin! Get your ass over here!"

Brute peeked around the SUV and watched a man lope toward them, hints of a family resemblance telling him that this guy was the mysterious brother who'd managed to become a minister in all of five minutes.

*

Elise ignored the man at her side. His large presence sent shivers and shudders of fear down her spine, but she had to push them away for Maya's sake. She assumed he was a lion since he was one of the Prima's guards, though he could have easily passed as a bear. With the odor of Maya's fluids and blood permeating the air, she couldn't quite find his scent beneath everything, but a lion was a good bet.

Brute could have easily reached over and hurt her. Hit her for…hell, the men in Freedom had rarely given her a reason. The minute her fox had retreated, the very second her skills as a Sensitive fled her mind, the men had…

She pushed the memories aside, shoved them down deep where they lived and slammed the door before they could escape again. She didn't have time to fall apart, didn't have a moment to spare for a panic attack.

Elise had a patient that needed her skills. End of story. It'd been a long while since she'd assisted in a birth, but shifters tended to have few problems when it came to babies. A push or two and then catch.

The SUV rocked a little as first Alex and then Gavin crawled into the vehicle. They'd lowered the seats so that Maya could stretch out, which meant the men were able to sit by her head. Without missing a beat, the Prima snatched at the men's hands and gripped them tight, squeezing with every new pain.

A glance at Gavin revealed that her brother probably hadn't really thought through his role in the whole thing.

Maya growled, her belly clenching.

Alex snarled after Maya's growl.

And then Gavin paled and swayed, looking more like a ghost than a man.

Elise snapped her fingers. "Hey, Gavin, we don't have much time here. Let's hop to it."

Her brother glanced between her and Maya, then cleared his throat. "Dearly beloved…"

Another growl.

Oh, look, a snarl, too.

"The good parts!" Maya roared.

Elise took a peek between Maya's legs. "You're gonna push with the next one, hon." She glared at her brother. "Get to the good parts."

"Uh, Maya… I don't know your last name."

The bones in Maya's face sharpened and Elise watched a peppering of golden fur coat the woman's legs. "No shifting! Gavin, you don't need last names. Maya, push-push-push-push."

The Prima hissed at her.

Alex roared.

Had Elise not been worried about catching a set of twins, she would have been scared. She reminded herself to freak out later. "I'm getting the head! Gavin!"

Gavin gulped. "Maya, do you want to marry Alex?"

Maya roared.

"That's a yes. Next?" Elise supported the baby's neck, cradling it while working the shoulders from Maya with the next push.

"Alex, do you—"

She glanced at the Prime and saw his flash his fangs at her brother. "That's another yes."

"By the power vested in me by the internet, I now pronounce you man and wife."

Baby number one slid free of Maya and suddenly Elise needed a dozen other hands. She got two. The big guy next to her reached for the little bundle, blanket spread across his palms and she hesitated a second.

"I got him. You wouldn't believe how many women decide to go into labor at the same time in Ridgeville. Sometimes men get drafted into playing catch. Just snip and tie the cord and I'll get him cleaned up."

A scream from Maya made the decision for her. "So help me god, I am neutering you. If you think that dick is getting anywhere near my gold-plated fucking vaginaaa…"

Elise wasn't going to laugh. She wasn't.

Brute disappeared with baby one and she focused on number two, repeating the process, easing the wiggly bundle into the world. Just as before, the big man was ready for the little one.

She didn't hesitate this time around. He'd managed one baby; she figured he could handle another. He was so tender, gentle as he cupped the child in his palms and held the bundle steady for her.

Elise wasn't going to examine the feelings that came along with seeing how tender he was. She wasn't. Period.

Plus she wouldn't acknowledge that, despite his size, he didn't frighten her like so many other men. Oh, she was conscious of his presence, his height, massive shoulders and barely restrained strength, but for some reason, she didn't think he'd hurt her.

Her attention was drawn back to a panting Maya. The lioness was covered in sweat and streaks of blood, proof of the recent birth, and Elise went to work cleaning her up. Within an hour, any tearing would heal and she'd be fully recovered from the birth, ready to take on the world. Or, at least, two screaming babies looking to be fed.

Alex still sat by Maya's side, her brother just opposite him. Had it been any other time, she would have teased the hell out of Gavin. His face was pasty-white and he swayed as if he'd pass out any second now.

Coos, oohs and aahs sounded from around the side of the SUV, but she ignored everyone. With quick, efficient movements, she cleaned up the Prima, set her to rights and got Alex moving. Sometimes, giving men orders was the only way they could be of any use.

Alex popped from the vehicle and rushed to the back to scoop his mate into his arms.

"We're never doing that again. Ever." His voice was rough, deep and tinged with worry.

Maya just patted his cheek. "Yes, dear." She signed and snuggled into her mate's arms. "Where are the boys?"

Elise watched the blood drain from the Prime's face and he stumbled, nearly dropping poor Maya.

"Neal." Alex had a penchant for roaring.

A man came around the end of the SUV, cradling one of the twins in his arms. "You rang?"

"Where are my sons?" More roaring and then the baby started fussing and that turned into a great big wail.

"Right here, Alex." Another stranger came around the corner, cradling the other baby. Wait. Not a stranger. She recognized Ricker from when she was rescued with Maddy.

Ricker was followed by Brute, and Elise found herself crowded by men on all sides, large bodies corralling her.

In that moment, memories assailed her. Males, lions, wolves, bears, all of them... they followed and chased her. Cornered her at the end of the hallway. Her feet bled, she'd raced over broken glass at some point. Did she break something? Her bloody foot prints had led them to her. She ran and ran and ran…

Barks and hisses followed her. She ran until her lungs heaved, body dying a little more with every step. The fox had retreated after the fourth man. It'd deserted her, turned its back on her human half and refused to share her strength. Elise couldn't even manage slipping into their minds any longer, the power of her beast gone in a blink.

But she kept running.

Faster.

Faster.

Faster.

Strong hands wrapped around her biceps and she screamed, clawing at the hands, fighting with human teeth and blunted nails. "No-no-no-no…"

"Easy, Elise. I've got you. It's Gavin hon, I've got you. Shh…"

Her brother's scent surrounded her, wrapped her in a calming blanket and she sunk into his strength.

"Gavin." She sighed his name, let his comfort slide through her body.

"That's right." She laid her head against his chest, felt the vibrations of his voice echo through her.

Distantly she heard others, males and females, talking over one another, but she couldn't worry about them. Gavin had her and he'd protect her. He would, he would, he would, he…

"Come on, hon. I've got my truck and I'll take you home."

Elise stiffened. "Ridgeville."

"Elise…" His voice held a warning, but she wasn't listening. Panic attack aside, she wasn't going back home. She needed to live her own life. Even if it meant hiding in her new apartment for a little while.

Or maybe a long while.

"Ridgeville."

CHAPTER *three*

"I don't have a short temper. I have a zero-tolerance policy for assholes." – Brute Mauer, Asshole Eradicator

Brute couldn't forget her. The sight of the in-charge woman barking orders as his Prima gave birth warred in his mind with the image of her cowering and clutching at her brother. Like a light switch, the memories flitted back and forth.

And he cursed himself and the situation that hadn't allowed him to savor her scent. The cat clawed at him, telling him that missing out had been a mistake. By sight, he and the beast wanted her, craved her whether she was growling or panicking. Both sides of the woman intrigued him, lured him.

And disappeared on him.

Brute had watched as her brother hustled her to his truck and settled her in the passenger seat. He'd stayed frozen near the rear of the SUV as the others decided on who was riding with whom. He had to watch and make sure she put on a seatbelt, 'cause he was prepared to march over there and put it on her if she didn't. Thankfully, it hadn't been necessary. His focus remained intent on the beat up truck when Gavin pulled onto the on-ramp and then into speeding traffic.

It took everything in him not to race after them, throw people into their seats and then floor it until he caught up to Elise.

But he hadn't. He'd almost patiently waited for the split with Neal, Carly, Ricker and Maddy loading into one SUV while the rest of the crew loaded into the other. Maya had bitched a fit about not having baby seats, but somehow, Alex had talked her into the truck.

Brute didn't even want to know what the Prime had promised the Prima for her cooperation.

And now, they were back in Ridgeville. Two of the couples and Gina dropped at their respective homes, and he was just pulling into the driveway at the pride house. With care, he helped the Prime, Prima and newborns inside. He made sure the coast was clear and they weren't bothered on the way to their room. He was determined to give them time to themselves.

Which left him with time to think about Elise. About her flushed cheeks and the way she nibbled her lip while deciding if he could be trusted. He had no doubt that she'd been wary when he offered to take one of the twins. And he was thankful when she'd brushed the feelings aside.

Then he thought about her shining brown hair and the way thin strands fluttered in the breeze. Mostly about how he'd wanted to tuck them behind her ears so they wouldn't bother her as she worked.

Right now, memories flowing through his mind, he cursed the fact that he couldn't add thoughts of her scent to the scenes.

With a shake of his head, he left the hallway and tromped to the first floor, heavy boots thumping against the wood stairs and then the marble tiles. Bypassing the formal dining and living rooms, he headed on down to the family room. Also known as: the man cave. The males in the pride had unofficially claimed the space as theirs and stuffed it full of comfortable leather furniture and more electronics than Best Buy, plus a small fridge they kept stocked with beer. Including light beer for Deuce. The pansy.

Male voices filled the entryway and Brute rounded the corner to find exactly what he'd expected. Harding, Wyatt and Deuce were scattered through the room, all slumped into their chairs, eyes glued to the TV.

No one's gaze cut to him, and Brute was thankful for the reprieve. He didn't want to talk about seeing his Prima's girl parts, or the ferociously timid woman he couldn't get out of his mind.

Some game was on the TV, but Brute couldn't focus on what he was seeing. An ache was building in his chest, and the need to see Elise and make sure she got to her new place okay was eating at him. He rubbed the spot with the heel of his hand, hoping that he could massage the feelings away.

The fucking cat wasn't having it. Nope, it craved the smaller woman, demanded that they go hunt her and bring her back to their den.

Not that their den was anything to write home about. He slept there. That was it. He'd been living in the apartment since he'd left home and it wasn't a home, but a place to lay his head. He might have to start looking for a new place if he planned on bringing his ma—

195

Fuck.

No. He wasn't one of those guys who'd settle down with a mate. Hell, most of the time, he could hardly get close enough to a woman to even see if she was the one for him. The ladies took one look at his size, the tattoos and bald head and ran as fast as their paws could carry them. He had no doubt Elise would be the same. The woman had probably only stuck around because she'd had to help Maya.

So lost in his thoughts, Brute didn't realize a full beer can was coming at him until it was too late. A flare of pain bloomed on his head and he turned toward the source, a snarl on his lips while his fingers shifted into claws.

Harding raised his empty hands. "Easy, man. I thought you saw it coming. Didn't mean nothing." The man's face was pale, eyes wide, and pungent fear poured off him. "I swear."

Brute forced his beast to calm, to remember that Harding wasn't prey. He was a partner. He was one of Maya's guards. Had to remember... Inhaling deep, he let the breath out in slow increments. He licked his lips, ran his tongue over the fangs, coaxing the cat into pulling back. A flex of his fingers, crack of his knuckles, and the claws receded. It took a few minutes for the lion to relax, but it eventually padded to the back of Brute's mind.

"Sorry." Another cleansing breath. "Just on edge."

Harding nodded. "Yeah, we get you." His gaze flicked around the room, landing on Wyatt and pausing on Deuce. "You want a new beer, man? The other one is sorta dented and shit from your head. Maybe you need the light stuff. Deuce could probably hit you with one."

Rolling his eyes, he let a smile form on his lips as he reached down and grabbed the damaged can, setting it on the coffee table before relaxing again. "Naw, I'm still not that much of a pussy. Gimme a Guinness or something."

A can was tossed across the room and he caught it this time around. No sense in letting the cat out to play again. Hell, he'd need to go for a run soon. While others could get by with shifting once a month, Brute had to go furry at least once a week. Cat was a prickly fucker.

"So, what was Maya's idea this time?" Wyatt spoke up, eyes never leaving the game. A closer look revealed that they were watching soccer. Damn, they were scraping the bottom of the barrel. They all tended to watch more violent sports and soccer was never bloody enough.

"We ended up catching her on her way back from Virginia with a woman and her brother." Brute popped the top on the can in his hand and took a deep drink of the bitter brew. "I figure the woman is joining the pride or settling in Ridgeville. Not sure about the guy. The chick had bags with her, so at least she wasn't kidnapped."

"True." Deuce added.

Brute had no doubt that Maya was capable of abducting someone if she thought they'd be better off with her. The woman was that loving…and crazy.

"What's the chick's name? Maybe the Prima has mentioned her before." Wyatt, always the thinker.

"Elise. Not sure what she is, but she's a pretty little thing. Short. Curvy. And—" Brute stopped talking when he realized that the room had gone quiet. Hell, they'd even muted the TV. "What?"

"Elise Mara?" Harding's eyes were wide, face pale. "Real, real short? Kind amber eyes? Dark hair?"

Brute shrugged, but on the inside, he was pissed that anyone else had laid eyes on sweet Elise. "Maybe. Not sure about her last name, but the description fits."

"And you're attracted to her? Brute, man…" Harding shook his head while Wyatt and Deuce groaned.

He glared at them all. "What?"

Deuce was the one to speak up. "Don't go there, man. She's… Remember the chick that Maddy and Ricker helped rescue from Freedom? That little Sensitive fox?"

Brute searched his memory, but finally nodded. The guards hadn't been part of that hunt, Ricker having handled it all, but he'd been briefed on what had happened.

Freedom, a shifter organization bent on destroying the hierarchies, had broken into Maddy's home and kidnapped her. After making the Sensitive calm the shifters in the compound, Maddy had been thrown into a cell with another Sensitive, an abused fox. Eventually Ricker had gotten them out of there, but not after Maddy had killed a guy trying to sexually assault the fox. From the hints they'd received, the fox had been held for two years and been raped and beaten repeatedly during that time.

"You're saying…" The lion roared at the mere idea of Elise being harmed in any way.

"Yeah, man. That's what I'm saying. You need to steer clear, yeah? I love you, man, you know that, but you're a lot to take. Especially for a woman. Even more so for one who's lived through Freedom's brand of hell."

The cat snarled in his mind and shoved at Brute's control. Without conscious thought, the bones in his face cracked and broke, reforming into the beast's muzzle. The lines in his cheeks sharpened while golden fur pushed through his pores. The lion wanted out, wanted to hunt down and slaughter everyone who'd ever hurt Elise. Hell, if they'd made her sad, they'd die.

And that thought right there was part of the reason that he'd steer clear of the little fox. Even if it killed him.

* * *

Elise could get through this, even if it killed her.

The way her heart was trying to break through her chest, she figured she'd be dead in the next handful of minutes.

Gavin had brought her to Drool and Dine so she could meet Seno, get her schedule and the keys to the apartment over the diner. Doing all this had seemed so simple in her mind. She'd worked hard with her therapists, even if they hadn't been all that helpful to her fox and Sensitive nature.

Now she'd come to the moment of truth.

Gavin escorted her from his car to the front door and held it wide, ushering her into the noisy space with a hand at her lower back.

"I'm gonna grab a table in the corner. I'm right here and you're safe. You hear me?" Her brother hadn't even bothered whispering. Nope, the asshole had to embarrass her by speaking loud enough for everyone to hear. She ignored the fact that nearly everyone's focused flicked to her, some people outright staring while others merely snuck a glance and then quickly turned away. "No one's gonna hurt you ever again."

199

Elise squeezed her eyes shut for a moment, shoving back the memories of when she hadn't been safe…when she'd been chained to a bed while a man shoved his co—

With a shake of her head, she banished the memory.

"Okay." Her voice was barely a whisper, but she knew he'd heard her when he brushed a chaste kiss to her temple.

Watching him stroll away from her, she ached to follow him, let her brother pull her into his arms and shelter her from everyone's stares. Instead, she squared her shoulders and practically stomped to the register. "Hi, I'm Elise Mara. I'm here to see Seno. I don't have an appointment, but—"

"No worries, girl." The woman waved off her words. A look at the waitress' name tag revealed her to be Alice, and Elise remembered Maddy telling her that the older woman was all bark and no bite. Literally. The woman was a wolf who couldn't shift without an Alpha's help. Since Alice had chosen to live in Ridgeville instead of the wolves' home of Stratton, it'd been a while since she'd shifted. "Why don't you take a seat there in the back? I'll getcha a cup of coffee and send Seno on out."

Without waiting for a response, Alice disappeared through what Elise assumed was a kitchen door, leaving her standing alone at the counter.

Okay, then. She could do this.

Taking a deep breath, something she'd been doing lot lately, she squared her shoulders and did as asked, settling into a booth a scant moment before one of the biggest men she'd ever seen approached her. God, he was almost as big as the man who'd helped her deliver Maya's twins.

If he was here, he could protect her…

Elise's eyes went wide. The guy seemed to get larger the closer he came and panic crept toward her, inching into her mind with every breath. She couldn't do this. Not here. Not now. She'd just arrived in Ridgeville and couldn't freak out in front of everyone yet.

Placing a hand to her chest, she pressed the spot over her heart, felt the rapid tattoo through her palm. Calm. She imagined the forest surrounding the town was lush and filled with life now. She could run and play in the trees. Gavin would be at her side. Gavin… Gavin was in the diner and would protect her. She could do this…

The giant slid into the seat opposite her, easy smile on his face. Stains decorated his shirt and, for the first time, she noticed he was also wearing an apron.

"Hey there, kiddo. I'm Seno." He didn't hold out his hand, instead keeping them loose on the table top.

Elise silently thanked him for that small concession. Fear still poured through her veins, pushing and shoving at her to get the fuck out of the diner and run as far and fast as she could.

"H-h-h," she swallowed past the lump in her throat. "Hi, I'm Elise. We spoke on the phone and…"

Seno nodded. "Yes, the apartment is all ready for ya. It needs a good cleaning and maybe a coat of paint. Whatever you lay out, just deduct from the rent."

"Oh, no, I can pay—"

Seno rolled his eyes. "Not happening, short stuff. I didn't have time to get someone in to fix the place up and it's

201

been empty since I mated Alice. I'm happy to have you, honey." The big man eased his hand across the table, nice and slow, and she watched as his much larger hand engulfed hers. The panic didn't overwhelm her with his touch, didn't threaten to shove her into unconsciousness, and she breathed out a sigh of relief. "You're gonna do fine here, kiddo. Alice and I will make sure of it."

And she believed him.

"Okay." Tears burned her eyes. "Yeah, okay." With her free hand, she brushed aside the tiny bit of moisture that had formed. "I've got my stuff, so I can move in today, if that's okay. When do you want me to start?"

Seno shook his head. "No, kiddo. I want you to get all set up, first. Settle in and—"

This time, Elise shook her head. "No, I'll spend some time cleaning today and get the place livable. My brother can hang out for a few hours to help with the big stuff, and then I'll send him home." She took a deep breath, calming her racing heart. She was voicing her desires. Seno wouldn't haul off and punch her or drag her into a room… "I need to have a routine, Seno. I need to start living my life. The first step was moving here. I want to start right away, I need to. Please."

The larger man stared at her a moment and she was sure he was going to give her a hard time. Instead, a broad smile broke out on his face. "I like you, kiddo. You're ready to bite back." He patted her hand. "You'll do just fine. You can start in the morning. It's our busiest time and Alice could use the help. It'll also give you a chance to meet some of your neighbors. They're good people here in town." Then his eyes narrowed. "But if anyone gives you grief you let me know. I don't tolerate foolishness and neither will the Prime. You promise me, young lady. Someone makes you uncomfortable, you come right to me. Hell, tell Alice if you hafta. But no one," he raised his head and turned to capture everyone with his gaze. "No one is gonna mess with this little lady. I won't have it," he snapped out the last sentence. "Now, where's my promise?"

Elise mustered up a smile for the big man. As scary as he looked, she sensed an innate goodness in him and his words kindled a spark of hope in her chest. Maybe…maybe things would be all right now. "I promise."

CHAPTER *four*

"The best things in life are worth waiting for. Unless you're an impatient fuck. Then, go hunting." – Brute Mauer, Ridgeville Pride guard who is thankful as hell that his parents are back from vacation.

Brute managed to stay away for two weeks.

They'd been the hardest two weeks of his life. True, he'd had his sisters to keep him some-what occupied. He'd chased after Honor, making sure the she-cat didn't bloody anyone while also ensuring that those guys sniffing after her didn't get close enough to do anything but sniffing.

Thank god his other sister, Emma, was normal.

He went ahead and thanked god again when his parents returned three days after he'd met Elise and he was able to pass his sisters back off to them. He was never having children. Ever.

But since he'd handed over the responsibility for Honor and Emma back to his mom and dad, he'd been lost. Oh, he still got up and watched over Maya and the twins when his shift came up. He still managed to feed himself in between drinking with the other guys.

The only thing he hadn't managed was getting a good night's sleep. Not when images of the delicate fox filled his mind. Once the Prima was up to it, he'd questioned her further about Elise, confirming she was the tiny woman who'd been in captivity for two years and had only been out a handful of months.

Damn. The things they'd done to her. He couldn't even let hints of the thoughts linger in his mind or he'd lose control. More than once he found himself waking in the middle of the night, half-shifted and heading toward his back door. The cat wanted to be near Elise, ached to protect her, period.

So far, he'd been able to keep the cat at bay with internal promises of going to the woman.

It'd been just fourteen days and the cat was at its breaking point. Brute the man either went to Elise, or the lion would do it for him.

So, he'd driven to Drool and Dine. Man, fucking Seno had a jacked sense of humor. But it was the best place to eat in Ridgeville and pulled a good crowd at every meal. Brute managed to hold off his arrival until what he assumed was the lull between breakfast and lunch, hoping to get a hint of her scent. By the way his beast acted, the pretty fox was all but claimed as their mate, no sniffing needed.

Fuck, he felt like a teen all over again, going to talk to the first girl he ever liked and asking her out. Hell it took him three tries to actually make it from his truck. First he'd forgotten to put the damned thing in park. Then he'd sorta overlooked cutting the engine. And, hey, unbuckling his seat belt was a good thing.

He hated the rush of nerves, hoping that he hadn't built up his attraction to Elise only to have it slammed down when he got a good whiff of her.

Stepping down from his truck, he strode toward the building, heavy boots thumping on the asphalt as he approached. He shoved one foot in front of the other, stomping to the front door and then he was inside, the welcoming scents of Seno's cooking surrounding him.

And then there was something different…something delicious and sinful, mouth wateringly good and both Brute and his cat wanted to bathe in the scent. Without hunting up the source, he knew it came from his delicate fox. She was in the diner, close enough for him to snatch and then hide until she agreed to their mating. She was his mate, his everything.

Pausing in the doorway, Brute swept the interior with his gaze, searching for her. Within moments, he spied his quarry toward the back, smiling wide at the customers at the table. A growl built in his chest as he recognized the seated men.

Harding, Wyatt and Deuce were all smiles while Elise served them.

He didn't like it, and the lion was ready to settle his problems outside. With claws and teeth. Taking a deep, calming breath, he waited until the sweet fox left their table before stomping toward them.

Damn piece of shit assholes told him to steer clear of Elise and here they were…

Before any of them could say a word, Brute shoved his way into the booth, pushing Harding into the corner. He glared at each of 'em, growling low so that they got a hint as to how pissed he was.

All three of them were looking a little pale and he was pleased with their reaction. "Hello, boys."

"Uh…"

"Hey…"

"What's up, man?"

Sure, they tried to play it cool, but the acrid flavors of fear teased Brute's nose. "Now, if I recall, I was supposed to steer clear of Elise because of her past and I'm 'a lot to take in'. All right, then. The question is, how are the three of you at once any easier than one of little ole' me?"

"You see…"

"The thing about it is…"

"Well…"

All three of them hemmed and hawed while he captured them with his glare. He readily admitted to being a scary fucker. It was his job. But the three of them together weren't any less frightening than him alone.

Seeing Elise approach, Brute tore his gaze from his fellow guards and watched her as she neared.

Damn, she was just as gorgeous as he remembered. Hell, more so now. He'd seen her stressed and in charge, barking orders while she worked, and then panicking when it was all over. But this…this Elise bowled him over. She was so open…so happy. Pleasure radiated from her entire body so much that she seemed to glow. Her hair shone in the sunlight, eyes danced and a wide smile graced her lips. Those plump, kissable lips. Shit, he needed her. Even in the dumpy uniform, her curves beckoned him, tempted and teased him.

Brute wanted to do nothing but sneak her away and hold her close for as long as she'd let him.

Each step brought her nearer and he picked out more details…like the hint of a dimple when she laughed or that there was a slight hitch in her step. Hell, now his cat was pissed about who could have possibly injured her to the point that she had a very slight limp.

Damn beast.

In another two steps, Elise's attention landed on their table, particularly Brute. Butterflies, fuck it, bats took up residence in his stomach while he waited for the fox's reaction.

He shouldn't have bothered.

Elise took the last two steps in a rush, reaching out and squeezing his hand the second he was within her reach and then said his name with a sigh. "Brute."

Just like that, the lion calmed. It slumped in relief in his mind, rolling to its side and then letting its head fall. It no longer growled or snarled at him. No, for the first time, maybe ever, Brute was a peace.

"Hey, Elise." They were frozen for a moment, her gaze locked squarely on his while he traced circles with his thumb on the back of her hand. That seductive scent surrounded him then and his nostrils flared as he inhaled, pulling more of her into his body. He nearly broke out into a shit-eating grin when he watched her do the same. Her tiny hand shook against his and he squeezed it in a gentle tightening of muscle before releasing her. "How have you been?"

A tiny pink tongue darted out to lap at her lips and then disappeared. He ached to follow it, delve into her mouth and drink in her natural flavors. "Um, good. Great. The town is real nice and Seno has been taking great care of me."

A growl built in his chest, his calm cat now pissed as hell that he hadn't been around to see after her. Brute suppressed the sound, sure that the little fox wasn't ready for his intensity.

Instead, he replied, "I'm glad to hear it. Real glad." He looked at the other three men in the booth, glaring at each of them. "You know, the guys were just leaving, but I don't wanna eat alone. Do you think you can sit with me a bit?" He gave her his full attention. "I promise I won't bite."

*

Shit, shit, shit.

And another shit.

He was here. As in, *here* here.

Fur brushed her mind, a gentle stroke that Elise wanted to grasp with both hands, but she kept the urge at bay. Her fox was interested enough for that tentative touch and she refused to fuck things up by pushing the issue. It wasn't the first time her timid animal had made itself known, but it was the first time in public.

Maddy had helped her search for her fox when they were alone in her apartment, but this…this was new and unexpected and…amazing.

Elise licked her lips and slowly pulled her hand from Brute's, mind racing as she took a step back. "Okay. So, you guys want anything to go?"

The three other men glared at Brute and then gave her smiles. She had no doubt their exit was caused by the big lion sitting feet from her, but she couldn't muster any sympathy. Not when her fox stroked her thoughts once again and showed interest in the larger man.

With grumbles, the men left her and Brute alone. He sat once again while she stood clutching her order pad. "Um… Did you want to order?"

"If you're eating with me and let me pay?" He raised his eyebrows and she felt nothing but snippets of hope from him.

Another thing her time with Maddy had returned to her. Nothing near her original Sensitive abilities, but at least feeling the emotions of others could help keep her safe.

His hope and happiness rubbed off on her and, for the first time since she'd come to Ridgeville, she sensed her future was a little brighter.

"Yeah, okay." She nodded. "What would you like?"

Smiling wide, Elise took down Brute's order, not bothering to hide her surprise when he wanted not one burger, but four. Then again, the man was huge, bigger than Seno. But she couldn't muster an ounce of fear of the man.

Not since she'd placed a tiny baby in his large hands and watched the gentleness that he'd shown. He'd towered over her, could have easily overpowered her without a thought, yet he'd cradled the small child as if he'd die rather than hurt him.

With a spring in her step, she headed to the window to pass off her order. It was time for her break anyway, and something in her ached to spend time with Brute. She'd known that he was the cause for everyone's fear, but she couldn't imagine why everyone felt that way. He was kind and gentle, with an innate goodness that couldn't be ignored.

They were all just jerks.

Elise passed the ticket to a bored Seno and then leaned against the counter. With it so slow, Alice was in the back, taking a break, so it was just her and the big boss.

"Five burgers?"

Her smile widened further. "One for me and four for Brute."

"Brute? Brutus Mauer? Aw, kiddo he's…"

Elise didn't care for his tone. "He's fine. He's nice, Seno. I don't know him well, but…" God, how did she explain something to someone who had no frame of reference. "He's just a good guy." She finished lamely. She made a fist and rubbed it over her heart. "You know how you tell me that certain customers are good people? He's one of my good people."

Seno looked skeptical, but finally slumped his shoulders in defeat. "Okay, kiddo, okay. I know he won't hurt ya. Not on purpose. But he's a big guy and…"

"Leave her alone and cook the damned burgers." Alice's voice came from the back, cutting into their conversation, and Elise couldn't suppress her laugh.

The giggle earned her a glare from her boss.

"Fine, fine. I'm cooking the burgers. You ladies getting your panties in a bunch and..." He kept grumbling while he worked, leaving Elise to her thoughts.

Her mind flitted, bouncing around. She recalled delivering the babies and Brute's care. Then his attentiveness while she helped Maya. His earnestness when he said he just wanted to help. The distance he gave while she worked, as if sensing she couldn't deal with someone close. She even remembered his body, tense and ready for action, when Alex had begun roaring at her.

Would he have stepped in? It seemed like it.

The cool brush of her fox's nose followed by a stroke of fur showed that her beast agreed. Elise suppressed the shout of glee as relief and happiness rushed through her. In the handful of minutes that she'd been in Brute's company, she'd had several interactions with her inner-fox.

Elise couldn't imagine being friends with Brute could be anything but good.

"Order up."

Blinking, she pulled from her inner thoughts and reached for the plates, placing them on a tray before hefting it onto her shoulder. "Thanks, Seno."

Not waiting for a response, she headed back toward the table...and to Brute.

In moments she was at his table, their table, and setting the tray down.

"Shit, Elise. You shoulda told me how heavy this would be. I could've gotten it." His voice was filled with worry and she rolled her eyes.

"I do this all day, Brute. It's fine. Get your fingers out of my way." She brushed his hand from the plate and then lifted it from the tray. "Just eat."

God that felt good. The fear that would have debilitated her before didn't make an appearance, didn't even poke its head of out its hole and nudge her. She hadn't been that blunt with anyone but Alice, Seno and Maddy since she'd hit town. Being that way while dealing with Maya's delivery was one thing, but this was the first time she was in a normal situation with someone she didn't really know and had reacted, well, normally.

Unloading the last of their plates, she set the tray aside and settled into the booth opposite Brute and just stared at the beautiful man. No, he wasn't really beautiful. Not like a supermodel or pinup. He was just…just Brute.

The bright lights shone against the smooth skin of his head and she followed the lines of his face to a strong jaw and soft looking lips. Part of her, the part that hadn't died while trapped by Freedom, almost wondered what his kiss would be like. Almost.

Her perusal continued to his broad shoulders, thick biceps and thicker chest. She imagined his dark shirt covered layers of muscle and couldn't fathom the strength he held. A man's inner cat was typically larger than his human body and if that was the case with Brute…the lion would be huge.

A delicate nudge by her fox proved that the idea didn't scare her nearly as much as it should have.

Without waiting for Brute, she dug into her burger, chomping down on the juicy sandwich as if she hadn't eaten in a million years. She still hadn't gotten over that aspect of her imprisonment. Freedom had fed her, sure, but only when they remembered her. Or rather, she was remembered by the right person. Plenty of men had her in mind when they wanted to rape her, but otherwise, she wasn't even a flicker of a memory to them.

Elise moaned as the first burst of flavor passed over her tongue.

If she hadn't been watching the man across from her, she would have missed the flash of pain that crossed his features. "Damn."

"Brute?" She set her burger down.

Then it hit her, lust. It was hot, burning her skin, and terror struck. She'd felt interest in the last two weeks, but this went so far beyond that.

"No..." Her voice was barely a whisper and she felt the heat of her blood leave her face but the fox... Her fox pushed against her. It wasn't a nudge like before, but an outright shove. As if the beast wanted to answer the lion's call.

Brute breathed deep and worry immediately replaced the desire. "Easy, Elise. Nothing's happening. I'm attracted to you, that's all. I won't move, won't even talk to you if you want. Just lemme sit here and eat lunch with you." She thought something more than attraction lurked just beneath his skin, but she kept her mouth shut. "Is that okay?"

Elise stared at him and forced her breathing back to an even tempo. His words had a ring of truth. He could have done something already if he'd wanted to. There was no doubt in her mind that Brute could have taken on every man in the diner, including Seno, and won. Hell, he probably could take over the pride without breaking a sweat.

So…so, she could have lunch with him. Have lunch with the man who had cradled Maya's baby with gentle hands.

Lunch? Yeah, she could do that.

CHAPTER *five*

"I feel like I'm playing a game without the instructions. So I'll just make it up as I go along. That means I win, collect two hundred dollars plus I've just sunk your battleship. Everyone else can put their left foot on blue." – Elise Mara, almost Sensitive, semifox and all around confused.

"He's here again, kiddo." Seno's voice cut through Elise's concentration, sending her fox scurrying into the back of her mind once again.

She and Maddy had been working diligently, meeting for an hour each day, luring her fox out while also blunting the sharp edges of her memory. For a month now, they'd labored together, sometimes doubling up their time in the last two weeks since Elise had a reason to get better now. Well, better was more of a relative term.

With each day that passed, each smile she shared with Brute, she was becoming convinced that he belonged to her. If only the damned fox would cooperate and help her confirm her suspicions. The little beastie was easing closer each day, but refused to stick around for very long.

"Thanks, Seno." She pushed to her feet, figuring her fifteen minute break was at a quick end. Brute had been visiting her each night after the dinner rush, sitting at the counter and chatting while she tidied, rolling flatware or marrying the salt and pepper. And in all honesty, she wasn't upset that her break got cut short, not when it meant spending a few (or more) safe minutes in his company.

"Well, uh," the big man scratched the back of his neck and then ran his fingers through his hair. "I'm sorta giving you the rest of the night off."

Elise narrowed her eyes. Seno wasn't a slave driver, but he didn't just send someone home out of the goodness of his heart. "What do you mean?"

"See… The thing is… Aw, hell. Brute wants to take you out and I gave him my blessing. He's been coming in here every night to see you—"

"You sure he hasn't been coming in for the pie? You make a really good pie." Her lips twitched as she suppressed the urge to laugh. That was something else Maddy had helped her rediscover…her laugh.

"Elise," Seno growled. "He's proved to be a good boy and he asked me to let you off tonight." The man straightened fully, impressing her with his full height. "I gave my blessing, told him to treat you right and that I'd gut him if you weren't smiling by the time you returned. By midnight."

"Blessing? Midnight?" She let herself glare at him. It was okay to disagree with people. They wouldn't hit her for having an opinion, least of all Seno.

"Well, it's not like your father is here and good girls don't stay out to all hours. In my day…"

Elise snorted. "In your day, a horse was transportation."

A yell from out front ended their little "discussion" and Elise bolted, slipping around Seno and practically skipping to the front of the diner.

Brute had asked... Well, he hadn't asked her, but he'd gone to her faux-father and gotten permission to date her at least. Gah. Date. She wasn't sure she'd ever really done that. Not well, at least. And then there'd been the years with Freedom...

She shoved that thought aside. The pain, terror and ache that came with the memories were not nearly as sharp, but they still poked at her with a very pointy stick.

Bursting through the kitchen door, Elise caught sight of Brute and her heartbeat stuttered in her chest. The man was gorgeous, no doubt about it. Even after spending so much time with him, her breath still caught in her throat and a nervous flutter settled in her stomach.

She had it bad. If only the fox agreed.

As if he was in tune with her, Brute's focus shifted from Alice and zeroed in on her. Beneath her gaze, desire heated his features and Elise felt a tiny shiver of arousal tinged with worry slither down her spine. Yes, she'd recovered in leaps and bounds with Maddy's help, but, but, but...

She placed a hand on her stomach and took a deep, soothing breath, willing her nerves to calm. The human therapists had barely done anything for her while the Sensitive lioness had put her back in touch with her fox and her powers as a Sensitive as well. She'd long ago thought both were lost to her.

The only hitch was that both the fox and her abilities only popped up around Maddy…and Brute.

And now, she'd go on a date, a real date, with the man who managed to tug the fox out of hiding.

"Hey," she closed the distance between them.

"Hey, back." His smile was easy, wide and open, and the delicate nudge of her fox's nose had her smiling wide in return.

"So, I hear Seno gave you permission to date me." She half-frowned and quirked a brow, nearly breaking the expression when his face turned a bright shade of pink.

"Well, he's a scary fucker. Didn't think there was a point in asking at all if he decided to kick my ass after I asked you. I'm not the best man for you, Elise. Getting his permission ahead of time seemed to be the best way to avoid bloodshed."

Elise sensed the truth in his words and got mad on Brute's behalf. "You are a wonderful man, Brute Mauer, and I'm gonna tell him so. The stupid, interfering, butt-sniffing—"

A large hand gently wrapping around her wrist stopped her. "Easy, sweet fox. There's no need to defend my honor." A smirk played on his lips, and Brute's thumb drew circles on her wrist while the anger that filled her fled as quickly as it'd arrived. "I've done some not-so-nice things in my life and I'm not known to be the nicest of guys."

"You're nice to me."

"Of course, I am. You're a very special fox who's wiggled into my heart."

Wiggled into my heart…

She wanted to believe him, wanted to believe that some of the feelings that were growing inside her were reciprocated.

Blushing, she looked away from his all too knowing gaze. "So, a date, huh?" Getting her body under control, she returned her attention to him. "Where are we headed?"

* * *

And an hour later, she was ready.

Brute had waited while Elise dashed to her apartment and changed into different clothes. They were just heading to a drive-in movie, something fun and causal where she could feel at ease surrounded by people she knew, but still have a little privacy with her…friend?

Elise's fox brushed her then growled as if she was unhappy with her train of thought. She hadn't been able to talk with her beast in over a year, but she figured she'd give it a shot. As a Sensitive (okay, semi-Sensitive) she could actually speak with her fox in addition to soothing shifters. She could also sense emotions and "dig" through other's minds to read their thoughts and memories.

The work with Maddy had her progressing in leaps and bounds, so the worst that could happen by talking to her inner-beast was she'd simply be treated to silence by the fox.

Boyfriend?

The fox snarled.

Well, unless you come out to play and tell me different, he's a friend.

221

That earned her a growl.

Quit it. Bad, fox. No treats for you.

That seemed to anger the damned thing even more and Elise did something she hadn't done in a long time. For two years she'd called for the fox, begged it to help her and return to her, but it'd hidden deep in her mind, taking her Sensitive abilities with it.

In the last month, she'd tried to coax it back into her life.

But if the darned thing was just going to snap at her and not help, she could go back to where she'd been.

Letting her eyes drift closed, she poked and prodded at the beast, nudging and pushing it until she could snap a wall in place, holding the fox at bay.

There.

The stupid thing still growled and snapped. It wasn't overwhelming, but muted now, giving her the chance to focus on the man beside her.

Brute turned into the drive-in theatre's parking lot with ease, paying the attendant and then navigating the mostly-filled rows before pulling into a space. He'd chosen an area that was toward the back, but not secluded, near enough to the concession stand that she knew there'd be a decent amount of traffic.

She'd be alone with Brute...but not.

Brute popped the truck into park and then turned to her, giving her his unwavering attention. "Here we are."

Elise nibbled her lip. "We are."

"I've got snacks in the back. Soda and stuff. Or I can grab you some popcorn or…" He was rambling, body twitching and knee bouncing.

She scooted across the bench seat and placed her fingers over his lips. "Hush. I'm fine. I can feel your worry buzzing and there's no need." She smiled to ease her intrusion, but it'd been unavoidable. His emotions pulled her in like a tornado and she'd been powerless against him. "I'm happy being with you Brute. Happier than I've ever been."

The anxiousness that filled him bled away in a blink, leaving a purring male in its place. Purring. Literally purring. Elise let her fingers slip from his mouth to trail along his neck and then rest on his chest, letting the vibrations slither through her. Gaze locked on his features, they remained still, seemingly tied together.

Her fox was growing increasingly aggressive, the little thing barking and growling, scraping at the internal wall she'd built to corral the animal. She hadn't been helpful before and suddenly the furball wanted out right this minute and not a second longer.

It scratched and clawed, fighting her shaky control until it scaled the wall she'd built and rushed forward, building into a solid presence in her mind. The fox, she could see it now in all of its red-hued glory, danced and yipped.

Elise almost broke down then, relief clogging her throat as she embraced her beast. It'd returned, fully and whole.

And then it began a repetitive mantra that scared her to her very soul, yet sent her joy flying.

Mate. Mine. Mate. Mine…

Gasping, she crawled back from Brute, putting as much distance between them as the truck would allow.

"Elise," he frowned. "What's wrong, sweet fox?"

Brute reached toward her and she panicked. No, she couldn't. She'd thought about it, what it'd be like if he was her mate. The feelings that had been building threatened to overwhelm her each day. She was attracted to him, truly attracted to the man. It wasn't some chemical, biological, mating imperative. It was a true pull between a man and woman, and one she could take at her own pace.

But with the furries involved? Already her fox showed her displeasure that Elise had pulled away. The beast wanted to whine and rub on their mate, join and claim him as theirs.

A claiming that would involve sex, fucking. It wouldn't be making love. Not after...

"No. I can't," she shook her head from side to side. "I can't, I can't, I can't..." The words repeated in her mind as she fought with the handle, yanking and pulling until it finally swung wide. She scrambled from the vehicle, ignoring Brute's call as she blindly ran between the cars and SUVs littering the area.

"Elise!"

Worry and fear beat at her, pounding at her mind with every step she took. She recognized Brute's feelings pouring through her, but she tossed them aside. The fox, unable to do anything to completely stop her, decided to steal her energy, fighting with Elise the only way the beast knew how.

Her limbs felt heavy, feet filled with lead as she put one foot before the other. She dashed toward the bright lights of the concession. Stomach churning, she silently begged for a restroom, a place she could hide and be sick in peace.

The rapid thump of boots on asphalt followed her and still she ran.

Stupid, stupid, Elise.

She should have recognized the signs, should have realized that the fox liked Brute a little too much. The gentle man deserved more than a damaged woman for his mate. He deserved so much more.

Elise burst past the final line of cars and into the wide circle of light surrounding the concession and straight into someone. Someone male. And large.

"What the fuck?" The stranger shouted as his food and drinks went flying, pouring over her and scattering on the ground. "What the fuck is your problem, lady?"

A glance at his expression, the rage that lived within his features and Elise did what she'd done for the past two years. Without thought she dropped to the ground and wrapped into herself, forming a ball. If she kept her head down, they wouldn't get her face. Just her back and ribs. They'd receive the brunt of the attack and it'd take a few weeks to heal and...

A snarl cut through the man's ranting and still she remained on the ground, relatively safe.

"Don't touch her." The voice was more animal than man, but she recognized it without a problem. A scant moment later, his scent overrode the soda and popcorn surrounding her, blanketing her in a web of comfort and safety. "Mine."

Elise dared to peek then, the stranger's yells quickly replace with gurgling gasps. Brute stood above her, his body between her and the other man, his hand shifted and wrapped around the stranger's throat as he held him above the ground. The man's feet didn't even touch the asphalt, legs flailing as he fought for air.

God, she couldn't let him kill a random guy. The situation was caused by her, her fear, not the man Brute was about to tear into.

She forced herself from the ground, ordered that damned fox to help her as she pushed to her feet and walked to her mate. No. She couldn't think of him that way. Not yet. She wasn't ready, wasn't… She shook her head; she could freak out about the mate thing later. Calming Brute was her priority for now.

"Brute…" Another step closer and she brought her hand to his shoulder blade, rubbing his back in soothing circles. "Put him down, Brute."

"Mine." His snarl surrounded her. Possession and protection were infused in the single syllable.

"I know, Brute. I know. He didn't hurt me though. I got scared. Put him down, Brute." She increased the pressure, sliding her palm up and down his spine. "You know Maya will be cranky if you kill him. Let's put the nice stranger down and then we can leave, yeah?"

The fox nudged her mind, as if urging her to do…something, and Elise did the only thing she knew how to do. Reaching deep inside, she poked at the well that held her abilities and gasped when they rushed to respond, nearly overwhelming her in the sudden eagerness. Not questioning the change for now, she delved into Brute's mind, stroked the massive lion within him and smoothed the beast's fluffed fur. It didn't object to her presence, not like the average shifter. No, it rubbed against her metaphysical hands and purred with her every touch.

The easing of the tension in Brute's muscles told her she'd gotten through to him. His shoulders slumped and he slowly lowered the stranger to the ground, releasing him fully as soon as the man's feet touched the asphalt. The stranger stumbled, but quickly caught himself.

Silence and tension strung tight between the two men until Elise had enough. She elbowed her eventually-to-be mate in the side.

"Apologize," she whispered.

"No," Brute whispered back.

Elise glared at him. "Excuse me?"

"He touched you. And yelled at you."

She looked at him like he had two heads. She had no doubt that another would suddenly sprout from his neck at any moment. "I ran into him and made him drop his food."

"Doesn't matter. He shouldn't have touched you." Brute turned his attention to the frozen stranger. "Apologize and I won't kill you."

"Are you kidding me?" She looked at the man. "You don't have to apologize. He's not going to kill you."

"Yes, I am."

Elise stomped on Brute's foot, her frustration increasing when he didn't even grunt. "No, he's not. Brute, give him some money. I'll pay you back when you take me home."

"I'm not giving him money and, even if I did, you wouldn't pay me back. I want to take care of you. You're my mate."

She wasn't going to punch her maybe-never-to-be-mate in public. "I know I'm your mate." She added a silent *butt-sniffer*. "But I would appreciate it if you'd give this nice gentleman some money and then I'd like to leave. Preferably before I die of embarrassment."

And that got Brute roaring. "You will not die!" The snarling lion turned toward her, the bones in his face sharp and chiseled. "My mate will not die."

God save her from possessive, protective, litter box using lions. She stroked his chest. "No, I won't die. I promise." She patted his shoulder. "Now, give the man money and take me home. I swear I won't die. Not even a little."

Brute narrowed his eyes but remained silent and then turned his back on her, digging out his wallet in the process.

Elise peeked around his big body and gave the white-faced stranger a smile. "I'm really sorry about this. We haven't mated yet and I've got issues and…"

Her growled at her. "There's nothing wrong with you, you're perfect."

"Yes, Brute." She'd placate him. This was the first glimpse of the "bad" side of Brute that she'd ever seen and she had to admit, he could be a bit scary. Except for some reason, she wasn't afraid.

And that scared her, but not nearly as much as it should have.

228

CHAPTER *six*

"Dude. You can totally kiss him. Just keep telling yourself that it's not a kiss, you're simply telling his lips a secret. Ta da! No more being freaked. I. Am. Awesome!" – Maya O'Connell, Prima of the Ridgeville Pride and totally married! Boo-yeah-mother-fuckers!

Brute pulled into the parking lot at Drool and Dine and popped the truck into park. From his spot, he could see the stairs in the back leading up to Elise's apartment. A familiar ache seized his chest. He'd have to let her go into her apartment alone. She wasn't ready to mate, he could feel it, but the lion clawed at him. They couldn't protect their sweet fox if she wasn't with them in their den.

Glancing at the door one last time, he turned his attention to the delicate woman at his side. He knew he'd acted like an ass earlier, but the thought of something happening to her, the idea that someone else had touched her, made his lion roar.

"So *that* happened." A smile played on her lips.

"Yeah, I'm sorry, Elise. I ruined our first date and…you know I'm your mate and your mine and he touched you. I'm not rushing you though…"

229

As before, she scooted closer and placed her fingertips against his lips. He ached to flick his tongue out and taste her skin. He restrained himself, and his lion, barely.

"Hush. I swear, I've never seen you this nervous. Yes, I'm your mate, but," she shook her head, her beautiful brown hair glinting in the dim light of the parking lot. "But, I'm not ready. Look at how I reacted just realizing you're mine." Her smile widened and she scooted closer. "I like that you're mine, Brute."

"I like that you're mine, too." He cupped her face, thumb tracing the line of her cheek. "I like that you know you're mine now."

"Yeah, the fox suddenly decided to come out and play." She wrinkled her nose and she looked so cute all scrunched like that.

Because, yeah, he was so gone for her it wasn't even funny.

"So, we take it slow."

Elise eased closer, barely an inch separating their bodies, and the heat of her seared his skin. "Right...slow..."

"Elise?" Arousal flared hot and high in his body, cock going from soft to hard at her nearness. He knew that the scent of his sudden need filled the cabin of the truck, but he couldn't do a damned thing about it. In the diner, he'd always kept his distance, but the confines of the truck didn't really give him the chance to move away.

"Kiss me, Brute? Just a kiss?" Her worry ate at him, her delicate fragrance tinged with a hint of bitterness that didn't belong. "I…"

"Just a kiss, sweet fox." He eased her closer, reducing the distance between them until he could brush his lips across hers. He gave her a tentative touch to gauge her response. He wouldn't push. He didn't want to frighten his mate before he had a chance to taste her. Hell, he never wanted to scare the curvy bundle pressed against him.

A tingle of electricity flared between them and Brute's lion purred his pleasure. They were touching their mate, holding her close with their skin against hers. The lion had been pushing him harder and harder with each day that passed, but he knew that his courtship of Elise had to be slow.

Brute increased the pressure on the next pass, flicking her upper lip with his tongue. He teased her, gathering her flavors with every graze.

Elise's mouth opened on a gasp and he took advantage, sweeping his tongue into her mouth and moaning as the flavors of strawberries and cream poured over his taste buds.

He sampled everything she had to offer, lapped and licked her mouth as a purr built in his chest. When his mate whimpered, he swallowed the sound and repeated the caress that had caused it. He wanted all of her noises, over and over and over again.

His sweet fox's weight slumped against him and he reveled in the press of her perfect curves against his body.

Brute kept his hand in place, regardless of much he ached to slide his palm over her until she purred right along with him. He had to take it slow, ease into a physical relationship that would end with their mating.

That didn't mean his cock wasn't pounding in his jeans.

He put gentle pressure on her head and tilted her slightly until he could deepen their kiss. He poured every drop of desire into the meeting of their mouths, showed her without words how he wanted her more than anything.

Elise whimpered and pushed closer, her breasts pressing against him, and he could feel the hardened nub of her nipples teasing him. He grabbed every ounce of self-control he possessed and kept himself from reaching for her, stroking and petting her until she writhed beneath him.

Breathing heavy, Brute eased their kiss, lightened the pressure of his mouth against hers and gentled the tangle of their tongues. He had to let her go before he did something he'd regret. Like lay her down and claim her in the front seat of his truck.

Gentle laps eased to sensuous brushes from his lips, and then he let his forehead rest against hers. Panting into her mouth he inhaled her scent and let it fill him.

"Elise…"

A rapid knock on the window wrenched them apart. Brute's face began shifting as golden fur pushed through his pores and his hands shifted to claws. He opened his mouth, exposing his elongated fangs, and hissed at the intruder.

Seno stood on the other side of the passenger window, eyes wide and face pale. He had his hands raised, one clutching a handful of envelopes. The large man stood frozen and the lion assessed Seno, growling when he couldn't get a good handle on the man's scent.

"What?" He snapped out the word, fighting to speak through his near-muzzle and elongated fangs.

"Just checking on my girl and dropping off some mail." The man's voice was soft.

"Mine." Elise belonged to him. She'd acknowledged his claim, even if they hadn't solidified the bond. He'd kept the lion on a tight leash, but the moment she'd agreed, the beast had become fanatical in protecting the woman and making sure everyone knew she was off limits.

Seno's eyebrows went up so high they nearly hit his hairline. "You okay with that, kiddo?"

Elise stroked Brute's thigh, and he took comfort in the soothing gesture. "Yes. My fox came out to play and confirmed what I'd been feeling all along. He's mine. We're just not totally there yet."

Brute could feel the heat coming from her blush and he growled. No one should embarrass his sweet fox.

"Easy, big guy." Elise tried to soothe her mate. "Seno, if you'll just set the mail on the ground and head out, I'm sure Brute can escort me to my door."

Yes. He could do that. Make sure his mate was safe. She didn't need some other male to watch after her. She had him. His lion would decimate anyone that threatened her. He would...

"Sounds good, kiddo. See you in the morning." The man bent down and Brute heard the soft shuffle of envelopes dropping to the pavement. "And, Brute? I think it'd be good to switch to decaf until you claim your mate."

Brute curled his lip, exposing a single, white fang and Seno spun on his heel, striding toward a truck on the other side of the parking lot.

A snort followed by a delicate giggle came from his mate and he nuzzled her, enjoying her happiness and feminine scent at once. "What's so funny, sweet fox?"

Elise snorted. "You. On decaf."

He mock growled and nipped her shoulder. Fuck, the cat wanted to sink his teeth into her and force the mating bite, but he couldn't do that to her. Regardless of the fact that her pulse doubled with his gentle nibble and the delicate scent of her arousal suddenly filled the air.

"Come on. Let's get you to your apartment before we start something we're not ready for."

"You mean I'm not ready for?" The sting of pain collided with her arousal.

"Never. I would never say anything like that. You aren't ready for that step and I'm not ready to even risk upsetting you, sweet fox."

Elise nodded and eased toward the door. Brute was quick to hop out of his side and rushed to her, snatching the mail Seno had left and then helping his mate to the ground. "Let's get you inside."

Brute kept his arm wrapped around her shoulders, holding her close as he led her to the stairs and then to her front door. Not wanting to start something they weren't ready to finish, he snagged one of her hands and brought it to his lips, brushing a kiss across her knuckles. "Good night, Elise."

"Good night." A soft smile touched her lips and the musky fragrance of her arousal perfumed the air, blocking out everything else.

It took every ounce of his strength to step away from her and put distance between their bodies. "Go ahead in. I'll wait to hear you lock up and head on home."

"I'll see you tomorrow?" She looked anxious, as if he'd leave her alone now that she'd admitted that they were mates.

"Of course. Now, go on in. I won't be able to sleep tonight if I don't know you're safe." He handed over her mail and watched her tuck it into her purse.

When she returned her attention to him, amusement twinkled in her eyes. "Based on the bat in your pants, I think you'll need a cold shower, too."

*

Not waiting for a response, Elise locked herself in the apartment before she could rush back into Brute's arms.

What a crazy night. She'd been freaked the fuck out at realizing Brute was really, truly, no mistaking it, her mate. Hence, the running. But even that had been over the top. She had to admit, with his frequent visits, she'd suspected that he wasn't popping by just because he was her friend. And now she understood his behavior.

Mate.

Wow…just…mate.

And sex. Fuck! They'd have to fuck.

The butterflies that always seemed to lurk in her stomach fluttered and flew within her, the imaginary bugs going to work as apprehension and fear coursed through her veins.

Pressing a hand to her stomach, she took a deep, cleansing breath. Brute wasn't like the others. He wasn't a Freedom member bent on destroying the shifter hierarchy or one of the furballs who felt raping a woman was their due. Already he'd proven his need to protect. The poor guy at the drive-in hadn't done anything but been in the wrong place at the wrong time and now had a few claw marks to prove it.

Elise's fox pushed forward, urging and nudging her, letting Elise know that the beast wanted to claim their mate. Hell if the furball had her choice, they'd be heading over to the man's home at that very moment.

But she needed to prepare.

Mate.

Stupid fox.

Mate now.

Elise growled. *I am not going to mate the man unless I know we won't freak out half way through it.* Stupid, stupid fox.

We won't.

She rolled her eyes. *And you know this how?*

He's mate.

Elise sighed. They'd just go round and round until she lost her patience and snapped at her inner-beast. Considering the fox hadn't voluntarily come out to Elise in years, she figured a nasty argument would set them back a ways. Shaking her head, she flicked on the living room light and froze.

Adrenaline poured into her bloodstream and the fox, having just barely retreated, shoved forward, lending Elise its abilities. Blood. So much blood coated the wall. Words were etched into the paint in the burgundy liquid…

Whore.

Die.

The furniture was trashed and the TV lay helplessly on the floor.

And so much blood.

Hands shaking, she reached into her purse and dug out her cell phone, not tearing her eyes from the scene before her. The fox catalogued scents, tried to sift through them to discover an interloper, but they couldn't find anything beyond the blood.

At least it wasn't human. Or shifter. Fox thought it was cow. Fresh, not frozen and that thought brought a giggle to her lips.

The moment her fingers encountered the metal case of her phone, she tugged on it and poked at the screen. The smartphone jumped into action. Before today, she would have called her brother. Now she had only one person in mind.

In one ring, he answered.

"Brute. I need you. Oh, god," she stifled a sob. "Please."

"What is it, Elise?" Brute's voice held a hint of worry and an abundance of growl.

She could hear the roar of his truck's engine and the squeal of tires and a snippet of her fear drifted away. Her lion was on his way. He was big and mean and could protect her and…

"I'm inside and… Blood. It's everywhere, Brute."

A snarl came over the line. "I'm coming across the lot right now."

Another squeal of tires was almost immediately followed by the rapid thump of her mate's boots on the stairs. Wrenching the door open, she threw herself into Brute's arms, the cat not even grunting under her added weight.

"I've got you. Shh…" He stroked her back and she shuddered against him, drawing strength from his embrace.

Elise inhaled his masculine scent, letting his presence soothe the debilitating fear that had arisen. The fox, just as on edge, reveled in the presence of their mate, fur smoothing with his arrival.

A growl from Brute reverberated through her. She realized the tangy scent of blood must have reached him. She soothed him the only way she knew how, stroking his chest and trying to wipe away his anger.

Brute pulled her closer and then swung her into his arms, cradling her against his chest. She squeaked in surprise, but readily relaxed into his embrace as he tromped down the stairs and to his truck.

"I'm gonna call Alex, Grayson, Seno and then Sheriff Corman." Brute sat her sideways in the driver's seat, staying close while he fished out his phone. "It's not human or shifter…"

238

"Cow," she provided.

"Right. Cow. But it's a helluva lot of blood."

Hands shaking, she reached for Brute, needing a connection to her mate. If he was around, nothing could happen to her. He'd protect her, wouldn't let anything hurt her.

"I couldn't smell anything other than the blood. But that's not saying much since I'm not too in-tune with my fox." A tear slid down her cheek and she hadn't even realized she'd been so close to crying. "But they wrote things on the wall. I'm scared..." The last was said with barely a whisper, but her mate must have heard it.

Brute squeezed her hand and stepped closer. Releasing his grip, he cupped the back of her head and brought his face to hers, staring into her eyes. "Nothing will happen to you. Nothing. I will die to protect what's mine and you, Elise, are mine."

Another tear leaked from her eye and she nodded. "Okay."

"Good." He released her, but leaned his hips against her legs, maintaining their contact as he woke his phone and began his string of calls.

By the time he'd finished with the Sheriff (also a shifter, apparently), Alex and Grayson had arrived with Seno pulling in immediately after.

Then growly hell broke loose. It started with Brute, and then the others responding to Brute, and then Brute responding to that until it became a vicious circle of whose dick was bigger.

Still slumped in the front seat of the truck, Elise reached out and stroked her mate's shoulder, sliding her hand down his back and then up again. Without second guessing herself, tendrils of her power slid into the air and into her mate, petting the lion he held within. The cat's fur smoothed beneath her ethereal hand, settling as the protective rage left it, and the tension in Brute's human body eased.

Feeling empowered by what she'd done, and with the fox urging her on, Elise reached toward the others. Joy filled her as she repeated the process on each male, only stuttering when she got to the Sheriff. Hyena… A shudder raced down her spine, memories of the hyena that had tortured her the most, threating to creep in. She shoved the feeling aside. This guy wasn't Jasper. He was just another hyena and living in Ridgeville with Alex's permission. She trusted Alex, so she'd trust this guy. Mostly.

The aggression in the air around them nearly disappeared, a general hint of calm filling its space.

Elise bounced, unable to contain her feelings. "I did it! Did you see?" She shook her ass in the seat. "Go me!"

Then the wind changed direction, blowing the stench of blood toward them. The happiness faded, replaced with the fear and apprehension from only moments ago.

Brute retreated from the circle of men and rested his back against her legs, grabbing her hand and pressing a soft kiss to the center of her palm. "I did, sweet fox. I'm so proud of you."

Elise leaned down and nuzzled his neck, inhaling his scent as she transferred hers to his skin. His fragrance, more than anything, swept away the dread that had threatened to overwhelm her again.

"Can we finish with the lovefest and get to work?" The Sheriff interrupted them and Elise's fangs pushed at her gums. She wanted to launch her body over her mate and bite the man who'd broken into their time.

It seemed her fox was getting back in the game.

Brute snarled and then filled the men in as she silently listened. Her mate could take care of this, take care of her. Too many thoughts bounced around her mind. Letting her male handle things lifted a weight from her shoulders.

"We need her to come down to the station for questioning." Sheriff Corman's voice overlaid Brute's explanation.

"No."

"You're not the law here—"

Brute cut the hyena off. "I'm her mate. I was with her all night and she came back to the mess upstairs. That's your statement."

A glance at the Sheriff revealed a set of glowing eyes. "She needs to come down—"

Her mate snarled and, finally, Alex stepped in. "I think the Sheriff can do his work here and Brute can bring his mate in tomorrow to give a statement. It's late and I'm sure Miss Mara needs to rest after her ordeal." The Prime's gaze encompassed them all. "And I want to get back to my mate and cubs. Sheriff, do what you can and then let Seno get a crew in to clean. Any questions?"

Through Alex's orders, Elise had kept an eye on the Sheriff and she didn't like what she saw. The man was livid, furious at Alex taking over and issuing orders. A frisson of fear consumed her and she fought back the sensations. He was just another hyena…not the one who'd tortured her. That male was dead, but this one…

She shook her head, clearing those thoughts. She couldn't harbor prejudice against an entire race for one man. He'd been the worst, but wasn't the only type of shifter to abuse her. Not by far.

Brute turned to face her. "Scooch in and we'll get out of here."

"But go where?"

Her mate cupped her cheek and traced her lower lip. "Somewhere safe."

Elise wasn't sure where "safe" ended up being. Not when she'd fallen asleep on the way there. She half awakened to listen to her mate and changed into an oversized T-shirt. Then again when a boxer clad Brute slid into bed beside her.

Bare skin met hers, the hair on his chest brushing against her arm and she instinctively pulled away. Only to be mentally shoved back by her fox. She was torn. The pain of her past collided and fought with the potential pleasure of her future, a future she'd never dreamed to have.

Without second guessing her decision, she eased closer to her mate and right into his arms, allowing him to pull her snug against his body. She melted along his length, laying her head on his chest and resting her hand over his heart.

"Elise?" Brute's voice was low, soothing as it flowed over her nerves. He would protect her, take care of her and defend her from the world.

She sighed and let her eyes drift closed. "Mate."

CHAPTER *seven*

"Apparently, surprises are only surprises if she smiles. If not, death looks really, really good." – Brute Mauer, Prima guard and a total novice at the mate thing.

Elise woke in small degrees, her drowsy mind drawing her toward wakefulness like a gentle breeze.

She first became aware of the musky, delectable scent of her mate surrounding her, then the feel of his arms wrapped around her body and the smooth, hot skin beneath her cheek. She lay in his embrace, absorbing his essence with every breath.

Mate...

The dim light of the room allowed her to see past the shadows and drink her fill. Her gaze traced his nose, along his strong jaw and on to the lips that she ached to taste once again. Reaching out, her fingers followed the same path, absorbing the silky feeling of his flesh.

So beautiful, yet so deadly. She had no doubt that her fierce lion would fight anyone that threatened her. Including the ass that had violated her apartment.

Elise's fingers continued to drift, over the thick column of his neck and along his chest, tracing the carved muscles of his body. So strong. So…hers. She paused and explored the swirls and lines of his tattoos, the thick expanses of colors and black that peppered his skin and begged for attention.

The subtle change in the tempo of Brute's breathing alerted her and she glanced at his face. He captured her with his gaze, lust-filled eyes snaring her, and she fell into him. Pure passion lurked in his expression and unknown desire beckoned her. More than anything, she wanted to wrap herself in him and live in his hold.

"Brute…" Elise whispered into the ever stretching silence.

She needed him. The truth of the thought slammed through her. The past couldn't be forgotten and she'd always have remnants of her history sneaking up on her, but she couldn't let past experiences mar her future. Not when she had her mate so close. The fox yipped in agreement, the little beast anxious to sink her teeth into Brute's flesh and claim him as theirs.

Pushing onto her elbow, she rose to stare down at her mate and increased the range of her exploration. No part of him was saved from her touch. She stroked his bare chest, slid her hand over his abs and on. A sliver of fear wound its way through her veins, but she shoved it aside.

Brute was not them. Never them. He wouldn't hurt her in any way and would die to protect her.

While he was shirtless, he still wore boxers, hiding him from her touch. She slipped her fingers beneath the elastic and let her hand rest above his cock, fingers sifting through the cropped hair there, and she willed her body to continue. She teased the base of his shaft, his cock already hard from her ministrations. She shoved away any remnants of her hesitation and encircled his dick, measuring his width. She had no doubt that he'd fill her, stretch her, like no other. Then again, Brute was like no other.

"Elise..." Emotion filled her mate's voice and the scent of his arousal flowed throughout the room. His large hand wrapped around hers and encouraged her to release him. He brought her palm to his lips and pressed a kiss to her skin. "This will be about you, sweet fox. Let me love you first." His husky voice sent a shiver of arousal down her spine and she forced herself to nod.

"Yes."

Brute slid from beneath her and eased her to her back so that their positions were reversed. His large body loomed over her, hovering and covering her like a blanket. A wicked smile split his features as he slid down the bed.

When he'd helped her into bed he'd left her with only one of his shirts and panties. She should be annoyed with him for coaxing her into so little while she was half-dead to the world, but she couldn't muster the hint of anger. Not when he settled between her spread legs and then flipped her shirt up, exposing the juncture of her thighs to his gaze.

"Do you know how wonderful you smell? Not just your natural scent, but your arousal, sweet fox. You're making all of that cream just for me, aren't you? All wet and sleek?" He rumbled, face growing closer to her panty-clad pussy with every word. He paused just above her mound, his gaze zeroing in on her with unerring precision. "Right, Elise?"

He was so right. All of it. With her fox restored, she was powerless against him. Every breath brought more of his inherent scent to her, arousing her further with each rise and fall of her chest.

"Yes. All for you." She couldn't suppress the moan that gathered in her chest. Not when he stroked her thighs, calluses scraping along her sensitized skin before settling on the waist of her panties. She'd worn a thin, lacey pair that barely covered her, and she knew the silken fabric was already soaked with her juices.

He slipped his digits beneath the elastic and tugged at the material. With no hesitation, she brought her legs up above her and together, allowing him to slide them free of her body. The moment he tossed the confection aside, his hands were back, spreading and lowering her thighs once again.

Now she was completely bared to his gaze.

"So pretty. So pink." He pet the juncture of her thighs, stroking the very edge of her lower lips and a tremble shook her. "Elise? You okay? We don't have to do this. If you're not ready…"

Oh, her sweet mate. He must have thought her shiver was based in fear, not arousal. She was quick to reassure him. "I want you, Brute. Take me. Mate me. Make me yours."

Growling, Brute lowered further, mouth hovering over her heat once again. He rubbed his cheek along her warm flesh, stroking and marking her with his scent. "Mine."

"Yours." She watched, rapt, as his tongue snaked out and flicked the seam of her nether lips. A new burst of arousal and want filled her with the second touch of his tongue. Another teasing of her slit, another gathering of her juices.

"Mmm… So sweet. S'good, sweet fox. I could get drunk on you." He settled more comfortably between her spread thighs then, easing down until he was nearly eye level with her weeping pussy.

That nimble muscle returned, sliding between her folds and slithering over her aroused flesh. He started at the center of her heat and then traveled north, ending his journey with a rapid flick against her needy clit. Elise groaned.

Brute repeated the caress. He once again started at her wet opening, circling the center of her desire before tormenting the bundle of nerves at the top of her slit.

"Oh, god, Brute. Please." She kept her gaze locked on his, hopefully projecting her level of desperation.

Her mate groaned, vibrations adding to her desire, and then gave her a little more of what she needed. He circled and teased her clit, round and round, sending her arousal burning hotter. He pulled her lips apart with his fingers, exposing her soaking pussy to the cool air and then got back to tormenting her once again.

Brute lapped, licked, nipped and sucked her clit as she writhed and moaned beneath him. He teased her with rapid flicks and then tortured her with slow, sweeping strokes. He kept her on edge, bringing her high and then helping her float back down.

Elise rocked her hips, chasing the pleasure that her mate promised. But the lion wasn't having it. Brute held her hips still and ceased stroking her with his tongue until she settled. The moment she relented to his silent demand, the pleasure was rekindled.

"Brute," she whined.

Her mate hummed against her and she moaned in response. So good. So hot and wonderful and...

"Please." She gasped when he gently scraped his fang over her clit.

That earned her another hum, the vibrations adding to her arousal. That hum then turned into a deep purr that filled every inch of her body. She felt the quivering shakes from head to toe, the sensations then centering on her nipples and pussy.

"Oh, shit." Elise arched, aching to follow his movements and drag herself to the edge of orgasm.

Brute purred louder then, harder until she felt like a tuning fork as wave after wave of his sounds danced along her nerves. Her mate was going to purr her to climax.

His tongue centered on her clit, circling round and round in a steady rhythm, the move joining with the steady tempo of his cat's purrs.

And still his focus was on her as they shared this intimacy. He lapped and licked her juices from her most private place, giving her more pleasure than she'd ever experienced. And she could feel her orgasm building.

It darted in and out of reach, nimble like her fox, making her body work for the elusive pleasure of release. Her nipples hardened and tingled, pinpoints of need in the maelstrom of ecstasy that Brute created.

And he continued.

"Brute. Gonna..." She gasped the words, syllables rising above the low hum of his purrs.

Brute seemed to take her words as a challenge and he doubled his efforts, going faster, harder, and their sounds grew louder in the room.

Elise cried out, overwhelmed by the level of bliss coursing through her veins. Her pussy tightened and pulsed, aching and begging to be filled by her mate. But that was to come…

The bubble of pleasure built within her body, stretching and filling her from head to toe. It stroked and plucked pleasure-tinged nerves, snatching at bits of bliss and hoarding them. Only they were soon to be released…

It grew and grew, larger with every breath and beat of her heart until she could barely stand the feelings swamping her. She stood on the edge, balancing on the razor sharp ledge that bordered unimaginable joy.

Brute sucked on her clit, let loose a loud purr and that was all it took. Elise was shoved over the cliff, falling into pools of bliss, and the sensations welcomed her. She screamed out her completion, Brute's name on her lips as her body convulsed and twitched. She no longer controlled her muscles, her orgasm having snatched away every ounce of power she possessed.

In minute degrees, Brute brought her back to earth, slowing his ministrations until she was a sated pile of bones.

But still she wanted.

Elise held out a hand for her mate, beckoning him. "Make me yours."

Trepidation etched his features, worry and fear filling the lines of his body as he remained kneeling. "Elise, I don't think..."

"I want to be yours, Brute. More importantly, I want you to be mine." She pushed herself into a sitting position and grabbed his face between her hands. "I don't want any other woman to try and take you from me." She stroked his shoulder, fingers ghosting over his skin. "I want to sink my teeth into you and mark you as my mate." Eyes on his, she begged. "Please, Brute?"

When she heard him groan, she knew she'd won. Even more so when he tugged on her shirt and helped her pull it over her head, leaving her bared to him. Worry niggled the back of her mind, anxiety that her curvy body wouldn't satisfy him. But one hard look at his features revealed the truth. She aroused him. The desire and need in his gaze was for her. And only her.

She eased back down to the mattress, smiling wide. "Come to me."

Brute slid from the bed for a moment to remove his boxers, then returned to kneel between her legs. She got her first look at his cock.

Oh, shit.

He was long and thick and, as she'd assumed, more than enough to stretch her. He'd fill her like no one before and his touch would banish her memories.

Brute stroked his dick from root to tip, tugging his shaft as his focus remained intent on her. "Are you sure, sweet fox?"

Elise gave him the only answer she had. "Yes."

"If you want me to stop…"

She shook her head. "I won't. I want my mate to claim me. Want *you* to claim me. So, get to the sexy times and bite me, kitty."

With a growl, Brute leaned over her, one hand still on his cock as he placed the tip at her entrance. Slowly, much slower than she liked, he eased his thick shaft into her heat. Inch by inch he entered her, stretching her almost to the point of pain as he slid deeper into her slick pussy.

More and more he fed her until his hips met hers in an intimate embrace and he groaned deep. "Perfect."

Elise arched, rocking her hips. "Yes."

"S'good." He sounded more animal than man. "So wet and tight."

"Need."

Brute eased his cock from her sheath and she whimpered at the loss, only to moan when he returned and filled her once again.

"So mine," he growled.

Again, a gentle glide out and a slow slide back in.

Elise picked up his tender rhythm, rocking her hips and meeting his teasing thrusts. With every joining of their hips, his body brushed against her exposed clit, stoking the fires of her arousal.

She gripped his shoulders, holding him as he claimed her body, branded it with his scent.

With each collision, his pace increased. In slow increments, the intimate glide of retreat and advance matched the beating of their hearts.

Brute gave and gave, handing her pleasure on a silver platter, and she gifted in return. They fed each other's need.

Elise's fingers became tipped with her fox's claws and she dug them into her mate's shoulders, tugging him toward her in a silent plea for more. Brute lowered, brought their chests together and she wrapped her arms around him. She was surrounded by his scent, his very being, and she'd never felt more safe, more cherished.

They shared their breath, panting as they worked toward release. Elise's body was responding to his increasing ministrations, pussy tightening and milking his shaft with his every entrance. The wet slap of their bodies filled the room along with the heavy scent of their combined musk.

And still her pleasure rose higher. Her moans and groans mingled with his, her bliss mirroring her mate's.

Brute's pants grew deeper, heavier, and she knew he was racing toward the edge of control. His pace increased yet again. The rapid tattoo of his hips meeting hers now overrode every sound in the space. The rhythmic meeting of his body to hers shoved her to the edge as well, and she couldn't hold her desperation at bay.

"Gonna…"

"Come on my cock. Gonna fill you, Elise. My mate." He grunted and she took his words as the ultimate permission.

She threw herself off the cliff and dove into the pleasure that awaited her. She embraced the fireworks that burst through her body and danced among the sparks of bliss that peppered her nerves.

The fox rushed forward amongst the waves of ecstasy and forced her canines to emerge. A single word occupied her mind and she followed the beast's urgings.

Claim...

Elise raised her head, opened her mouth and sunk her teeth into the vulnerable flesh of Brute's shoulder. His blood burst from the wound and filled her mouth. She suckled the wound, savoring the delicious flavors. Her saliva mingled with his life's blood, tying them together for all eternity and finally the fox within relaxed, secure that Brute belonged to them.

A sharp sting of pain laced her shoulder and she felt the final string of their connection fall into place as Brute claimed her. His saliva slithered into her and she was comforted by their new connection.

Her orgasm was still soaring high, dancing through the clouds as gentles bolts of pleasure strummed her veins and then began floating back to earth. Brute's hips slowed his blissful assault, bringing them back from their haze of ecstasy in slow waves until she felt grounded once again.

Sated fully, filled with emotions she had no interest in exploring, Elise released her bite on Brute's shoulder, wincing as her mate did the same. Her mate. He was well and truly hers now.

They'd shared something she hadn't ever dared hope to experience, yet she had. Those men hadn't taken her life. They'd beaten and battered at her soul, but with Maddy and Brute, it'd been repaired.

Her mate nuzzled and lapped at her wound while she did the same, easing his pain and savoring the masculine flavors of his blood on her tongue.

Mate… Ours…

Yes.

She relaxed and let satisfied lethargy overtake her. "Mmmmate…"

A deep, vibrating purr traveled through her and she smiled. Apparently his cat was satisfied, too.

Brute rolled them until she was settled against his side once again, her body curled into his. With a sigh, she let her eyes flutter closed.

Of course, hours later, their delicate peace had to be destroyed by a sudden pounding on the bedroom. "Hey, Brutus! Before you start boinking again, Mom wants you."

Elise stiffened and pushed away from Brute's chest, staring down at him, horrified. "Where are we and why is your mother here? Who was that?"

The man blushed. "At my parent's. Because she lives here. My sister Honor."

Elise swung her leg over Brute and rolled from the bed. She ignored the wet squishy feeling that came from condom-less sex and glared at her mate. She took a deep, cleansing breath. Then a few more, 'cause one just wasn't cutting it. "So, you brought me to your parent's house because it was safe—"

"Dad was a guard before Mom forced him to retire and Grayson lives across the street. Neal and Carly have a

256

house one block over." He rushed out the words as if they could save him. "I've just got an apartment."

"Shut it. I can't believe we mated in your parent's house." Her heart thundered and blood rushed to her face. "Oh, god. I'm a screamer. Your parents and your sisters heard me didn't they? Oh god, oh god, oh god." Brute rolled from the bed and took a step toward her, but she backed away. "No touching. I already want you and we are not having sex in this house, never, ever again. Hell, I don't know if we'll ever have sex again. Period."

"Hey! Now that we have the no boinking thing established, are y'all coming to breakfast or what?" Honor's voice cut through the room and Elise prayed the floor would open up and swallow her whole.

Any time now.

CHAPTER *eight*

"It sounded like a good idea at that time. And I figured I could apologize later. Apparently that only works in theory." – Brute Mauer, Prima guard, now wondering if there's a mate handbook.

Sitting in his parent's living room with just his dad, Grayson and Neal, Brute was realizing that bringing Elise to his childhood home *might* have been a mistake.

Strike that. Listening to his mother, sisters and Carly carry on in the kitchen made him realize he'd really fucked up. He probably would have been forgiven for bringing her to his parents for safety's sake. If that was all he'd done. But following through with the mating even when he knew his family was down the hall...that had probably been the nail in the coffin.

And Honor hadn't been any help.

Tearing his gaze from the hallway, he returned his attention to the others in the room. It'd been too much to hope for that his mate would abandon the women and come to him.

Two sets of eyes were focused on him and him alone. His father looked disappointed in him. Neal was smirking. The ass. And Grayson's attention was firmly fixed over Brute's shoulder and the hallway beyond.

Brute had to deal with Grayson first. He reached out, making sure his hand was within the Second's line of sight, and snapped his fingers. "Hey, over here, buddy."

Grayson bared his fangs and hissed at him.

Okay then. "Dad, are you aware that Grayson thinks he's Honor's mate? Honor, your totally underage daughter who has yet to experience her first heat."

That comment seemed to wrench a snarl from Grayson and his father just frowned at him. "Yes. He came to me the moment he recognized their relationship, but that's not the issue right now, Brutus," Brute winced. "The problem we're facing is who's threatening your mate and how we'll deal with the situation."

Brute's dad grabbed an envelope from the end table and twirled it in his hands, watching the spinning the packet. "Son, this was sitting on the porch when I went to get the paper this morning. I'm not gonna lie, I've looked at what's inside, but I didn't show it to anyone else. That'll be your call. If I give you this, I need you to stay calm. You hear me?" His father's attention turned to him. "No roaring. No shifting. Nothing to disturb the ladies in the kitchen, is that understood? Find your beast and put a leash on him. Harder than you ever have before."

Oh, god. His dad knew better than anyone that his cat was fierce and ready to shove forward at the blink of an eye. It'd taken years upon years and countless mentors to get him to the point that a bout of road rage didn't turn into a blood bath.

So, yeah, he had a tiny control issue.

Doing as his father asked, Brute ducked into his mind, found his lion and built thick steal walls around the cat. He added layer after layer, rising higher within his head until he could barely feel the beast prowling beneath his skin.

Task done, he blew out a slow, cleansing breath. "Okay. I'm good."

With those few words, his dad handed the envelope over. Hands shaking, he lifted the flap and pulled out the contents. Pictures. The first showed a frightened Elise, dirty, bare and curled into a ball in an empty cell.

He flipped to the next: his naked mate tied to a bed.

Then the next: a nude male hovering over her, his cock almost fully embedded in his mate's body.

He flipped through the rest: image after image, male after male, violating his delicate Elise. Rage filled him. The cat roared and the pressure of the beast's fight for freedom forced a harsh breath from his chest. By the time he came to the end, he'd seen twenty men in all, but he had no delusions that the number was significantly higher. With his emotions running high, he wasn't even sure he could trust his mind any longer. One of the bodies seemed familiar…that birthmark, a tattoo… The memory poked at his mind, but he couldn't grasp the thought.

Then, the last image came and his heart froze. A sleeping Elise, her perfect bow-shaped mouth curled in a tiny smile, her body snug beneath a flowery quilt. A closer look at the image showed him things he recognized, furniture that was known to him. Yes, it was a picture of a fully-clothed Elise…in her apartment above the Drool and Dine.

Breath stilled in his lungs, Brute aligned the pictures, edges straight, and then slid them back into the envelope with infinite care. Focus equaled strength. He had to busy himself with minute details while he held the cat at bay.

Ease the pictures in. Lower the flap. Press the crease. Slide the flap into the envelope. Set the packet on the table. I can do this...

"No one else sees these." His voice was harsh, torn and wrecked. "No one."

Brute's father grabbed one of his hands, covering his fingers and squeezing. "There are a few with faces, Brutus. Those should be shown to Sheriff Corman, Ricker and Alex. They may be able to identify them and hunt them down."

"No." No. No one could see his mate that way.

"Elise, then. See if she could give us names."

Tears stung his eyes. And why did his chest hurt? Breathing. He wasn't breathing. "No."

Grayson spoke next. "Brute, we can all protect her. She's part of the pride now. But we need to know what we're up against." Brute forced his attention to the Second. "None of us caught a scent from her apartment. The cow's blood overpowered everything else. So, we need whatever information we can get."

"No." He only held one word in his mind: no. He'd keep repeating the word until it got through to them.

Brute couldn't reveal these images to anyone, he couldn't show others what she'd been through, couldn't accept that he hadn't been there to save her. His mate had suffered so much. He couldn't force her to relive that time.

"Brutus." His father snapped. "You only have so many choices here. Do you want to keep your mate safe?" Yes, yes he did. "You show the images to them in full or just the faces that are visible. If you don't do that, you show the pictures to Elise and see if you can get any information from her. Period. We can't help if we don't know what we're up against."

No-no-no-no... With a ferocious roar, Brute's beast tore through the wall of steel in his mind and rushed forward, shoved its way through his mind and his shift tore through him. Between one heart beat and the next, he went from man to lion. His clothes shredded as his body reformed. The sudden pain of the shift forced a deafening roar from his maw.

The cat watched the men retreat, stumbling over furniture to put space between them. They were afraid. Good. They hadn't listened and now they'd pay for their denials.

He was lion. He was cat. Men should heed him or...

The rapid patter of feet on tile had his attention shifting from the males to the hallway as four females crowded the space.

"Get back!" His father screamed at the women. Ah, fear tasted so delicious on his tongue. He licked his lips.

No. He shook his head. He couldn't eat his father. But the tantalizing scent of terror came from the other two males as well. He took a step toward the other men, looking at each in turn, trying to decide who would suffer first for their refusal to listen.

"Brute?" The voice was so soft, almost a song to his ears, and he tore his gaze from the males, searching the cluster of women for the one who called to him. "Mate?"

Mate. Yes, he had a mate. A sleek fox who called to him like no other female. He had to protect her. There was someone threatening his mate. A growl formed, echoing through the room and he curled his lip. His claws extended and then curled into the carpet as his muscles tensed. He wouldn't let anyone harm her. He had to stay alert. Lion could take care of what belonged to them. Sweet fox was theirs and...

"Brute?" The women shifted and a single female stepped free of them, taking a step forward.

Ah, mate. Her scent beckoned him. Delicate and sweet and she still carried his essence as well. Lion remembered claiming their mate only hours ago. Yes, this fox was his.

Brute padded toward her and nuzzled her stomach, purring against her curves as he covered her in his scent. His. And when a delicate giggle reached his ears, he chuffed. Yes, his mate liked him.

Along with rubbing, he nudged and prodded her until she was backed into a corner, his body between her and the rest of the room. A whisper-soft shuffle sounded behind him and he spun, snarling and baring his fangs. They shouldn't move. Shouldn't come closer to what belonged to him. The fox was his. *His.* No one would threaten his mate.

Brute's father was closer now. A chair no longer separated them and he snarled, the sound echoing off the walls.

"Brute!" His mate's voice was loud and sharp...and followed immediately by a thump to his forehead. "No, bad kitty."

He turned his head and focused on her. Didn't she know he was a lion, the fiercest in the pride? He could challenge

Alex and become Prime if he wanted. Others feared him to their very bones.

"Brute. You can't get growly with family, so quit it."

Brute huffed. She just didn't understand.

"I mean it, mate."

"Elise, I wouldn't—" Neal's voice overrode Elise's.

Brute growled and bared his fangs at the man. That earned him another thump, this time on his nose. When he turned back to Elise, she pinched and twisted his ear and he whimpered in response.

"No more growlies. Do I need to give you catnip to calm your kitty ass down?" She released his ear and then crossed her arms over her chest. He couldn't help but stare at the way the position pushed her plump mounds up. "If you don't quit it, I'll shift and bite your ass in a not good, very bad way." His mate narrowed her eyes. "I'd do it now, but that gets too close to bestiality."

"How about he shifts back and you nibble his ass then? 'Cause I'm all for that show. Brute's got a cute butt." Carly's laughing voice filled the room and then Neal snarled.

Thank god for his mother. The woman would get Neal under control and… "Enough. Brutus Mauer, I don't know why you're furry, but you shift back right this minute." Brute huffed and his mother stomped. "I mean it young man. I put you on this earth, I'll take you right back out of it. How many times have I told you that shifting isn't the answer? And in the house no less. You would have thought you'd learn after Ian treed your snarly butt." His mother tsked. "I thought I raised a smarter boy."

With a final growl, the cat relinquished control and Brute the man pushed forward. The shift took twice as long, but eventually he was on two feet once again.

"Oh! God! My eyes! It's brother junk. Ew! I'm blind!" Emma screeched and spun, hiding her face against his mother's shoulder, and his sister Honor was quick to follow. The males in the room looked everywhere *but* at Brute, and Carly...

"Carly, quit looking at my mate." Aw, his sweet fox had a bit of a backbone.

"What? A mated girl can't look?" The little rabbit blinked with wide, not-so-innocent eyes.

"No." Neal's snarl was followed by the male stomping across the room. The lion wrapped his arms around the smaller woman and shoved her head against Neal's shoulder.

"What a killjoy." Carly's words were muffled. "Hey, I have an idea. Let's worry a little more about Brute becoming a homicidal, furry ass and less about Carly ogling junk." Neal's growl was so loud and deep, Brute felt it in his bones. "O-kay. How about the fact that Brute got treed by Ian when he was sixteen? That's fun. A sweet little bunny chased the big, bad lion up the old oak. Yay."

A delicate snort came from behind Brute and he turned to look at his mate, single eyebrow raised.

"A bunny? Really?" Elise stepped forward and wrapped her arms around his waist, pressing all of her luscious curves against him, resting her head on his chest. "Don't worry, kitty. I'll keep you safe from the scary bunnies. I hear they're crunchy. Like candy."

"Hey! I heard that!" Carly's voice was louder now, but still muffled by Neal. "Didn't we give you enough chew toys in your welcome basket, fox? Now you're threatening innocent little bunnies? Didn't you get the memo that rabbits are no longer on your list of munchables?"

"Screw all that. I just wanna know if Brute's junk is still hanging out."

He'd kill Honor. Later.

"Honor Mauer!" His mother's voice held the perfect balance, of anger, love and exasperation.

Brute rolled his eyes and then tipped his fox's head back with a finger beneath her chin. "Welcome to the family, sweet fox."

Apparently, Emma was riding the same crazy train as Honor. "Seriously now. Is someone gonna answer the question? Bro-junk? Is it still flopping around or are we safe from the attack of the weenie? And how much does it suck that my first weenie sighting is my *brother's*? Ew!"

Elise was smiling, laughing with his family, and it pierced his heart. Because what he was about to ask of her would wipe the happiness of these few moments away as if they'd never existed.

CHAPTER *nine*

"Everyone dies at some point. I just help things along every once and again." – Brute Mauer, Prima guard and wishing a few choice people would die already.

Elise was in a daze as Brute led her through his apartment. Memories still tumbled and turned in her head, the faces of her rapists flashing in her mind. So many… So many names, so many men.

And Brute had seen them.

She followed her mate, forcing one foot before the other, yet the shame of her past still pulsed through her body. She remembered them all. Maybe not their names, but definitely their faces…

And she'd had to relive those moments, those painful snippets of time, with her mate and other pride members.

After they cleared the room of Brute's family, Carly had sat to her left, fingers twined with hers, while a newly clothed Brute curled around her on her right, lending her strength as she flashed picture after picture to Alex, Grayson and Sheriff Corman.

That's Laramie. He's a lion. I was there a year before he came to me…

The one with the tat is Jasper. A hyena. But Ricker and Maddy took him out during my rescue…

He's another lion. His name starts with a "J". Jennings? Jensen? Jenner?

Tension in the room had exploded then, but she ignored it, too lost in her memories. She needed to ask Brute about it, though. Especially since the males had each eased toward furry-dom as she spoke.

Polar bear. I don't know his name, but he helped kidnap Maddy.

Wolf. He didn't usually come alone. This is Owen, but he tended to have Elijah with him.

And on and on and on until they came to the last one in the stack, the final image and she saw that the man had been in her apartment at least once before he'd destroyed it last night. He'd broken in as she slept, stood over her and taken pictures. That single photo had been worse than the others combined.

Because it shattered her peace. Every hint of safety that she'd acquired since coming to Ridgeville had been dashed with one four inch by six inch piece of paper.

Just…gone.

Elise didn't even process her surroundings. Distantly she recognized that her feet were bare. Did Brute take off her shoes? Her toes dug into carpet. Then slapped against a hard surface. Wood? Tile? Then carpet and something hard and cold again. Maybe this was tile?

270

The flare of bright lights had her blinking against the sudden glare, and she looked at her surroundings to find herself in a huge bathroom nearly the size of her apartment bedroom. The large space was sparsely decorated in neutral colors of brown, brown and more brown. One corner was occupied by a glass walk-in shower while the opposite held a large garden tub. Part of Elise yearned to surround herself in hot water, but the other half of her just wanted crawl into a bed and hide.

"Come on, sweet fox. Let's get you clean." Brute's voice was soft and gentle as he tugged on her borrowed shirt and she lifted her arms so he could pull it free of her body. Next went the shorts he'd worn when he was in middle school, and then she was left bare to the room.

She let him lead her to the shower, stepping in at his urging and waiting while he closed them into the glassed area.

The sudden rain of the shower had her jerking in surprise and her mate was quick to reassure her. "It's okay. We're just gonna clean up and then I'm gonna make you breakfast. How's that sound?"

Clean. Yes, she needed to get clean. They'd touched her and did things to her and…

"Yeah," her voice came out strangled and she coughed to clear the lump in her throat. "Yeah. Need to get it off. All of it." Tears stung her eyes. The morning had been like reliving her years with Freedom. True, she'd repeated her tales to Maddy and her therapists, but never with Brute. And now he knew so much… "Want to get clean and then you'll claim me again?"

She needed it. Needed to have those memories erased and replaced by her mate.

"Elise I don't think..." His hesitation was clear in his voice.

Elise snuggled close, resting her head over his heart. "Please, Brute?"

"Okay, baby, okay." He stroked her back, running his fingers along her spine until they came to rest just above her ass. "I'll give you whatever you need."

Yeah. Yeah, she had no doubt he would.

Brute shifted, hand sliding over her skin, and she let him draw her into the warm spray, soaking them. She felt some of her tension melt away. Here, in the safety of Brute's arms, she had nothing to fear.

Her back to the shower, she leaned against him as he soaped his hands and then slid them along her body. The delicate scent of his soap surrounded them and she settled into the comforting embrace. This was Brute, her Brute, and he was taking care of her.

Before long, he turned her, front facing the gentle mist of water, and he repeated each caress, fingers dipping and stroking her curves as he cleaned her. She rested passively against him, reveling in her mate's care. A whimper escaped when his touch retreated, but he'd merely dropped to his haunches and treated her legs to the same treatment as her chest, soaping and rinsing her skin. His fingers seemed to pay special care to the juncture of her thighs and delicate tendrils of arousal surrounded her.

"Brute..." Her voice was barely a whisper, but he'd heard.

"Right here, sweet fox." He came to his feet and cuddled against her back, arms wrapping around her waist, his hardening cock nestled against the crease of her ass. "Right here."

Elise turned in his embrace and absorbed his features, recognized the concern, fear and...love? God, she hoped so. Mating didn't equate to love, she knew that. But his daily visits to the diner, his understanding and caring, had practically forced her to fall in love with the fierce lion.

"Take the memories away." She blinked away the tears in her eyes. "Please."

Brute leaned down and she let her eyes flutter closed when he brushed a soft kiss across her lips. His natural scent tickled her nose and she inhaled his raw essence, savoring the comfort that came with his closeness.

"Not here, Elise." He whispered against her lips. "Not against a wall. I want to take my time with you. Show you how well I can love my mate."

God, the tears kept coming.

Elise pushed into him, rose to her tip-toes and deepened their barely-there kiss. She licked at the seam of his lips, tongue gently caressing his mouth, and she delved deeper into him when he opened for her. She lapped and drank in his flavors, let them slide over her taste buds, and she felt her fox stir in response. The small beast had retreated as they'd looked over the photos, hiding from their shared pain.

Eventually, Brute engaged her, mimicked her every stroke and giving as well as taking.

His cock hardened fully against her belly, telling her without words that he was more than ready to help dispel her memories. She wanted to bathe in his scent, let his

273

every touch wipe away any others. She didn't want to be able to recall anyone's touch but Brute's. Always Brute's.

Slowly, she eased from him until their lips were once again gently brushing. "Need you…"

"Yes," his voice was deep and husky.

Not releasing her, he reached and shut off the shower then helped her leave the glass enclosure. Dripping on the bath mats, Brute was quick to snag a nearby towel and dry her, then him.

In moments, they were merely damp and Elise reached for him, twining her fingers with his. "Bedroom?"

Brute tilted his head toward an open door and she took that as an invitation.

On trembling legs, she led him toward the master bedroom, carefully padding over the tile and then into the cavernous space that Brute called home. A large, dark wood bed dominated the center of the space. Masculine hues were sprinkled throughout the room, and she could see hints of her mate in every corner.

At the bed she paused, looking over the soft surface, imagining the two of them rolling and loving one another.

Brute's warmth enveloped her and she leaned against him for strength. "We don't have to do anything, sweet fox. We can crawl beneath the covers and nothing more."

Oh, her sweet, sweet lion.

Elise shook her head. "No. We're making new memories. Our memories. I need our lo—" Brute's hands stilled and she swallowed. "I need us to replace everything else."

Her mate turned her until she was faced with a simple choice: stare at his chest or look into his eyes. She decided to take the risk and meet his gaze, and hope blossomed in her chest. There...in his eyes...she saw what she'd be hoping for.

"Do you need our love to replace it all? Is that it, sweet fox?" His voice was soothing and gentle. "Because it's yours. I'm yours." He cupped her cheek as he stared at her and his eyes glistened in the dim lighting. "I love you, Elise. More than life, I love you."

The tears that had been a blink away for the last half hour finally fell, trailing down her cheeks as the weight of his feelings blanketed her. "I love you, too."

Reaching up, she ghosted her fingers over his face, absorbing his features by touch, and then finally settling her hand on his neck, tracing the underside of his jaw with her thumb. "Make love to me, Brute."

Elise stepped away from him and crawled onto the bed, her mate quickly following and then stretching beside her. She fit her length along him, curving into his larger body and drawing on his strength.

She traced the lines of his face, fingers dancing over the curves and dips of the muscles on his chest and abdomen. She traveled further south until she brushed the short curls of his groin. His cock was still hard and waiting for her.

She slid her palm over his length, not grasping, just playing as she discovered him once again.

This was a reconnection, a rebirth, of what they shared. It wouldn't be tainted by the others. She and Brute wouldn't be ruined by her past.

She wrapped her fingers around his width, encircling him and letting his warmth fill her palm.

The chest beneath her ear stilled and then picked up a new quickened rhythm, and she smiled against his skin. With a gentle move, she stroked him, traveled to the base of his cock and then to the tip, running her thumb over the slit to gather the bead of moisture.

She'd never done this, never taken control and discovered a man's body. And now, Brute was submitting and giving her what she didn't even know she'd desired.

She rubbed that little droplet over the head of his dick and then brought his thumb to her mouth, lapping at the salty flavor of her mate. "Mmm…"

"Damn, baby." His curse turned into a deep groan when her hand returned to his shaft, squeezing him just below the crown.

Elise returned to her explorations, stroking and petting him, watching for his reactions as she discovered what brought her mate pleasure. He throbbed and twitched against her, dick seeming to have a mind of its own as the flesh sought her touch.

More and more of his pre-cum seeped from his slit, giving her lubrication for her travels. Down and then back up, a twist, a squeeze and then back down again. She let her fingers reach even further, stroking his balls and feeling them draw tight beneath her touch.

"Elise." His voice was both a plea and a prayer.

She ignored him. No, she didn't ignore him. Not really. She simply tormented him further.

Hot skin was beneath her cheek and she turned her head, raising it so she could lap at the smooth, brown nipple near her mouth. She licked the nub, once, twice and again, smiling when it hardened from her ministrations.

With each touch her body prepared for him. Her pussy moistened, growing slick with her desire for her mate. Her clit throbbed within her folds, aching for his attentions, and her heat became wetter with each breath. Her own nipples hardened, mirroring his body's response.

She wanted him. Craved his possession like a drug and ached for the connection of their bodies.

But still she continued tormenting him. Sharp nails scraped along her arm, his shifted claws making themselves known and showing her how she'd affected him.

Elise resumed her torture, returned to stroking his throbbing length and nibbling and lapping his nipple. True, her body demanded completion, but she enjoyed the power she held.

She hadn't had that for the last two years, hadn't held the reigns and called the shots. Now she could.

Another tug, another twist, another squeeze.

Brute's breathing came in harsh, heavy pants and she could see that his other hand had shifted to a claw as well, the nails shredding the blanket beside him. A glance at his face revealed a pleasurable torment.

"Brute?" Her mate grunted. "Want to ride you." She whispered the words against his moist flesh and then blew a cool breath over his nipple, smiling at the further hardening. "Can I?"

A harsh breath escaped his lungs. "Anything."

With a last lingering pet, she released his cock and rose to her knees. She straddled his hips. Instead of lowering to his cock, she remained raised, hovering over his straining erection.

Elise stared down at her mate, the male she'd be with for the rest of her life, and was in awe. He held a strength that she couldn't imagine and yet he was so gentle when he touched her. Scars peppered his body, proof that he wasn't afraid of a fight, yet he never once touched her with anything other than love.

And that's what she saw shining in his eyes. Love.

With trembling hands, she stroked his chest, traced the various pale remnants of his wounds and pet each dip and curve of his skin over muscles. Brute twitched and moaned beneath her, but didn't move. He lay passive as she took the time to discover him, learn his body as well as she knew hers.

She counted the valleys between his abs, sliding over the tensed muscles until she once again met the juncture of his thighs. His cock was hot and hard, straining for her and she finally gave in.

Careful of his sensitive flesh, she positioned the head of his cock at her weeping opening and let her pussy kiss the tip of his length. She circled her hips, tormented and teased them both with the hint of contact.

"Elise…"

She eased down, letting the crown slip into her, and she lowered a fraction more. An inch in, then back out, another in, retreat… She tortured them both with the hints of possession.

Eyes trained on her mate, she watched as he shredded the blanket beneath him, claw-tipped fingers fisting the soft covering. His muscles were tense, straining with the effort to remain still.

And she loved it. Loved all of that constrained power, her self-restrained warrior.

Unwilling to wait longer, she lowered her body, taking her time as inch after inch of Brute eased into her heat. The searing brand of his cock burned her from inside out as she accepted him.

Further and further she traveled until her hips came to rest upon him, his dick fully embedded in her sheath. Completely possessing him, she paused and met his gaze, absorbing the love he showed and returning it in kind.

Elise's pussy pulsed, spasming around his length, and her clit twitched in response. She ached for release, was desperate to come with her mate.

Ever so slowly, she rose above him, letting his cock stroke her inner walls while she moved higher and then she retraced her movements. A gentle fall along his length stroked nerves inside her pussy, and a gentle shudder traveled along her spine.

She moaned and repeated the intimate caress, up and then down again. She moved her hands from Brute, stroking herself from hips to waist and then to her breasts, cupping their fullness. She found her nipples and she plucked the hardened nubs, teasing herself further.

Another shudder, harder than before, slithered through her and then settled around her pussy. Her cunt responded with a quick tightening of muscles which pulled a groan from her mate.

"Yes…" She hissed the word, enjoying the bolts of pleasure that poured into her.

Another up and another down, cock stroking her just right as she snatched snippets of bliss from Brute.

Her mate's hands released the mattress and came to rest on her thighs, callused skin sliding higher until they rested on her hips. He squeezed and kneaded her flesh but didn't force a rhythm.

"God, you're beautiful. So lush. So gorgeous."

Elise pressed down hard, grinding her pussy against him and moaning with the pulse of pleasure from her clit.

Brute snarled. "So mine."

"Yours." She gasped and repeated the move: up, down and a hard circle of her hips.

Again and again, her cunt spasming around his length, clit twitching with the bliss, the move elicited from her body.

"Need." God, she needed.

Dropping her head forward, she let her eyes drift close and focused on her release. Sparkles of light danced behind her lids like fireflies of pleasure that danced in and out of reach. They grew brighter with every grind of her hips, but not quite enough to lead her over the edge.

"I can give you what you need, sweet fox…"

Brute's voice was rough and she raised her head to look at her mate, revealing heavily sharpened features. Oh, the cat wanted out to play. His claw-tipped hold shifted along her hips, thumbs sliding over her vulnerable skin until they rested just above her slit.

"I can stroke this pretty clit while you ride me. Want that? Let me make you come, mate." He purred then, vibrations traveling along his cock and then into her, stroking her aroused nerve endings and making those pretty lights burn higher.

"Yes."

Elise kept her motions sure, gaze intent on Brute while his entire focus was on the juncture of her thighs. Those deadly digits moved again, teasing the top of her slit, dancing between her lower lips and then away again. He tormented her with that peek-a-boo touch. In and then out, the pad of his finger petting her clit before disappearing again.

"Brute…" She couldn't withhold the whine in her voice.

"I've got you, mate." He purred again and she gasped, pussy clenching hard around him. "Tell me, is it the purring or my fingers, Elise? What's getting you off more?"

"Both." She gasped.

"Hmm?" He pressed hard against her clit, a fierce, rough circling pressure.

"Both!" Elise pinched her nipples, adding that sliver of pain to the pleasure her mate was drawing from her body.

So he purred some more.

His thumb continued circling the bundle of nerves hidden within her folds, round and round, as she rose and fell along his thick length. With every lowering the head of his cock stroked her G-spot, drawing her bliss out even further.

"That's it mate. Come on my cock. Use me."

Elise whimpered and did as he asked, took her pleasure while giving in return. His cock twitched and pulsed within her sheath, and her pussy in turn stroked him with rhythmic touches.

His thumb never quit, never ceased as she increased her pace, fucking herself on his thick long cock. She relished the feeling of his possession, moaning and gasping with every slide of his dick within her heat.

"Brute…" She needed. Needed so bad.

Pleasure was tickling her nerves, plucking each one in turn and traveling through her with lightning speed. She ached to embrace the feelings. Bliss emanated from her cunt, wrapping around her hips before traveling along her limbs. Muscles tensed and twitched as the sensations tormented her.

And still she went on.

"Take what you need. Come for me."

Those sparkling lights nearly blinded her then, glowing brighter and drawing her toward the edge of release. She lost control of her limbs as she fought for her orgasm. She chased the pleasure, fought to find the ecstasy of climax until it hovered just before her.

So very, very close…

Brute's cock throbbed and twitched within her and pain-tinged pleasure flashed across his features, telling her without words that he was close to coming as well.

"Come for me, mate." She gasped out the words, the first uncontrollable trembles of orgasm surging through her. "Come for *me*."

Heaving breaths escaped Brute's chest, but his touch never faltered. No, it continued in a steady rhythm. His mouth opened wide and he released a deafening roar that filled the room. Her fox answered in kind.

Her beast wailed within her mind, answering her mate's call, while Elise's human body was overcome with the pleasure of climax.

Her limbs tensed and twitched, filled to bursting with the ecstasy of release. Her pussy milked Brute's cock, pulling more and more of his seed from it. She felt him fill her sheath with his cum.

And on it went.

Her shattering release overcame her body, stealing control of every cell until she was a jumble of overwhelming spasms as her passion crested. Higher and higher her release climbed, tossing more pleasure through her body with every step.

Sweet blissful death overtook her until she couldn't control herself any longer. She arched her back, the lava-hot waves overtaking her, and screamed as the pinnacle of her orgasm slammed into her body.

With the peak reached, she slowly began the descent, chest heaving as she panted and her lungs searched for air.

Brute slowed his touch, easing the pressure until he withdrew his thumb from between her thighs and returned his hands to her hips.

Gaze entirely focused on her mate, she saw the love shining there, saw his bone-deep desire for her, and knew without a doubt that this male would care for her like no other.

"Mate…" She reached for him, stroked his chest and let him take control when he brought her hand to his mouth. He pressed a kiss to her palm and then placed it along his cheek.

"Mate…" His voice was hoarse, from shouting or emotion, she didn't know. But then a tear slid along the cheek of her big, bad, fierce mate and she wasn't left to wonder any more.

CHAPTER *ten*

"We're all given skills in life. Mine is how to kill people. Deal with it." – Brute Mauer, Ridgeville Prima guard and growly badass.

Two weeks. Two weeks since the asshat that had trashed her apartment and tried to destroy her life (again) had made an appearance.

And, other than worrying about that guy, they'd been the happiest weeks of her life. She'd moved in with Brute rather than go back to her apartment. They'd cleaned her temporary home from top to bottom, but the only place she wanted to be was at her mate's side, in his bed, every day. They'd started looking for a house. Brute had encouraged her to get her nursing license in North Carolina since she enjoyed healing others so much. Plus, Ricker had just begun his job of training shifters for the council and that tended to get bloody.

And now she'd get to go on her first run with her hunky lion. It'd been postponed after the whole picture thing. With the guy having not reappeared, Alex gave the pride run a green light.

And, holy cow, it was a lot different than a skulk gathering. The foxes tended to arrive in a handful of cars at midnight, hide behind trees to shift and then run for a few hours. After which, they'd go back to their cars and leave. No talking. No socializing. And definitely no munchies.

Brute pulled into a dirt parking space and cut the engine as she stared at the gathering. There were easily fifty lions, and who knew what else, wandering around the clearing. Small groups were sprinkled throughout, but it was a particular cluster (right next to the food table) that caught her eye.

Maya, Carly, Maddy and Gina were grouped together, taking turns rubbing Carly's burgeoning belly while laughing and having fun.

"Elise? You ready?" Brute had been worried about her all day. All. Day. If she didn't love him so much, she would've killed him.

"I'm fine. It's not like you're feeding me to your pride. Besides, we're sticking with the big guys, right?" She gave him her best "let it go" smile.

"Right. But the man hasn't been caught. We could come to the next one—"

"Brute, I'm going out there, getting furry and running. I know he's still loose, but I also know that my mate, and my pride, will protect me. Right?"

Her mate huffed, looking annoyed and defeated at the same time. "Right. Let's go, then."

Mates. Gotta love 'em cause you couldn't kill 'em. At least, that's what Maya said. She also demanded that dead things be dropped at her feet as proof of her mate's love, but Elise was happy to pass on that custom. Dead things? Ew.

Not waiting for Brute, she slipped from the truck, hopping to the ground and then pushed the door shut behind her. With a smile to her mate she headed toward the gathering of her friends, anxious to reconnect and have some "girl talk".

"...so I've decided that the dead thing at my feet is going to be Alex. Who's with me?" Maya raised a chicken wing in the air. The woman was still "eating for three" and justified it by saying that she was breast feeding and needed the calories. Elise thought the woman just liked chicken wings. "All in favor, say aye!"

Elise froze mid-step and looked at the other women. Conspiring to kill a Prime outside of challenge was a death sentence. When none of them spoke up in agreement, she let out a sigh of relief.

"Fine," Maya grumbled, nibbling on her drumstick. "Rain on my parade then. I just want a prize. A mouse even." The Prima picked up a celery stick. "I'd say rabbit, but it might end up being Carly's brother and then where would we be?"

Carly snorted. "Better off."

Maddy seemed to realize that Elise had walked up and she wiggled free of the others, arms outstretched and embracing her in a tight hug. She could feel the tingles of the other woman's power brushing her mind and Elise couldn't hold back her smile.

"I'm fine, *mom*. But Brute may end up being the dead thing at Maya's feet if he doesn't relax a little."

Giggling, Maddy eased the hug and stepped to the side. "You know I've got to check on my sister from another mister." All chatting stopped and three sets of eyes focused on them. More specifically, Maddy. "What?"

"It's that damn Urban Dictionary. She's trying to be cool again." Carly shook her head with a sigh.

"Honey," Gina pointed at Maddy. "Embrace the dorkiness. You are the Queen of Dorklandia." Gina took a bite of her celery stick. Lions and greens? Weird.

Maya ripped into her chicken wing, ignoring the barbeque sauce left in its wake. "Exactly. Hey! You get to have two titles. Queen of Munchlandia and Dorklandia." The Prima's eyes narrowed. "How is it you get two and I get none? Off with her head!"

Elise leaned toward Gina and whispered. "Is she always like this?"

"I think it's sleep deprivation. Between the babies and Alex, she's running on fumes." The lioness shuddered. "Babies. Ew."

Unfortunately, Maya heard them. "My babies aren't ew-ey. They are sweetness and light. They are also poop factories, but Alex deals with that end." The Prima cupped her boobs while still clutching her chicken wing, rubbing that sauce all over her chest. "I handle what goes in, he handles what comes out."

"Maya? Um…" Elise waved at the woman's abundant chest. "You got some…"

The Prima looked down and sighed before returning her attention to them. "They're ginormous and get in the way of everything." She paused for a moment, eyes going wide.

"Dudes. I'm the Queen of Booblandia. Score!" A roar ended their conversation and all eyes shifted to the center of the clearing where Alex now stood.

"Oh! Show time." Maya handed off her chicken wing to Gina, plucked a napkin from the picnic table and wiped up. "'K. Gotta get this party started."

Maya squeezed through their circle and made it all of five feet before she spun and jogged back to their group, gesturing for Elise to come closer. "So, the thing about it is…"

Elise raised her eyebrows.

"Remember the whole thing we did before I popped out the babies? With the heart and blood and woo hoo you're in the pride?" Maya nibbled her lower lip.

"Yeah." She'd thought it'd been sudden, but hadn't been sure how prides operated.

"Well, I kinda didn't tell Alex about it. He gets all puffed up about being the Prime and welcoming new members and yada, yada… So, just play along and I'll give you a carton of Half Baked ice cream. Deal?"

"Make it three." Elise smiled.

"Two and it's my final offer. Alex thinks I need to rock the healthy thing and has my stash locked down. Three would clean me out."

Elise sighed heavily, pretending to be put out. "Fine. Two."

The Prima stuck out her hand. "Shake on it and you three are witnesses. You renege and I'm totally giving you puppy chew toys for every gift-giving occasion for the rest of your life. For both you *and* any kidlets."

A quick handshake and then Maya was gone, jogging to the center of the clearing and throwing herself into Alex's arms. The Prime caught his mate with ease, spinning her around, their lips locked, and then lowering her back to the ground. Even from where she stood, Elise could recognize their shared passion and love in the embrace.

Looking around the space, she found Brute on the opposite side and their gazes clashed. Lord, she loved that man.

And based on his expression, he felt the same. Through one look, they shared their love, their caring, and most definitely, their physical need. Without hesitation, she broke away from the girls and headed toward her mate, anxious to be at his side, in his arms. She walked ten feet, then twenty, then...

"Elise Mara!" She froze with a squeak, Alex's voice vibrating through her.

Slowly, she turned toward Alex, her Prime (almost-ish), and a smiling Maya. "Prime?"

"Come forward." Damn the man was arrogant when he was all Prime-y. She'd gotten used to the laid back version of the lion.

Looking over to Brute, she hoped her mate would save her. Or hell, come with her. The hope was dashed quickly with a shake of his head and a quick brushing gesture, urging her to get her ass in gear.

Lovely.

Straightening her spine, she walked toward the center of the clearing on shaking legs. She did not do the whole "being the center of attention" thing. Couldn't they just let her hide amongst the kitties? Yeah, she was a fox, but she was itty-bitty. No one would have noticed her and…

"Kneel."

Maya elbowed her mate and frowned at him and Elise almost giggled. Almost. Apparently the Prima didn't care for his tone either. But Elise couldn't disobey him and did as he asked.

"Tonight we welcome fox, Elise Mara. Several of you have voiced your doubts over accepting her into the pride and I have listened." Alex's voice met silence. Mostly.

A low growl followed by a snarl echoed across the wide area. Apparently Elise wasn't the only one who'd been surprised by the Prime's statement. Brute did not sound like a happy kitty.

Fear curled in her belly. She'd made a home in Ridgeville, conquered many of her demons and looked forward to building a family with Brute in the small town. And now they'd have to start over… Tears built in her eyes and she blinked them back. She could cry later.

Maya elbowed Alex. "Stop it, you big bully." The Prima leaned down, winked and then whispered. "It's fine honey. He just likes to put on a show." Alex frowned at Maya. The Prima just giggled before stretching up and pressing a quick kiss to his lips. "Well, you do."

The Prime rolled his eyes and then continued. "I have listened and I think you've lost sight of what it means to be Pride." Alex paused, his gaze traveling over the circle. "To be Pride is to think of the many and not the one. With two Sensitives within our ranks, our cubs will find ease during their first transition instead of pain. With Elise in our arms, we shall settle disputes with words instead of fang and claw. And above all, she will calm those around her when our first thought is to destroy. This fox is a gift, and we should each be thankful that god has guided her to us."

Maya had totally been right. Alex seemed to be all about the politician-esque grandstanding.

"Elise Mara, give me your hand."

She did as asked, extending her arm and baring her wrist. A quick flash of a blade was the only warning she received before the sharp edge slid along her skin. Blood welled from the wound, and she watched as Alex repeated the motion on his own arm.

Alex pressed their wounds together. "Blood to blood, heart to heart, fur to fur, I welcome you to my pride."

The roars and growls of the gathered lions rose and filled the clearing, and Elise was sure she heard the squeaky chitter of a specific bunny amongst the welcoming vocalizations.

But then a singular word rose above the din, louder than all others.

"No!"

Oh, god. She knew that voice... She'd never forget it.

Wrenching her arm from Alex's hold, she rose to her feet and spun to face the speaker. It was...it was one of them and she wouldn't let it happen. No. Never again. He wouldn't. She had Brute and...

She backed away, tripping over Alex and Maya in her bid to flee. She stumbled and fell to the ground and then crab walked away from the man. Her heart hammered and pummeled her chest, pumping adrenalin through her body with every flex.

And for once, the fox fought. She snipped, snarled and barked at the male, ready to show that his assault wouldn't be tolerated. But fear still rode her hard. It pulsed like a living thing beneath her skin.

She wouldn't, wouldn't, wouldn't...

Elise's back collided with something large and solid, unmovable, and she looked up to find her mate towering over her. His large hands wrapped around her biceps and pulled her to her feet. Without hesitation, she clung to him, doing her best to burrow beneath his skin and hide. "Brute. He's one of them. Don't let him... Please."

Brute nudged her behind him and she fisted the back of his shirt, unwilling to release him. As he strode forward, she followed, trusting her mate to take care of the male.

God. The man had to be part of the pride.

She wouldn't stay. Not ever. Not with the sick fuck free in town.

Standing alongside the Prime and Prima, Brute stilled and Elise risked a look around his massive body.

The male was just as she remembered. He was tall and lean with a glint of evil that had never left his eyes. Yes, he was one of the many.

The fox wanted to feast on him, gnaw on his bones and then let the scavengers pick at what flesh she'd leave behind.

"What's the meaning of this, Jenner?"

Yes. Jenner. Brute had mentioned his sister's crush on the lion, as well as Maya's friendship with him, but she hadn't connected the male to her time with Freedom. She couldn't imagine that someone in the Ridgeville pride would have been involved in the movement, involved in her pain.

And then her thoughts returned to the pictures, the images she'd been forced to look over and the tension that had filled the room when she'd gotten to that particular photo.

"You weren't supposed to let her in. You were supposed to banish her." Jenner's eyes collided with hers and his fear threatened to overwhelm her. Oh, hate was present, but panic was coursing through his veins. "She's not a Sensitive, Prime. She's just a broken whore."

*

Brute would kill him. The way his mate trembled and shivered against his back had been enough for him to justify roughing the cub up a little, but his words... The male would die.

He's another lion. His name starts with a "J". Jennings? Jensen? Jenner? He knew he'd recognized that birthmark, that tattoo. He just hadn't been willing to accept the truth. They all hadn't been willing to even entertain the idea that a pride mate would hurt another.

The cat rushed forward, prowling beneath his skin, scraping his claws along his muscles and snarling for blood.

Brute would be glad to deliver.

Beside him, Alex stilled, body just as tense and alert, and Brute had no doubt that the Prime had connected the dots they'd all been unwilling to examine. "Explain yourself, Jenner."

He knew that tone, the one that said blood would be spilled without hesitation if he didn't like the answer he received.

Jenner took a step forward and his mate pushed against him even harder, body seeming to fold in on itself. "Don't let him…"

"She couldn't help Alis—" The lion cut off the word and spit on the ground. "She's simply worthless. A useless dog that can't even summon her powers. How's a broken whore going to benefit the pride? Didn't I show you that?"

Brute growled and took a step forward only to have his movement halted by Alex's large hand coming to rest on his forearm. "And when would we have seen that?"

Again, low and calm with no evidence of his rage. And Brute had no doubt that the Prime was seething. The male was pushing the proverbial "line in the sand" with their leader. Much more and Alex would see Jenner's accusations and ranting as an outright challenge. To the death.

Even if Brute knew what Alex was doing, trying to get Jenner to admit his involvement with Freedom and Elise's torture, he didn't have to like it.

"You saw her when she was rescued. You know what she was like. And you know she's brought trouble to town." The male growled. "You saw the pictures."

Brute felt the jerk of Elise's body, a rough shudder that was followed by a low whimper.

"Alex…" He hated the warning in his tone. He'd never wanted to challenge his Prime, but if the man didn't do something about the fucker before them…

"I see."

Keep talking mother fucker. Keep hanging yourself so I can gut your ass for touching my mate.

Out of the corner of his eye, he saw a grim-faced Grayson enter the clearing with the Sheriff mirroring the Second on the opposite side. Behind Jenner, the rest of Maya's guards emerged: Harding, Wyatt, Deuce and Neal tense and ready. Even better, Ricker stepped out as well. All of them showing support for their Prime in a wide, loose circle.

Which was as it should be.

Silence reigned in the clearing. Not even the wind dare break the quiet until Alex spoke up once again. "And what do you know of Elise's rescue? How could you know anything about her state after being stolen back from Freedom? She hadn't stepped foot in Ridgeville until a month and a half ago." Alex took a step closer to Jenner. Brute mimicked the move. "Better yet, what do you know of pictures, Jenner?"

Rage poured through Brute's veins and his beast rode the wave. Fingers turned to claws, hair sprouted from his pores and the crunch and crack of bone signaled the shifting of his face from man to lion.

296

Because there was one reason, and one reason only, that Jenner would know anything about Elise's rescue and the recent appearance of pictures.

He'd been in the compound, probably raped his gentle mate. He'd been behind the destruction of her apartment and the arrival of the pictures that had nearly destroyed his sweet fox.

He's another lion. His name starts with a "J". Jennings? Jensen? Jenner?

Jenner...

"Alex..." The two syllables barely made it pass his lips, muzzle fighting to push the word from his body.

Again the hand stilled him.

"Jenner, it seems you know more than you should. It seems that you have a first-hand accounting of Elise's time in captivity as well as the destruction of her home. In addition, it *seems* you know an awful lot about pictures that were recently delivered to her." Alex's voice remained level as he spoke while Brute's desperation for blood rose.

"Of course I do! I was there. I—" The lion snarled.

"I see." Alex turned his attention to the rest of the lions, sweeping his gaze across the gathering. "Will the pride bear witness?"

"We will." The voices echoed, resonating in Brute's bones with the power behind their conviction. They must have come to the same conclusion as he and Alex. Even if they didn't know the details, they had acknowledged a portion of Jenner's guilt.

"Wh-What?" Jenner was sputtering, the first hint of fear entering his features as he backed away from the Prime.

"Then hear me. These will be the last words from the pride to your ears, Jenner Mattson. You are no longer of the pride. May the pride's blood freeze in your veins, may the pride's heart still in your chest and may the pride's fur leave you cold."

"So witnessed." Again, the chorus.

"No! Don't you see? It's her. Not me, *her.*" Jenner folded to his knees. "Don't you see? Alistair just wants us to be free and she was supposed to help. But she can't because she's broken. You don't understand—"

"Sheriff Corman, please take the nameless and secure him for the council."

"Yes, Prime." The Sheriff stepped forward, but before he could grab the man, Jenner went on the offensive.

With a roar Jenner rose from the ground, face contorting with each beat of his heart, and Brute recognized the impending shift. "It's her. You'll see. It's her!"

The man was heading right for him, but the eyes were trained on Elise.

"Not gonna happen." Brute pulled free of Elise and tore his shirt and pants from his body, cloth rending easily, and then the cat came out to play.

Jenner mirrored his shift and went on the attack. Brute tackled him in one leap, fangs bared and mouth gaping wide. He'd tear out the man's throat, feast on his blood.

The other lion met him with claws and teeth and he snarled and snapped, stretching and reaching for fur.

Then Jenner pushed back and danced away. Brute followed, crouched and ready to spring. His claws dug into the dirt, ground sure to give him the extra leverage he'd need for the next attack.

They circled, wary and watching. He hunted for the perfect strike only to be thwarted by an impatient opponent.

Jenner raced forward, rising to his hind legs when Brute countered the assault. The lion's claws found home in Brute's shoulder, but he ignored the inconsequential pain. The scent of his own blood filled the air and his cat was aching for retribution. The other beast would die.

Now Brute went on the offensive, leaping at Jenner, roaring in pleasure when his nails sunk into flesh and tore at the vulnerable tissue. Lines of red followed in his wake and triumph filled him at the sight of the wound he'd caused.

Limping, Jenner hopped away on three legs, his tawny fur now burgundy as the injury bled.

Brute didn't wait, didn't give the male a moment to recover before he was on the lion again. He kept the pressure up, following, striking, cutting and hurting Jenner with every swipe and flex of muscle and claw.

Jenner would die.

The assault continued. Slice. Bite. Tear.

Brute's mouth was filled with blood.

The lion he fought was fighting a losing battle, and part of him was proud that the other beast wasn't giving up even if it was a lost cause.

No one would threaten what belonged to him and live. No one.

Then, Jenner stumbled, his muscles unable to keep him upright, and Brute pounced. He dug his nails into the male and wrapped his mouth around Jenner's neck, teeth sliding into the flesh with ease as he applied more and more pressure.

Beneath him, the other cat went lax, but it wasn't enough for Brute's lion. Not when it meant that letting him live would leave a threat hanging over Elise.

Die. Die. Die.

"Brute!" Alex's voice rose over his growls and Brute froze. "Release him."

No.

"We need him alive, Brute. You've begun avenging your mate. Let the council get information from him and then you can finish it." Brute felt the power behind the Prime's words, but still he resisted.

Has to die.

"Brute?" Elise's voice, gentle and sweet, floated to him. "Listen to Alex. Let Sheriff Corman deliver him to the council."

Brute whined, but kept his mouth in place. He didn't wanna, damn it.

The soft pad of feet over the grass approached and a delicate hand stroked his flank. "Please, Brute. I don't want you to kill him. At least not today. What if he knows something that can help others? What if there are more Sensitives and he can help us find them?"

Brute huffed and released the lion, quick to push his mate away from the injured male, not trusting that the fight had fully left Jenner. He prodded and poked until they were back beside the Prime, and they watched as Sheriff Corman went to the prone beast.

Quiet surrounded them. Well, mostly.

"Do you see that? Brute left something dead-ish for Elise. Why can't you bring me dead things? What's up with that?" Brute could always trust Maya to lighten a situation.

Alex sighed and pinched the bridge of his nose. "Maya…"

A snarl grabbed their attention and they watched as the Sheriff subdued a struggling Jenner, hitting him with a Taser. The jolt of electricity forced the male to shift back to human. Blood still marred his body, but most of the wounds were no longer visible. "Wait! I'll tell you everything! Don't take me—"

The man would be tired, but he'd live.

Unfortunately.

With the threat no longer present, Brute shifted and pulled his mate into his arms, burying his face in her locks and inhaling her sweet scent. Peace surrounded him, soothing his beast and placing a blanket of calm over his body.

"Damn, looks like Brute will have to start over with the killing thing." Maya poked Alex. "But at least Elise got closer to getting dead things than me. What's up with that?"

Alex sighed. Again.

The Sheriff led away a staggering Jenner and silence reigned in the clearing, tension and worry filling the space. Brute chided himself over ignoring his gut when it came to Jenner. Hell, he, along with Alex, Grayson and Sheriff Corman had disregarded their feelings. None of them had wanted to even think that a pride mate would be involved with Freedom. That a pride mate would inflict such pain on another.

Maddy filled the quiet with two quick claps, tearing Brute from his thoughts. "Okay then, I think we've had enough of that." The small Sensitive smiled wide and raised her hands above her head. "Let the run begin!"

The woman dashed toward the trees, Ricker hot on her heels.

Alex's roar followed them. "I start the run, woman!"

"Maybe next time!" Her giggles flitted back to the gathering.

Alex glared at Maya, and Brute wondered if he'd now have to step in and protect the Prima. "Do you realize that I haven't started one of our runs since you gave Maddy 'bad ass' lessons? Do you?"

"Of course." Maya smiled and sidled up to the Prime, sex in her every feature. "But you love me anyway. And if I didn't do things that annoy you, you'd never have a reason to punish me." Maya wiggled against him. "Wanna spank me?"

Brute rolled his eyes and turned his back on the couple, hugging Elise tighter. "Come on, sweet fox. We've got a forest with our names on it."

The Prima's squeal tore through the clearing. Then the rapid tattoo of feet on grass surrounded them as the pride followed their Prime's lead and got on with the run, leaving the two of them alone.

Elise rested her head against his chest, small palm resting over his heart.

Brute grasped her hand and brought it to his lips, brushing a kiss over the petal-soft skin. "He's gone now."

"I know."

"And with the information the council gets from him, I'll hunt down every male that's touched you." A growl entered his voice, the cat in full agreement with his plan. He'd dismember every man that had hurt his precious mate.

Elise giggled and nipped his chest. "My fierce little furball."

"Little?" With her wiggling, his cock twitched and came to life, hardening against her softness. "I don't think there's anything 'little' about me."

His sweet, delectable, evil mate reached down and wrapped her hand around his stiffening dick and stroked him, tugging on his length until he was rock hard. "No, I don't think there is."

"Elise…"

A wicked gleam entered her eyes. "What? Gonna spank me?" She rubbed her thumb over the tip of his cock. "Gotta catch me first."

Elise bolted, clothes flying behind her as she ran toward the tree line and he watched as curve after curve was revealed to him, smooth skin that he ached to taste. Over and over again.

Five feet from the edge of the forest she dropped to all fours, body shifting as she moved until his lush mate was replaced with a sleek red fox.

She yipped at him and ducked behind a tree, teasing him.

God, how he loved her.

And now, he'd teach her just how fierce he could be. Twice. Okay, forever.

End of Fierce in Fur

DEUCES WILD

CHAPTER *one*

"Life is not WYSIWIG. There is no 'what you see is what you get' thing going on. Because, hey, people wear clothes and stuff. Or they're liars. So, get 'em naked or shoot them. Just don't get blood on the carpet." — Maya O'Connell, Prima of the Ridgeville Pride and a woman who's decided that twins are overrated and that two is never ever better than one.

Deuce wondered when the curvy little woman standing at Alistair's back would make her move and rip out the polar bear's jugular.

He guessed five minutes. This was unfortunate since he had a good hand and he figured he'd be winning pretty soon. He, Alistair—leader of Freedom, a shifter antiestablishment militant group—and two others had been sitting around the poker table for a few hours. Deuce was one flip of a card away from taking the last of the man's money in this game of Texas Hold 'Em. The turn had been revealed and Alistair had raised. The rest of them called, easily meeting the new amount. Now he needed the river card to come through for him and he'd win the pot.

But the woman standing behind the leader and flanked by two guards looked like she'd happily end the polar bear's life.

She was beautiful, despite the bruises and dried blood peppering her face. Deuce fought the attraction that had been prodding him since the moment he'd walked into the room and settled in a chair. Regardless of her wounds, she stood tall, glaring at Alistair anytime he chanced glancing at the female.

With the room filled with heavy, sweet cigar smoke, he couldn't catch her scent. He wasn't quite sure if she was a shifter or simply a human who'd caught the leader's eye. Based on her fresh, deep bruises and the dirty looks she kept flashing to the room, the woman hadn't been too keen on being taken.

He'd heard the rumors about the woman, speculation that she was anything ranging from a senator's sister to the relative of a powerful shifter family. Deuce figured the latter explanation was closer to the truth.

He leaned forward, grabbed his quickly emptying can of light beer, and swallowed a mouthful of the bitter brew. Even after all these years, he had trouble getting past the taste of the specially formulated liquid.

"Can't believe you drink that shit." The grumbled words easily cut through the smoke-filled room. It was the hyena on his right. Big fucker. Without a doubt, he was twice as wide as Deuce. But Deuce had training on his side and the other guy knew it.

Deuce's fangs burst from his gums in a flash and he hissed at the larger man. His lion purred in approval. He'd been going through this shit from the moment he'd joined Freedom, constantly having to prove his dominance over the others. It had gotten him this far, securing his place in Alistair's inner circle and closer to his ultimate goal.

"Enough." Alistair's voice was quiet and Deuce's beast wanted to turn his feral attention to the polar bear. In truth, the man wasn't as strong, fast, or lethal as he and his lion, and it'd take no time to take him down.

But he couldn't make his move, not yet, not when so much was still unanswered. He had a lot more intel to gather for the council. A lot more.

The woman suddenly moved, dived past her guards, and attacked the seated leader. She wrapped her fingers around Alistair's throat with a flash of claws and encircled his neck, tips digging into the flesh at his throat.

Damn it.

Alistair's men forced her to relinquish her grip, and then shoved her back, her body colliding with the wall and cracking the smooth surface.

Deuce swallowed his fury, pushed the lion in an effort to keep it from emerging. His beast lurked beneath his skin, rippling along his muscles. He forced his heart rate to remain steady, urged his cat to control itself. They couldn't afford to let their true feelings show.

He hated violence against women, but there was nothing he could do. Not yet. He had a job to do and he couldn't sacrifice his mission. He studied the men bracketing the woman and committed them to memory. When his job was complete, he'd visit those two in their jail cells. Privately.

Rage filled every line of the polar bear's features and the man wiped at his bleeding wounds with a napkin. Placing the crumpled, red-tinged bit of cloth on the table, he rose and gave his back to the room. Alistair took two striding steps, blocking the dazed woman from Deuce's gaze. The sound of flesh against flesh echoed through the silent room. Based on the thud, he figured it was a backhanded slap rather than a punch.

"Bitch." Alistair spat the word and then, as if nothing had occurred, returned to his seat, easing into the padded chair.

The leader reached out and flipped the river card, appearing not to have let the interruption bother him in the least.

Deuce. Funny, last card revealed happened to be a wildcard.

Deuce took turns in observing the men surrounding the table from beneath his lashes, checking them all for tells he'd observed during their play. The guys to his left and right had nothing. Alistair remained.

He hadn't discovered anything about the polar bear that would clue him in on the man's hand. No flick of his eyes, throb of a vein, or dilation of his pupils. Nada.

A glance at the chips in front of Alistair revealed that the man didn't have enough to even hit the minimum bet. Deuce wasn't sure what the shifter was up to. He should have folded before now. Unless he'd been praying for a miracle.

With the last card faceup, the leader was set to begin this round.

"It seems I'm at a slight disadvantage." The polar bear smirked. "Let's make it interesting. We each go all in and since I'm a little short on funds, we'll sweeten the pot with Miss Martin. Agreed?"

Lust coated the features of the men beside him, the scent of their desire managing to override the sweetness of the cigars, and they both nodded. Not that they'd win. Deuce's stomach churned at what Alistair might be trying to do.

His loyalty had been tested, day after day, from the moment he'd made first contact. He couldn't blame the man. Deuce had been a guard to the mate of one of the strongest and most influential Primes in the country, Alex O'Connell. But he'd abandoned that life and had embraced his time with Freedom.

Alistair's gaze was locked on Deuce as the next words left his mouth, as if the man spoke to him and him alone. "I made a promise that Miss Martin wouldn't enjoy my bed, but no mention was made of anyone else's."

He somehow knew Deuce had a winning hand and Alistair was going to force him to win, force him to drag the battered woman back to his room and…

He refused to let the disgust that filled him enter his features, pushed down the bile rising in his throat. He couldn't blow it over a woman. He'd figure something out. Somehow, some way.

The woman fought against the guards restraining her, fire burning bright in her eyes as she tugged against their hold. A rapid chitter passed her lengthened teeth and he still wasn't sure of her inner animal.

At least, based on her sounds, she wasn't a rabbit. He'd had enough of those little furballs (and not having them for dinner) when he was part of the Ridgeville pride. They'd shared their territory with a colony. Then the Prima's best friend, a rabbit named Carly, had mated one of the other pride guards. So he could easily identify those scratchy noises.

One by one, they pushed their chips into the center of the table, signifying their bets. Then they flipped their two cards, watching and waiting to see who'd take home the prize.

Tension rose in the room, heating the space and assaulting Deuce's nose with the heavy scents of desire and anticipation. The musk of sweat joined the acrid aromas and he simply wanted out. Out of the room. Out of the house. Out of Free—

No, not yet, not when he was still missing so much. Alistair's crimes were unquestioned, but they needed to know the man's plans. They needed Deuce to gather information and hand the leader over to the council.

Alistair and his antiestablishment militant group, Freedom, were a threat to all shifters. He fought against the hierarchal structure that kept them all sane and controlled, believed they should each be self-governing and able to live free of another's rule. The council, and ninety-nine percent of the country's shifters, knew the man was an idiot. A crazy idiot who tried to get his point across by injuring innocents. The problem was his methods drew attention.

Humans were aware of shifters and allowed them to self-police, but Alistair's actions threatened the uneasy peace with the non-weres. Murder tended to piss people off. His job was to directly tie Alistair to Freedom's activities. Hard, cold physical evidence. He said, she said wasn't gonna cut it.

Deuce's gaze fell on Alistair. His focus was met with a smug smile from the leader and he let his attention waver to the other man's cards. Damn it. Deuce had won. If only it'd been cash. Now he had to drag the female to his room, keep her from unmanning him, and find a solution to their problem, because he wasn't about to rape a woman.

"Looks like Deuce takes the pot." Grumbles and growls met Alistair's pronouncement, but the leader let the sounds roll off his back. With a smirk, the man gestured behind him. "Come claim your prize."

Forcing his features to take on a cool mask of indifference, Deuce pushed back from the table and strode around the gathered men. At his approach, the woman glared and then spit, sending a glob of saliva through the air to land on his cheek.

"Charming." He wiped the fluid from his face and then wrapped his hand around her bicep, tugging her from the guards' grasp. "I've got her."

The woman fought; he had to give her credit for that. Even after the beatings she'd suffered, she still dug her heels in and struggled against him. She wouldn't win, of course, but he admired her inner fire.

Deuce dragged her through the doorway and down the hall, keeping his grip tight so she couldn't break free. He really didn't feel like running. At the steps, he finally gave up with pulling her along and simply tossed her over his shoulder in a fireman's carry, hand across her thighs so she wouldn't fall.

At the top, he turned right and stomped to the end of the hallway, anger and frustration going into every collision of his booted feet with the plush carpet.

Damn it, he didn't need this.

He pushed into his bedroom and kicked the door closed behind him, thankful for the relative privacy. He'd been given one of the few sound-insulated rooms in the mansion, his rank within Freedom affording him that luxury. It wouldn't keep everything from the outside world, but words would be muffled.

Deuce tossed her onto the bed and watched her lush body bounce, breasts jiggling with the movement, and he forced himself to look away from her curves. He needed to focus. Alistair expected him to rape the woman, and he had to find a way to get around the silent order.

The moment her body stilled, she went into action. Her mouth opened, releasing a screaming chitter, and she came at him, small claws extended and teeth bared. He had to admire her tenacity.

He easily countered her attack and shoved her back onto the soft surface, forcing her to lie supine beneath him as he pinned her arms beside her head and body with his.

Still she screamed and bucked, fighting him for all she was worth.

This close, he could see the busted blood vessels in her right eye, the depth of purple that stained the area surrounding the milk-chocolate-hued orb. He noted the fresh blood staining the corner of her mouth and the fist-sized abrasion on her chin. Her nose had been broken, the bridge crooked and never reset. Blood caked her upper lip and he imagined her nostrils were filled with the dried remnants of her nosebleed.

Alistair had obviously worked over her face pretty well. He wondered about the rest of her body.

But she hadn't been raped.

At least, he didn't think she had been. "Hush."

The smoke from the game cleared his nose and he could finally breathe, catch hints of aromas that didn't involve cigars. It was then he caught her scent.

And he seized her flavors. He captured the essence of dewy pines and honeysuckle and...mate. Oh, god, not now. Not when there was so much at stake and he couldn't keep her safe. He'd worked so hard to get to this point.

Those brown eyes, even filled with burning rage, called to him. Her bruised lips begged for whisper-soft kisses. He wanted to tend to every bruise, every scrape, cut, and injury. He'd kill Alistair, tear the polar bear limb from limb for injuring his mate.

Deuce's lion roared in approval, anxious to secure their mate and then return to destroy the leader.

The woman's lush body cradled him, abundant breasts cushioning his chest, and the heat from the juncture of her thighs burned him. His cock hardened from her closeness, responding to her scent and mere presence. He wanted to strip her, lick, taste, and nip every inch of her flesh and then slide deep into her pussy. He'd slip his fangs into her shoulder and claim her as his, coat her in his scent so everyone would know she belonged to him.

"I'll kill you." Her words came out in a strangled, raspy voice and he noticed the handprints that wrapped around her neck.

"I know you'd try." The sour scent of her fear reached him and he shoved the cat back. They couldn't play, not now, not when so much danger lurked.

"Then I'll kill myself."

313

A raging roar filled his mind and Deuce fought against voicing the feelings that filled him. His gums ached, pushing against his flesh, and he kicked the lion back this time. He didn't have a moment for finesse when dealing with the cat, and he'd suffer the consequences of his actions later when he let the beast free. He doubted his little mate could handle an incensed lion.

His mate. His lush, curvaceous mate.

Deuce took one last deep breath. He knew he'd have to climb from her, force himself to retreat and show her she could trust him, at least a little. That final inhale brought even more to his senses, more of her alluring fragrance along with hints of her inner animal. Her… "Squirrel? You're a squirrel?"

She narrowed her eyes but nodded.

Great.

A lion mated to a squirrel. And he'd teased one of the other guards back in Ridgeville about claiming a bunny.

Damn, he missed that place, missed his friends—

No, he couldn't think on that, not when he had to deal with his current situation.

Deuce huffed. "Okay, I'm gonna move off you and go stand by the door. Screaming isn't going to solve anything. Got it?"

Her glare remained in place and she agreed with a quick jerk of her head.

Fighting against the lion's demand that he remain near their mate, he tore himself away from her and did as he promised. He didn't stop until his back met the solid wood of the door.

Beneath his gaze, Miss Martin pushed into a sitting position and he noticed the wince that bolted across her features, the way she clutched her ribs. Fury tore through him, unadulterated rage over how his mate had been treated.

Alistair would die.

The moment she hit vertical, she stilled, wary, and her eyes remained trained on him.

"I'm Deuce, Deuce Karn. Lion." Her lips formed a tight white line when she remained silent. "I can call you lady, squirrel, or Miss Martin. Or you can give me your name." He stuffed his hands in his pockets, trying to look as harmless as possible. It wasn't easy.

Being a lion, he hit just over six feet and the rest of his body matched. His shoulders were wide, barely fitting through the average doorway, his body swathed in heavy muscle from head to toe.

"Elly." She bit off the single word.

He nodded and forced himself to relax. His mate's name was Elly. Scrumptious Elly Martin.

"Okay, Elly, we're gonna get you out of here." He hadn't realized his true intention until the words passed his lips.

"Really?" She quirked a brow. "Do tell. We'll scurry out and no one will stop us?"

Deuce wiggled his arm, intensely aware of the watch strapped to his wrist.

A watch given to him by the shifter council before he'd embarked on his mission.

"Not quite. We'll move fast, but we'll have an escort."

He wasn't ready to suffer through his debriefing, unsure of how his superiors would take his actions.

"Right." She snorted. Well, almost. The quick inhale was immediately followed by a fierce, bone-jarring cough. Elly bent over, mouth wide as hacking wheezes racked her body, arms wrapped around her middle. The sheen of tears sliding down her cheeks broke him and he rushed to her, embraced her shoulders.

Reaching for the bedside table, he snagged a tissue and pressed it into her hand. She grabbed it without hesitation and held it to her mouth. It felt like hours before the attack ceased and he noticed blood coating the tissue when she pulled it from her lips.

Internal bleeding.

Deuce checked his watch. If he called them in now, he'd have an hour to get her ready for movement.

He crumpled the tissue and stalked to the garbage can, tossing it into the trash before returning his attention to her. "I have a plan, but you'll have to listen."

"And why should I trust you?"

He gritted his teeth. Part of him respected her strength in dealing with the situation. She hadn't stopped fighting. Not when Alistair beat her nor when the bear had handed her over to Deuce to be raped.

"Elly, I'm gonna get you out of here. Alive and in better shape than you are now." He softened his tone. "I have a few friends, but I need you to trust me for a little while."

Deuce couldn't reveal his true mission, couldn't tell her that, based on information obtained from a rogue Ridgeville pride member, he'd infiltrated Freedom. He'd been undercover for ten months, monitoring the group from the inside and feeding intel to the council through his handler, Stone Redd. He'd managed to keep his nose pretty clean, but he couldn't see a sure-fire way to get his mate out of the mansion unharmed.

Unless he called in Stone.

A hard pounding on his door interrupted his borderline plea.

"Deuce, man, how's that pussy?" Alistair's voice boomed through the solid wood.

In two steps he was gripping Elly's shoulders. "Scream," he hissed.

"Wha—"

Damn it, he'd have to scare her, force her to give him the reaction he needed. He wrapped his hand around her throat and bared his teeth, driving the lion to lend his assistance. The beast balked at his demand and Deuce wrestled the cat into submission. Fangs burst from his gums and his fingers turned into deadly claws.

Elly's eyes widened and a bloodcurdling scream rose from her throat. "No!" She scratched his arm, true fear in her eyes, and she fought against him. "No!"

"Give it to her good, man."

Deuce released his hold, heart breaking as she crab walked across the bed and away from him. "Fuck off, asshole!"

A deep chuckle was the only response he received as he listened for anything, or anyone, else that may linger on the other side of the door.

Deuce returned his attention to the sweet squirrel and held up his hands, palms out, trying to show her he wasn't dangerous. "I needed him to believe I was hurting you. That's all. I didn't injure you, Elly. I scared you a little, but it was necessary."

He could see the trembles that traveled through her body, but couldn't do a damn thing about them. With a sigh, he let his shoulders slump. He'd fix this thing between them. Later. Like when he got her to safety.

"Alistair is going to come back. He's going to want to come in here and look for proof of our...encounter." He swallowed the bile that rose into his throat. "And I need you healed enough to move without agony."

"I'm not—"

He shook his head. "No, you're not. He pointed toward the small door on the other side of the room. Go into the bathroom, wash up, and shift. At least twice. I know it's gonna hurt." Carly had griped, more than once, about going from big curvy woman to little furry bunny. It wasn't an enjoyable experience. "But I need you in the best shape possible."

"What about..." The trembles had left her body and he took it as a sign she was beginning to trust him. Just a little.

318

But what about proof? He knew what she asked and the necessity sickened him. He needed the scent of sex to fill the room, the musky aroma of cum to permeate the air.

"I need at least…" He glanced at his watch. Any other day, with his mate so close, he'd get hard and come in less than a minute. But with danger looming over their heads? He wasn't sure he'd even be able to perform. "Give me fifteen minutes."

If he couldn't finish the job in that amount of time, it wasn't happening.

"Are you gonna…" She gestured toward his groin and he gave her a half smile.

"Yeah."

Pale pink tinged her cheeks, visible in spite of the purple spots coating her skin. "Oh."

"Go clean up." He stepped away from the bed, putting space between them, and she took advantage of the distance. She grunted but moved with surprising agility when making her way off the bed and into the bathroom.

He waited until the door closed with a low *snick* before turning his attention to his groin, particularly his soft cock.

Fuck.

*

Elly fought the tide of panic that had been running rampant through her from the moment Alistair had snatched her from her home in Colwich, West Virginia.

319

She knew why the leader had kidnapped her: her father was the colony's Alpha. But he was also the brother of a member of the council, which made her the council member's niece. From what she'd overheard, Freedom was trying to get the council to back off.

She'd been shuttled from Freedom location to Freedom location until they'd finally settled her at this mansion with Alistair.

Shit. Alistair McCain. A panic attack lurked at the edge of her consciousness, waiting to pounce the moment she eased her control. Pain, fucking agony, throbbed and pulsed in time with her heartbeat.

But she'd been strong. She'd fought her guards, the men who'd groped her when no one was looking. Oh, she'd ended up with a fat lip, black eye, and broken nose... God, she wished she could smell the air around her.

Terror had gripped her the moment she'd been captured, but her father's teachings and strength bolstered her the instant a gun touched her temple. His words had floated through her mind at that moment, the memory of him having knocked her down while they sparred.

There's fighting and there's dying. Martins die fighting. So get off your ass and hit me, damn it.

With the door standing between her and Deuce, she took a moment to breathe, to release a bit of the tension she'd been carrying. She leaned against the solid surface, letting her body slump against the wood. Part of her wanted to believe the lion, ached to put a little trust in him.

He hadn't touched her, raped her. He'd... Her heart skipped a beat. He'd lain on top of her, his hips pressed intimately against hers, and his hardness had been

320

unmistakable. But he hadn't pushed. He'd obviously quickly recognized his body's reaction to their closeness and then rolled from her.

What would he have done had he known her body responded to his?

Elly's pussy had warmed with his nearness, her body reacting to him, and she hadn't been able to figure out why. She'd been near hot guys before—shifters didn't exactly come in "ugly"—but it had been nothing like her response to Deuce. It'd been instantaneous, a blink, and she ached to rub all over him.

She pushed away from the door and pulled at her clothes, anxious to push her feelings aside. She needed to get clean and shift, and if Deuce was to be trusted, she'd soon be free.

Groaning, she tugged on her T-shirt and lifted it over her head, biting back a cry when her ribs protested. She knew what Deuce was doing out in his bedroom, knew the man was creating the scent of sex and cum.

He's jacking off. He's stroking himself until he comes and—

She wondered what he was thinking about. Her? He'd gotten hard when he'd lain atop her. Was he imagining her battered body? Maybe he pictured her bruise-free.

She pushed the thoughts from her mind and her inner squirrel chittered in agreement. The little beastie, for some reason, trusted Deuce and urged her to hurry things along so they could get back to the massive lion. Her squirrel was determined to scamper back into the man's presence.

Even with her fury, she'd recognized her attraction to him. She appreciated his barely constrained strength, piercing green eyes, and long dark hair. His body bore scars of past fights and more muscles than she'd ever seen.

But his beast would eat her as an appetizer. A crunchy little snack.

Divested of her clothes, she turned on the shower, and it only took a few brief moments to warm. Beneath the spray, her body lost some of its throbbing tension, water washing away dirty blood and some of the worry she'd been carrying.

A man intent on harm wouldn't have sent her to get clean and heal. He wouldn't have "handled" the issue of scent on his own.

She'd lend him a little trust. For now.

Before long, she stepped out of the shower, clean and anxious to shift and heal her body. Parts of her wouldn't be the same. She had no illusions her nose would suddenly straighten and be perfect once again with a shift or two. And she wasn't sure she'd ever want it corrected. The flaw would be a daily reminder of her strength. She hadn't given up, not once.

Refreshed from her shower, she stood before the mirror and cataloged her injuries. The nose was obvious, as well as the black eye and bruise on her jaw. The handprints on her throat weren't very pretty. A boot print—or four— peppered her ribs. There was another on her hip. A glance at her thighs revealed much of the same.

Well, she could always get a job as a punching bag.

Taking a deep breath, she called her squirrel forward, coaxed it into seizing control and changing her body to that of her animal. Her shift wasn't pretty, or painless, but it was a gift she hadn't ever regretted. Running through the forest, hopping from tree to tree and connecting with nature was priceless.

Painful pinpricks slithered over her skin. The crack and pop of bones filled the room. Her body reshaped, jabs of agony shooting through her as muscles shortened and molded to her new form.

The torture continued, the world growing while she shrank, and eventually she was eight inches tall. Panting, she lay on the bathroom carpet for a moment, catching her breath, begging for the strength to shift back to human. The difference between one hundred seventy-five pounds and five pounds was a lot. Now she had to do it in reverse.

She rested on her side and the residual hurt slowly eased from her body, the pain no longer plucking her nerves. She scented the air, disappointed her sense of smell was still on the fritz. Maybe she would have to get the break fixed.

She rolled to her feet, flicked her tail, and poked her squirrel—they had to get a move on. The little beast grumbled but relented control, allowed the shift to reverse itself. The crack and crunch of bone was different this time, limbs stretching and reaching as she returned to her five foot five inch height. Her breasts became bountiful once again; her hips spread wide and thighs filled out until her chunky frame reemerged.

Damn it. Every time she shifted, she prayed to come back the tiniest bit thinner.

The squirrel clicked and chittered as if saying "dream on." Little furry beyotch.

Elly needed to focus. She still had to repeat the process, growing a tail and then back again. A glance in the mirror revealed that most of her bruises were gone, but the ache in her ribs remained. Her nose was tender, and just like when she was shifted, her sniffer was out of commission.

Okay, once more.

She beckoned the squirrel closer, coaxing it to help her along once again, but a curse from the other room broke her concentration.

"Motherfucker." Deuce was growling. "Cooperate, damn it."

A heated blush overtook Elly's body. Was he having…trouble? No. She shook her head. No, he'd been perfectly hard when he'd been atop her, his thick cock pressed against her stomach. He shouldn't have problems—

"Fuck, fuck, fuck."

She wondered if fifteen minutes were up. Wondered if she should—

No. Just no. He'd been kind and promised to help her get free, but that wasn't reason enough to help things along. Guys had been jerking off alone for centuries. She was sure he could complete the job by his lonesome.

"Goddamn it." His growl was deeper, heavier, and sprinkled with a hint of animal.

Maybe he couldn't take care of it himself.

She nibbled her lower lip, surprised at the lack of pain, and wondered if she should go out there. She wouldn't sleep with him. But she could…something.

No. Could she?

Growls, grumbles, and groans reached her, frustration growing more and more prevalent in his sounds.

He wasn't doing it for the pleasure of the act; he was trying to help save her. She'd recognized the truth in his words. If Alistair returned and the scent of sex didn't hang heavy in the air, there'd be trouble.

She had to get touchy-feely with the enemy.

Or was he?

Elly didn't want to examine her feelings, didn't want to admit there was a chance he wasn't quite the foe he appeared to be.

Another growl came through the hollow wood and she pushed away her hesitation. She grabbed her clothes, yanking them on as fast as she could, and then rushed into the bedroom.

And froze.

Deuce was still dressed in his T-shirt and jeans, boots still tied to his feet. But his cock, his large, soft cock was in full view.

"Damn it, Elly. I said fifteen minutes." He propped his hands on his hips, apparently comfortable with his exposed dick. Well, she supposed, if she had a prick and it was that big, she would be pretty relaxed too.

She tore her gaze from his groin, forcing her squirrel to come along with her since the stupid thing wanted to keep ogling his package, and then waved toward his, uh, flagpole. "You haven't…"

A pale blush filled his cheeks. "No. You can't smell anything?"

"No." She licked her lips, glancing at his cock once again. Beneath her studying stare, his shaft twitched and thickened. "But, uh—" How did one go about offering *services?* "Um, with me here…" She gestured to his now half-hard cock. "You're uh, yeah."

This had been a mistake. It'd sounded wonderful behind closed doors, but in reality, she was so not this girl.

"Elly, for the love of god, please go back into the bathroom." He didn't sound angry. No, it was more desperate, needy.

"I-I want to help. Not all the way help, but a little." She glanced at his thick dick, length jutting from his jeans. "A little, not so little help."

"Elly, you can't… I don't… I'm saving you, damn it. I'm not about to molest you."

She took a step toward him and he sucked in a shallow breath, held it as she continued her approach. She made him hard and he needed to be hard to come, and he needed to come just in case…

Elly closed the distance between them until she was tucked against him, his arm over her shoulders. She reached for his straining erection and wrapped her fingers around his thickness. A soft hiss encouraged her and she tightened her fist for the barest of moments before beginning her illicit seduction.

It was wrong, wicked, and then somewhere in between. She shouldn't want to touch him, shouldn't want to give him pleasure, but she couldn't help herself. He'd scared her, but everything about her situation frightened her. Yet he'd done nothing *to* her, was actually trying to prevent intimacy.

That singular truth set her free. If it were any other time and place, she would have thanked god for his reaction to her presence. She decided to embrace the situation.

She slid her hand along his length, stroking his cock from base to tip and back again. On her next rise, she squeezed just below the head and ran her thumb over his slit, gathering the bead of moisture that'd formed there.

"Elly." The word was somewhere between a plea and a moan.

Elly did it again, down, up, squeeze, and stroke.

"Fuck, yes," he hissed, and a part of her liked that he responded in that way.

For her body was reacting to him. Her pussy heated once again, aching and moistening with a flutter of desire. She was torn between scorn and worry and longing.

But he was simply one of her captors.

Who's helping me escape.

She wouldn't dwell on her feelings. Getting him off was a necessity. Nothing else. She could examine her body's responses another day. Or rather, another night. Beneath the covers.

Using his sounds as a guide, she increased her pressure and pace, splitting her attention between the beautiful cock in her hand and his face. Pure pleasure coated his features, something between bliss and pain sliding over his expression as she jerked his dick.

Before long, Deuce's hips moved in tandem with her caress, compelling her to increase the force behind her ministrations. He upped the speed until he was fucking the circle of her fingers. The precum leaking from the tip of his cock lubricated his passage.

It was Deuce's words that made everything so much worse. The syllables that reached into her jeans and rubbed her mound, flicked her clit and sank deep into her core.

"Yes… Give it to me… Fuck your pussy… So deep… Take my cock…" He was panting, body heaving and jerking in an ever-increasing rhythm. "God, Elly… So hot and tight… Gonna come in your cunt… Gonna…"

Her pussy spasmed, the barest hint of an orgasm, and Deuce came on her hand. She imagined the musky scent of his release filling the air as his creamy cum spurted from his cock. His hips lurched and body shuddered as the last remnants of his climax slithered through him until he stood still, panting beside her.

Gingerly, she released his softening cock and held her cum-soaked hand away from her body. It'd been…something. And she wasn't quite ready to dissect her feelings. She didn't want to think of the tremors of her barely there orgasm when she'd heard her name on his lips and his desire to come in her… No. She wasn't thinking about it.

"Elly." His voice was strangled, full of remorse, and she shook her head. She refused to look at him, embarrassment leaching into her body now that all was said and done. "I'm sorry." Deuce left her side, snatched up a few tissues, and handed one over. "You can't wash your hands…"

She couldn't wash her hands because then his scent would be gone. Right.

Elly nodded, still not trusting her voice.

"I-I contacted my friends as soon as you went into the bathroom. They should be here in thirty minutes or so."

Thirty minutes? That meant she'd spent at least twenty with her hand on his cock, stroking and pleasuring him until he came.

She gulped and nodded. "Okay."

"Why don't you see if you can shift one more time?"

"Okay." She fled for the sanctuary of the bathroom.

*

Deuce crumpled the wet tissue in his hand, shuddering at the wet squish it made in his palm. Damn it. Shock had kept him immobile when she'd appeared, his protests dying on his lips when she approached, and then all thoughts simply fled at her first touch.

His mate had pleasured him, stroked him with her small delicate hand until he came all over them both.

God, now that all was said and done, he was sick to his stomach. Bile burned his throat and he pushed back the sour fluid. He couldn't believe their first encounter had been in a home owned by Freedom and done purely to keep her safe.

The wet tissue in his hand cooled and he remembered he had to spread the scent around the room, fill the space with their apparent fucking. He rumpled the bed, tearing the blanket and sheets from the mattress, and then rubbed the delicate paper over the fabric. He continued by knocking things over in the room, rubbing his drying cum on random spots.

A deep inhale confirmed that the air was permeated with his heavy musk.

He checked the wall clock. Ten minutes.

He'd broken his watch, popped the back, and destroyed the tracking device the moment she'd stepped into the bathroom. The council had several contingency plans and the watch was part of 'em. The only reason for the chip inside his watch to cease working was if he'd been found out, and then they'd bring his internal tracker into play, zero in on him, and send in the cavalry.

Another look. Eight minutes. Elly was still in the bathroom. Damn it.

He took a step toward her hideaway. He needed her prepped and ready to run as soon as the alarms sounded.

Only more pounding stalled his progress. "Deuce!"

Fuck. Alistair.

He stomped toward his door and wrenched the thing open, uncaring that his dick still hung in the breeze. "What?"

The bear's gaze drifted into his room, into the space showing evidence of a struggle, then encompassed his

330

body and finally returned to his face. "Good. You got it done. Where's the whore?"

He gritted his teeth and fought back the challenging snarl building within. "Bathroom. I didn't want her blood staining my shit."

"Smart." The leader nodded. "When you're done playing with her, send her on out to the living room. The other guys wanted to get a little taste and I promised—"

The alarm saved the bear's life. One more word and Deuce would have ended the man and damn the consequences.

The whirling whine of the siren assaulted his ears, the sudden blinking red lights near blinding him with their intensity.

From the corner of his eye, he watched his bathroom door open a crack.

No. Stay in there a moment longer, Elly.

He couldn't let Alistair see her healed and healthy. He couldn't arouse the man's suspicions.

The polar bear's roar shook the air, trembling vibrations traveling through the wood, and a half-shifted maw barked orders. "Fucking council. Keep her here. I won't have her taken."

With that, the still-transitioning male raced off, leaving him alone with his mate. He pushed the door closed and tucked his cock back into his jeans, ignoring the wet spots that remained.

Deuce reached for the emerging Elly and wrapped his fingers around her wrist. "Come on. Time to go."

331

A tug had her following him to the door and he wrenched it open. A peek down the hallway revealed that they were alone, the occasional shout and pounding of feet the only hints others had entered the mansion.

He moved into the barren area, one destination in mind.

Five doors down to the library. North corner.

They passed the main stairwell and a glance revealed the Freedom members and council soldiers engaged in battle on the first floor. He couldn't see Alistair, but the polar bear's roar was unmistakable.

Hopefully someone would kill the man.

With more speed than finesse, he yanked his mate after him, breaking into a jog as the library door came into view. A twist of a knob granted them entrance and he closed the door behind them. Hopefully no one observed them.

"Deuce?"

"Shh…" He kept them moving, racing past row after row of books and along the northern wall.

The click of the door had him pausing in his tracks, stilling, but then he picked up his pace. Someone had found them.

He skidded to a stop in the corner and tugged on books.

The Great Escape. Tom Sawyer. Huckleberry Finn.

One of the columns of books clicked, shifted, and then slid aside to reveal a darkened stairway. Movement from the corner of his eye drew his attention and Deuce turned his head.

The man before him had him freezing.

"I'll fucking kill you. You goddamned traitor!" Alistair McCain.

And he meant every word.

With a fierce shove, Deuce pushed Elly into the darkness and dived after her, hitting the pressure plate that would close the portal once again.

Snarls and roars of rage followed, but the door snicked closed, separating them from Alistair.

Rolling to his feet, he reached down and pulled Elly up. "Come on, time to go."

"Deuce?" Fear tinged her voice and he stopped long enough to give her his attention.

"I swear to you, Elly. I'm getting you to safety. On my life, I'll get you out of here." He pressed his hand to his chest, assuring her the only way he knew how. He'd die for the woman before him without hesitation.

Not waiting for her response, he turned his attention back to the descending stairs and led her into the pitch black. The noises of battle receded the farther they traveled and, eventually, the hallway dumped them into a massive room.

Dim lighting illuminated the space, giving Deuce the ability to avoid various boxes that littered the area.

In moments, a body separated from the shadows. "Deuce? Who's your friend?"

"Stone, this is Elly. Elly, this is my friend Stone. He's with the council and he's going to get you out of here."

A draft, gentle blowing air, stroked Deuce's back and he watched as tension jolted through his handler. "You didn't."

"Stone, you don't understand…"

"You wouldn't."

"Listen, she's my ma—" That was the last syllable that left his mouth. The final word he'd tried to voice before the butt of Stone's assault rifle collided with his head and sent him tumbling to the floor.

CHAPTER *two*

"Too bad there's not a lost and found for people." — Maya O'Connell, Prima of the Ridgeville Pride, who was missing one of the twins. If only she could tell them apart and knew who'd wandered off. Kidlet tattoos were in their future.

Elly had slept for twenty-four hours. Twenty-four. At least, that's what they'd told her.

Now, awake and fuzzy headed, she ached to slip back into unconsciousness. It was easier than facing her family.

Coffee cup in hand, she sat slumped in a cushioned chair, the scents of its previous occupants wafting over her. A sweating tiger, his fear clogging her nose, had been interrogated. Then a wolf.

She traced a watery stain on the left arm. Her mother's tears. She wondered what they'd told her mom as she sat in the comfy seat. Had she been informed of Elly's wounds? Her treatment? The fact that she still breathed?

Apparently it'd been iffy for a moment or two.

She remembered Deuce—gentle, gorgeous, careful Deuce... He'd saved her, dragged her from Freedom's hellacious clutches, and brought her to the council's soldiers. Stone, one of Deuce's supposed friends, had slammed the butt of his gun into Deuce's head and she recalled pouncing on the warrior, pummeling him with her fists.

He hadn't done anything *wrong*.

But then... Things got fuzzy. She'd been on top of the stranger and then...she wasn't. Searing pain blossomed in her side, her back, her thigh.

Pop, pop, pop.

She'd never forget that sound.

Elly hadn't been conscious of anything. They'd told her about the rest of the rescue. That they'd carried her through underground tunnels to a helicopter waiting a mile away, gotten her to a hospital, and then waited for her to awaken.

Now she was sitting in what she'd deemed the "what the fuck" room.

What the fuck are they doing?

What the fuck have they found?

What the fuck is Deuce?

Okay, that should be where the fuck is Deuce.

Deuce... Her squirrel chittered, the angry tone recognizable. Elly and her squirrel wanted their lion. He'd

336

saved her and he could damn well hold her hand. She'd held his dick, damn it. He could return the favor.

The only memory she snuggled tight against her chest was of the lion. He was her one and only bright spot during her time in hell.

The echoing sound of footsteps reached her. *Click-thump-click-thump.*

It was too heavy to be a woman, the rhythm wrong for high heels.

A man, then. A council member? Her uncle? Her father?

The doorknob turned, the latch releasing with a gentle slide of metal against metal. When the wood swung wide to reveal her visitor, recognition slammed through her. He was the one, the man who'd struck Deuce, the one she'd scratched and pummeled.

"Miss Martin." His voice was deep, deeper than any she'd ever heard. Then his scent enveloped her. The ability had returned when she'd awoken. The crooked ridge along the bridge of her nose remained, however. The nurse told her she'd fought when the doctors recommended fixing the break. "I'm Stone Redd." He reached out, something in his hand. "Here's my card. I'm—"

Yeah, she'd wanted to keep the imperfection. It reminded her of…

"Where's Deuce?"

Stone paused midmotion, a nearly imperceptible stutter, before going into action once again. He pushed the door closed and a low *click* signaled that the latch caught.

His scent drifted toward her, smelling of heavy forests and fresh rain. Gorilla. "He's fine. Recovering."

Liar. Lies stunk of rot and garbage, filling up a shifter's nose with the noxious fumes.

"When can I see him?"

Stone eased into a chair similar to hers, his seat opposite her position. Again with the stilling, and she imagined the gears of his mind tumbling while he picked a new lie. "Prisoners aren't generally allowed visitors. Especially their victims."

Victims. She was a victim, yes, but not Deuce's.

"I don't think you understand. Deuce never... He didn't—" Pain strangled her, choking her until it hurt to push words past her lips. How could they ever think he'd harm her?

"Ma'am, we have a therapist on staff. She specializes in rape cases and we have her on standby for you. Would you like me to get her?" Worry and anxiety replaced the stench of his lie.

"Rape?" Elly spat the word. "You think..."

Oh, god, *no*.

"Miss Martin, should I get the doctor? I don't want to traumatize you further. My questions can wait." The unease increased and Stone squirmed beneath her gaze. The big bad gorilla looked afraid of the squirrel.

It was almost funny. Almost.

"Deuce didn't... He never... I wasn't raped. Period. Now, where's Deuce?"

"I see. Perhaps it's best if you speak with the doc now. Maybe after you two talk we can continue our interview."

Elly shook her head. "No, I can tell you what happened, beginning to end, without someone here to hold my hand." She could. She would. And she wouldn't shed a single tear. She had to be strong, tough, if she was going to get Deuce's location out of the man. She had a feeling weakness wasn't going to convince them her lion hadn't done anything wrong.

Her lion?

The squirrel flicked her tail happily. Her little beastie wanted the man, ached to be in his presence once again, and she had to question her squirrel's response. They hadn't been able to scent Deuce, but she wondered...

"I'll make you a bargain, my story for Deuce."

Stone shook his head. "Ma'am, it's policy that victims aren't granted access to perpetrators. We've had some unfortunate incidents in the past. The information he has is too important for one of your family members to engage in vigilante justice."

"You don't understand." She gritted her teeth. "He. Didn't. Rape. Me. I wasn't raped. Period. I was beaten, bruised, and a bone or two was broken, but I wasn't—" She choked on the word. If it'd been anyone other than Deuce who'd won her in that card game, she had no doubt she'd have been violated. "I wasn't raped."

Stone eyed her, uncertainty clouding the air, and her heart sank. He had the look of a man who was immovable as a mountain. "Let's just start at the beginning and we'll see how the interview ends."

Elly kept her squirrel's snarl at bay. "Fine." She took a deep, cleansing breath. Stone plucked a tissue from the table and held it out to her. She waved it away. She wasn't going to cry. She had to do her best to convince the gorilla that she was fine. *Fine.* Or he'd never tell her where to find Deuce. Even if he was in jail, she wanted, needed, to see him.

See that he was whole and well and hers…

Letting her eyes drift closed, she opened the door to her memories, allowed them to rush forward.

"It was the seventeenth— What's today?"

"Twenty-eighth."

"Wow." She whispered the word. "Time flies when you're getting the shit beat out of you, huh?" She chuckled then, blinked her tears back. "Okay, the seventeenth. I'd gone to bed early. I was opening the library the next day." She waved a hand. "Anyway. I don't know how long I slept, but I woke up to the muzzle of a gun pressed against my forehead."

The powder clinging to the pistol had overwhelmed her senses.

"Metal's cold, you know? Chilly. So, a gun to the head, and I went with him. Quiet. It's very, very quiet when you're kidnapped. I'd never known that. It's like you suddenly can't hear anything but your heart and the man with the gun." An involuntary shiver overtook her. "I don't know how long I was in the car. An hour? It could have been five minutes."

"Could you recognize your kidnapper if you saw him again?"

She nodded. "I can describe every man that hit me. Every. One. That guy backhanded me when he took me out of the car. I think I struggled then. It'd finally occurred to me that there were no sirens blaring, no police chasing us. I was alone."

Alone until Deuce. Alone until he'd gotten her out of hell and then they'd taken him from her.

"What happened next?" Stone was writing on a notepad, a small recorder resting beside the pad of paper. Funny, she didn't remember him pulling that stuff out.

But it didn't matter. What mattered was getting through the retelling and then she'd see Deuce. She was convinced that if she just gave them what they wanted, they'd let her see the lion. She'd prove to them he was a good guy and her uncle could get him released and…

Elly spoke about the first house, then the next, and the next, and on and on until she got to when she'd met Deuce.

"You're lying." Stone's expression was understanding yet sad.

She shook her head. "No." She wasn't. She just didn't want to talk about what they'd shared. It'd been dirty, yet…yet not. "I'm not. Not really. I'm telling what I want to tell and the rest doesn't matter because I wasn't raped."

"Okay." He nodded with slow deliberation. "Maybe not raped, but sexually assaulted. Your situation left you vulnerable and he took advantage." He glanced at his notes. "I think I have enough for now. Let's get the doc in here and—"

Another shake of her head. "No, you don't understand. You don't *get* it. I want to see Deuce. Take me to him."

"I'll be right back."

Stone didn't return.

CHAPTER *three*

"There's listening and then there's listening. So, listen (not listen) and then do whatever the hell you want. What are they gonna do? Spank you? Wait, that might be fun…" — Maya O'Connell, Prima of the Ridgeville Pride, who isn't really listening.

One month later…

Deuce was an easygoing guy. Not the type of lion to gut first, ask questions later. That was Brute's job. The man, one of the Ridgeville Prima's guards, had become especially touchy since his mate, Elise, got pregnant.

No, Deuce wasn't quite that bad. At least, not until today.

He'd had enough.

Enough of the council's vague answers.

Enough of Stone dodging him and his calls. He'd practically chased the man across the country.

Deuce had been their do-boy—fed them information and had been in deep with Freedom for almost a year. And they kept giving him the runaround when it came to Elly.

Fuck. That.

Deuce stomped through the forest, following the path that had been worn into the ground from the constant comings and goings.

Ricker, Ridgeville pride member and ex-tracker for the council, had setup a training program in Ridgeville. With the increased aggression of Freedom and attacks from the Humans for Shifter Extermination, the Ridgeville Prime had agreed that males across the country needed to be trained in combat. The main training location was deep in Ridgeville's forest.

And luckily for Deuce, Ricker had a special guest instructor for the week: Stone Redd.

The grunts and groans from the grounds reached him. The low sounds spurred him on and he picked up his pace, breaking into an easy, loping jog.

Two hundred feet from the clearing, a familiar scent joined the trees around him.

"Deuce. What brings you here?" As if Ricker didn't know. The man had heard him ranting and raving for twenty-nine days, six hours, and fifty-four minutes. Damn, he hadn't seen Elly in a long time.

Had she even thought about him? He hadn't been able to get her out of his mind. His lion had been going bat-shit crazy, roaring, snarling, and even pouting while Deuce tried to get information on Elly. And no one was talking. He knew their opinion, knew they believed he'd assaulted her in some way, and not a one of them believed a single word he'd said to the contrary.

Ignoring Ricker's presence, Deuce didn't slow. Hell, he increased the pounding tempo of his booted feet hitting the dry leaves littering the forest floor.

"This isn't going to solve anything, man." Yeah, Ricker was trying to reason with him. Right.

Deuce rounded the last turn, pulling into a straightaway, and he put on more speed. His lion was more than willing to lend a hand, give him a boost, and sent him practically flying over the ground.

Distantly he heard Ricker, heard the tiger begging and pleading, but all Deuce recognized was rage. Rage at the council. Rage at Stone. The man had been his handler for ten months. Ten. Months. He'd gotten closer to the fucking gorilla than any other. Stone had been the only friendly face in a world of psychopaths and he couldn't give Deuce the benefit of the doubt.

Oh, the council "forgave" him for all of his actions while he was in Freedom. It was "understandable" and "necessary behavior to ensure his acceptance."

But they wouldn't tell him about Elly Martin. His mate. No, she was one of his "forgiven transgressions" and should be allowed to heal in privacy.

It seemed like he'd flown over the land, the heavy *thump* of his boots against the ground rolling into a single never-ending sound.

The path opened into the clearing and he spotted Stone among three trainees as they sparred.

It'd taken one hundred seventy-three rebuffs to get him to this point. One hundred seventy-three inquiries that had ended without any information about Elly brought him to the clearing.

He was going to beat the information out of Stone.

Deuce didn't slow, rage spurring his pace, and Stone turned to face him at his approach. The man's eyes widened slightly as recognition dawned. But the gorilla didn't have a chance to get out of the way. Not when he leaped at the man, going airborne and putting his size behind his blow. He flew through the air, fist pulled back, and then he brought it forward, his speed, weight, and muscle aiding the strike.

His fist collided with Stone's jaw, the *crack* echoing through the area. The gorilla stumbled, tumbling and then rising to one knee as he shook his head. Deuce rolled over the grass and then sprang to his feet, ready to take on the other man. The first strike had been a cheap shot, something to get Stone's attention. He'd have to fight the man in earnest now.

"Damn it, Deuce." Ricker skidded to a stop.

"Fuck off." He shook out his hand, knuckles throbbing. They hurt, but the pain was worth the discomfort. Especially considering Stone had a difficult time standing.

"You can't just kill my instructors," the tiger grumbled. Ricker sure had turned into a whiny shit since he'd mated.

"I've had enough, Ricker." The gorilla finally rose and Deuce stepped closer, arms up and hands balled into fists, ready to take on the other man. "Especially when this asshole is standing between me and my mate."

"Mate?" Ricker's surprise was evident.

346

But Deuce was distracted by Stone as black fur slithered from the man's skin, coating him in the proof of his beast.

"Good hit." The gorilla wiped a trail of blood from his chin and pushed to standing. "And we've discussed your supposed mate. You've done enough damage already. You've been pardoned for what you did to Elly. Leave it at that and move on, Deuce. If you keep pushing, someone's gonna push back."

The lion in him roared. It'd been a bit satisfied after hitting Stone. Yeah, he'd been aching to do that since the gorilla had slammed the butt of his gun into his head during the raid and knocked him out. He'd been trying to tell Stone about Elly, explain the circumstances and that she needed to be protected because she was his mate. All Stone had done was scent the sex surrounding them and sent him into dreamland.

Since then, Stone's word had been law when it came to the Elly "situation" and no one within the council or at headquarters would give him information.

Enough.

His beast rushed forward, pushing past the barriers Deuce erected and tossing his humanity aside. Fur sprouted in a jarring rush, gold coating his body in a tsunami of pale color. The crack and pop of bone filled his ears, mouth reshaping to a muzzle. His lion's fangs burst from his gums. He flexed his hands, and fingers shifted to claws, tipped in razor-sharp nails that he ached to dig into the gorilla's stomach.

He'd torture the man, force him to give Deuce the information he needed. He might even let him live. Maybe.

Stone formed his own set of fangs, just as deadly of the lion's. Muscles grew and bulged beneath Stone's midnight fur, giving the man his gorilla's power. Damn it. He hated Stone's upper-body strength. Approaching the man hand-to-hand might have been a mistake. He should have shot Stone with a tranquilizer dart and then tied him up, beat information out of him that way.

Stone rushed him, fangs bared, and struck out. Deuce managed to duck the attack and counter with a punch of his own, fist colliding with the other man's stomach.

It didn't slow the gorilla. Not when Stone went for Deuce's jaw and rocked his world.

Fucking gorillas were strong as hell.

His vision blurred, lights dancing before his eyes, but he managed to get a bit of his own back. A return punch to Stone's face was met with a lovely crunch and blood flowed from the gorilla's nose.

"Asshole." Stone took a step and swung, the hit connecting with Deuce's mouth.

He spit, the copper tang of his blood enraging the cat even more. "Tell me what I need to know and I won't fuck up more of that pretty face."

Stone roared, the deep baritone so different from a lion's sound of rage. "So you can rape her again?"

A haze of red covered Deuce, encircled him in a blanket of molten fury, and suddenly he and his beast were in perfect agreement: Stone wouldn't walk away. He'd suspected others believed he'd harmed Elly. And he wondered if they thought he'd raped her, but no one had said the words aloud.

The idea he'd harm any woman, let alone his mate, in such a way sent his ire rising to a breaking point.

Closed-fist strikes became open-handed swipes, nails grazing midnight fur and sinking into the flesh lurking beneath. Right, then left and right again. One-two-three, duck, left.

Stone countered, attempting to fight off Deuce's approach, but a strange wrath-induced calm had overtaken him. There was no pain, no ache or burn of the gorilla's strikes. No, there was simply red and his lion's desire to see more and more of the pretty fluid.

Dimly he heard shouts, saw others coming near, but he frightened them off. The kill was his, by right. The gorilla had challenged his honor, had been keeping him from his mate. The lion felt he should die and Deuce readily agreed. The man had held out this long, had reported his opinions to the council. It was Stone's fault Deuce wasn't with Elly.

All.

Left.

Stone's.

Right.

Fault.

Left.

Stone stumbled, falling to the ground, and Deuce saw his chance, saw the opportunity to level the gorilla once and for all. If he was dead, he couldn't...

The depth of his bloodlust eased, sliding and slipping away until it no longer existed. Colors returned to his vision, the burgundy haze ceasing to overshadow his sight, and the grass became green once again.

Deuce's lion receded, drawing back with a purr of contentment as the desire for the gorilla's death drifted away on the breeze. Which left him with a bloodied, near-dying Stone. And guilt.

He shook his head, wondering where this sudden calm came from, and the answer soon eased into his line of sight.

"Maddy." He barely recognized his voice, the deep timbre now grating against his nerves. Maddy. One of the pride's Sensitives. The woman held the power to delve into another's thoughts. And soothe a person's inner beast.

Another wave of calm overtook him.

"You okay, Deuce?"

He nodded.

"Good. Go ahead and get him to the doc, guys."

Blurred shapes eased toward Stone, moving as if through water when they went into action. And then he realized he was crying.

Crying.

Tears swam in his vision, blocking the reality of his actions from his gaze, but they couldn't be washed away. He'd almost killed Stone. And for what? Why? Frustration? He should have tried to talk to the man again, made him understand. Maybe if he'd…

A slap, the strike of a small hand against his cheek, jerked him from his regrets. "Stop it."

Damn, Maddy could hit for a girl.

"Madison…" Ricker's growl had him freezing.

Deuce had already tempted fate once that day in his fight with a much stronger gorilla. He wasn't about to take on a mated tiger.

"Oh, shut it." Maddy sure had taken the Prima's badass lessons to heart. "It's your fault and Stone's fault and the fucking council's fault we're standing here right now." Maddy growled. "And why?" The lioness lowered her voice, pretending to sound like her much larger mate. "'Because, Madison, this is council business and it's nothing to worry your pretty little head about. Get back to taking care of the bun in your oven.'" Then she hissed, baring her teeth at her advancing mate. "Well, *fuck* and *you*. Asshat."

The still-glaring Maddy stood between Deuce and the trainees as if she were a momma protecting her cub.

The others carted Stone away, the man conscious and growling but alive nonetheless. Relief coursed through him. If the gorilla was conscious, he'd probably live.

"Damn it, Madison." The tiger's jaw was clenched.

"Fuck you, Ricker." She said the words in the same tone as her mate's and Deuce couldn't hold back his smile. Ricker had bitten off more than he could chew when he mated the sometimes-sweet Sensitive. "It's my turn to talk and you are going to listen. Then you're going to tell Deuce what he wants to know or I'll dig into your head and take it."

Ricker's golden eyes narrowed. "You wouldn't dare."

"Try me, litter boy."

The blood on Deuce's body was beginning to dry on his still-present fur, the viscous fluid matting the hair, but he kept his mouth shut. He had too much guilt eating away at him. With Maddy's gentle touch, the rage at being separated from Elly had lessened and now he was left with the results of his actions. His heart hurt, beating an aching rhythm over what he'd done.

His knees went weak, the knowledge stealing his breath from his lungs, and he ached to go to his friend.

He'd nearly killed Stone.

Maddy turned toward him, smiling wide as she came to his side and clasped his hand, wrapping her dainty fingers around his blood-soaked paw. "You stop it too. It's as much their fault as it is yours. Albeit you're a little bloodier in sorting things out."

He quirked his lip. Yeah, "little" was an interesting way to describe things.

A low growl snared her attention and the tiny lioness bared her fangs, hissing at the big, bad ex-tracker. The man was twice her size, but that didn't intimidate her.

"You do not get to make a sound, jerkasaurus. I'm going to do what I've been begging to do since you told me about Deuce and you aren't gonna do shit. Wanna know why? Because I am the keeper of the vagina." Then she turned back to Deuce, smile wider than before. "Now, this won't hurt a bit. Mostly."

That was all the warning he received before Maddy used her powers to dig into his mind, and then he was thrust into the past. Thrown into his memories and forced to relive his brief time with Elly.

The card game.

His room.

His mate.

His plan.

His hand.

"Okay, we'll skip a tiny bit. That's a little too much information. Congratulations on the equipment, though. Nice size." Maddy's low murmur intruded on his internal movie. And her words were followed by a snarl from Ricker.

The alarms.

The rescue.

And then nothing.

Maddy ripped free of his mind and he stumbled, fighting to catch his balance while the small lioness verbally tore into her massive mate. "You men are the biggest, most fucknacious, assholicious jerkazoid fuckheads on the planet!"

"Now, Madison…" Ricker backed away from his raging woman.

The short lioness stomped her foot. "No. You were all wrong. *Wrong.* And too stupid to ask for help. Instead, you simply believed everyone else—true criminals—instead of your friend. And when I offered to read him to prove you were *wrong*, you said no because you men couldn't risk truly being *wrong*. Well, fuck you very much." A low, rumbling growl filled the space and Ricker backed away from Maddy. Hell, he did as well. The woman was freakishly scary.

"Madison—"

"Do you know where Elly is?"

"Now, Madison—"

"That means you do. You've got two seconds to tell Deuce where he can find his mate—the mate that he cared for and did everything he could to keep safe—or I will take it from you. And I won't be gentle, Ricker. I'll make it hurt in a very painful no-hard-on way." Madison believed him, and the relief made his knees weak.

"Mate?" Deuce didn't miss the surprise in Ricker's voice, as if the words were getting through to him.

"One, one thousand."

"Colwich, West Virginia."

He knew where she was and for the first time in twenty-nine days, seven hours, and eight minutes, he could breathe.

* * *

It'd been a month since her rescue and Elly still looked for Deuce everywhere she went. It didn't matter to her that she was in her Podunk of a hometown. Or that the lion would have to be insane to come to the territory of a council member's family, even if the council member was a squirrel.

She missed him, as fucked as that sounded. They'd spent over an hour together and she ached to be in his presence once again. Her squirrel was beyond pissed when the council had invaded. She'd watched one of the soldiers slam the butt of his assault rifle thingy into the side of Deuce's skull. Deuce had been demanding that she be taken care of. And for a moment, the man looked as if he was going to reassure Deuce. The stranger had tugged the lion close, mouth open, but quickly shoved the lion away and struck him. It'd been lights out for Deuce and three words from the unknown man had followed.

"You sicken me."

She'd tried to stick up for him, tried to tell anyone who'd listen that Deuce had taken care of her. Yes, he was part of Freedom, but… But, but, but…

Elly relaxed into the bench, enjoying the gentle wind that carried the park's scents to her. She ignored the essence of her guards. Her father and uncle had assigned her "protection." At least until Alistair had been apprehended and "dealt with." She translated that as until the polar bear had been cut into tiny pieces. But they'd told her he'd be taken care of.

She hoped it was sooner rather than later. She was tired of being followed around, tired of the pity she'd seen on her guards' faces whenever they looked at her. And damn tired of being afraid.

The flavors of fresh-cut grass, cool water from the fountain, and roses that snaked up the arbor teased her nose.

Her nose. She reached up and traced the crooked line of the bridge, the pad of her finger running over the slight bump indicating the break. It'd never straightened after her shifts and she hadn't worked up the nerve to voluntarily endure the pain of another break.

It served as a reminder. Not of her time in captivity, but of Deuce. Of his kind eyes, gentle hands, and worry over her comfort. Not to mention his strength, carved muscles, and the arousal that'd thrummed through her in his presence.

She couldn't get him out of her mind and she wished she'd gotten a hint of his scent instead of only his taste. The embarrassment over her actions burned her cheeks. She'd tasted him, just a little, when he sent her into the bathroom to shift again. She'd brought her fingers to her lips and let her tongue snake out to lap at the evidence of his release. A tiny bit.

The delicious, salty fluid slid over her taste buds and her squirrel had gone crazy inside her, demanding that she go back into the room and ferret out more. It shoved and poked at her, more aggressive than Elly had ever witnessed.

When she'd finally agreed to listen, finally allowed herself to trust in her beast's instincts, the alarm had sounded.

Elly coveted those memories, the feeling of him resting against her palm, the pleasure that coated his chiseled features, and the heady flavors of his essence.

Memories don't keep your bed warm or your body hot.

No, they didn't.

She needed to let the man go.

Maybe after she talked to Stone one more time. Stone Redd had been one of the soldiers who'd busted into the mansion and rescued her. He'd also been the man to knock Deuce out. But other than that, the man had been a friend. Of sorts. Mostly he'd deflected her whenever she'd asked about Deuce. She was gonna corner the man if it was the last thing she did. He could at least tell her if Deuce was alive.

She reached into her purse and tugged her cell phone free. From memory, she typed in Stone's number. She would have put it into her phone's address book, but that would have been too close to permanent. Having him on speed dial would have been like conceding defeat. She didn't need the man's number in the phone, not if he was going to tell her where to find Deuce. She'd never have to talk to the gorilla again once he told her what she wanted to hear.

Four rings and it went to voice mail. Like the other thirty-two times she'd called, one call for every day she'd missed seeing Deuce.

"This is Stone Redd. If you need immediate assistance, please dial zero now or leave a message…"

"Stone, it's Elly Martin calling about Deuce Karn. Can you please call me back? I need to know that he's okay. That he's not—" She swallowed past the lump in her throat. "That he's still alive. He didn't do what you said. I swear. The council is wrong and—"

The beep let her know she'd spoken too long. Again.

"Cat on the brain?"

Elly dropped her hand and jerked from her thoughts, raising her attention to face the person intruding on her lunch break.

357

Recognizing who stood before her, she glared at his smiling face. Sometimes she hated having brothers. Unfortunately, he was one of seven of the annoying things. "I have no idea what you're talking about, Joey."

"Uh-huh." He slumped on the bench beside her. "Pull the other one. Dad's worried because you're still asking questions about him."

Ignoring her brother, she picked up her forgotten sandwich, taking a nibble and enjoying the sweet flavors of the peanut butter and jelly. Maybe if she ignored him, he'd go away. This was her time, damn it. Her bit of normalcy that she'd snatched back from Freedom, and he was ruining it by intruding. It'd taken her two weeks to work up the courage to each her lunch in her favorite spot. Two weeks of panic attacks and fighting with her own mind.

She still hadn't managed to sleep in her bed overnight. Occasional naps, but most of the time she slept on the couch. Maybe if Deuce were at her side…

"You need to get past it, Elly-belly."

She clicked her teeth at him. She hated that nickname, the "endearment" she'd been saddled with when she was just a child and she'd been more "belly" than "Elly."

"You need to go fuck yourself." Couldn't people just let her *be*? She'd told her family about Deuce, even going so far as to beg her father to intervene on the man's behalf when it came time for his punishment.

It hadn't made a difference. They kept telling her to move on, release her worry and get back to living life. Forget about the man.

Her family was not touchy-feely. But they were men and she couldn't hold that against them.

Men endured captivity, healed from the physical wounds, and then pretended the rest had never happened. Men weren't nearly raped. Men didn't have to accept they weren't anywhere near a match for their captors. Men…were men.

But the pain lingered in Elly's heart. The terror caught her in the middle of the night.

"You've become a raging bitch since you got back."

She snorted. Nah, she'd finally found her balls. Back there in that room, scared for her life, she'd found 'em and put 'em to good use. She wasn't about to go backward now.

Plus, being a raging bitch helped her pretend everything was fine when she was in public. She could fall apart in the privacy of her own home. In the shower. Where her guards couldn't hear her sob.

"And you've always been an ass. Funny how that works." She took another bite of her sandwich, smiling when a group of frolicking kits scrambled atop the fountain wall and then one sweet girl tumbled into the water. Poor thing.

"Damn it, Eloise. Pay attention."

She quirked a brow. "Really? You think busting out with my real name is going to get me to listen? Try again, *Josiah*."

With a sigh, he leaned against her, dropping his head to her shoulder, and his familiar warm, woodsy scent drifted over. "You know we're all worried about you."

"And I'm worried about Deuce." She shrugged, but Joey was unwilling to be dislodged. "It's life. Y'all get to haul your worry around with your 'poor Elly' and boohoos. But it's nothing for you when you go to bed at night. It still lives in me and you guys don't get to dictate how I deal with things. You don't get to tell me what to do when it comes to this. Leave it. I love you, Mom and Dad, and the rest of the family. But if you keep pressing this every time we see each other, it's not gonna end well. Back off."

She said the words without malice, no hint of her anger and frustration tarnishing the syllables. It wasn't a threat, merely an FYI.

Another sigh, but at least he lifted his head from her shoulder. While she'd ended up short and plump like her mother, her brothers had taken after their father. That meant they all topped six feet and weighed over two hundred pounds.

"Fine. I'll talk to the gang." He pushed up from the bench. "But I'm not making any promises. Uncle Carl is telling Dad you're still calling. Which worries him. And that worries Mom. And that—"

"Sends you boys into a panic. What, did she start crying?"

"Yes, you little shit." The words were said without heat, a rueful smile on his lips, and she grinned in return.

"Okay." She gave him a mock salute. "Your duty has been done. You've asked me to quit, I said no, and now you've got your marching orders. You can safely tell everyone you tried your best, but your sister has turned into a stubborn bitch."

"Well, I wouldn't say bitch."

Elly quirked a brow. "You already did."

"Oh. Yeah."

She grabbed a potato chip and threw it at him, striking him in his chest. "Good-bye, Josiah."

Before she could jerk away, he ruffled her hair. "Bye, Eloise."

With that, her brother strolled away, hands stuffed in his pockets. He worried. Probably more than anyone else since he was only a year older than her.

But she couldn't fight their worry and couldn't guarantee them that she'd brush off her concern for Deuce. Hell, she should call a spade a spade. She was near obsessed with the bad-boy lion. True, they'd only spent a short time together, but she felt something more…just more.

With a sigh, she gathered her leftovers and stuffed it all back into her lunch cooler. Another hour over and it was time to get back to work. Not that she didn't enjoy her job. Being the small town's librarian gave her a chance to see everyone.

The old biddies came in the mornings with their knitting and sat around chatting as they held their book club meeting. Then the mid-afternoons brought Elly the children, squirrel kits and lion cubs who loved hearing stories and tearing the kid's section apart. The local pride and her colony lived in relative peace—there was no controlling drunk-ass men—and the town proper was a solid no growly zone.

The place didn't fall quiet until the teenagers showed up, those kids having learned enough to not cause trouble for

Elly or they'd find their happy asses outside the doors. Then they'd have to explain that to *their* parents.

Bag in hand, she traipsed across the park, enjoying the last few rays of sunshine until she was closed back up in her air-conditioned building.

Elly waltzed through the automatic doors and then got behind the counter, waving at her coworker as the woman ran past her. With a laugh, she settled at the front desk, ready to spend the next few minutes surrounded by quiet. Well, until the kits and cubs showed up to tear the place apart.

The heavy rumble of an engine destroyed the relative silence, but it was Miss O'Leary's gasp that drew Elly's attention. "Ma'am?"

The woman was ancient, a hundred if she was a day, and Elly always worried the lady would decide to keel over by the Stephen King section.

"I just can't believe it." Miss O'Leary shook her head, loose jowls swaying with the movement, and her gaze was focused on something in the street.

She wasn't going to tell the woman she looked like a basset hound. She wasn't. First it was because she'd been taught to respect her elders, and then because she doubted a lioness wanted to be thought of as a dog.

"Believe what?" Elly got up from her desk. It wasn't like the place was hopping with readers.

"That boy." She clucked her tongue. "Can't believe he's showing his face here after all these years."

She followed the old woman's line of sight and her gaze landed on a large man astride a motorcycle across the street. Clad entirely in black, the man had to be sweating up a storm. "Who?"

"That Karn Junior. He hasn't been in town for years. Left before your colony came and settled in Colwich. Sixteen years, maybe."

The man threw his leg over the bike and dismounted, straightening to his full height. Damn, he was big. Yeah, the leather added a little to his bulk, but it couldn't have been that much. He was probably caked in muscles when all that clothing was stripped away.

"Are you sure, Miss O'Leary?" The woman was blind as a bat.

"Of course I'm sure. I bounced that boy on my knee. I should hope I'd know him when I see him."

"He hasn't even turned around."

Miss O'Leary harrumphed.

With a roll of her eyes, Elly kept watching. She followed his movements, the smooth way he handled the heavy motorcycle, the ease with which he kicked out the stand and let it rest against the asphalt.

The actions, so effortless, so familiar. The stranger whipped off his helmet and set it on the back of the bike. Then he turned around, giving her an unobstructed view of his features.

"Deuce."

"That's it." She snapped her weathered fingers. "The boy never did like being called Junior and refused to answer to Little Karn. Told everyone he wanted to be called Deuce." Elly sensed the old woman's regard. "Didn't know you knew the Prime's son."

"Prime?" She swallowed, dread building in her chest.

"Of course, that's Karn Pierce's boy."

Karn Pierce. Right. The Colwich Prime, leader of the local pride, and biggest asshole known to man.

Lovely.

Deuce obviously didn't go by his real name with Freedom. He'd told her his name was Deuce Karn.

"Well, fuck." The words were out of her mouth before she could call them back.

"Oooh. Miss Martin said 'fuck.'" Elly recognized the high-pitched voice as belonging to one of her regular rug rats.

Double lovely.

CHAPTER *four*

"The words 'wait here' should always be taken as a suggestion because men really should know better than to try ordering women around. Especially if they don't wanna see their balls in glass jars."
— Maya O'Connell, Prima of the Ridgeville Pride and glass jar aficionado.

Deuce looked around his deceased grandmother's home, noting the thick layer of dust that littered every surface. If the woman had been alive, she would have whipped his ass from one end of the house to the other and back again.

He was back in his hometown. Back in Colwich. Back… He shook his head. He'd deal with his family later. Then again, it would probably be sooner than he hoped. The minute his father and brothers heard about his return, they'd be on his doorstep. He prayed Elly would still give him a chance after she learned about his past.

Everything had remained the same as the day his grandmother had died. Back then, he hadn't had the strength to touch a single thing. No, as soon as the funeral had ended, he'd left, unable to continue facing the past.

Another look around the place and he realized he wasn't going to get it all done in a day. Lugging the box of groceries through the entry and on toward the back of the house, he stopped in the kitchen. More dust.

He tugged on a nearby drawer and found his grandmother's stack of towels. A little musty, but mostly clean. He dusted a spot on the counter and settled the box on the cleared bit.

Now, on to the rest of the room. He needed a clean place to eat and a decent place to sleep. The remainder of the place could wait for tomorrow when he could find someone to get the home into shape. He wondered if there'd be anyone in town willing to step across the threshold.

Glancing down the hallway, Deuce noted his footprints in the dust he'd disturbed. He'd pay them a lot.

With a sigh, he got to work, tugging out another handful of towels and wetting a few in the sink. First he'd wipe away the bulk of the dust and then he'd get to sterilizing things with the antibacterial wipes he'd purchased. The scent would drive his lion crazy, but it couldn't be helped.

He couldn't bring his mate back to a filthy den.

He paused in the middle of wiping the counter. His mate. Damn. Until two days ago, he wasn't sure he'd ever see her again.

Eloise Adele Martin.

Elly to her family and friends.

Deuce's dick hardened in his leather pants. Memories of the feel of her small hand wrapped around his cock assaulted him. She was so tiny and perfect, snuggling against him as if she'd been made to stand at his side.

Then again, she had.

Thinking about Elly kept his mind occupied while he cleaned, surfaces shining by the time he'd worked through the small kitchen. The refrigerator was busy cooling, freezer lowering to the right temp so he could buy some perishable groceries in the morning. He couldn't live on instant noodles and warm soda.

At least in Colwich he wouldn't have to drink light beer along with the rest of the guys. He wouldn't drink at all. No uncomfortable discussions about drinking in the tiny town. Especially considering their opinion of him.

Deuce looked around and was satisfied with what he'd accomplished. It wasn't the best, but it'd do for now.

On to the bedroom.

Leaving the kitchen behind, he tromped up the stairs, noting their disrepair. He'd have to get a few guys in here to do some repairs as well. He hated that he'd let his grandmother's home fall into such poor shape.

Then again, he hadn't anticipated ever setting foot in the place again.

Halfway up the steps, the rough pounding of a fist against the front door grabbed his attention and he sighed. At least he'd gotten the kitchen squared away. He could always see if the bed-and-breakfast would rent him a room. He didn't think he'd get a chance to clean upstairs.

Deuce turned and retraced his steps, mentally preparing for the coming confrontation. His lion stretched and roared, letting him know the beast was right along with him. He'd been in town long enough for the gossips to get to work, and if he had to guess who he'd find on the other side of the front door…

He turned the knob and let the wood panel swing inward. "Dad."

His father looked old. Sure, the man had a lot of years on him, but his face was haggard, pale, and drawn, with more wrinkles than seemed possible. The once wide and powerful shoulders were slumped and narrower. Right along with the rest of him.

Of course, the barely concealed hate was still present. "Karn."

He despised that name. Almost as much as his father despised him. Huh. "What do you want?" There was no sense in being polite and pretending his appearance was a social call.

"You gone."

A movement behind his father drew Deuce's attention and he found his brothers pacing the front yard. "Uh-huh." He turned his gaze back to his dad. "How's it feel to want?"

"Listen here, you no good—"

"Piece of shit. Right. I got it." He nodded. The words weren't anything new. He would have thought the old man could come up with a few different names to call him over the years. "Thing is, this house belongs to me. Me. Not you, Eaves, or Felix. If Autumn—"

"Don't you say her name." His father took a step forward, yellowed teeth bared, and Deuce countered the move, flashing his fangs and letting his eyes yellow at the threat.

"You don't have the right to even think about her after what you did."

Pain tore through him at the memory, flashes and snippets of that night slipping through his mind. But the beast shoved them away, locked them back into the vault where they belonged.

He shook his head, breaking free of the pain. "I'm not leaving, Dad. I'll stay out of your way, won't go into your territory, but right, wrong, or indifferent, this is my house."

"I want you gone." His father's growl was low, threatening but weak.

Deuce's was not. His sound filled the entryway and spilled into the yard, rolling through the space with ease. The crunch and crack of bone from his partial shift followed until he was near bursting with muscle and power.

"And I said I wasn't leaving." The words were garbled but recognizable nonetheless.

"Are you trying to ruin what happiness she has?"

The question hit his heart, but he wasn't about to back down. He'd talk with Autumn himself. If his sister didn't want to see him, wanted to keep their secrets after all these years, so be it, but he'd hear the words from her mouth.

"Dad?" His brother Eaves' voice was deeper than he remembered and the power of his lion gave him the height and weight he'd been missing when Deuce left. "Someone's tearing down the road."

His father growled once, low and threatening, and Deuce's lion couldn't have cared less. He recognized he was

369

stronger than his dad and could take the man in a fight. He didn't want it heading there, but his father's hate of him ran bone deep.

A small four-door car whipped into his driveway and parked beside his father's truck, and then the driver was running. Right for him.

Her curves were as he remembered, lush and begging for his touch. Her long hair flowed behind her as she rapidly closed the distance between them, strands catching the afternoon light, almost glowing in the waning daylight. And that smile—he'd seen it once, at their rescue, and dreamed of it every night.

That smile was back.

Deuce's sweet squirrel had returned.

"Elly." Deuce's voice was gravelly and deep, reminding him of the threat that still remained on his porch. He turned his attention from his mate and glared at his father. "You need to leave."

His dad's attention wasn't on him, but on his squirrel. The old man snarled, baring those aged teeth once again, and Elly froze at the bottom of the porch steps. "Get out of here, *prey*."

Fuck no. He shoved his father aside and Deuce placed his body between his mate and his dad. "You will *never* speak that way to her again."

Golden fur coated him in a rippling wave and his fingers shifted into claws. The cat was pissed. Adrenaline pumped through his veins in a rapid *thump, thump, thump*. Flooding him with additional strength. No one would ever refer to his mate as prey. Ever.

His father glared at him, narrowing his dull yellow eyes, and spit on the ground at his feet. "Leave before it's too late, boy."

Deuce kept his gaze focused on his father and brothers, remaining bodily between them and Elly while they returned to his dad's truck and left his property. The cat remained alert even after their departure, tense and waiting to see if another threat would appear.

A small hand against his back sent a shiver down his spine and, as quickly as his lion had jumped to the fore, it retreated. With Elly's touch, relief and a soothing calm enveloped him.

"Deuce?" Her voice was timid, musical despite her worry, and he turned toward her, anxious to feel her in his arms once again.

The bruises were gone, purple no longer marring her delicate features. The bridge of her nose still had a tiny bend, residual effects of her break, and anger suffused him. Alistair had escaped during the raid, running with his brother and a few of his top supporters.

The subtle scent of honeysuckle wrapped around him in an arousing embrace and his cock throbbed, desperate for her warmth.

She was so damned beautiful. And so damned his.

He ached to touch her, feel her supple skin beneath his palms. But he'd wait. He wouldn't grab her. Not yet. Not when the air was still clouded by lies and—

"You're my mate." Awe tinged her voice and her chocolate eyes were wide in surprise. "You're mine."

371

*

"And you're mine." The words washed over her, consumed her with the truth.

She'd craved him for the last month, worried and wondered, unable to figure out why an hour spent with a stranger affected her so much.

And now she knew.

Elly ached to crawl into his arms, revel in the heated, woodsy scent that clung to his skin. Her squirrel chittered and danced inside her, thrilled at finding their other half while another part of her broke at the time they'd wasted apart. The council, Stone included, had brushed aside her inquiries and informed her that Deuce was no longer her concern. He'd be punished for his offenses against her. They hadn't cared when she told them there were no crimes.

She took a step forward, reaching out to him, anxious to touch him once again. "But... How... If you knew... Is it safe for you to be here?"

That worried her the most. Had he come to Colwich due to Freedom or her?

Deuce grimaced. "It's safe. And the rest is a long story."

He clasped her hand, twining their fingers. He tugged until she was pressed against him, snuggled tight with his arm draped over her shoulders.

She buried her face against his chest and inhaled, drew his natural flavors into her lungs. Desire snaked through her, crawling over her skin in a ghostly caress, and all she could think about was completing their mating. She wanted to sink her teeth into his skin, suck, nibble, and then claim him as hers. She couldn't wait to feel his fangs slide into her shoulder and mark her as belonging to him.

When he gripped her shoulders and nudged her back, she whimpered, body drawn to his like a magnet. She didn't want to let him go, didn't want there to be any space between them. She'd waited and waited...

Deuce glanced back at the house and then returned his attention to her, worry etched in his features. "We can't stay here tonight."

She raised her eyebrows. "Of course we can. It's your home and I'd prefer to do the whole mating thing in a bed." She peeked around him. "Unless you've got another house hidden somewhere." She paused, invitation to her bed on the tip of her tongue. "We could go to my place, but..."

"But they wouldn't be happy about their little squirrel mating with the town pariah." His lips quirked in a rueful smile.

"Probably not." She still wasn't sure what Deuce's great sin had been, but Miss O'Leary had made it clear that he was persona non grata in Colwich.

"And this place hasn't been cleaned in sixteen years. I hadn't planned on finding you until I could bring you back to a proper den." A frown marred his features and she reached up, brushed away the lines between his eyes.

"You've known all this time."

"Yes. The second you walked into my room."

"And you didn't say anything." Awe filled her at his level of control.

Deuce cupped her cheek, stroking her lower lip with his thumb, and his gaze bored into her. "I needed you safe. Your well-being came before anything else."

She pulled back and punched him in the arm, smiling at his wince. She doubted she'd really hurt the massive lion, but she was glad he at least attempted to look injured. "Took you long enough to come get me."

Pain flitted across his face. "I've been searching for you since the moment I regained consciousness. There are things you don't know. I'm not really with Freedom. I was undercover, and the council wouldn't give me any information and then Stone—"

"Stone? Stone Redd? He knew…" She'd take him at his word, at the truth ringing easily in his statement. It was the rest that irked her. She growled, an odd sound coming from a squirrel, but she growled nonetheless. "I'm gonna kill him."

Deuce leaned down, brushed his lips across hers in a chaste kiss, and she melted into a puddle of goo. Well, not really, but she couldn't feel her feet any longer.

"I almost did. Let's try getting a room at the B and B and then we can talk about things and mate." He pulled her tighter against him, pressed their fronts together, and she could feel the solid length of him against her. "Not necessarily in that order."

Elly snorted and rolled her eyes. "Yeah, yeah, come on, kitty. Grab your stuff and I'll follow you."

In minutes they were on their way, weaving through the slow traffic of the small town and then pulling into the parking lot of Rosie's Bed-and-Breakfast. The second Deuce's motorcycle quieted, he was at her door, holding it open for her as he helped her climb from her little car. He held a pair of saddlebags in his free hand. The moment she was on two feet, he tugged her into his arms, brushed another one of those shiver-inducing kisses across her mouth, and she let him take her weight.

Lord, if they ever truly kissed, she'd go up in flames. *Poof.* No more Elly.

"Come on, kit." He grabbed her hand and tugged her toward the large home that served as a vacation spot. The Victorian building was massive, boasting fifteen suites, two large sitting rooms, and a full formal dining room.

Arousal thrummed through her, growing with every step closer, the reality of what was to come pumping through her veins. Her inner beastie danced happily, bouncing around, tail twitching and flicking. The squirrel was beyond thrilled with their mate.

Deuce didn't hesitate to push open the front door and step into Rosie's, holding the door open for her to enter after him. His gaze swept the place and took in every detail.

The rhythmic click of high heels on solid wood announced someone approaching and her mate was quick to nudge her behind him.

She poked him in the back.

He reached around and squeezed her hand in warning.

This time she let her finger shift, just enough to transform her nails into sharp claws, and poked him again. Take that!

He simply tightened his hold.

Jerk. She got his need to shield her. Really. Mostly. Her father was the same way with her mother. Didn't mean she had to like his behavior.

The *click-clack* neared and then abruptly ended with a shuffle of feet. "Deuce Pierce?"

Rosie. Well, at least they'd been greeted by a friendly face.

"What the hell do you think you're doing here?"

Or not.

"My mate and I are here to rent a room for a few days…"

Yeah, Elly could see how they'd need at least a handful of days to take the edge off. Her body felt as if it were on fire with desire and she couldn't wait to have him deep within her, stretching and filling her pussy over and again.

"Mate?" Rosie's voice was filled with disbelief and Elly nudged Deuce aside.

"Hey, Rosie." She smiled wide, full of pride at being with Deuce.

Rosie took a step toward them, worry evident. "Elly. Did he kidnap you? Are you okay? I can call your family—"

Elly narrowed her eyes. What was with the people in the damned town? "No. He's my mate. My *mate*. Why would I want to be separated from him?"

Her friend licked her lips, gaze flicking to Deuce and then back to her. "Do you know what kind of man he is? He—"

She raised a hand and silenced the woman. "I know that he's a man who puts my safety above his own. I know that he was made for me. That's enough. Are you gonna rent us a suite or not? Because we can easily drive to the next town and—"

"No, no." Rosie stepped back and moved around the small counter nearby. "I've got a secluded room at the end of the hall with its own exterior entrance."

Exterior entrance. Right. Without a doubt, Rosie hoped that she and Deuce would avoid the main areas of the place.

Elly felt the tension in Deuce's body, his muscles strung as tight as a bow, and she ran her hand along his spine. She stroked him gently, silently urging him to calm as they waited for Rosie to complete their paperwork and hand over the key.

Thankfully, they didn't have to wait long. It looked like the woman wanted the two of them out of the lobby as soon as possible.

She had no problem with that since if people didn't start treating her mate better, Elly was going to go badass squirrel on them and gnaw at their Achilles tendons. Then, once she got them down, she'd go to town on their asshole-ish asses.

Nom, nom, nom...

As if able to read her thoughts, Deuce squeezed her hand to snare her attention. "Bloodthirsty thing, aren't you?"

Elly stuck out her tongue, transfixed as his eyes flared to a darkened gold and the scent of his heated arousal seared her.

377

"The room is this way." Rosie broke through their connection.

Deuce was the first to look away and then move, drawing her along in his wake as they traversed the interior of the bed-and-breakfast. Before long, they were standing in front of their assigned door, Rosie unlocking the room and then handing Deuce the key.

For a moment, Elly thought that'd be the end of things. Rosie would go on her way and they wouldn't see her for a while.

Only, the woman had to say something else. "This is a dry establishment. There will be no alcohol or drinking here."

Elly turned her attention to her mate, watched as his expression shifted from arousal to rage in an instant and then was replaced with a distant mask devoid of emotion. "Understood."

Worry churned in her belly, warring with anger at how Deuce's family, and now Rosie, treated her mate. She had no doubt there were things she didn't know about her lion, but she judged Deuce by his actions. And those actions, coupled with his assurances that all was not as it appeared, earned her unwavering trust and faith in him.

She didn't have all the details, but she couldn't imagine her other half would be some evil jerk looking to take over the world while hurting everyone on his way to the top.

The tension she'd just brushed away was back. It thrummed through him in barely perceptible vibrations and she squeezed his hand, letting him know that she was at his side. Always.

"Thanks, Rosie. We'll let you know if we need anything." Elly practically spat the words, more than ready to be alone with Deuce and away from the hostile, judgmental assholes.

She pushed open the door and dragged her mate into the space, thankful he slammed the entrance closed in their wake.

"Elly…" His voice held a mixture of sorrow, anger, and need, and she couldn't help but answer.

Elly rose to her tiptoes and wrapped her arms around his neck, forcing him to lower, and then she laid her lips against his. It wasn't gentle by any means. No, she needed to show him she didn't care, wasn't concerned in the least about the town's hostility, Stone Redd, Freedom, or the council. They were nothing compared to Deuce and Elly together.

She moaned against his lips. She slid her tongue into his mouth, lapping at the flavors hidden in his depths and groaning when he returned the caress. They tangled, searching, giving and taking as their kiss continued. Heat suffused her, slithering through her body, delicate roots of arousal increasing and spreading along her veins. Excitement surrounded her and she ached for Deuce's touch. Nothing mattered but him. Them.

Her pussy responded to his nearness, growing slick with evidence of her desire, and her clit throbbed with the need to be stroked. Her nipples hardened to sensitive nubs.

Elly wanted his hands, his mouth…everywhere.

Deuce's hands tightened around her, pulling her inexplicably closer, aligning them from chest to knees, and the evidence of his arousal was hard against her.

Groaning, he broke their kiss, slowing the erotic rhythm until their lips barely touched.

"Elly… There's so much I need to tell you before we do this."

She kissed him again, a gentle meeting meant to soothe rather than arouse. "I don't care about what you did with Freedom or why the hell the town thinks you're some kind of monster. I know you're a good man, Deuce. And nothing, *nothing,* in your past could make me turn away from you. So get over it and mate me already."

With a groan, he kissed her again, taking control and leading instead of being led. He delved into her mouth and she went along for the ride, enjoying his carnal possession, the tangle of their tongues and shared flavors. She moaned and writhed against him, pussy desperate for him, and having his thick, hard cock so close simply teased her even more.

Deuce's hands traveled south, moving past her lower back and then on to cup her ass, knead the globes, and sending further bits of growing ecstasy over her nerve endings.

Her squirrel nudged and prodded her, small nose poking at the back of Elly's mind, encouraging her to get on with the show already.

Apparently Deuce's lion had the same opinion. In the next breath, he held her ass tightly in his hands and then lifted her, urging her to wrap her legs around his waist. Elly did so willingly, reveling in the feeling of his thick cock nestled between her thighs, pressing intimately against her heated pussy.

"Mmm…" She used her new position, rocked against his thick length and let his shaft massage the juncture of her thighs. She cursed their clothing, furious that his leather and her jeans separated them.

She felt him move, every jarring step sending another nibble of arousal through her pussy. In a half dozen strides they paused, and then her world tilted and her back suddenly rested against the soft cushion of a bed.

Deuce growled against her lips. "Now I have you."

He trailed his lips along her jaw and skimmed her neck, yanking a blissful gasp from her chest. "You've had me from those first moments."

The words had him stilling, pulling back, and she whimpered at the loss. "In that hellhole?"

"In that hellhole, Deuce. When we were rescued and then every day while I harassed the council and Stone for your whereabouts. Every. Day. I didn't know you were my mate, but I wanted you." The words were nothing but the truth and she didn't hesitate to hand them over to him.

That had her lion growling, eyes darkening, and the seductive flavor of arousal surrounded them. It mixed with the salty musk of her cream and created the alluring scent of sex and need within the room.

"You're mine." He snarled the words, fangs now long and shining in the waning light.

Golden fur pushed through the pores on Deuce's arms, coating him with evidence of his inner beast. Those fingers that'd stroked her with such passion shifted until claws tipped each digit. And then he moved, bringing his hands to her shirt. She watched as those nails slid through the fabric with ease, exposing her to the room's cool air.

Self-consciousness speared through her. She had no doubt that he was attracted to her and they *were* mates, but would he still feel the same when presented with the proof of her curvy body? Clothes could mask some of her lovely lumps, but there was nothing to hide behind when she was nude.

"Goddamn, you're beautiful. So pretty and so mine."

Well, that answered that question.

Another slip of nails through cloth, and her bra parted, breasts easily bouncing from their bindings. He held her mounds in his palms, cupped them with those deadly hands. He traced the hardened nubs of her nipples with his callused thumbs, circling the sensitive buds and gently flicking them with his claws.

She arched into his touch, increasing the pressure and easing some of the ache growing within her. He eased farther onto the bed, sliding one of his thick thighs between her legs and nudging her pussy.

"Ooh, yes." She moaned and rocked against him, enjoying the pressure of his body against hers. She rolled her hips, reveling in the sensations that he evoked, soaking in the pleasure.

"That's it, kit. Take what you want." His voice was more animal than man and the deep vibrations plucked her nerves, slipping through her like molten lava and searing her from inside out.

Deuce pinched her nipples, adding the tiniest bite of pain to her increasing pleasure, and she gasped with the sensation. She moved against him, writhing, searching out more bits of ecstasy. Damn it, she wanted more. Her pussy throbbed with the need to be filled, spasming and practically begging for his cock, while her clit trembled and twitched within her wet folds.

"You smell so good. You're hot and slick for me, aren't you, my Elly?"

She whimpered. "Yes."

"Hmm…" His hands left her breasts and she whined, earning her a cocky smile from her soon-to-be mate. "Let's finish unwrapping you."

His claws came into play again, slicing her jeans, rending the fabric with ease. Then her panties suffered the same treatment until she was completely bared to his gaze, cool air wafting over her heated flesh.

"Gorgeous." He was focused on her center and she could feel the weight of his stare.

The urge to cover herself, slide her hands over her exposed breasts and pussy, roared through her but she pushed it back. A large part of her wondered what a gorgeous man would want with a chubby librarian, but his expression said it all. The lion was hungry. For her.

"Scoot back, kit." He nudged her, urging her farther onto the bed, and she complied, centering her body on the blanket and resting her back against the pile of decorative pillows.

"Perfect," her mate purred.

Deuce prodded her thighs apart, positioning her legs as he desired until she was spread before him. Her heart thundered in her chest, anxiety and desire battering against each other as she waited for his next touch.

It wasn't long in coming.

No, her still-clothed mate knelt between her thighs, bringing his face level with her exposed pussy.

He breathed deep and released the air with a moan. "Need."

Deuce leaned forward and nuzzled her inner thigh, his scruffy cheek scraping against her supple skin. His lips grazed and danced over her flesh, easing closer and closer to where she desired him the most.

Then… Then his tongue tapped her needy heat, slipping over the seam of her soaked pussy in a barely there caress.

"Yes, Deuce." She opened her legs farther, silently enticing him to continue his explorations.

He eased closer, palms sliding along her inner thighs until she felt his fingers play with her sex lips, stroking along the delicate aroused flesh. He teased her slit, massaged her labia, and then delved into her in teasing strokes. With every touch, he nudged her arousal higher, burning her from inside out. Up and down the seam, gathering her cream.

She watched as he pulled two digits into his mouth and sucked them clean. "Delicious, kit. Absolutely delicious."

His eyes blackened with need and, beneath her gaze, he leaned forward and brushed his tongue against the top of her slit. He teased and tormented, the delicate flutter taunting her with what could be.

Her clit twitched and throbbed, the promise of release so close yet so far. With the next lick, he eased fractionally closer to the bundle of nerves. The following teased the very tip of the nub. He slid over her pleasure spot and she cried out.

"There! There there there there…"

A chuckle rose from between her thighs. "Do you know how good you taste, kit? All hot, sweet, and salty for me." He lapped at her clit, the tip of his tongue finding the concentrated bunch of nerves with ease.

Lick. Lick. Flick flick flick. He repeated each caress, setting up a rhythm that her body craved. Her pussy clenched and spasmed, aching to be filled with his cock. She was desperate to feel him sliding in and out of her sodden sheath with an ever-increasing pace.

"Fuck, yes. Please, Deuce." She cupped her breasts, kneading her flesh and plucking her sensitive nipples. "Lick me."

Deuce growled in response, the vibrations traveling through her like lightning and settling around her pussy, setting off nerve endings. Now he truly focused, tongue tapping her clit in a steady rhythm, the constant pace easing her toward her release.

She pinched and plucked her nipples in time with his ministrations, drawing on the pleasure he created with his talented tongue.

Suddenly fingers stretched and filled her desperate pussy.

"Fuck, yes!" She rocked against his invasion, taking pleasure in his fingers.

"That's it, kit. Fuck yourself on my hand."

She snapped her teeth, her pleasure plummeting with the absence of his tongue. "Back to it, furball." She released one of her breasts long enough to snap her fingers. "Less talk, more tongue."

God, didn't men know to keep things going if she was gonna get to the finish line?

"Yes, ma'am." He chuckled and lapped at her clit with a long, lingering lick. "That better, mate?"

This time she bared her teeth at him.

He got back to business.

Score one for the squirrel!

Then she figured, fuck the squirrel. Especially when his fingers slid in and out of her wet hole, stroking her inner walls and dancing over her G-spot with unerring precision.

"Oh, that's it." She gasped, arched, and rocked against his hand.

Elly panted and moaned, following his every shift, thrust, and retreat, fighting for her release. The early tremors of her climax plucked her muscles, stealing her control, and she let the sensations wash over her.

Deuce growled against her, sending additional quakes of pleasure along her spine. Her pussy clenched and tightened on his fingers, milking him as she couldn't wait to milk his cock. She was desperate for his dick, that thick length filling her.

"God… Deuce…"

This time he snarled. His fingers pressed more insistently against her G-spot, his touch spilling molten ecstasy directly into her. Her heart stuttered, the muscle pounding against her ribs, and she couldn't catch her breath.

It was too big, too high, just...too much. Her pussy continued its rhythmic spasms around his thick fingers, his tongue still giving her immeasurable pleasure.

Her breasts were heavy in her palms, aching, and part of her wished his talented tongue was lapping at her nipples, teeth nibbling the hard nubbins. Then he scraped a fang over her clit and she was pretty damned thankful he remained between her thighs.

"Yes... There... Suuuckkk..." And he did just that, latching on to the bit of flesh and giving her exactly what she craved. That added sensation was enough to thrust her to her peak.

She arched and froze, hanging by a thread, and then she broke, the raging storm that had been building finally unleashed. Her body was no longer her own, but a tree bending with the wind, unable to do nothing but ride the gust of air as she rose higher and higher. The pleasure swelled, ebbed, and flowed around her until she was lost.

Deuce continued tormenting her, fingers never stilling, tongue continuing without fail. She sobbed and screamed, babbled and whined. It went on and on, her gasping for breath while she suffered through his ministrations.

No, not suffered. She gloried in his touch, snatching every bit of pleasure he handed over, and she never wanted it to end.

Well, until it became so much that it bordered on pain. She whimpered, jerked and twitched, shifted, and she couldn't decide if she wanted to get closer or farther away.

"Deuce…" She jolted, released her breasts, and clutched the comforter beneath her. *"Deuce…"*

He eased his attentions, bringing her down in gentle increments until his tongue simply rested against her aching clit, fingers still in her sheath. Finally, his mouth lifted completely and she met his eyes, saw the burgeoning emotion that mirrored her own.

"Deuce?"

He slipped his digits from her body and a residual spike of desire stabbed her. He rose to his elbows and leaned over her hips and nibbled her stomach, nipping her curved belly.

"Yes, kit?"

"I think I may kill you if you don't claim me now."

He quirked an eyebrow but remained silent.

"I'm not kidding. Really. Death and everything." Her squirrel was in complete agreement. That single orgasm wasn't nearly enough for her. No, she wanted his sharp teeth sinking into her flesh while his fat cock slid deep into her pussy.

"Of course." He nipped her. "Anything my mate wants."

"Right answer." She stretched and relaxed into the soft mattress beneath her. "Perfect answer."

Deuce hopped from the bed and then he was peeling away the layers of fabric and leather. During her captivity, she hadn't taken the time to truly appreciate his body. Not like she could now.

His jacket was dropped to the floor, leaving behind a tight, thin shirt that revealed all. It clung to his carved muscles and she held her breath as she waited for the hidden flesh to be exposed. She didn't have to wait long. The shirt disappeared in a rending and shredding of cloth and it drifted to the ground like broken petals on the breeze. She counted the lines of his abdomen, drooled at the thought of licking and tracing every one. Including those lovely dips at his hips, the contours that led to the Promised Land.

She licked her lips, her sated desire flaring back to life.

"See something you like, kit?" He hooked his thumbs into the waist of his leather pants.

Elly moaned and he smirked. Jerk.

Hot jerk.

But still a jerk.

Until he got back to undressing. He leaned down and flipped the buckles on his boots and his feet were bare in moments. Which left the slacks.

"Don't hurt the pants." She barely recognized her voice as words were pushed past her partially shifted teeth. Damn, her little beastie wanted him. Bad. Elly had to admit that she craved him just as much as the furball did.

He paused. "No?"

Elly licked her lips. "No. Definitely not."

His smirk turned into a wide, knowing smile and she couldn't have cared less. Not when he popped the button on his pants. Or when he lowered the zipper. Or even when the thick cock that had been teasing her sprang from its confines.

Elly was a lucky, lucky squirrel.

CHAPTER *five*

"The number one rule for sex is that gals get two for a man's one. If that ain't happening, he sucks in bed. Kick him out. Really. Just plant your foot on his ass and—" — Maya O'Connell, Prima of the Ridgeville Pride and a woman who needs to learn that talking about sex in front of twins is a no-no.

Deuce was a lucky, lucky lion.

God. Damn.

He stared at his mate, cataloged each and every dip and curve of her scrumptious body. Her skin was smooth and flawless, pale as milk. His mouth watered and he couldn't wait to taste the rest of her. Her cream had been like ambrosia and he had no doubt her skin would be just as sweet.

Elly still cradled her abundant breasts in her palms, as if holding them in offering. Her tapered waist led to her wide hips and he imagined her riding him while he gripped her, guiding her movements as she took her pleasure. He couldn't wait to have her thick thighs wrapped around his waist as he fucked her delicious pussy and claimed her.

The woman was a walking, talking temptation. And all for him.

His fangs lengthened further, pricking his lower lip, and the coppery tang of his blood slithered over his taste buds. Soon it'd be her blood coating his tongue as he claimed his sweet mate.

"Damn it, Deuce." Her words came out as a mixture of chitter and growl.

Maybe not so sweet.

He nudged his leathers past his hips and let them pool at his feet. A quick step and kick had him free of his clothing and nude before Elly, bared to her gaze. He wondered what she saw, how she felt when she looked at him. Did he please her?

He knew his body was honed and muscled. His job as a guard to Ridgeville's Prima required it. Then, when he'd gone on to Freedom, being one of the biggest and baddest was a necessity. But there were the scars...

Lines of burned, puckered flesh snaked across his chest and over his shoulder. Proof of his past and mistakes never forgotten. Added to those were claw marks, bites, and gashes he'd acquired while with Freedom. He'd had to fight his way to Alistair's side. And then fight to stay there.

All in all, it made for a rather patchwork body. When she stayed quiet, unease slithered through him.

The room was still, Elly's easing pants and his deep breaths the only sounds in the space. His gaze remained intent on her, searching for any hint as to her feelings. He wanted her more than air, but he needed her to ache for him. The fact they were mates couldn't be changed, but he needed her to return his desire.

"Gimme." She held her hands out, eyes sparkling as her gaze raked over his body.

Well, that answered his question.

Smirking, he brought his hands to his chest, let his callused palms run over his muscles, along his abdomen, and then pause at his cock. He cupped his balls with one hand, encircling his shaft with the other, and stroked himself from base to tip. Up and down, he tugged on his dick, taking a bit of pleasure as he teased his little squirrel.

"See something you like, kit?" He repeated the motion, pausing at the tip just long enough to press against his slit. He tightened his fist, the gentle pressure beneath the head giving him an added hint pleasure. Oh, he wanted to slide deep into Elly, but this snippet of teasing was a nice bit of additional foreplay.

"Yummy." Elly's pink tongue danced over her lips and he wanted to follow it into her mouth, taste her flavors once again. A single kiss wasn't enough. Hell, a million kisses wouldn't satisfy him.

Deuce rolled his balls and tugged on the sac, unwilling to come from his own touch. Not yet. Not until he was deep within her and filling her with his release.

Unable to wait a moment longer, he released his grip and crawled onto the bed to kneel between her spread legs. With his free hand, he traced her outer thigh, gripping her and encouraging her to wrap one leg around his waist.

"Ready for me, mate?"

Elly opened even further for him. "Yes. More than anything."

With care, he nestled the head of his cock against her wet heat, groaning when the opening of her pussy kissed and suckled the tip of his dick. Poised to take Elly, he leaned over her. With his weight braced on his hands, he lowered until only inches separated them.

Emotion, hints of love, and piles of caring slammed through him when he met her gaze. "This is forever, Elly. Forever mine."

Her features were filled with feelings that mirrored his. "And you'll be forever mine."

Deuce didn't wait then, didn't hesitate. He eased his cock into her waiting pussy, slid into her in a gentle thrust, spreading her slick heat. The silken velvet clutched him, caressing him the deeper he went, and he kept his focus on his mate. Waves of pleasure slipped across her features. Etchings of bliss, ecstasy, and joy overtook her with his possession.

She tightened around him, milking the first few inches of his cock with her snug pussy, and he groaned, dropping his forehead to rest against hers.

"Damn, baby. You're so tight. So wet for me." His breathing quickened, the insane urge to push into her until he was balls-deep nearly overwhelming him.

"And you're big and thick. Stretch me. Feels s'good." She moaned as he fed her more of his length, pushing deeper.

Inch by inch he filled her, enjoyed the snugness of her pussy, until his balls rested against the curve of her plump ass.

Elly brought her other leg up to wrap around his waist, holding him close, and he rocked against her, reveling in the tiny mewl that escaped her lips.

"Deuce…" She said his name with a whine.

He shifted his hips, ensuring he rubbed against her clit with his movements.

"Oh, god." She gasped.

He did it again, this time pulling out ever so slightly and then pushing in, thrust-rock-retreat-thrust-rock-retreat.

Elly met his every driving entrance, tilting her hips to receive him, panting with each slide of his cock within her sheath. The wet, lewd sounds of their sex mingled with the breathless puffs.

"More." The word was no more than a soft wheeze of air. "Need more."

"Anything." Deuce pushed up, put space between their upper bodies, and searched for better leverage.

He repositioned his hands, sinking his partially shifted claws into the soft mattress, and increased his pace, the length of his strokes. He slid out until the tip of his cock remained inside her pussy and he slammed back into her. The bed jolted and jerked with his thrusts. Each push into her tight cunt jiggled her body, sending her breasts bouncing. The lush mounds called to him, lured him until he couldn't help but lower his head.

His hips never slowed as he captured one of her turgid nipples, pulled the nub into his mouth, and flicked the tip. He suckled and nipped, toyed with her as he fucked her sweet pussy.

The musky scent of their sex filled the air and he drew in the flavors. It was the mingling essences of their bodies that proclaimed to one and all that they belonged together.

With every suck, her pussy tightened around him as if begging him to come deep within her. He ached for release, pleasure gathering and thrumming through his balls, extending to his cock. His dick twitched within her, the slick friction drawing his orgasm closer. He retreated and thrust forward once again, their hips meeting in sweaty, wet slaps of skin against skin.

Deuce scraped his fang over her nipple and was rewarded with her walls closing in on his dick in an undulating spasm. He repeated the caress, was gifted with another pleasure-inducing tightening.

His balls drew up high against him and he felt the pounding of his heart between his legs.

But he held on. He needed his mate to come with him, pull his release from his cock while he sank his fangs into her waiting flesh.

"S'good. Hot. Deuce."

Deuce released her nipple with a soft pop, smiling against her wet flesh when her tiny claw-tipped fingers fisted his hair. "No!"

"Shh, kit. I don't want this other nipple to get jealous."

Elly arched her back, pressing her other breast into his mouth. "Yes, yes, yes, yes!"

He captured her neglected nubbin and gifted it with the same treatment, nipping, sucking, and grazing it with his tongue. He moaned, convinced the nipple had a direct line to her pussy. With every pull, she tightened. With every nip, she rippled. And with every scrape, she fisted his cock and held on for dear life.

Deuce sucked hard, smiled against her mound when she screamed and arched into him, back bowed as babbled words filled the air. Her nails dug into his scalp and hints of his blood mixed with the scents of their sex.

He released her and pulled away, smiling at her wailing "no," and not bothering to grimace when she eased her grip and smacked his chest.

"Gonna come, kit. Fill you with my cum. Bite your pretty neck." He increased his pace, ignoring the sweat that gathered on his brow and dripped onto her luscious chest. "Want that, Elly? Want to be mine?"

"Fuck, yes. Yours. Forever. Need."

He gave her what she needed. What they needed. His thrusts came with more force, hips meeting with punishing drives that drew moans and groans from them both. She scratched and clawed him, leaving shallow furrows along his arms and shoulders, and he loved his wildcat. Er, squirrel. But it wasn't *love* love. Not yet. It was too soon. There was no way he could lo—

Her scream overwhelmed his thoughts, drew his focus, and then she was motionless beneath him. Her mouth hung open on a silent yell, body poised at the edge, and he slammed into her, working to shove her over the cliff so he could join her in ultimate bliss.

His balls were begging to release their burden, pleasure surrounding him, coursing through his veins, and his lion roared in protest. But he held back. He refused to seek his pleasure before her.

But it took one, two, three more thrusts, and her form became a mass of trembling spasms. Muscles twitched and tightened, pussy milking him to near pain, and he let go, let his body do as it desired. His hips jerked, jolting, and his climax overcame his almost iron-clad control.

He roared, lion refusing to be silenced as his orgasm cut through him. The cat pounced and shoved him over the edge, pleasure shooting along his spine, and his balls let go. His dick swelled within her sheath, pulsing against her walls, and wave after wave of his cum shot from the head of his cock. Right into her waiting pussy.

Another of her screams joined his, her climax going on and on as he rode his release.

Then it was time to strike, time to join them while the ecstasy still traveled through her.

He opened his mouth wide, fangs bared, and sank them into her waiting shoulder. He growled, moaned as the seductive flavor of her blood flowed over his tongue. He dug his teeth into her flesh, marking her as his for all to see.

She belonged to him now in an unbreakable bond. She couldn't change her mind. Not now. The truth couldn't separate them.

Deuce's balls continued to empty, cock pulsating until the pure pleasure bordered on pain, and he withdrew his teeth, lapping at the wound until it closed.

Still buried in her tight pussy, he pushed up until he could look into her satisfied face. She smiled at him, eyes glazed with passion.

Elly was his. Forever.

He stayed within her regardless of his softening cock, unwilling to leave her loving warmth.

There was that word again. The one he refused to acknowledge heedless of his true feelings.

"Hey." Her voice was soft, tremulous, and her eyes glistened with gathering tears.

Releasing the blanket, he reached up and wiped away a single droplet. "Hey, no crying, kit." He kissed away the next. "You can't regret it now. You're mine."

She shook her head. "No. Happy tears. Promise. Happy-happy." She smiled wide and pulled him toward her.

He didn't hesitate, opening to her when she forced their lips to meet. They shared a languorous kiss, mouths and tongues stroking and caressing without the heat of arousal marring the meeting.

With a final lap, she pulled away. "Very, very happy tears."

Satisfied with her words, the conviction that filled her tone, he eased from her, tugging her along as he settled on his back. He pulled until she lay half across his body, and her curves snuggled against him as he cuddled her close.

Elly sniffled and nuzzled him, rubbing her soft cheek against his chest, and already his cock showed signs of coming back to life.

Damn, he'd just been inside her and he wanted to crawl into her once again.

She slid her leg along his, her smooth skin caressing him until her knee nudged his dick. "Mmm…"

"Minx." He brushed a kiss across her temple.

"Squirrel." Elly smiled against his chest and he couldn't resist smacking her ass, eliciting a squeal from his mate.

"None of that. You tired me out, woman."

She snorted. "I doubt it."

"Hush." Deuce shifted her until she lay fully across him with her warm pussy nestled against his cock. "We haven't actually talked and we're gonna do it, damn it. There are things you need to know…"

"Uh-huh." She nibbled his chest, little teeth pinching and biting him, but not breaking skin.

He tried to keep going, tried to talk to his new mate. Really. But when she licked his nipple and then scraped her teeth across the nub, he couldn't think. The sensation went straight to his cock and then, well, his cock went straight. He'd never believed his nipples were sensitive, but her every touch went right to his dick.

"Elly." He meant her name to hold a warning tone, but it sounded more like a plea to his ears.

Since she giggled in response, he figured that's what she'd heard as well.

There went his big, bad reputation.

A zing of pain slid through his chest and a hiss burst from his lips before he could tamper down his reaction. When the scent of his blood hit the room, he didn't doubt that his mate had sliced through his skin. And damn if it didn't take his cock from half-hard to rocklike in an instant.

"Eloise…" Maybe her full name would deter her. He was going to confess all, explain the town's reaction to him and his time with Freedom. Really.

Then she wiggled. A simple shift of her hips. Yup, there went his brain, right down to his dick, and all he could think about was sinking into her once again. He hadn't had such a quick recovery time since he was a teen, but Elly drew him like no other.

She wiggled again and her belly caressed his length. She mumbled against his chest while alternating between licks and nips.

"Mine." Lick.

"Claim." Nip.

"Wanna." Nibble.

Elly continued slithering down his body, lips caressing him as she continued her southward journey. The soft skin of her belly and chest bathed him in a silken caress and he fought against the need to rock against her. He'd had his way with her, claimed her as he desired. It was only fair he gave her a turn.

Because he wanted her bite more than his next breath. So he'd "suffer" through her ministrations.

Elly traced his hips, dipping into the carved lines he'd worked like hell to achieve. Having a beast inside him didn't automatically translate to having a lean, muscled body. Based on her whimpering little moans as she nibbled him, his mate approved.

The closer she eased toward his cock, the harder he became, his dick long and thick and ready for whatever she'd give.

Her moist tongue neared the base of his shaft and his sex twitched, pulsing with need to feel her mouth on him. He forced himself to lie passive beneath her, his lion in full agreement while they waited to see how she'd torture them.

Low chittering clicks and growls came from his gorgeous mate, gentle licks slipping in between the sounds. Her delicate hands stroked his thighs, nails scraping his lightly furred skin, and he spread his legs wider, encouraging her exploration.

And she did.

Slowly she worked her way to the base of his shaft, lapping at his dick like a lollipop. He couldn't suppress the soul-deep moan that gathered in his chest. He gritted his teeth and fought the urge to thrust, move, and force her touch where he desired.

Deuce was rewarded when her gentle touches traveled up his shaft, searing him with the heat of her mouth. While she loved his shaft, her small hands explored him further, cupping his balls and encircling his length. The grip on his cock followed in the wake, stroking him as she tasted.

When Elly reached the tip he thought he'd go mad with need. His cat, content moments ago, snarled at him to take control, flip them, and slide back into her wet heat.

But this was her claiming. He'd taken what he desired and now it was time to give back.

For a little while.

All thoughts left. Elly's sweet bow-shaped mouth opened and that lovely pink tongue lapped at the head of his cock. The tiny droplet of precum that'd formed disappeared into her mouth and then she returned, moaning against the head of his dick.

"Yes, that's it, baby. Suck it." His claws dug into the bedding and he realized he'd owe Rosie a new mattress before they checked out.

Elly did as he asked, increased suction on the spongy tip of his shaft, suckling him and tracing the edge with her tongue. She licked and drew on the head, taking him farther and farther into her mouth. More and more of his cock disappeared into her moist cavern and he sank into the pleasure.

She played along the underside of his cock, tracing the sensitive vein and then teasing below the head. She rose and fell along his length, hand working in tandem as she stroked and sucked his dick. He managed to keep his hips still while she teased and tormented him.

She cupped and massaged his balls, stroking the sensitive flesh, rolling them in her hand and adding to his growing ecstasy with every touch.

"Yes. That's it, Elly. Take me. Claim me, kit." He ached for nothing more than to be marked, was more than happy to beg for her to sink her sharp teeth into his flesh.

Elly's pace increased, her sensuous slide turning into a rapid rise and fall. His balls hardened and rose against his body, pulsing with the need to release his cum, and she continued her tormenting caresses. Faster and faster she moved, the slide of her palm along his shaft made easier by her saliva until it almost felt as if he was snug in her pussy.

Almost.

Deuce's orgasm approached, thundered through him while she kept up her pleasurable torture. Up and down she traveled, shining locks fanned around him as she brought him toward ecstasy.

And still she continued. Pace upping with every breath until the bliss gathered and encircled his hips, joined in her ministrations, and it felt as if a million tiny hands stroked his cock. His dick twitched, pulsed, and grew within the circle of her fingers and the sudden rush of orgasm ran toward him.

"Elly…" He couldn't help but warn her. God, he was going to come, spill his seed within her waiting mouth, and the only thing better would have been to spend himself inside her slick pussy.

Elly moaned, the sound adding to his pleasure, and then his release was there, roaring through him like a lion racing through the savannah. He felt his dick twitch with the first string of cum, saw her lift her mouth from his cock, and the ecstasy was joined by a searing pain.

It rocketed through him, adding to the joyful release of his climax, increasing his enjoyment until he could barely see straight. The rapid stroking of his shaft was unending.

But nothing was better than seeing his sweet mate between his legs, her mouth pressed tight against his inner thigh, and the feeling of her razor sharp teeth buried in his flesh. She licked and sucked at the wound, drawing out his release, the pain multiplying the bliss tenfold.

Now the only thing he had to figure out was how the hell he could show off his mating mark. What could he do, drop trou in the middle of the street?

The rush of his orgasm eased and Elly slowed her ministrations, her touch easing until her hand cupped his spent cock. Her tongue brushed his new wound one last time and then she rested her cheek against his thigh. Her eyes sparkled with satisfaction as she stared at him, a sweet smile on her lips.

Fuck it. He was so proud of his mark, he'd walk naked down Main Street to show off her bite.

Even better, he'd take a picture of it and have the thing framed and hung in his house.

His house.

That brought reality crashing home. They really needed to talk. Really.

When she snaked out her tongue and lapped at his wound one last time he realized that talking was overrated. They could discuss things...tomorrow.

CHAPTER *Six*

"If the man can't stick around after a night o' nooky, fuck him. Not, like, fuck him again. More like a 'get the fuck outta my bed' thing." — Maya O'Connell, Prima of the Ridgeville Pride and woman who no longer wakes up alone. She has twins; they always manage to climb into bed at some point. It's Alex's fault, though. He's a pushover.

Elly woke with a moan, little aches and pains jolting through her as she stretched. A heavy weight across her middle reminded her of the man beside her.

Deuce.

Her mate.

Her forever.

She peeked over her shoulder, watched her lion sleep in the growing light in the room. While resting, he looked so sweet, so vulnerable. The lines of worry and pain didn't mar his features and she resolved to do whatever she could to ease some of his burden. She didn't doubt that much of his emotional hurt stemmed from the town, his family.

She'd fix him. Fix him and love him and...

A lump built in her throat and she swallowed past the bundle of feelings. Mating didn't mean auto-love, but she couldn't overlook the care he'd shown her, the way he'd tended for her both within Freedom and again once he'd found her. From what she'd gathered, Stone Redd had been keeping them apart. She wondered what her Deuce had done to get the gorilla to talk.

Elly hoped it'd been painful for the other man.

Like Stone-in-traction kind of pain.

Damn, the lion had made her a bloodthirsty herbivore.

Taking one last glance at her mate, she eased from beneath his arm, wiggled until she was able to roll from the bed.

A quick look around the room revealed that her clothes were in utter tatters, turned into scraps of fabric by Deuce's claws before they'd made love. Well, the first time, anyway. Her pussy was deliciously raw after their night of passion and she couldn't wait to have him within her once again. She wasn't sure she'd ever get tired of sharing her body with him.

"Hmm…" She let her eyes flutter closed, remembered that last time they'd come together. Him behind her, slamming into her as he told her how beautiful she was to him. How he loved her curves and he'd paddle her ass if she decided to go on a diet and try to become a twig. He wanted her as she was.

A low snort drew her attention and her growly lion snuggled her pillow close, nuzzling the soft, downy cushion.

How could she not love him?

The tempting scents of breakfast teased her and drew her toward the room's interior door. Sweet cantaloupe, watermelon, and berries called to her, beckoning her to venture into the common areas. She knew Rosie didn't want them downstairs. Well, not Deuce anyway.

For now, she'd do as the woman asked and head below alone. But if she and Deuce were going to live in Colwich—

Wait. Maybe they wouldn't. True, his family and hers called the small town home, but there was no reason the two of them had to stay. They could go anywhere. Her apartment was rented and she was pretty sure Granny Pierce's place had been empty for some time. Hell, until now, she hadn't believed the home was owned by anyone. It was just a landmark mentioned in directions for as long as Elly could remember.

"Go down Main, turn left on Jenkins, and then a right by old Granny Pierce's place. It's been sitting empty since…"

Shaking her head, she pushed aside thoughts of the future. Her only focus now needed to be her and Deuce and breakfast. Looking around the room, she hunted for something to wear and her gaze fell on her mate's saddlebag. A quick dig resulted in a folded, wrinkled shirt. She pulled it on and was satisfied that it'd cover her enough for the trip downstairs when the hem brushed her knees.

A snuffle and a moan drew her attention back to the bed and she met Deuce's sleepy gaze.

"Wh'r goin'?"

She padded back to him, lay across the mattress, and brought their lips together. They both had morning breath, so it didn't matter. She licked his lips and delved into him, gently tangling her tongue with his in a lazy meeting of mouths.

Her arousal thrummed in a low murmur over her skin, but this kiss wasn't a precursor to sex. It was easy and sweet. A soft good morning.

Until he shifted and managed to somehow wrap his arms around her waist and drag her to him.

"Much better," he mumbled against her lips and returned to their kiss. A lick here, a nibble there.

Her nipples pebbled within her borrowed shirt, pressing against the soft, worn cotton. She was tired and sore, but none of it mattered when he gave her this. It wasn't just lips and tongues interweaving. It was more. She felt the emotion that wafted toward her, the scent of attraction, deep feelings, wrapping around her in an embrace.

The emotions enveloped her, delved into her soul, and she returned them.

His hands wandered over her, sliding along her spine and moving to cup the plump mounds of her ass. He squeezed and kneaded, the shifting of flesh wrapping around her and traveling straight to her clit.

Deuce pulled from their kiss, chest heaving, and she mirrored his condition. Damn.

"You're mine, sweet Elly. My little kit." His words were a whisper, but she felt them down to her bones.

Elly nuzzled his jaw, continued her tender travels until her face was pressed tight against his neck, and she breathed deep. His scent was so strong, so hard and soft and soothing. She wanted to bathe in him roll in his flavors until they coated her from head to toe.

"Yours. And you're mine. Bit you." She nibbled his neck. "Claimed you."

Deuce chuckled, the rolling tenor sending shivers through her body. "Let's just hope no one wants to see the mark, kit."

She pulled away, faking a pout and pushing out her lower lip. "You don't want people to know you're mine?"

He smiled wide. "Never that. I just don't feel like dropping trou and nearly flashing my dick to everyone I meet." He leaned forward and nipped her lip. "Especially any women that question me. I *am* a hot commodity." He sobered. "Not here, but elsewhere. Here I'm—"

Elly placed two fingers against his lips. "Here doesn't matter. You. Me. We matter. They don't. And as for women, I'll nibble off important bits if they even think of touching you."

Her squirrel was in total agreement. She'd get over the taste of blood.

Deuce gave her a wicked grin. "Important bits? Does that mean I'll get to see you with another woman? That idea has merit…"

She rolled her eyes and smacked his chest. "Dork."

"Your dork."

Elly's stomach grumbled, keeping them from falling into a bout of mushiness. "Lemme go grab some breakfast from downstairs and then we can pick up where we left off."

He sighed and flopped onto the mattress. "Defeated by a bagel. What's the world coming to?"

She eased over and bit his nipple. "Nah, more like a chocolate muffin."

With a growl, he reached for her, but she jerked out of the way and danced toward the door. "Put some clothes on and, as soon as we finish eating, we can work on your grandmother's home. Get it livable while we figure out what to do with the rest of our lives."

She winked and dashed through the room's door. Then she was striding down the hallway, feet bare and not making a sound as she padded through the bed-and-breakfast. Quick as her squirrel, she'd dart in and out before anyone could catch sight of her. Well, maybe it would be more along the lines of "as quiet as her squirrel." She wasn't generally all that quick on two legs.

She tiptoed down the stairs, on the lookout for Rosie. Except she shouldn't have bothered since the woman met her at the base, and anger pinched her features. Elly stopped short, waiting for the woman to speak.

"I thought I made it clear I didn't want y'all down here." Venom filled her words and slapped Elly in the face.

"No, making it clear would have been you telling us you'd take our money, but you didn't want us stepping foot in the rest of your little establishment. This is a bed-and-*breakfast*, Rosie. Unless you feel like delivering, I'm going into that dining room and making up a plate for me and Deuce."

The woman stepped closer, eyes glittering, and Elly refused to back down from the weaker squirrel. Elly had her father's strength and she'd be damned if another in her colony would intimidate her.

"I don't want him here." The woman's voice was low and she hissed.

"And I want to scratch out your eyes because you're being a bitch, but I'm restraining myself." Elly's teeth pushed against her gums and lengthened, the squirrel super pissed at the confrontation.

"Do you know what kind of man you're hanging around with? He—"

"Is my mate, *juvenile*." If the woman wanted to act like an immature squirrel, Elly would call her one.

"You were telling the truth?" Horror covered Rosie's features.

"Yes, so I suggest—"

Rosie grabbed her hands, expression pleading. "He set his own sister on fire, Elly. *Fire*. The man is a drunk who almost killed family and his father kicked him out of the pride for it. He'll end up killing you."

Elly shook her head. No. No way would her mate do something like that. Never. She'd never believe Deuce could harm someone, especially his sister, in such a way.

She'd met Autumn, seen the woman limping through town, always smiling. The gentle female was a picture-perfect lioness. Deuce wouldn't, couldn't, hurt his own sister.

There was no question as to whether Autumn had suffered an injury long ago—her limp attested to some sort of accident no one ever discussed. But at Deuce's hands?

"No, you're wrong, Rosie. He's too gentle. I can't see him—"

Elly's defense was cut off by an earth-shaking roar that had the pictures on the walls vibrating, images rattling and bouncing against the drywall.

In her heart, she knew it was her mate. And he was pissed.

Abandoning Rosie, Elly spun and ran, breaking into a sprint as she raced to her mate's side. God, what had happened? Had the townsfolk decided Deuce should be punished for some supposed crime against his sister?

She recognized Deuce had at some point been involved in a fire. His scars attested to that fact.

A heavy thud reached her, the sound spurring her to run faster. Which wasn't saying much since Elly, jiggly butt and all, wasn't really a runner. She was not down with cardio and her body was making it known.

The thump was followed by silence and that worried her more than Deuce's echoing roar.

She skated around the corner and sprinted toward their room, worry and anxiety pumping through her veins. Adrenaline wove into the mix when she caught sight of the suite.

The place was a mess, bedside tables overturned, television broken on the carpet, and pictures hanging haphazardly on the wall. It looked as if a tornado had hit the place.

And there was no Deuce. The exterior door hung from its hinges and Elly raced forward, ignoring the slivers of pain that assaulted her feet from the broken glass littering the floor.

Deuce was gone.

She crashed into the stairway railing and then thumped down the stairs, soles stinging with each collision of her torn flesh against the mesh surface. She ignored the inconsequential aches.

The squeal of tires pulled her gaze to the edge of the small lot. She watched as a red truck swing around the corner of the building, flying out of sight.

But she'd seen enough. Just enough.

Elly spun, intent on chasing down the vehicle. She retraced her steps, tromping up the stairs only to have her way blocked by Rosie.

"What's going on, Elly?"

She shoved the squirrel aside. She didn't have *time*.

"Elly? What the hell happened here?"

Shoes, shoes, shoes...

"Eloise! Who's going to pay for all of this?"

Shoes! She tugged on her sneakers, wincing as the insoles collided with the bottoms of her feet. Didn't matter, though. Nothing mattered but getting to Deuce.

"Eloise Martin!" Rosie jumped in front of her, blocking her exit. "You can't just leave—"

415

Elly let a hint of her gathering rage seep from her control. She allowed her inner beast to come out and play just a bit. Her fingers re-formed into claws, nails razor-sharp and ready to do damage. Without hesitation, she wrapped a hand around Rosie's neck, squeezing until the woman squeaked. The tang of her blood permeated the air and she ignored Rosie's attempts to dislodge her.

"I need a gun." She pushed the words past her shifted teeth. The squirrel wanted to bite the other woman, hurt her for hindering them.

"I—"

She tightened her hold. "Two, actually."

"But—"

"And what ammo you have on hand." Her daddy had taught her to shoot—the daughter of a colony's Alpha needed to be able to protect herself—so she was a good shot. Her father had always told her to look twice, shoot once. But who knew how many she'd be facing?

It wasn't just the local pride Prime that had taken her mate. No, Elly's own daddy had been in the back of that truck while one of Deuce's brothers drove.

"Elly—"

Elly held the woman still and leaned close, baring her teeth before speaking. "Because of the town's ignorance and stupidity, my mate is in danger. Every business owner in Colwich has at least one gun. You have two because Bobby Lords sold you his Glock last week. I want both the shotgun and your handgun. Now." As an afterthought, she added one more item to her list. "And pants."

When Rosie nodded, Elly released her, followed the squirrel as she practically ran through the house and back to the front lobby, only stopping long enough to grab a pair of jeans. Thank goodness Rosie was as curvy as Elly.

In seconds Elly was in her car. Both guns were loaded, ready to go, and she tucked additional shotgun shells in one pocket and an extra mag for the handgun in the other.

She was getting her mate back come hell, high water, or blood. She knew, *knew*, deep in her heart there was more to the town's version of events. There had to be.

Elly tore out of the parking lot and raced along the back roads leading out of the town proper. Smooth asphalt led to dilapidated concrete and, eventually, hard-packed dirt. Her father wouldn't try to contain a lion in the family home in the center of town. They were headed to the pride house.

It took her a good twenty minutes, but she swung into the pride's driveway and she tore the hell out of the gravel while she sped toward the main building. The assholes had taken her *mate*. Her own family had run off with the man who belonged to her.

The squirrel was out for blood and wouldn't be satisfied with anything else.

By the time she slid to a stop in front of the steps, both her immediate family and Deuce's were gathered in the yard.

Without hesitating, she grabbed the shotgun in one hand and tucked the handgun in the waistband of her pants. She kicked her door open and jumped from her car. She leveled the gun at the main source of her rage, sure the lion was the instigator, and asked a simple question.

"You took Deuce. Don't bother to deny it. Now, tell me why shouldn't I kill you."

Burning fury turned Karn Pierce's body red and the man bared his wicked fangs.

"Eloise Adele Martin." Elly brushed away her father's shout. She had eyes for one man and one man only.

"I'm waiting, cat." She kept her tone even.

"Fucking *prey*." The Prime took a step forward and she pulled the trigger, shattering the lovely post to his right, turning the wood into kindling. Pretty.

The lion jerked and hissed at her, color rising higher.

"I'm waiting, cat."

A roar. Another stride forward. The next step on the stair exploded in a ball of concrete and dust. "Control your daughter, Martin!"

"The next one will cost you a knee, cat." She didn't let her gaze waver, didn't let a single person distract her. "Daddy, why don't you tell Mr. Pierce how good I am with this gun? Just on the off chance he thinks I'll miss."

Her father cleared his voice, the normal smooth tenor now wavering. "She's right. My girl looks twice, shoots once, and always hits her target, Pierce." He stuttered his next words. "M-m-maybe this wasn't such a good idea. Baby girl, we wanted to protect you from—"

"Daddy, if you don't wanna make Momma a widow, I'd shut your mouth." Fuck, the gun was getting heavy. "Now, give me my mate before I start putting holes in bodies."

"He's getting what he deserves." Karn spit on the ground, gob of saliva striking the step with a low thud.

"What have you done?" The lone woman's voice was enough to tempt her from her goal and she saw Autumn move toward her father. "Daddy, what have you *done?*"

"Now, baby girl…" While Karn hedged, one of Elly's brothers stepped into her line of sight.

"Elly-belly…"

"Joey." She spat his name. Her favorite brother turned traitor.

He must have seen the fury lurking in her eyes as he held up his hands, palms out. "I didn't know he was your mate, Elly. Dad didn't either. The Prime knew we weren't happy about your obsession with the lion and Karn wanted the man gone because of what he did to Autumn. We thought we'd help each other out. We can get him back. I know you're mad, but we can—"

Oh. Fuck. No.

"Mad? You think this is mad?" She shook her head. "No, this is beyond mad. But you'll see that soon enough."

Elly returned her focus to Karn, gave all of her attention to the Prime and his daughter.

"The boy ruined your life. Your grandmother protected him for a while, but he ran before he could suffer for it. It's late in coming, but he's getting what he deserves."

The color drained from Autumn's face, leaving her paler than death. "Oh my god. *Oh my god.*" Even from her spot

419

fifty feet away, Elly could see the lioness' tears. "You…
It's all my fault. It wasn't him! It was me. He didn't—"

One of the Pierce brothers came up behind Autumn,
stroking her shoulder, but the she-cat didn't let the touch
linger. She spun and shoved at the man, sending the lion
crashing against the side of the house. "What did you let
him do?"

Everyone's focus was on Autumn, Elly included, and she
felt like she dawdled at the edge of a cliff and simply a
gentle wind could push her over the brink. Emotion
charged the air, and it felt as if even nature held her breath.

Autumn returned her attention to her father, tears now
making tracks down her cheeks. "You and this fucking
town are so damned *stupid*. Do you think Deuce did this?"
The woman gestured to her leg. "That he went and got
shit-faced and then tried to drive a car with me in it? It
wasn't him; it was me. I went to that fucking party." She
shoved her dad. "I drank until I could barely walk and
decided to drive home. I skidded off the road and hit that
tree." She waved behind her. "Your prefect little sons?
They stood by and wrung their hands like little bitches
while Deuce pulled me out of a goddamned burning car!"

The Prime's face burned bright, eyes now golden, his lion
making its presence known.

"And then he took the blame. He decided he'd rather take
your anger, the town's scorn, than have you beat me once
I healed." Elly felt the heat of Autumn's hatred for her
father from where she stood. "Because that's what would
have happened, wouldn't it, Daddy dearest? You would
have beaten me to death, and Deuce knew it. You hit
Momma for burnt toast, so what would you have done to
me?"

420

The backhanded slap echoed through the air, the crack of flesh against flesh grating on her nerves. Autumn's head jerked to the side, nearly toppling her with the force of the blow, and Elly caught a flash of red dripping from her lip.

Then she moved without hesitation. She couldn't disable the Prime completely. No, she couldn't knowingly do that to the man no matter how much he deserved the pain. Instead, she lowered the shotgun and yanked the Glock from her jeans.

Look twice, shoot once.

And one was all it took. The *pop* rang in her ears and, beneath her gaze, a lovely spot of red blossomed on Karn's knee. The lion went down in a howl of pain, clutching his injury.

Elly ignored the sound.

"Autumn? Get the fuck in the car."

"Wha—" The woman's eyes were wide, face pale.

"Do you feel like being around when your father recovers?"

Autumn shook her head.

"Then you're coming with me." Elly turned the gun on her father. Her fucking *father*. Tears stung her eyes, but the moment Deuce's fangs had pierced her skin, he'd become her whole world. He was her family now. And the man who'd sired her had taken him away. "Where is he?"

Joey stepped toward her, drawing her gaze. "Elly, I can take you there. Let's get away from here and make a plan and we can get Deuce back."

"Back from where?" She heard the coldness in her voice and couldn't care less.

As Joey crafted his response, Autumn ran toward her car, limp slowing her progress, but the woman seemed determined to join her.

"Deuce's father had us turn him over to Freedom."

Elly shot out the Prime's other knee.

CHAPTER *seven*

"They say pain is weakness leaving the body. Fucker, pushing two babies the size of watermelons out of a hole the size of a lemon is not weakness. Why don't you try it? Here, I'll catch." — Maya O'Connell, Prima of the Ridgeville Pride. Yes, she loves her babies. No, she won't ever-never, you'd have to kill her first, have babies again.

A fist slammed into the side of his head and he almost smiled. The asses could beat him until he could barely walk, but he'd be walking out of their hideout without a doubt.

He had too much to live for now.

Poor Elly. His mate had to be panicking. He'd kill them for worrying his little squirrel.

Then he'd move on to his family. Or rather, his father. He hadn't been able to believe his eyes when Elly's dad and his own brothers came for him. Then the worst came crashing down when his dad showed up and took him to Alistair McCain, Freedom's leader.

And hadn't those two been buddy-buddy.

That'd been about two hours ago, the midday sun heating the interior of the house as more time passed. Yeah, his gentle female was probably crying her heart out and there was no one in town who'd stop to help her. Not when they found out it was him they'd be assisting.

The old lie still lay heavy in his stomach, but the sacrifice had been worth every moment of disapproval and hate he'd endured. Autumn wouldn't have lived through another round of their father's cruelty. But Deuce was a big boy, over eighteen, and could walk away once the "truth" came out about the accident, the fire.

Which was what he'd done. He'd moved into his grandmother's home, cared for her until she passed, and then left Colwich behind for good.

Until Elly…

Another fist to his temple, the strike knocking him to the ground, and a booted foot collided with his belly. He heaved, stomach rebelling against the treatment, and he spit blood and mucus onto the wooden floor.

Deuce didn't bother trying to sit up. They'd knock his ass down again. Dicks.

Alistair knelt beside him, his oily black hair falling forward until it made a greasy curtain around them. "I don't particularly care for traitors."

He smiled wide, exposing his fangs, not doubting his white teeth were covered in blood. "I don't particularly care for psychopathic assholes. So I think we're even."

The polar bear spit on him, the warm glob of saliva slid down his cheek, and he rose to his feet. "Gimme a knife. I wanna hear the kitty scream for me before I kill the traitor."

Deuce shook his head and laughed. Nah, he wasn't about to leave his Elly. "Traitor? Your own family doesn't believe in your cause, Alistair. How do you think I got in with you? You think I just happened to meet you in that bar? Or did your cousin Jenner send me?"

Rage mottled the bear's features. He needed the man to go into a destructive fury. He'd waste a good bit of time tearing apart the room and would leave Deuce alone for a while so he could cool off. He'd seen it more times than he could count during his stint with Freedom.

"It was smart to get your cousin into the Ridgeville pride. Real smart. But you probably didn't plan on him going bat-shit crazy over that Sensitive we stole back from you. Yeah, Elise mated to one of the Prime's guards and it sent him over the edge. He's had a good time in the council's jail. Gave us all kinds of secrets. Did you wonder why your dear cousin hadn't called in a while?"

Deuce saw the next strike coming and relaxed into the blow, let the pain flow over and through him, biting back the curse that flew to his lips.

"You lie."

"Do I?" His left eye had swelled shut, leaving him half blind. Didn't matter. He needed enough vision to get him to one of the cars in the back of the house. He hadn't trained with fucking Stone for nothing.

The crazed man stared down at him, eyes intent, and Deuce didn't hide a thing, let the bear see the truth in his eyes. Well, eye.

"Fuck!" Alistair spun on his heel and stomped from the room, slamming the door behind him, the low click of the lock resonating through the room.

At least he'd been left alone.

Deuce tugged at his bindings, the rope digging into his wrists as he fought the restraints. He could feel the fibers cutting into his flesh, the new rush of blood permeating the air, and he struggled to ignore the additional pain. It'd been part of his training before he went undercover with Freedom.

They taught him how to endure.

He withheld the groans and grunts that filled him, unwilling to draw the attention of any others in the house. He'd seen two more from Alistair's inner circle as well as the leader's half brother, Niall. Out of everyone he'd met, he'd liked Niall the most. Well, more like hated him the least. The man wasn't in Freedom by choice. No, he'd promised his dying mother he'd look after his younger brother. Only to have that vow damn him to life as an outlaw.

Deuce yanked against the twine, working at the rope and urging it to stretch. The skitter of nails on wood had him freezing, muscles tense and still.

Skitter-skitter. Stop. Skitter. Skitter-skitter. Stop.

The noise was too small to originate from one of Alistair's men. The man typically kept company with other larger shifters, carnivores that could easily destroy. No, this was much, much smaller.

Then a scent bowled over him, one he'd come to recognize, and his cat rushed at his control, fighting his internal bonds in an effort to escape.

Skitter-skitter.

Fluffy fur brushed his bound wrists, soft and delicate and Elly's.

He'd tan her ass for this. As soon as he got them clear of the house and to safety, he'd bend her over his knee and blister her bottom.

The rope around his wrists vibrated, was tugged and yanked on by his tiny mate, and he imagined her in her tiny squirrel form, gnawing at the cords.

Nibble, nibble, sneeze. Then more nibbling.

At one point, he was pretty sure she gagged. He couldn't blame her.

More tugging, biting, and fighting until he was able to flex and break the last shreds of his bindings.

Blood rushed into his arms, stinging pinpricks filling his hands while he stretched his muscles and worked feeling back into the blood-deprived extremities.

He pushed himself up, resting once he was vertical, and then he rolled to his feet, silent as he moved. No sense in drawing attention now.

Of course, there was still the squirrel.

His little mate sat on the ground, perched on her back legs, worried little frown on her squirrely features, and nose twitching as she scented the air. She darted toward the window and back to him—scramble, return, and scramble again.

Part of him ached to go through the room's door, tear apart the guards, and fight his way to Alistair.

But the other half of him realized his first plan had been to escape and get to Elly. He had his chance.

Tightening his lips, he made his decision, unwilling to risk recapture or, worse, them taking hold of Elly again. He nodded at his tiny mate, following her with silent steps.

As he approached the opened window, he spotted a handgun resting on the sill. At least his mate had come somewhat prepared. She scampered up the wall, gaining height with ease, until she was prepped to hop out the portal. She paused, waiting for him, and he kept his pace steady, silent.

Until he hit that board. That single board just about every room with wood floors held. The one that creaks.

Deuce stilled, foot planted, and his heart thundered as he prayed no one had heard the revealing sound.

Even Elly remained motionless on the windowsill, her small eyes wide.

Then it seemed the world exploded. The room's door burst inward, Alistair leading two of his men into the space, and Deuce centered himself for a fight. Escape was no longer his plan. No, now it was ensuring his squirrel got away.

Alistair was the first to attack, the first to land a blow to his midsection. One of the goons hit his knee, sending him to the floor.

Deuce returned the attacks, striking out as he was able, landing a few punches of his own while he regained his feet. The scent of the others' blood joined that of his own and he smiled when bones crunched beneath his fists.

Somehow he managed to knock the bigger of the two goons out, the man falling like a tree after a vicious hit.

That left him with one other guy and Alistair himself.

He could take them. Yeah, he bled from a dozen or more wounds, but he wasn't about to let them get their hands on Elly again.

Because as sure as the sun rose in the east, his mate was probably still sitting by the window and waiting for him.

A glance over his shoulder revealed he was right.

Her ass would be red for days. *Days.*

The distinctive click of the hammer being cocked went straight to his bones, chilling him from inside out. He turned and stared down the barrel of a revolver pointed right at him and inches from his head.

Things just got real.

Pure mad fury filled the polar bear's eyes and Deuce waited for the blow.

Deuce didn't fear death, didn't regret his life in the slightest. He'd sacrificed a lot for his sister, but it'd been out of love and she deserved a long life.

But if he died in this crappy room in this run-down house, he'd always regret not telling Elly how he felt about her. It didn't take years to love someone. Or months. Or weeks. Or days. No, it took three words.

"I'll kill you."

Alistair's finger tightened on the trigger. Deuce watched the end of his life draw nearer, and he prayed to every god he could think of that Elly would get away.

A thundering *boom* filled the small space and Deuce watched, transfixed, as Alistair McCain, leader of Freedom and the most evil man he'd ever encountered, fell to the ground in a heap. A dead heap.

Blood pooled beneath the lifeless body, the puddle growing with every millisecond. The remaining goon gaped, staring down at the man who'd led Freedom, and Deuce took advantage of the man's inattention. He balled up his fist and struck, knocking the guy out with a single blow.

Panting, adrenaline pumping through his veins, he turned toward his mate, his sweet, gentle squirrel, and simply stared at her.

She stood, naked as the day she was born, hair flowing around her shoulders and arms outstretched, gun in her hands. Her weapon was trained on Alistair's still body and Deuce eased toward her, wary of her reaction to taking another's life.

Instead of anguish or pain in her features, he saw only a mixture of anger with a hint of happiness.

Elly turned her head to look at him and gestured at the dead man with her gun. "Bring him back. I wanna do it again. Maybe shoot his dick off and let him bleed a bit before I decorate the wall with his brains." She stomped, distracting him with her bouncing breasts. "Damn it. Now."

The thunderous pounding of feet reached him and he snatched the gun from her hands, swung it around and aimed at the gaping doorway.

Niall McCain rounded the corner first and stopped short when he laid eyes on Deuce. Immediately he raised his hands, palms out.

"Deuce." The man's voice was cautious.

"Alistair is dead and I'm taking my mate out of here. You wanna come after me for it, that's fine. But right now, I'm going through that window and none of you are gonna stop me."

Niall nodded, gaze shifting to Alistair's immobile form and then back to him. "Okay. But you and yours are safe. I never agreed with what my brother was doing, Deuce. You know that. You tell the council."

He did. He knew. "Fine."

Deuce backed into Elly, shoving her through the window while he kept his gun trained on the men. The moment she was outside, he passed the weapon to her so she could keep them covered while he crawled out. He refused to turn his back on the house until they hit the woods and were out of sight, unwilling to allow any vulnerability.

A hundred feet into the forest, Deuce spun and hauled Elly against him, smashing his lips onto hers with a bruising force. His lion was raging, roaring at him to reclaim their mate and assure her well-being. She'd been in danger, vulnerable, and they hadn't been able to protect her. She'd been... And almost...

He shoved his tongue into her mouth, forcing his way inside her and taking what he desired. He licked and lapped, tasted her, relearned her flavors, and thanked god she was still there for him to touch. His cock hardened within his jeans, body heedless of the wounds he carried.

He had one thought: her. Elly was his world, his everything, and he'd almost lost his mate.

His squirrel leaned into him, pressed her body against his and opened for him. She surrendered and took what he forced upon her. He fisted her hair, tugged her head into position as he desired, searching for a way to deepen their kiss.

Her tongue dueled with his, languorous against his frantic need, and his mate clung to him, digging her small nails into his biceps. She whimpered and moaned, whined and writhed as if even being skin to skin wasn't enough.

The snap of a twig threw him from their kiss. Deuce raised his gun, zeroing in on the sound's source with unerring precision to find he held a gun on his own sister.

"Autumn?"

"Uh…" The lioness stared at the ground, cheeks pink. "Yeah, can we get going? I'm sure there are lots of bad guys and stuff, plus Joey said he's seriously 'tired of staring at my sister's junk.' Direct quote, so don't kill me."

"Joey Martin?" Deuce growled, but the gentle stroke of Elly's hand over his chest had him swallowing the sound.

"It's fine. We'll talk about it once we get to safety." His mate's voice was calm, soothing to his beast.

When she twined her fingers with his, he allowed her to lead him toward the nearby vehicle. He let her nudge him into the front seat and he watched her don one of his shirts and a pair of unfamiliar jeans.

She couldn't keep him from punching her brother, though.

The crunch of her brother's nose breaking did make him feel better.

It wasn't until the man brought his hands to his face, attempting to staunch the flow of blood, that Deuce noticed Joey's new jewelry.

"Elly, why is your brother handcuffed?"

Anger pinched his mate's features. "He was at your father's and knew what my dad and yours had planned. He offered to come along to help, but I don't trust him."

"I see." His rage had lowered to a simmering anger while he'd been held. "And Autumn?"

His sister was pale and he saw the faint tremors racking her body. "I told them, Deuce."

Deuce's heart stuttered and then thundered. "Told who what?"

"Everyone. Everything. Dad knows. Elly's family was there, so they do too." A grin eased some of the pain coating her expression. "Your mate shot out Daddy's knees."

Shock jolted him and he swung his gaze back to Elly, eyes wide and mouth hanging open. "She what?"

Elly shrugged. "It was only with a nine millimeter. It's not like he won't heal. I had a shotgun. He should be thankful I didn't hit him with *that*." She glanced at him and then returned her attention to the road. "I was *this close* to taking out your brothers, and mine, for going along with your father's plan, but I was worried about getting to you."

"You—"

"Took care of it. If I had enough bullets, I'd take on the whole fucking town. How could they believe—"Elly's knuckles went white as she gripped the steering wheel, claws now tipping her fingers. "I know we haven't known each other long, but even I know you never would have…"

Elly brought the car to a stop at the next intersection, sitting at the empty four-way stop. Taking advantage of the pause, he reached out and took her hand, swept away the tension.

"Elly?"

She turned to him, tears shimmering in her eyes.

"Do you have any idea how much I love you?"

She shook her head, denying him, and one of those salty droplets escaped.

He brushed it away, ignoring the pain that accompanied the gesture. "More than anything, I do."

A loud, obnoxious honk destroyed their embrace and his mate broke away with a gasp, pulling through the intersection and then on toward the center of town.

"Well, that was a great Kodak moment." Joey's nasally drawl made him want to hit the man again. "So, where are we going and when do I get to lose the handcuffs?"

Deuce voted for sending the squirrel to hell and never on the handcuffs.

He was overruled.

Damn it.

CHAPTER *eight*

"You should always have a freezer full of ice cream. You never know who's gonna stop by." — Maya O'Connell, Prima of the Ridgeville Pride and mad ice cream lover. Hard-core, fat kid-and-chocolate-cake kind of lover.

Where ended up being Autumn's home. They stopped off at Elly's to grab a few necessities, a couple of guns to add to his sister's collection. He wanted to be prepared in the event his father managed to turn the tide and gathered a posse while they figured out their next step. He could take care of himself in a fight, but a gun or two kept things from escalating that far.

Loaded up, they head to his sister's, where he was able to get clean and slide into some of the clothes left behind by his brothers.

He also attached Joey to the radiator in the living room.

The squirrel had not been happy.

Deuce didn't give a fuck.

And at least the man could keep an eye on the front of the house. Getting out of Colwich was a no-brainer. Deuce wasn't sure how the Ridgeville Prime, Alex, would feel about adding another lioness to his pride.

In the kitchen, he settled into one of the chairs and held a bag of frozen peas to his face. His body would heal more rapidly than a human's, but he wanted to hurry the process along with a cold compress. No sense in dealing with an eye swollen shut if he didn't have to.

Elly padded into the room and eased onto his lap, laying her head on his shoulder while she curled into him. He brushed a kiss across her temple and wrapped his arm around her waist, happier than he'd ever been. Even through the pain and heartache that plagued him, his joy shined through.

Autumn plopped into a nearby chair and turned her attention to the spread of weapons on the table. Methodically, she checked each one, popped out the magazines, filled those that could take a few more bullets, and prepped each for use.

Of course, the silence had to be broken by Elly's asshole brother. "Hey, can I get a beer or somethin'? If I've gotta sit around and wait for you to kick my ass, the least you could do is gimme a drink."

Autumn huffed and he knew his sister was about to lose her patience. "We've got water or tea."

"That's it?"

Beneath his gaze, the lioness' teeth elongated. "There is no alcohol in this house. Ever."

Joey's grumble floated toward them, but he answered. "Water, then."

The gun she'd been working on slammed against the wood table with a heavy *thunk* and his sister rose from her chair. Her movements were jerky and quick and then she was gone, stomping down the hallway with a glass of water in hand.

"No alcohol?" His mate's voice was soft, almost timid.

"No. Since then... None of the Pierce siblings drink."

"But... When you were with Freedom... I saw..." She snaked her arm across his body to rest against his other shoulder and nuzzled his neck.

"You saw me with what you thought was a can of ultra light beer." He shook his head. "It wasn't. It smells like beer, tastes like beer, but it's essentially water. No alcohol content. I drink it instead of getting questioned when I refuse to have a beer with the boys. They think light beer is pansy shit so they don't touch my stash and can't catch me in the lie." He shrugged. "It's a pain in the ass, but beats having to go over my history every time I decline. When I go to a bar, I'm the designated driver, but at home, I drink the other stuff. I just can't. Not after what happened to Autumn. She'd been at a party drinking and we'd followed her, saw firsthand what happened. I shouldn't have let her go to that damned party. Should have stopped her. Should have done *something* so that she wasn't covered in scars and walking with a limp."

"Oh." Silence descended, the quiet broken by the mumbling of his sister and Joey in the front of the house. As if she could sense his pain, she cupped his cheek and urged him to turn his head. Those beautiful brown eyes were locked on him and love filled his heart. "You are a good man, Deuce Pierce, and none of it was your fault. None. Bad shit happens to good people. People make

439

choices. Your sister is in the other room today, reaming my brother a new asshole, because you dragged her from a burning car and lied to cover it all up. If you don't stop beating yourself up over this, I'll kick your ass."

He grinned then, his heart already lighter with the depths of her love. "You and what army?"

Elly narrowed her eyes. "Fine, no nooky then."

Growling, he leaned forward and nibbled her neck, rubbing his scruff along her sensitive skin and nipping her. He let her giggles fill him and lift his heart. "You sure about that?"

"Uncle! Uncle!" He relented and Elly laid her head on his shoulder with a soft sigh. "So, we need a plan."

"I thought we'd—"

"Yo, lovebirds, we got company." Joey's voice cut off their conversation and he pushed Elly from his lap, helping her stand.

In a flash, they each had a gun in their hand and were heading toward the front of the house. Autumn dashed past them to the kitchen and quickly returned, also armed.

Elly was the first to reach a window, back resting against the wall while she peeked through the curtains. Deuce took up position near her, adrenaline pumping through him while he waited to see who'd decided to risk their lives with a visit.

Two SUVs were parked on either side of the driveway as a third screeched to a stop in front of the house. The recognizable sound of a door opening and then slamming shut reached him. That was followed by a voice he knew all too well.

"Damn it, woman. I told you to keep your ass in the car. The. Car." The roar from Alex, Ridgeville pride's Prime, preceded the appearance of his mate, Maya. The frisky lioness stomped around the SUV, skirting her snarling mate as she approached the house.

"Hello! Anyone home? The cavalry has arrived!"

"Damn it, woman!"

Maya stopped and faced Alex, hands on her hips. "You keep repeating yourself. Are you coming down with Alzheimer's? Already? I'll make you an appointment with—"

"Maya…"

Deuce knew that tone and pushed away from the wall, intent on getting to the couple before their "cavalry" mission got derailed by a blow-up argument. Those tended to end with sex. Wherever they happened to be at the time.

Deuce was not a voyeur.

"You guys stay here," he called over his shoulder while jogging toward the front door. Of course, Elly was hot on his tail. He'd remember to spank her for that later. At least Autumn stayed put. "What the hell are you guys doing here?"

Both of them shut it and turned toward him, Maya with a blinding smile and Alex with a frown.

With Deuce's appearance, others from the pride poured from the SUVs and they surrounded him and Elly, all talking at once.

Ricker grumped at his mate, Maddy, over jumping from the car before the area was "secure." The man was an ex-tracker for the council and had endured his fair share of encounters with Freedom and risky situations. Deuce didn't blame the man for bitching at his not so timid badass lioness. Maddy's frown meant the man wouldn't be enjoying his mate's attentions for a while.

Brute was losing a fighting battle with his little fox, Elise, as she kept jumping in front of him and he kept pushing her back. The man was more protective, and scary, than any other lion Deuce had ever met.

"I'm gonna bite you on the ass if you don't let me by." Elise's tiny growl was muffled but still audible.

"Promise?" Brute had the look of a well-mated man.

Neal's bunny mate, Carly, kept biting him.

"Okay, guys, let's—" Carly was cut off by Neal's hand slapping over her mouth.

She bit him.

"Carly."

"What? We should—"

Another muffling grip. Another bite.

"Woman." This time his voice was a whispered hiss. "Alex is the Prime. You are a bunny. You women need to let him

call the shots at some point before one of you ends up lunch."

That quieted the little rabbit. At least it seemed like the woman had enough of biting her lion.

Maya's two remaining unmated guards, Harding and Wyatt, stood at the back of the group, each holding one of the Prima's twins.

Only the Prima would bring her kids along on a mission that required the "cavalry."

Alex's roar cut through it all and everyone quieted. The Prime turned his attention to Deuce. "So, you look pretty free for a man who's been handed over to Freedom."

He smiled, ignoring the sting of pain from his split lip. "Yeah, I've mated a one-woman SWAT team." He glanced around the group. "Who called you guys?"

Maya wasn't silent for long. "Your sister. She gave us the deets—your dad is a dick, by the way, but Alex won't let me beat his ass—and directions. So, since you're all safe and sound, do you think she's got ice cream?"

Alex rolled his eyes and Deuce bit back his smile. "Not sure if she does or not, but you guys can come on in. Elly's brother is handcuffed to the radiator, but otherwise, it'll just be us and my sister."

Elise managed to wiggle past Brute. "Can I poke him with a stick?"

Deuce pinched his nose. In the short time he'd been away, he'd forgotten what it was like around the pride's women. "No, there is no poking with a stick. He did help a little with my rescue and I haven't figured out what to do with him yet." He shook his head. "Come on, you guys can grab something to eat and then get back on the road."

"We're not leaving." The four women spoke over each other and the men groaned. At some point, the men in the pride had handed their balls over to their mates.

Deuce included.

Their pronouncement set off another round of arguing and he sighed, pulled Elly into his arms, and rested his chin on her head.

"Are they always like this?" His mate whispered the words, but the males surrounding them answered anyway.

"Yes!"

Then they went back to arguing.

The only thing that stopped them was two more cars joining their little party in the yard.

One carried his mother and the other held a woman who looked like an older version of his mate.

Great. Mothers.

In a blink, babies were passed off, women were pushed back and told to keep their asses put unless they wanted a spanking. The males formed an impenetrable line before the approaching ladies.

Elly groaned and thumped her head against his chest. "My mother."

"Mine too."

"They look really pissed."

Deuce nodded. "Probably figured out what our dads got into."

The women's voices carried past the wall of men.

"I want my baby girl!"

"I want my son. Move aside. Don't make me turn you over my knee, young man."

"I will gnaw your dangly bits until not even god can bring 'em back."

Carly leaned toward Deuce. "I like that one. Can we keep her?"

Hell. His life was hell. Maybe they could find a shifter-free town and settle there. Nothing said he and Elly had to go back to Ridgeville. Nothing.

"Enough!" Alex's roar set off the car alarms, but it did quiet everyone. "We are going into the house—"

Maya raised her hand. "To have ice cream."

Alex's glare at Maya could have killed. "And will discuss what's been going on and decide where we're going from here." The Prime stepped aside and motioned their parents to precede him.

The moment the women scooted past Alex, Deuce and Elly were swept into a barrage of hugs, apologies, and promises of retribution against their respective fathers and brothers. When the mommas weren't happy, no one was happy.

The world became a volley of assurances, threats, and some downright vicious planning until Alex managed to wrangle them enough so they were on the way to Autumn's home.

The moment Elly's mother crossed the threshold of his sister's house, the woman stomped over to her handcuffed son and kicked him, sneaker-clad foot colliding with the man's hip.

"Momma!"

"Don't you 'Momma' me, boy. I brought you into this world and you better give me a damned good reason not to take you out of it. You tried to get your sister's mate killed. Killed! The one man made for her, and you and your brothers tried to take that away from her." Mrs. Martin leaned down and pointed her finger at her son. "I thought I raised you better."

"Can I poke him with a stick *now?*" Elise's question probably saved the male squirrel from his mother.

But it was Maddy's next words that stunned everyone to silence. "Did anyone else notice that the little squirrel is pregnant? Or is it just me? I guess she doesn't get to be a snack now, huh? That sucks."

Deuce froze for a moment, shock holding him immobile, and he turned toward his mate. "Pregnant? And you came in after me?"

Alex cut in. "If it makes you feel better, Maya challenged a tigress when she was carrying the twins. Obviously those two made it into the world okay."

"Did you beat her ass black and blue?" Deuce had visions of spanking Elly until she couldn't sit for a week. He was already upset with her over coming into the house, but pregnant… Even if she hadn't known at the time, it was still a huge risk.

"No," Maya harrumphed. "It was really red though."

Elly looked at him with wide, faux innocent eyes. "Um, I love you?"

"And I love you. But you'll still get a spanking."

"You wouldn't want to hurt the baby—"

Maya again. "Oh no, spankings don't hurt the little ones. Promise."

The announcement of the baby—damn, a *baby*—elicited another round of hugs and snuggles.

Eventually lions, squirrels, fox, and single rabbit got settled in the living room. Deuce was able to expand on the happenings since he'd left Ridgeville and by the time he was done, the mothers were in tears.

The two women glanced at each other, apparently communicating without words, and then turned to Deuce and Elly.

"I left your father." Their voices were a chorus.

Before either of them could comment, Joey butted in. "Mom? Wha—"

Mrs. Martin raised her hand to silence her son. "No. The man I mated wouldn't have done what he did. That man may have said he didn't agree with his daughter's choice, but he wouldn't have had her mate hauled off and delivered to Freedom. Never."

"Mom, we didn't know that's what Karn planned. We just wanted... You know he—"

The older squirrel narrowed her eyes and gave Joey a hair-singeing stare. "You know Karn Pierce is a son of a bitch—beg your pardon, Mrs. Pierce—and you know what the man is capable of doing. The person you *don't* know is Deuce and you went ahead and got stupid because of some rumors from dumbassed backwoods assholes. Well, you can keep on listening to them without me. I'm done with all you boys and your father. When you stop wearing your ass like a hat, you can call me. I'll be living in Ridgeville."

"Uh..." Deuce wasn't sure what to say about that.

"Me too. I know your brothers have protected Autumn all these years at your expense. I don't agree with it, but I accept it. But it's time I got out from under him." His mother jerked her head in a quick nod. "He tried to kill my baby. I've put up with a lot of abuse from that man, but my baby..." Tears glistened in his mother's eyes, but she brushed them away.

Heart pounding, he turned to Alex, question on the tip of his tongue. "Prime?"

When in doubt, go formal.

Alex pinched the bridge of his nose and Deuce recognized the lion's growing frustration. He'd come to the small town to save Deuce and was ending up with two extra squirrels and two more lionesses. He didn't envy the man.

"Fine. Get everyone packed up and moved. For now, until we can have the ceremony at the next run, you're welcome in the pride." Deuce allowed his gaze to flick to his mate's mother and then back at Alex. "Yeah, even if she is a squirrel, she can join us. We'll just warn the pride that squirrels are now off their list o' munchables. They'll be pissed though. First rabbits, then foxes, and now squirrels. I swear to god, if anyone mates a deer, we're going to be in trouble."

CHAPTER *nine*

"Naked in a room full of shifters is okay. Boinking in a room full of shifters is creepy." — Maya O'Connell, Prima of the Ridgeville Pride, and woman who has been tempted by creepy. What? Alex is hot with a capital "do me."

Elly looked around the clearing, eyes alighting on the group of shifters. Fuck, gathered lions... Well, and the lone fox. Elly, her mother, and Carly were the only veggie lovers in attendance.

Eep.

"And then I poked him with a stick! Elise wanted to, but I got there first." Carly's voice broke into Elly's worries and she turned her attention back to the circle of women. And the veggie platter.

She took a moment to observe the ladies, focus going from the Prima, Maya, and on to the two pride Sensitives, Maddy and Elise. Then there was Carly, a generally snarky, occasionally bloodthirsty, and insanely loyal rabbit. The cluster was rounded out by Gina, a lioness who'd lived a difficult life. She was still getting over Jenner, a lion who'd betrayed the pride and was Alistair McCain's cousin. *Was* being the operative word.

451

Alistair man was dead. And she was glad.

But the nightmares…

In those, she hadn't shifted fast enough, hadn't transformed from four feet to two and killed Freedom's leader. The terror consumed her in her sleep more nights than not and Deuce talked of her going to a therapist to work through everything.

Not that Ridgeville had one, but Alex told her the council would give her whatever she needed in thanks for her actions.

She was being thanked for killing someone.

"I kicked him." Maddy's triumphant shout drew her and she smiled.

Elly had heard the story of Maddy's transformation from doormat to badass.

"And almost broke your toe." Maya snorted.

"Pft on you." Maddy again, blowing a raspberry at the Prima.

Which was another thing Elly was trying to get used to. Everyone was so laid-back with the leaders. They were respectful when it was needed, but otherwise, the Prime and Prima were like any other couple.

And that was pretty cool.

Smiling, Elly returned her attention to the clearing, scanning the area and hunting for her mate. Deuce had been so good with her, always attentive and quick to meet her needs now that they knew of her pregnancy. She hoped he'd calm down a little as the months passed.

She found him on the opposite side, standing in a huddle with Maya's guards. Their heads were bowed and she made a mental note to ask him about the conversation when the run was over. They looked so serious.

"Oh, look, Stone can walk again." Carly's voice held more than a hint of über bitch.

At the mention of the gorilla's name, Elly turned toward the approaching male. When she'd first been rescued, he'd been helpful and caring during a time it was needed most. Then he'd done his damnedest to keep her and Deuce apart.

Forgetting any consequences, she marched right up to the man, cocked her arm back, and let her fist fly. She aimed for the man's face and was pretty damn happy when blood flowed from the man's nose.

"Damn it, Elly." He cupped his face, eyes darkening to black.

Whatever.

"Your mate already put me in traction." His voice was muffled behind his hands.

"Really?" She brightened at the idea Deuce had taken out some of his anger on the gorilla. "How did I not know this?"

Maya tapped her on the shoulder. "Not that I'm not opposed to beating up a man for no reason, but is there a reason?"

Elly crossed her arms over her chest. "Yes. He—"

"Aw, Elly, take pity on a guy. Deuce kept it to himself. Can't you do the same?"

Carly stepped forward. "He kept what to himself? You mean Deuce was the one who kicked your ass?" The rabbit turned to Maya. "Alex told Neal that Stone had gotten attacked by one of the council enemies."

"Uh, yeah, that's what Ricker said too." Maddy added to the conversation, but something didn't ring true in the woman's words.

They all turned to stare at Stone and the gorilla held up his hands, palms out. "Don't look at me. I did some stupid shit that hurt Deuce and Elly, but your men are the ones who did the lying."

"They lied." Maya's voice was a low growl and the woman spun on her heel. She stomped across the clearing and straight for her mate, the rest of the women trailing in her wake.

Stone, nose no longer bleeding, moved to stand next to her. "I should find another pride."

The second Maya reached the group of men, she began yelling, arms waving, and Alex backed away from his mate.

Elly nodded. "Yes, you should find another pride."

"Damn." He paused. "Do you think you and Deuce will get around to forgiving me or should I get used to broken bones and bruises?"

454

She sighed. "If he already kicked your ass and put you in the hospital, I suppose I can get over it. I'd refrain from lying in the future, though."

From the corner of her eye, she watched him rub the bridge of his nose and smile when a loud yell floated toward them. "Yeah, I see that."

They stood in silence, watching the women, Gina included, tear into the group of men. It seemed like forever before Deuce made his way toward her, smile in place.

His gaze shifted to the man beside her and his grin turned into a thunderous frown. In a half dozen strides, he was at her side, nudging her until he separated her and Stone.

"Need something, monkey?"

Elly peeked around her overprotective mate.

Stone rubbed his head, running a hand through his midnight-black hair. "No, man. Just wanted to apologize to Elly. You know I didn't mean to keep you two apart. I thought—"

"You thought…" Deuce took a deep breath and let it out slowly. Over the past two weeks, he'd been dealing with so much stress with their families he'd taken to counting to ten when he got pissed. Elly secretly believed he should up it to one hundred, but kept her lips zipped. "I'm moving past it. There are more important things in life than dwelling on what can't be changed." She nudged her way beneath his arm and leaned against him, smiling when his free hand settled on her still-flat stomach.

"I know, man, congratulations." Stone's words rang with sincerity. Silence descended, only broken when the gorilla took his leave. "Well, you guys have a good run. I'm gonna head on out and get on my way to Georgia."

With that, the man strolled away, hips rolling in an easy gait, and Elly turned to her mate. "Why's he headed to Georgia? I thought he was helping Ricker train here."

Deuce shook his head. "Not anymore. Alistair's brother, Niall, contacted the council. The man still holds his brother's beliefs about how shifters should live. He doesn't think we should be bound by prides, packs, or any other shifter collectives. He still thinks being forced into a group or facing charges isn't right. But he never agreed with Alistair's actions. He told the council of a compound in Georgia where quite a few women have been held, most of whom are Sensitives."

Her mate paused and she let his words sink in. Sensitives. Those women held a power that was meant to be used to benefit shifters. But Elly knew Alistair used them as sex toys and assisting in keeping his Freedom members calm. Elise had recounted some of her time in Alistair's clutches and her heart broke for what they were enduring. Possibly at that very moment.

"Alistair's dead, but his legacy lives on." Tears clogged her throat.

Deuce dropped a kiss to the top of her head. "Yes."

"Is the council gonna help them? Give them somewhere to stay and heal and—"

"They plan to send some here if they're willing. Maddy helped Elise recover and the two of 'em hope to assist others. Plus, Maya has already put in a request for hedgehog 'if available.'"

Elly rolled her eyes. Only the Prima. "That woman is crazy."

"Yeah, but just the right kind of crazy for those women. She'll turn them into badasses like Maddy while Maddy and Elise work on their emotional states."

"If I can have your attention, please!" Alex's yell halted their conversation. "Can the Martin and Pierce ladies come forward, please?"

Nervous anxiety replaced the sadness that had plagued her at Deuce's information. She hated being the center of attention, hated everyone (okay, carnivores) staring at her. But, it couldn't be helped. Per Maya, she had to do the whole "kneel blood thingy."

So she was gonna. Soon even. Probably when her legs decided to work.

Deuce's nudge got her moving and she turned to frown at him before doing as he silently asked. Barefoot, she padded across the empty clearing and toward the waiting Prime. The Prima's guards and their associated mates formed a semicircle behind the two pride leaders, the two unmated lions, Wyatt and Harding, standing next to Alex and Maya.

By the time Elly made her way to the group, her mother, Autumn, and Deuce's mother were already kneeling in the grass.

Right. Kneeling.

She trembled, tremors jolting through her body, but she got her legs to obey. With more awkward falling than finesse, she thumped to the ground and swayed.

Thank god her mother was next to her and managed to grab her arm before she fell. Good lord, she was committing herself to living with a bunch of lions. Squirrel to the slaughter.

They were gonna eat her in a bad way.

"I promise we won't." Alex's voice was a deep, laughing rumble.

Dear god, she'd said that out loud.

"Yes, you did."

"That too?" Oh, look, she realized she was speaking that time. "Can we just get on with this?"

She hadn't meant to piss off the Prime. Really. But she did.

"Maya." His teeth were clenched. "We talked about this. No more teaching the women to—"

"Okay, okay. New rule: no ordering the lion-o around." She even saluted.

Shaking his head with a sigh, Alex seemed to gather himself and got on with the show.

"Welcome, pride!" Roars, a chitter, and a bark answered the Prime's words. "These past weeks have been troubled, but there's a new future on the horizon. Change has been rapidly unfolding and all of it for the better. Part of those changes is expanding our pride and accepting these women into our hearts. I welcome Autumn Pierce, sister of Deuce Pierce. I welcome Eloise Martin, mate of Deuce Pierce. I welcome Amya Pierce, mother of Deuce Pierce. And finally, I welcome Rowan Martin, mother of Eloise

Martin. With these women, our pride shall grow. They bring the knowledge of the elders and the fruit of youth."

Maya had been right about Alex's politician-esque grandstanding.

One by one, the Prime went down the line, greeting them, making the cuts in their arms, pressing them together and repeating the ceremonial words. By the time he got to Elly, she was sure she'd pass out.

She was an herbivore for a reason.

Alex was before her, hand outstretched, palm open, and the other clutching a ceremonial blade. "Elly?"

Trembling, she extended her arm, flinched when his warm fingers encircled her wrist, and winced when the knife sliced through her skin. He pressed their bleeding flesh together and repeated the binding words.

"Blood to blood, heart to heart, fur to fur, I welcome you to my pride."

Elly wove, swaying when the Prime released her, and she tilted her head back to look at her smiling mate. "Deuce?"

He dropped into a crouch beside her. "Yes, kit?"

"Am I allowed to faint now?"

Chuckling, he rolled to his feet and leaned down, helping her to stand. "Not yet." He nuzzled her neck, sending a shiver of arousal through her. "Maybe after I make you come a time or ten."

"Now?" She was all about coming now, about having him deep within her. An orgasm or ten sounded much better than fainting.

"As soon as Alex starts the run."

Yeah, that made sense. They couldn't get down and dirty with the pride standing around.

"Okay everyone," Maddy yelled over the cheering group. "Let the ru—" Ricker slapped his hand over the woman's mouth and his hissed admonishment could be heard by all.

"We talked about this. No sex unless you pretend Alex runs things. That means no giving directions to the pride."

Alex growled, glaring at the couple, but turned his attention back to his lions…and the one rabbit. Oh, and the fox. Then there was Elly and her mother…the two squirrels. Damn, she forgot Ricker was a tiger.

They could almost start their own zoo.

The Prime raised his arms into the air, pulling everyone's attention from the arguing couple. "Let the run begin!"

The rustle of clothing, giggles, and moans filled the silence. Elly kept her gaze averted, trying not to stare while the pride stripped. Squirrels tended to be solitary animals and stripping and shifting typically happened behind bushes or trees. They only came together after they were ready to scamper on all fours. A peek from beneath her lashes revealed that most people were nearly naked, some bare, and a lot of them getting frisky in front of everyone.

The members of the pride who had surrounded Alex were shifted. And Elly tried really, really hard not to laugh at the sight of a white bunny perched on the back of Neal in his lion form.

Really. No laughing.

Before long, Elly and Deuce were alone in the clearing, the crowd having flowed around them as the shifted animals disappeared into the surrounding forest.

"Still feeling like fainting, kit?" Deuce nuzzled her and, with everyone gone, the scent of his arousal was unmistakable.

Her clit pulsed, body reacting to his closeness and scent, and the only thought filling her was how to get Deuce naked as fast as possible

"No. I've got a few other feelings now." She nipped his chest through his shirt.

"Come on, then." Deuce twined his fingers with hers, stepped out of her arms, and dragged her across the clearing. "There's a nice secluded spot with our names on it."

"How far are we talking? Over the river and through the woods or more like parking lot to burger joint?"

With that question, Deuce spun and tossed her over his shoulder, arm behind her knees to keep her from tumbling off. The sharp pain of his hand colliding with her ass had her gasping.

"Hey!"

"Hush." Another smack.

Elly grumped. Ideas of how to punish the man rolled through her mind with every thudding stomp toward their destination. Before long, Deuce stopped and lowered her to the ground, giving her a chance to absorb her surroundings.

"Holy shit." Her voice was barely a whisper. The small pool before her was edged in blossoms of every color and the lush green grass called to Elly's inner squirrel. Didn't she want to shift and play? Frolic through the dew and hunt for yummies?

"This is my favorite place and I wanted my favorite mate to see it." Deuce's thick, deft fingers tugged at the hem of her shirt and she raised her arms, allowing him to strip her.

"Your only mate." She said the words without heat, the comment now a joke between them. Plus she was too distracted by her surroundings to care about much else. The bunch of red flowers seemed to ease into the grouping of purple and those flowed into the layer of yellow. She padded toward the pool, peeking in, and she noted the smooth stones that decorated the bottom.

Her shorts went next, her mate's fingers slipping beneath the waist, and the elastic made it easy for him to slide the fabric over her hips. Then she was nude, bared to nature. And to Deuce.

After weeks of making love, exploring and tasting each other's bodies, embarrassment had no place in their mating.

Elly tore her attention from the water and turned toward her lion, let her gaze drift over his now bare form. She lingered on his gentle smirk and on to his heavily muscled chest, flat stomach, and farther south. At some point, while he'd stripped her, he'd also removed his clothing.

Yum.

His cock was already hard for her, long and thick. Her pussy responded to his nakedness, his nearness, growing damp and pulsing with need. Her nipples pebbled, not from the cool air, but from arousal.

She wanted him. Again and again. And then again.

She took a step toward her mate, fingers tingling with the need to touch him, but he nudged her backward. One pace and then two, farther and farther until the warm water of the pool surrounded her feet.

"I guess we're skinny-dipping?" She let him back her up another step.

"To start." He prodded her farther. And farther still until the warmth enveloped them.

On Deuce, the water rose to his hips. On the much shorter Elly, it hit her breasts.

Elly reveled in the heated water, squirrel rejoicing in the impending lovemaking. Thankfully, she didn't have to dream of the sensations for long. No, not when Deuce gathered her close, lifted her against his chest, and slanted his mouth over hers.

He slid his tongue into her, lapped at her, and suckled her tongue. She mimicked his every move, sucking, licking, nibbling. With each flex of muscle, her arousal heightened, body burning for her mate.

At his urging, she wrapped her legs around his waist and moaned when the searing heat of his cock pressed against her slick pussy. She rocked her hips, aching for the pleasure of his ownership.

The water flowed around her, slid over her body, and then her back was resting against the hard, smooth surface of a rock.

Deuce's lips feathered over hers, kisses alternating between raging passion and gentle stimulation. "Sweet mate…"

"Deuce." His name burst from her lips with a gasp. He'd nicked her lip with his fang and then lapped at the injury, sending tingles of ecstasy dancing through her.

She was perched between her mate and the stone, held immobile by the pressure of his body, and she abandoned the need to cling to him. She relaxed her muscles and trusted in her mate to keep her from drowning.

Drowning during sex equaled bad.

"Need you, kit." He rolled his hips, his thick length sliding along her spread sex lips and stroking her poor flesh.

"Take me." She gripped his shoulders, nails digging into his skin, and her mate growled against her lips. Her lion loved it when she gave him a hint of pain, revealed her desperation for him.

Growling, he shifted his hips once again, and she felt the broad head of his cock against her entrance. With one punishing thrust, he filled her, shoved his way into her weeping cunt, and she screamed with his fierce possession.

"Deuce!"

His response was a snarl.

Her mate withdrew and pushed forward once again, filling her, stretching her pussy. She moaned when the ridges of his cock massaged her inner walls, gave her pleasure, and petted her in those perfect places. He repeated the forceful caress, retreat, and advance, his hips meeting hers in a press of skin against skin.

The water surrounding them splashed and danced around their bodies with his every flex.

Deuce buried his face against her neck, kissing her skin and nipping her flesh. He grazed her, hints of pain adding to the growing ball of ecstasy that centered around the juncture of her thighs.

She clung to him, content to enjoy his ministrations and use her body as he desired. This was her mate, her one, the man she loved, and she reveled in his passionate touches.

"More. Deuce, more." She scratched and clawed him, fought to bring him closer, to eliminate any space between them.

"Pushy." He growled and bit her, sting of pain slamming down her spine, and the scent of her blood joined the fresh flavors of the forest.

"Yours." His next thrust was bone-jarring yet caused her heat to clench, need rocketing through her.

He bit her again and she couldn't resist the need to return the favor. Her teeth lengthened, sharpened, and she slid them into his shoulder. She lapped and licked at the sluggishly bleeding wound, savoring his natural flavors.

The cut she'd created seemed to spur him on, his hips moving faster than before. He pummeled her with his cock, shoving his way in and out of her pussy, fucking her needy cunt with a fierce passion.

Elly gripped him, face pressed against his shoulder and tongue still stroking his injury. His taste was unrivaled, sweet, hot, and seductive as it flowed over her taste buds.

She let him do as he wished, rhythm now punishing and constant. His attentions shoved her toward the edge of orgasm and she let the wondrous feelings envelop her. Nothing was better than her mate's cock inside her. Nothing.

She sank her teeth into him again and his pace increased, his growls now rolling into snarls, the sounds vibrating through her and wrapping around her nerve-filled nub.

He didn't stutter in his tempo yet the power behind each thrust grew. His cock stroked that perfect place, his hips collided with her clit just right, and his efforts sent her rocketing to the edge.

Pleasure wove its way through her body, stroking her nerves, plucking her muscles, and circling her cunt. She spasmed around him, milking his length, and each contraction increased her pleasure.

"Come for me, kit. Come on my dick."

"Fuck, fuck, fuck." She whimpered, held him close while her body fought to do as he demanded.

"That's what I'm doing, Elly." She heard the smile in his voice and she nipped him. "Fuck, kit."

His cock seemed to swell inside her, twitch and pulse. That extra sensation sent her over the edge, pushed her into flying oblivion, and she came with a scream, his name on her lips.

She lost control of her body, muscles twitching and shuddering with the pleasure that filled her veins. Wave after glorious wave consumed her and she could do nothing but ride the sea of bliss he'd created within her.

Distantly, she felt her mate shudder and jerk, his hips moving against her in massive thrusts. One… Two… Three… He stiffened, cock pressed deep into her throbbing cunt. His dick swelled, then pressed against her inner walls, and she shuddered with the added pleasure the action created.

Warmth flooded her pussy, setting off another round of bliss-filled aftershocks, smaller orgasms that rolled along her spine.

Panting, she slumped against him, let herself rest, and trusted he would hold her close.

Deuce lapped at her wound while she did the same, ensuring she closed the cuts she'd created with her teeth. Nothing tasted better than his blood, but if she thought about it for too long, she'd get squicked out.

Elly nuzzled him, enjoyed the feel of his damp, heated skin beneath her cheek. "Love you."

Deuce nipped her. "Love you too, kit."

"Mmm… I'm really glad you won me in that game, lion-o."

He nipped her again, nicking one of her cuts, and her pussy tightened with the renewed sensations. "Lion-o?"

"Yeah, Maya's rubbing off on me." She smiled against his shoulder. "She's been teaching me to play poker and I figure I'll be able to beat you in a game pretty soon." She

467

leaned back and stared into his eyes, recognized the pure love shining in their depths. "What do you say? Aces high, deuces wild?"

"I'll show you wild, minx." He rocked against her, cock hardening within her sheath.

She wanted to remind him she was a squirrel, but then his kissed her, did that thing with his tongue. Yeah, she didn't care anymore.

A roar reached them, the sound unmistakably Alex, and she pulled away from her mate. "Shouldn't you go see if he needs help?"

Deuce shook his head. "He's the big, bad Prime. I'm sure he can handle things. If not, the ladies will be sure to tell him how to fix whatever has gone wrong. They're good that way." The next roar had her mate stilling, a curse immediately following. "Damn it. Maya's pissed."

And that ended their waterlogged lovefest.

Damn it.

*

By the time Deuce got Elly out of the small pool and both of them dressed, snarls and growls were reaching them with scary regularity. Something had the pride in an uproar. Particularly the women, considering more than one foxy howl and bunny screech had drifted their way.

"Come on, kit." His mate followed him along the path and back to the clearing and pandemonium.

A glance around the space revealed the source.

Their families.

Elly's father and brothers stood to Alex's left, screeching at the Prime, while his father and brothers stood at the lion's right, roaring.

Behind the Prime, Maya was being held back by Wyatt and Harding. The men were really trying hard to suppress their laughter, but the smiles couldn't be ignored. Snarky Maya, the woman who held her twins with such care yet had a wicked tongue, was spewing curses that would make a sailor blush.

"Listen, you nut-eating suckshits, I will gut you like a fish, toss you on a spit, and we'll have charred varmint for dinner. I'll turn your fluffy little fucktails into a *hat!*" The woman wasn't done. She turned her ire to Deuce's family next. "And you! You little ass-sniffing, butt-licking, hair-ball-hacking pieces of dog shits better run before I claw out your eyes and make a necklace out of your intestines." She fought against her two guards. "Lemme go! I wanna eat those sorry excuses for bipeds. Goddamned squirrel and lion are on the menu tonight!"

Another glance at Alex revealed that the lion was having a hard time keeping a straight face as well. Hidden behind the four people, he found the remaining guards, plus Ricker, standing before their mothers.

Thank fur for that.

The Prime looked over his shoulder. "Enough, Maya."

The Prima's lips tightened, but she kept her mouth shut. Then Alex turned back to the interlopers. Deuce hated the idea of thinking of them as family. Not after what they'd done to him and Elly.

At the time, he'd just wanted to get the hell out of Dodge with their mothers and forget they ever existed. Apparently the men weren't keen on letting that happen.

Nope, not at all.

Karn along with Elly's dad, Bradic, glared at the Prima, mouths still moving, and through their ranting, one thing was clear.

They wanted their women back.

"Enough!"

The clearing fell quiet.

"If I understand correctly, you"—the Prime turned toward Bradic Martin—"would like your wife back. You, the man who handed over your daughter's mate to be 'taken care of,' and your sons would like their mother back. Those same sons who assisted in 'taking care of' their sister's mate. Is that right?" Bradic opened his mouth, probably to respond, and Alex held up his hand. "That was a rhetorical question. I already know you boys are idiots. I don't need you to speak to confirm my opinion."

Deuce wanted to laugh, but he held the urge in check. The Martin men's faces burned red.

Alex turned to Deuce's family, his father and brother's already half-shifted golden fur coating their skin and mouths in the middle of transformation from lips to snout.

"And you, the men who have turned an entire town against Deuce as well as handed him over to Freedom, would like Rowan and Autumn to be returned to you." He paused for a moment and tension crackled in the air. "Tell me, Karn, when was the last time you hit your wife?"

470

Alex's tone seemed conversational, but Deuce knew of the rage that lurked just beneath the surface.

His father glared at the Prime. "That's none of your business. A man has a right to discipline his wife. Sometimes it takes a tap to keep them in line. Nothing wro—"

Alex moved in a blur, closing the distance between himself and Karn in a blink, and the echoing crack of the Prime's hand against flash reverberated through the still air. "And I don't think there's anything wrong with that, do you?"

Deuce could sense the rage pulsing from his father, felt the trembling anger that preceded the man's fury.

Karn lunged for Alex, fangs bared and claws extended, but Deuce's brothers kept him from attacking the obviously stronger Prime.

"Dad, chill. Take it easy." His brother's voice held the familiar soothing tone he'd heard throughout his life.

"Gentlemen, the fact of the matter is, these ladies have joined the Ridgeville pride and need my permission to leave." He felt the weight of Alex's deadly stare and fought the shiver that ached to snake down his spine. "And I refuse to grant it. They belong to me, and I protect what's mine." He focused on the Martin men. "I believe that you and your sons are simply the stupidest men I've ever come to know."

Alex turned and beckoned Mrs. Martin forward. Elly looked so much like her mother that he felt he was looking at an older version of his mate. And that made his lion that much more protective of the little squirrel. "If you can convince Rowan to return to you, she has my blessing. That said, only one of you can enter my territory at a time

471

and only for four hours each day. Even then, only if she would like to speak with you."

Bradic grumbled but nodded. "Yes, Prime."

The Prime focused on Deuce's father. But it wasn't the man who looked out through those eyes, but the lion. "The Martins were spared because I believe they didn't know of your full plans. They merely listened to gossip and wanted to protect Elly. But if you three step into my town again, approach any member of my pride, I will gut you where you stand."

Part of Deuce ached with the knowledge that he'd never see his brothers again, hurt for the severing of that familial connection. But the truth stood at his side. If they'd succeeded, he wouldn't have his mate or the cub she carried. All it would have taken was a simple call from one of his brothers. Yet they hadn't and he'd nearly lost his life and his mate for their weakness.

"You can't do that!" His father frothed at the mouth.

Alex stood tall, arms crossed over his chest, his power as Prime wrapped around him like a cloak. "I can. I will. I have." Alex gestured behind him once again and the remaining guards stepped forward. "Please escort the Pierces and Martins from town."

Deuce's blood burned like fire, an ache thumping through his chest. He wanted to shove his father down the street, watch him be kicked out and barred from Ridgeville. It was only a small hand stroking him that soothed the beast.

"He's not worth it." Her words speared into his soul, his mate having guessed his thoughts.

"No, you're right, he's not."

472

Brute, the largest of the pride's lions, and Ricker flanked his father, keeping pace as the man limped through the clearing. Obviously his mate's shots had done a decent amount of damage and they hadn't healed properly.

Good.

Karn continued his stilted journey, shoulders slumped, and it wasn't rage that lurked in Deuce's chest. Nor heartache over the loss of his father.

No, he looked down at his mate, the gentle swell of her growing belly, and it was love and hope that filled him.

Well, that and the yearning for a poker game. He wondered what he could win this time around.

End of Deuces Wild

If you enjoyed Ridgeville Series Volume Two, please be totally awesomesauce and leave a review so others may discover it as well. Long review or short, your opinion will help other readers make future purchasing decisions. So, go forth and rate my level-o-awesome!

By the way... here are some links to help you hunt up the rest of the Ridgeville series:

Ridgeville #1 – He Ain't Lion (FREE)
http://bookbit.ly/halzon

Ridgeville #1.5 – You're Lion http://bookbit.ly/ylzon

Ridgeville #2 – Ball of Furry http://bookbit.ly/bofzon

Ridgeville Series Volume One – Ridgeville 1, 1.5 & 2
http://bookbit.ly/rdg1zon

Ridgeville #3 – Head Over Tail http://bookbit.ly/hotzon

Ridgeville #4 – Fierce in Fur http://bookbit.ly/fifzon

Ridgeville #5 – Deuces Wild http://bookbit.ly/dwzon

Ridgeville #6 – Sealed with a Purr
http://bookbit.ly/swapzon

Ridgeville #7 – Like a Fox http://bookbit.ly/lafzon

Ridgeville #8 – Big Furry Deal
http://bookbit.ly/bfurdzon

About Celia Kyle

Ex-dance teacher, former accountant and erstwhile collectible doll salesperson, New York Times and USA Today bestselling author Celia Kyle now writes paranormal romances for readers who:

1) Like super hunky heroes (they generally get furry)

2) Dig beautiful women (who have a few more curves than the average lady)

3) Love laughing in (and out of) bed.

It goes without saying that there's always a happily-ever-after for her characters, even if there are a few road bumps along the way.

Today she lives in Central Florida and writes full-time with the support of her loving husband and two finicky cats.

If you'd like to be notified of new releases, special sales, and get FREE ebooks, subscribe here: http://celiakyle.com/news

You can find Celia online at:

http://celiakyle.com

http://facebook.com/authorceliakyle

http://twitter.com/celiakyle

COPYRIGHT

Published by Summerhouse Publishing. Ridgeville Series Volume Two: Head Over Tail, Fierce in Fur, Deuces Wild. Copyright © 2014. Celia Kyle. ALL RIGHTS RESERVED. This book contains material protected under International and Federal Copyright Laws and Treaties. Any unauthorized reprint or use of this material is prohibited. No part of this book may be reproduced or transmitted in any form or by any means, electronic or mechanical, including photocopying, recording, or by any information storage and retrieval system without express written permission from the author.

This is a work of fiction. The characters, incidents and dialogues in this book are of the author's imagination and are not to be construed as real. Any resemblance to actual events or persons, living or dead, is completely coincidental.

This eBook is licensed for your personal enjoyment only. This eBook may not be re-sold or given away to other people. If you would like to share this book with another person, please purchase an additional copy for each recipient. If you're reading this book and did not purchase it, or it was not purchased for your use only, then please return to Smashwords.com and purchase your own copy. Thank you for respecting the hard work of this author.